HELL'S
FAIRE

HELL'S
FAIRE

JOHN RINGO

Copyright © 2003 by John Ringo
Sluggy Freelance copyright © 2003 by Pete Abrams

A Baen Books Original

Baen Publishing Enterprises
P.O. Box 1403
Riverdale, NY 10471
www.baen.com

ISBN: 0-7434-3604-0

Cover art by David Mattingly

First printing, May 2003

Library of Congress Cataloging-in-Publication Data

Ringo, John, 1963-
    Hell's faire / John Ringo.
        p. cm.
    ISBN 0-7434-3604-0 (hc)
        1. Space warfare—Fiction. I. Title.

    PS3568.I577H45 2003
    813'.6—dc21

                                                                2003041680

Distributed by Simon & Schuster
1230 Avenue of the Americas
New York, NY 10020

Production by Windhaven Press, Auburn, NH
Printed in the United States of America

10 9 8 7 6 5 4 3 2 1

Dedication

For the Barflies.
Here.
It's done.
Now lemme alone! ☺

PROLOGUE

Monsignor Nathan O'Reilly, S.J., had to admit that there were good and bad aspects to being a consultant to the President of the United States. One excellent aspect was that his access to what limited intelligence the President possessed about humanity's "benefactors" had been tremendously increased. Much of it had already been available to the Bane Sidhe, presumably through penetration of human computer networks. But it was useful to the Société to be able to both support their ancient "allies" and, admittedly, ensure that they were not being given the run around.

The negative aspect, of course, was that *semi*-professional paranoiacs and conspiracy True Believers assumed that a Jesuit as a counselor to the President meant some deeply laid conspiracy involving pyramids, Atlantis, aliens and lore of the ancients. The professional paranoiacs and security officers of the FBI, CIA, NSA, and other agencies knew that there were no ancient conspiracies. Any who insisted that Monsignor Nathan O'Reilly, Ph.D., Counselor to the President for Galactic Anthropology and Protocol, S.J., was involved in a millenia-old conspiracy would find him or her self in a rubber room quicker than you can say "Quick, get the tinfoil beanie!"

A fortunate attitude, since in this case the wackoes were right.

But his position also gave him a cachet in dealing with certain categories of people. Such as his current visitor.

Before his desertion from United States Special Operations Command, Lieutenant Commander Peter Left had been a medium-height man with the build and charisma of a blond, blue-eyed demigod. O'Reilly's visitor was almost invisible: Brown hair, brown eyes, apparently lightly built, and his face had none of the commander's movie-star good looks. The standard indentification scans for entry to Cheyenne Mountain had even revealed different palm prints, facial IR patterns, voice print, retinal scans and genetics. Nonetheless, Monsignor O'Reilly had no doubt that he was talking to the third in command of the Cyberpunks.

So far the talk wasn't going well. Regardless of any convergence of interests between them and the Société, the Cybers existed to defend the U.S. Constitution against the Darhel and the politicians allied with them. Both the alliance and the orders it had spawned were entirely without basis in that document—without treaty, without article, without amendment; based solely on findings, declarations and standing orders—and so, totally counter to it in law and in spirit. As Left had just explained in quietly angry detail.

"When we presented our superiors with proof of the Darhel's intentions, it was clear that they had been compromised. So we had to go outside sanction; there was no one left to obey. If we now start taking orders from some nebulous, Galactic-controlled conspiracy, we will be worse than those we oppose. Your proposal is, frankly, insulting."

"The Société is not 'Galactic controlled,'" O'Reilly said with a smile. "We're independent of the Bane Sidhe. But each group has complementary strengths. The Bane Sidhe provide us with intelligence and access to Galactic technologies . . ."

" . . . And you provide the Bane Sidhe with assassins," Left practically spat. "The Darhel at least don't cloak their recruiting in high-minded phrases. Just because the Galactics can't do their killing for themselves, doesn't mean we have to be their lapdogs."

O'Reilly fixed the Cyberpunk with a glare. "Okay, you arrogant jackass. Is that the way you want to play it? You and your precious Constitution that is as dead as a doornail if we don't get the elves off our backs? You are fumbling in the dark for answers that we had when Gilgamesh was in diapers! I can show you the personal diary of Marcus Antonius, senior Centurion of the Fourteenth Roman Legion, one of the most cold-blooded killers you'd ever hate to meet, who decried in his personal writings the fact that humans were so often at odds when they should be combining their forces against the Darhel, the Old Ones as he knew them.

"You act to save 'America' and its precious Constitution, a constitution written in part by Société members. The Société has one mission and one mission only: Permit the human race to thrive and grow free of the Darhel! And right now, the Darhel are the biggest threat to your Constitution. So are you going to work with us or are we going to run around in the shadows at odds with each other? Those are the choices. Binary solution set. Get over it."

The commander considered him calmly for a moment then nodded. "What do you want and what are you willing to trade for it?"

"You're right that the major needs are for direct action personnel," O'Reilly said with a nod. "This war has sucked down the available pool of personnel and we have a need for teams, on-call teams . . ."

Left shook his head. "We cannot act directly against the Darhel. It would violate the Compact. While it may not be in direct support of the Constitution, we feel that the Compact is in everyone's long-term interest."

"The Compact, and your actions to bring it about, is what impressed me about you," O'Reilly said. "Although I think you pulled up short. Five Darhel for General Taylor is a poor trade. Fifteen. Twenty. A hundred if possible."

"I tend to agree," Commander Left said with a thin smile. "However, five was the best we could do without . . . excessive sloppiness. We considered being sloppy as payback for framing us for the Tenth Corps hacking, but it wasn't necessary. If, when, we have to repeat the lesson, five will be about the most we can guarantee. And since they would be willing to kill the occasional important soldier in exchange for five senior Darhel, we stated plainly that if the person is specifically protected it becomes an all-out war. But the point is, we cannot move against the Darhel. So what would you need teams for?"

"There are other actions that need the 'human' touch. Subtly guarding selected individuals for example. We actually get very good intelligence on Darhel intentions and can often intercept assassinations. But we need counter-assassins to do so. We also occasionally need pickups where angels fear to tread."

"Did you know about the termination of General Taylor in advance?" Left asked quietly.

O'Reilly nodded. "Certain cells were informed in advance along with the warning that using the information could reveal a source. On the balance, protecting General Taylor and possibly losing the source was not a good strategic decision. So we allowed it to happen."

Left's mouth tightened. "Like Churchill and Coventry. I understand the logic, but the Cybers reject that degree of realpolitik. Frankly, you may want to reconsider allying with us. If we do join up, we will expect a higher degree of . . . moral consideration, *Jesuit*. Call us paladins, but if you play realpolitik and dump one of *our* teams, or let one of *our* operatives die, we will hunt you to the ground or die trying. So, do you still want to do this?"

"Yes, we do," O'Reilly said with a sigh. "That, the Cyber Creed as we call it, was much discussed. One view was that we can work around it. Some sources will be more vulnerable, but if need be, we'll have them disconnect and we'll recover them. We lose the ongoing info, but not the source."

"Unfortunate, but you can't use people as pawns," Left said coldly. "Politicians doing that have brought us to this."

"Another view," O'Reilly continued, "was that we shouldn't ally with you because of that loss. That was mostly from certain Bane Sidhe factions, the Tongs and the Franklins. You want underhanded and realpolitik, the Franklins make the Darhel look warm and fuzzy. The third view, from different Bane Sidhe factions, the Société and other groups within the Mother Church, was that it is a refreshingly moral approach, and the long-term benefits outweigh any short-term consequences."

"Jesus," Left said with a laugh, "how many groups of you are there?"

"Quite a few, apparently," the monsignor said thinly. "If there is a civilization of any size, you will find the Bane Sidhe somewhere in its cracks."

"Okay, you need assassins and counter-assassins. What do we get?"

"Oh, we'll ask for other things than that," O'Reilly admitted. "That a guy with a 'wanted: dead' poster can walk into High Command proves just how capable the Cybers are." In support of that capability, O'Reilly offered clean AIDs for the Cybers to study. Access through Indowy contacts to Fleet's entire records database, and profile generators to better the Cybers' ability to identify good candidates for recruitment. Access to the Société's safehouse network, in every surviving major city, and even off-planet. "Weapons, money, documents, you name it, we can provide it."

"And, wow, all we have to do is kill perfect strangers," Left said, shaking his head. "I'll take it back to Cyber command. But I don't like it that so many of your cells are known to the Indowy. We will not permit executive connection to them: I meet an Indowy and we'll consider the bridge burned. Understood?"

"Understood," the monsignor said with a nod. After a moment he smiled. "One question: Do you still have females in your organization?"

"A few," Left admitted. "Cyber training is very physical, but it has as much to do with the mind as the body. Why?"

"Oh, just a thought," O'Reilly chuckled. "The Société looks at the long haul and we were discussing recruiting. It so happens we have a mission that has an immediate priority. I did mention where angels fear to tread, yes?"

CHAPTER ONE

Go tell the Spartans, passerby
That here the Three Hundred lie
Obedient to their commands.

—Simonides of Ceos
Inscription at Thermopylae

Near Asheville, NC, United States of America, Sol III
0215 EDT Monday September 28, 2009 AD

Major Michael O'Neal checked the holographic schematic he had thrown up and nodded as the Banshee banked to the right and dropped; now the fun started.

The shuttle he was riding in looked like a black scimitar scything across the cloudy Appalachian sky. The combination of human, Indowy and Himmit technology had created something that was neither the best nor the worst of the three worlds, a ship that was somewhat stealthy, somewhat armored, somewhat maneuverable and somewhat fast.

Of course, compared to anything from pure human technology, the Banshee III was a marvel beyond words.

The stealth shuttles had had an uneventful voyage until reaching the area of the southern Shenandoah. There the Posleen invaders, who held virtually all of the Atlantic and Pacific seaboard, had made an incursion in the area of Staunton. And *that* required the scimitar-shaped ships to drop to below the level of horizon and begin evasive maneuvers.

Over the past five years the Posleen had landed in waves throughout the world, overrunning virtually every defense. The few survivors of Western Europe were now huddled in the Alps, eking out a retched existence among those upland valleys. The Middle East, Africa, most of South America, were either in Posleen hands or in such a state of anarchy not even radio communications were coming out. The only survivors in Australia were in the far western territories and roaming the desert interior in a post-apocalyptic nightmare. China had been lost only after loosing nearly a thousand nuclear weapons in the long retreat up the Yangtze Valley. Others survived in the highlands of the world, holding passes against the enemy. But few of those scattered groups were a coherent defense. Everywhere, one by one, the civilizations of the world had fallen to the remorseless invaders. With one small exception.

In the United States a combination of geographic luck—the Posleen tended to land in coastal plains and the U.S. had defendable terrain features inward of all the coastal plains—and, frankly, logistic and political preparation had permitted the U.S. government to retain control, to retain a condition of "domestic harmony" in a few areas. Of these, the most vital were the Cumberland and Ohio basins due to their industrial might and breadth of agricultural resources. The vast plains of Central Canada were still safe, and would remain so as long as the Posleen were resisted at all, for the Posleen were almost incapable of fighting in snow. But those plains, and the various western areas in human control ranging from the Sierra Madre to the Canadian Rockies, could produce only a small number of crops, mostly grains. Furthermore there was little or no industrial infrastructure in comparison to the might found in the Cumberland and Ohio.

The Cumberland, the Ohio and the Great Lakes regions were the heart and soul of the defense of the United States. Losing the Cumberland, furthermore, would open all of that up to conquest.

And with one thrust the Posleen had placed all of that in jeopardy. For years the major blow had been expected at Chattanooga, where little would stand in the way of a break-out. This battalion, and others, had defended the cities that were scattered down the range of the Appalachians, each of them, at one time or another, assaulted in force by the enemy. Only a few weeks before the battalion had been in a hair-raising battle on the Ontario Plain. But this time the Posleen had surprised everyone, striking an unnoticed and lightly defended sector, and throwing the defense of the entire Eastern U.S. into flux.

O'Neal and his forces had passed over southern Pennsylvania and through West Virginia without incident. But now, approaching the jumbled mess of western Virginia, North Carolina and Tennessee, it was time to get down and busy.

From this point forward the Posleen were pressing hard or already over the Appalachian Wall. The battalion would actually be forced to fly between two Posleen thrusts; besides the attack through the Gap the Posleen were pressing in on two flanks of Asheville. If the Posleen were able to reach the embattled city from the rear, the end would be assured. On that flank, the mountains above Waynesville would be the key, but they were a problem for others; the only thing the First Battalion Five-Fifty-Fifth infantry had to worry about was surviving as a plug.

O'Neal nodded again as another turn was faintly sensed. The shuttles used just a touch of inertial compensation to reduce the impact of their course corrections. Too much and they stood out like light bulbs to the Posleen. Too little and they smashed their passengers into jelly. Mike switched to an external view and by the light of the waxing moon he could see the mountains flashing by overhead; the ships were down in a valley, following its wandering path and only the occasional shudder passed through to the humans.

Soon enough they began an ascent, traveling at over five hundred knots and not much more than a hundred feet off the ground. The shuttles rapidly shot to the top of the next ridgeline and then, in a maneuver that looked flatly impossible, dropped down the back side in exact parallel with the slope. At no time did their speed increase or slow; it stayed a constant fifty kilometers per hour under the ambient speed of sound.

Mike noted another checkpoint and looked off to the left. Somewhere out there was Asheville, awaiting the dawn of a new day, a city still inhabited by over a million civilians and six divisions of infantry. Behind it were two Sub-Urbs with a combined total of five million souls. And all of it was in the vise of a nutcracker.

He sighed and brought up a collection of tunes; a little music seemed appropriate at a time like this.

Might as well share the misery.

"What the hell is that?" Lieutenant Tommy Sunday asked as a strange keyboard melody started on the command override frequency.

"'Don't Pay the Ferryman,'" SPC Blatt said. The Reaper's armor had a purple and pink holographic teddy bear on the front of it and when the music started, the bear jumped to its feet and began to dance, shaking its fat little belly in time to the music. "The Old Man must be *really* depressed."

The Grim Reapers were the heavy weapons suits of the ACS. They were designed for long-range indirect fire or heavy-duty close-in support and generally carried four weapons (versus the standard one rifle of the Marauders). These might range from anti-ship heavy grav-cannons to long-range auto-mortars to flechette cannons capable of spewing millions of rounds per minute.

The Reapers' suits were bulkier and slower than the standard Marauder suits, looking a bit more fat bellied than the "muscle" look of the Marauders, but given that most of their weapons had much higher ammunition bulk than the Marauders, that was all to the good. The flip side was that their armor was lighter, so getting into direct fights with the Posleen was usually a losing proposition.

"Christ," PFC McEvoy cursed, rubbing at his nearly bald head. He'd detached the gauntlets of his suit and his hand made a rasping sound over the short, thick stubble. He leaned forward as far as he could and looked to the doors at the front of the compartment. "I hope it's not that whole 'we're all a gonna DIE!' playlist.

If I hear 'Veteran of the Psychic Wars' one more time I'm gonna puke."

The shuttles were small, designed to carry thirty-six troopers and two "leaders" in no particular comfort. Each "suit segment" was rigid, with clamps to hold the suits in place against the worst possible maneuvering and designed to swivel and fire the troopers out into a hostile environment. This did not make for the most comfortable of seating.

"Nah," Blatt replied. "James Taylor next. Betcha five creds."

"Sucker bet," McEvoy replied. "I hear the Old Man's daughter was in the Gap."

"Ah fuck me," Blatt said, shaking his head. "That sucks."

"She's tough," McEvoy said, leaning forward to spit into his helmet. "So's his dad from what I hear. They might make it."

"That is questionable," Sunday said, looking up from his hologram. "According to seismographic and EM readings, there have been multiple nuclear detonations in the area of the Gap. And we're about to make the area extremely unpleasant ourselves."

"I didn't think we'd opened up nukes yet, sir," Blatt commented. He started to put his gauntlets back on as a timer in his suit tinged. "Twenty minutes."

"We have recently," Tommy answered, putting on his helmet. "But these appear to be secondary explosions."

"Oh, that's okay then," Blatt said. "As long as they're not targeted on us or anything . . ."

"Yeah," McEvoy agreed. "The last time I worried about nukes was the first time I got hit by 'em."

"Any suggestions?" the lieutenant asked.

"Lay flat," Blatt said with a laugh.

"Yeah, getting tossed through the air is the worst part."

"I'd think having your arms and legs ripped off would be the worst part," Tommy commented.

"Well, the only one who's survived from *that* close is the Old Man, sir," Blatt pointed out. "You don't wanna be that close; getting an arm blown off *smarts.*"

"Agreed," Tommy said. "Been there done that."

The lieutenant was new to the armored combat suits but not

to battle; up until a few weeks before he had been an NCO in the Ten Thousand, the most elite unit short of the suits. The Ten Thousand was armed with captured Posleen weapons and other devices and shuttled from crisis to crisis, thus in his time in the unit Tom Sunday, Jr. had seen more than any trooper short of the ACS. And he had managed to survive and rise in rank to staff sergeant. All of which spoke for his versatility and ability to take cover when the shit hit the fan. But even the best soldier tended to run out the law of averages from time to time.

"Which one, L-T?" McEvoy asked. The officer was new to them and they hadn't had much time to get to know him.

"Right, just above the elbow," the lieutenant said. With his helmet on it was impossible to tell where he was looking but McEvoy was pretty sure it was directly at him.

"Ah," the Reaper said. "Just asking."

"You're right," the lieutenant said. "It smarts. So does taking a shotgun flechette in the chest. Or getting your right kidney taken out by a three millimeter that was, fortunately, going too fast to do much more damage. And getting caught in your own company's mortar fire sucks. So does getting shot in the back by a cherry radioman who panics. All in all, I imagine it's really unpleasant to get blown through the air by a nuclear explosion."

"I guess so, sir," the gunner said, swinging his heavy grav-gun from side to side to ensure it tracked smoothly. "All things considered I guess wearing armor *is* the way to go."

"Ah hell," Blatt said, changing the subject. "It looks like you were right. Here we go with 'Veteran of the Psychic Wars.'"

"He's something pissed at those Posleen," McEvoy said.

"I'm sure he's not the only one," Sunday said quietly.

Captain Anne Elgars looked at the motley group gathered around the small fire and sighed. The captain appeared to be about seventeen and had a heavily muscled body with long, strawberry-blond hair. She was, in fact, nearer to thirty than twenty and had until recently been in a coma. Her recovery from the coma, the musculature, odd skills and personality quirks that had arisen from the recovery, were mysteries that were only starting to be illuminated.

There were two other adult females, two soldiers and a group of eight children in the small, wooded dell tucked into the North Carolina mountains. The women and children had been in a Sub-Urb, an underground city, when the Posleen struck the Rabun Valley and swiftly pushed most of the defenders aside. Through a combination of luck and ruthlessness the three women had reached the deepest areas of the Urb, intending to escape through the service areas, when they happened upon a hidden installation tucked into the Urb. It was there that they had been "upgraded," their wounds repaired, and imparted with both increased strength and some basic weaponry skills. They had also found an escape route.

Trying to make their way to human-controlled areas they had first been cut off by the advancing Posleen and then encountered the two soldiers, Jake Mosovich and David Mueller. Now the question was where to go now that the easy route was closed.

"It's agreed?" Elgars asked, her breath ghosting white in the frigid air. "We'll head for the O'Neal farm and raid the cache?"

"Don't see any choice," Mueller replied. He was a bear of a man, not only tall but wider in proportion, with a thin shock of almost white blond hair. The master sergeant had been running around snooping on Posleen since before the first invasion and he had regularly found his ass in a crack, enough times that he'd frequently asked himself why in the hell he kept doing it. But none of the other times did he have to worry about getting three women and eight children out of the crack. And in this case, the crack included that the children, at least, were likely to die of exposure if something wasn't done.

"There wasn't anything to use at the Hydrological Station." The Posleen raided for loot, then destroyed every trace of previous habitation. While the station hadn't been leveled it *had* been emptied. As had every other building they had checked.

Shari Reilly grimaced. "It's still nearly fifteen miles," she said. "Even carrying the kids, I don't see how we can make it."

Shari had been thirty-two, a waitress and single-mother of three, when the Posleen dropped on her hometown of Fredericksburg,

Virginia. She was one of the very few survivors from that town and was resettled, along with her three children, in one of the first underground cities. It had been placed in an out-of-the-way valley in western North Carolina, despite a lack of roads to supply it, for two reasons: it was unlikely the Posleen would attack into such rugged country, and the local congressman was the chairman of the appropriation's committee.

As it turned out, after five years of battering their heads everywhere else the Posleen *did* attack up the Rabun Valley. And Shari Reilly had, again, been in the wrong place at the wrong time.

Story of her life, really.

"I'd like to find out what happened to Cally and Papa O'Neal," Shari admitted quietly. The group had previously visited the O'Neal family farm and she and Papa O'Neal had gotten along *very* well, to the point that he had asked her, and the children, to come live with him. With the Posleen having overrun the area that plan, like so many others in her life, had been nipped in the bud. But she still felt it necessary to find out what happened to the O'Neals.

Wendy Cummings shrugged and shook her head, pulling a lock of hair out of her eyes.

"We're still in the same boat," she said, gesturing at the gray skies. In the last few hours the sky had begun to darken. While the women, with their new upgrades, could probably survive the environment, the children were without any shelter or heavy clothing. Getting them both was the second highest priority, the highest being to keep them out of the hands of the Posleen.

Wendy was the main point of contact between the other two women and sometimes she felt like the only thing holding the group together. She was a well-endowed blonde, another survivor of Fredericksburg, who had until recently been stymied in her desire to go off and kill Posleen like her boyfriend was doing. She was doing it now, whenever the Posleen came in view, but killing Posleen while carting kids around took all the fun out of it.

Still, a mission was a mission.

"We need to get the kids some clothes and we could use some supplies," she continued, gesturing at the two soldiers. "Even with what the sergeant major and Mueller supplied, it's not enough."

"There was plenty in the cache," Mueller noted. He slid a little more dry wood into the fire and looked up at the sky. "If we move fast we can make it to the O'Neal house by midnight."

"Later," Mosovich replied. The sergeant major was the antithesis of his subordinate, slight and wiry. But he had been beating around the bush when Mueller wasn't even a gleam in his father's eye and could carry loads that were frankly astonishing. What he would not do, in these conditions, was lie. "Even with their girls' . . . improvement, we can't carry all the kids that far. And in a few hours it's gonna start raining, cold rain. And by morning we might be looking at sleet."

"You think we should try something else?" Mueller asked.

"No, but we're not going to make it there before morning." The sergeant major looked at the children and shook his head. "We'll try like hell, but we won't make it."

"We'll make it," Elgars said, getting to her feet. "But not if we debate about it all day. Sergeant Major, I'm apparently the ranking officer, but I don't know what in the hell I'm doing. How are we going to handle that?"

"Well, ma'am," the recon specialist said with a faint grin. "I'll make suggestions and you give the orders. And if you don't give the orders I suggest, you'd better have a damned good reason or I'll shoot you."

"Works for me," she said with a laugh. "And your suggestion is . . . ?"

"Let's move out," he replied. "It's not going to get any easier as it gets darker."

"Can I say just one thing?" Shari asked.

"Sure."

"I really *hate* the Posleen." As they started off, a gentle, cold, mist began to fall.

Tulo'stenaloor cursed and shook his crest. The senior commander of the Posleen forces assaulting Rabun Gap had been fighting the humans for nigh on ten years. And over the time he had developed a healthy respect for their abilities. Outnumbered though they were, outgunned though they were, the humans were

clever about using well-honed skills and an almost devilish ingenuity to defeat the assaults of the Posleen.

But the current group was really starting to annoy him.

"I hate humans," he grumped. "What do we know of this cursed
metal threshkreen 'unit.'"

The Posleen had first met the humans at the planet Aradan
5, what the humans called Diess. Up until that encounter the
advance of the host had been continuous and without major
check. There were three races that they had encountered in near
space and none of them, not the little green Indowy nor the taller,
slim Darhel, nor the insectile Tchpth, would give fight. Sometimes the Darhel would fight, but not well and not long. Mostly
it was a matter of simply rounding them up and butchering them
for dinner.

Until Aradan 5.

Tulo'stenaloor had been there, when the host had met its first
defeat. It had been a nightmare. Each time they thought they had
the humans defeated something had hit them from a different direction. It was necessary to dig the humans out like abat or grat and
they stung worse. The host had taken fantastic damage *before* a unit
of these demons-be-damned metal threshkreen had arisen from the
ocean of the world and destroyed his first oolt'ondai. He still
remembered the unholy destruction visited upon his fine collection of genetic specialists, ripped to shreds in bare seconds. Other
threshkreen, who had at first fled before the host, had stopped and
formed a wall of fire that seemed unbreakable. Faced with an
implacable foe to the side and an impossible foe to the front, the
host had fled. He had barely escaped with his life, limping off planet
in a simple in-system ship, and it had taken him *years* to recover
from that debacle.

"It is led by a human named 'Michael O'Neal' who is one of
their Kessanalt. The term the humans use is a 'hero' or 'elite.' And
this is their finest group of metal threshkreen."

Generally other species, and Posleen that had become too injured
or old to be of use, were referred to simply as "thresh" or "food."
Threshkreen was "food that stung." *All* humans should be called
threshkreen; even their *nestlings* fought.

"Do we know their plan?" Tulo'stenaloor said. "We need to push as many oolt'os through the pass as we can; we cannot afford to be trapped here."

"They intend to open up the area with nuclear bombardment. . . ." the S-2 answered.

"*What?*" Tulo'stenaloor snapped, his crest rising. "Why didn't you tell me?"

"The area they will be able to cover is limited," the intelligence officer pointed out, bringing up a map. "They will be firing ballistic systems from the northern regions and from the sea. Few of them can even be targeted on this area and most will be destroyed by oolt Po'osol. So all of them are targeted on a relatively small area. Given that most of the blast will be trapped by these accursed hills, we should take minimal casualties. They intend to land in this area forward of the original defenses, where 'Mountain City' once stood. Their fire will only fill that gap in the mountains and the immediate areas of the pass."

"So we'll lose less than two oolt'ondai," Tulo'stenaloor nodded. "That is fine. But we need a response, a 'counter-attack' as the humans would use. Prepare one of the elite oolt'ondai and all the remaining tenaral for an assault upon them as soon as they are on the ground. And two oolt'pos."

"We are almost out of trained forces," the S-2 pointed out.

"I'm aware of that," Tulo'stenaloor said dryly. "But if we can't keep this pass open until others are breached, it will all be for nothing. We need to crush these metal threshkreen before they can get dug in or we'll be trying to kill them two days from now. Have the oolt'ondar move immediately to the hills above the landing zone, in this gap where they will be out of danger from the heavy fire. Tell them to wait to attack until the unit lands and is in the process of unloading."

"The humans are in two groups, estanaar. They have two 'resupply' shuttles filled with antimatter following them."

"That should be an interesting target," Tulo'stenaloor said with a rise of his crest. "Have the oolt'ondai wait until those shuttles land in particular, but ensure that they are struck. That is most important."

"Very well, estanaar," the officer replied. "What shall we tell Orostan?"

"Nothing for now," Tulo'stenaloor said. "He has his own problems. And more than enough forces at the moment; it is when he hits resistance that he will need those passing through right now. Get the oolt'ondar moving immediately; ensure they are heavily weaponed. As the humans would say, they must 'load for bear.'"

Cally O'Neal looked at the pack and shook her head; she wanted to load for bear but there was just too much to carry.

She had spent half the night curled up in a ball, alternately sleeping fitfully and waking up to cry. She wasn't very good at crying—it really ticked her off when she did—but she had a lot to cry about.

When the word of the Posleen invasion had come, both of her parents were recalled to duty. Because her mother was considered "off-planet," Cally's older sister, Michelle, had been moved to safety on a distant Indowy world. Cally had been left behind in the care of her grandfather on the family farm in Rabun County in north Georgia. The farm just happened to be about five miles on the *good* side of the Eastern U.S. line of defense.

The Posleen had hit the Wall at Rabun Gap several times over the last few years, but this was the first time they had ever succeeded in breaching it. Now they were all over the place and she was alone in a friggin' cave, behind the lines and without the comfort and advice, not to mention combat support, of Papa O'Neal.

It was not the Posleen who had killed Papa, though, or at least not directly. Something had hit one of the landers when it was passing over their valley and the antimatter containment system had failed. The explosion, equivalent to a one-hundred-kiloton nuke, had come as she was moving back to the deeper shelters. But Papa O'Neal had still been in the outer bunker.

She had found him later, or at least an arm, which was as far down as she could dig, but it was still and cold. She had covered it back up and headed to Cache Four where she had spent the night.

The cache had everything a person on the run could need. Papa O'Neal had spent plenty of time opening up Viet Cong tunnels and he knew what the best ones stocked. He had simply updated the list to the times.

The first thing she donned was her body armor. The Class IIIA armor was custom made—nobody made body armor for thirteen-year-old girls—but she carried it without thought; she had spent so much time already in her life in body armor it was like a second skin. The armor was studded with pouches for ammunition and grenades, and they were all filled.

The base of the armor had latch points for more equipment and she had a holstered Colt .44 magnum on one side and a combat knife on the other. The .44 was a revolver—she just didn't have the wrists for a Desert Eagle yet—but she was nearly as quick with a speed-loader as most people were with a magazine. She also had two quart canteens—they would supplement the camelbak built into the back of the armor—and a buttpack with an absolute minimal of survival materials.

In the pouches she had her basic load, 180 rounds of 7.62, five fragmentation grenades, five white phosphorus grenades and two smoke. She probably wouldn't have an opportunity to use the smoke, but if she needed it she would need it bad. With the armor, pistol, ammunition pouches and grenades she was already looking at over forty-five pounds. Which was half her body-weight.

Around her neck she had a set of night-vision goggles. They were lightweight and had binocular zoom capability, both optical and electronic. As such they had it all over standard helmet monoculars. But, with the weapons sights she wasn't sure she should carry them. And the helmet she had just put on seemed like an unnecessary extravagance. Papa O'Neal was always adamant about it when they were going in hot against Posleen, but if she was on the move she wasn't sure she could afford the extra weight.

She thought about Papa O'Neal and a lump rose in her throat. He had always seemed . . . invincible, immortal. He had fought in just about every brush-fire war that existed for nearly two decades then came back to the farm when his father died. With her mother dead and Dad off with the ACS, he had been all she had and for him it seemed like a chance to make up for never being there when her father grew up.

He had taught her, intensively, from the first day she arrived. And she, in turn, had been an apt pupil. Demolitions, close combat, long distance shooting, she had taken to all of it as if only having to be reminded. It had seemed a very odd pair to the few people who knew them, the ancient mercenary and his towheaded granddaughter, and jokes had been made, carefully out of his hearing, about "the farmer's daughter." The jokes had tended to die, though, rather than increase as she "blossomed" and turned into a real Appalachian belle, albeit one that walked around with a panther's stride and a pistol on her hip. And they had stopped, or at least changed fundamentally, after she shot the sergeant major.

The command sergeant major of the 105th had been quite taken by the twelve-year-old beauty in the hardware store. So taken that he had finally trapped her in the nuts and bolts section, which at the time he thought very appropriate.

When a simple "go away" had been insufficient, and when the fat old soldier had his hand down her newly filling blouse, Cally had simply drawn her Walther and shot him in the knee. Then walked away while he rolled around on the ground screaming like he'd actually been hurt or something.

It wasn't like it was the first time she'd shot a man, and the other time had been far messier. An assassin, an acquaintance of Papa O'Neal from his Phoenix days but young again courtesy of a bootleg rejuvenation, had come recruiting. When it was clear that Papa O'Neal was uninterested in becoming a hired gun for whatever shadowy group Harold had represented, it was also clear that the assassin had revealed too much to let them continue breathing. Cally had realized things were going wrong when Papa's right hand had started twitching like he was reaching for a gun that wasn't there, a sure sign of agitation that she had used to good effect while playing poker against him.

Aware that things were about to go from bad to worse, and dismissed by the normally paranoid assassin as an irrelevant eight-year-old loose end that would soon be tied up, she shot the visitor in the back of the head while he was drawing on Papa O'Neal.

Therefore, shooting a fat old sergeant major was no big deal.

A point that she made to the judge, without reference to the previous shooting which had, fortunately, never come to the attention of the authorities.

Her self-possession was almost her undoing. The sergeant major was vociferously defending himself on the not inconceivable charge that she had propositioned him and then shot him when he wanted to pay too low a price. In fact, he was trying very hard to get her charged with attempted murder. However, Cally quickly demonstrated that if she wanted to kill him she could have done so with ease. And no one could be found to back up the sergeant major's assertions about extracurricular activities. In the end the former sergeant major found himself in a penal battalion and Cally's picture was circulated around all the nearby military encampments where it made a nice pin-up with the caption: "WARNING! JAIL-BAIT! ARMED AND DANGEROUS!"

She hadn't had much self-possession after finding Papa O'Neal's body. She had covered the arm back up and stumbled to the cache to cry her heart out. But as the night went on, she had recognized that she had to leave. There was a full-blown battle going on to the north from the sounds of it, and the Posleen flowing through the Gap were spreading out. She had to head to the human lines, or at least find somewhere further away to hide. The Posleen would pass by something like the cache at first, but later they would come back and dig like badgers if there was any sign of materials or people. So she started to pack.

She didn't know how long she would be moving, so she had to take food. And the nights were getting colder, so she needed some snivel gear. Papa O'Neal could probably make do with just a poncho liner but she wasn't nearly as tough, or well insulated, as the old soldier, so she packed a sleeping bag. Extra water, fuel tabs, spare ammo . . . There was just too much. Even with what she packed if she was in the woods more than five days things would start to get hard.

She stared at the pile, unsure what to take and what to leave, until the floor flipped up and hit her on the face.

CHAPTER TWO

Then it's Tommy this, an' Tommy that, an' "Tommy, 'ow's
  yer soul?"
But it's "Thin red line of 'eroes" when the drums begin
  to roll,
The drums begin to roll, my boys, the drums begin
  to roll,
O it's "Thin red line of 'eroes" when the drums begin
  to roll.

—Rudyard Kipling
"Tommy"

Rabun Gap, United States of America, Sol III
0242 EDT Monday September 28, 2009 AD

The external viewers had adjusted the night to sixty percent of daylight ambiance. The wood-shrouded hills were dark and cool under the gibbous moon and the Gap valley was occasionally visible as the shuttles crested the ridges.

Then everything went white.

The weapons were the sole survivors of a massive salvo fired from the northern tier of what was left of the United States. The

Posleen assault on Earth had shattered almost every other industrialized nation but through a combination of foresight, ruthlessness and terrain the United States had managed to hold on to productive areas in the eastern Midwest, what had come to be known as "the Cumberland Pocket." It was comprised of most of Tennessee, Kentucky, Illinois, Ohio, Iowa and Michigan. In addition there was a northern tier of states—Minnesota, North Dakota, Wyoming and Montana—that were above where the Posleen could effectively campaign.

It was from these latter that most of the nuclear weapons had been fired.

Nuclear missiles from silos throughout the Midwest had been recovered and moved to safety ahead of the Posleen hordes. Violating numerous treaties, they had been converted to mobile launchers and now were positioned throughout the northern tier of states, most of which remained in human hands, and even up into Canada. Many of them would not have the angularity to reach the target area—their "minimum range" was still too long—but a few would. In addition, while most of the nuclear ballistic missile submarines had been converted to transports, a few of them retained their missiles. All of these weapons, enough to gut any country, were available to support the ACS airmobile.

But Posleen antimissile systems were tremendously effective; practically anything that crested the horizon that was under power or maneuvered would be destroyed. So the only viable choice was to try to saturate the defenses. However, it was not just the innumerable weapons on God King saucers that could engage the missiles; as they reached apogee they were visible to the thousands of landers still scattered across North America. So out of the thousands of nuclear weapons that were fired, only a handful survived to enter ballistic trajectories and become mysteriously invisible to the Posleen targeting systems.

Those handful would be more than enough.

The salvo of reentry rounds landed in a triangle pattern, one directly in the Mountain City Gap and the other two in the passes to the north and south. Each of the explosions was one hundred kilotons, almost ten times stronger than the weapon that hit

Hiroshima, and wasted a circle three thousand meters in diameter, smashing every tree and scrap of brush to the ground or incinerating them and tossing them into the column of fiery gas that reached to the heavens.

The blast of fire and pressure reached out and scoured the ridges to either side, ripping up the trees and smashing them into tooth-picks, flattening the maturing forests and ripping the soil out to the bare rock all the way to the tops of the hills.

"Sergeant Major." Jake's artificial intelligence device still had the toneless tenor that was the "factory" default. He had never both-ered to personalize it. The AID was a Galactic introduction, a small, black, formable piece of what looked like plastic but that was, in fact, a continuous computing unit. The devices were fully AI and linked together in a seamless web of data that stretched across an entire planet. In this case the AID had picked up a piece of information from the net and after a nanosecond's consideration determined that, yes, this was something that its human needed to know.

"Multiple incoming nuclear rounds targeted on Rabun Gap. The unit is outside the zone of direct danger, but anyone looking in that direction will experience flash-blindness."

"Holy shit," Mueller muttered. They were traversing one of the innumerable ridges in the area and while the Gap was quite some distance away, the fireball would not only be visible, it would seem like it was right on top of them. The ridgeline was a knifeblade of rock, made slippery by the rain.

"Down," Jake snapped, pointing over the edge of the ridge to the north. It wasn't a cliff, but it was steep.

"How?!" Shari snapped, shifting Kelly higher on her back and freeing an arm to brush hair out of her face. As far as she could tell, one step to the side and she and the girl were both going to slide a couple of hundred feet to rocks.

"Carefully," Mueller replied. He was carrying both Tommy and Amber but he nonetheless started to shift down the steep hillside. But in a moment he stopped and shook his head. "Jake, it's not going to work."

"Why?" Mosovich said then cursed. "I'm a senile old fool: ground-shock."

"We can make it down, but . . ."

"It'll flip us off the side," Mosovich said, looking around. The ridges in the area were usually fairly easy slopes to either side; just their luck they were on one of the knife-edge portions.

"AID, how long?"

"Five minutes," the computer replied. "Many of them have been destroyed, but between three and twelve will probably hit. None of them will hit between our present position and the Gap."

Jake eyed the thin trail along the top of the ridge. In about a hundred meters it started to curve south and flatten out.

"Ma'am, my advice is to run!"

"Cool," Sunday whispered, watching the expanding mushroom cloud into which the shuttle was apparently going to fly.

"Yep, that's the real and the nasty, sir," Blatt said. "Finally the kind of support we're *designed* for."

"Three minutes: Standby for deployment," Captain Slight said over the company frequency. "I hope like hell everybody's awake. If not you're about to be woken up the hard way."

Sunday's chair suddenly straightened then rotated in two directions so that he was standing up, facing backwards.

"All troops," Major O'Neal said, "prepare to deploy."

The shuttles suddenly accelerated past Mach One in a series of barely felt sonic booms, approaching the last hill. They continued to accelerate as they hit the first compression wave from the nuclear explosions and began to noticeably rock in the turbulence.

"WHOOOEEEE!" Blatt yelled. "Comin' in hot and ROCKIN'!"

As the shuttles crested Oakey Mountain they began firing the combat suits at the ground, starting from the back of the shuttle and working forward.

Tommy felt the slam of ejection over his inertial compensators and bent his knees as the ground came at him at nearly a thousand miles per hour. His on-board compensators and the disposable inertial pack that he was wearing combined to slow his speed to just below the speed of sound before he entered ground effect where a Terran bounce pack included in the inertial set slowed him even more.

The ejection was noticeable but hitting the ground *hurt*. He was still going at over two hundred miles per hour and felt the shock through his whole body as the suit automatically tucked and rolled backwards.

He went through two more rolls, mainly due to the slope, before the suit was able to establish control and throw him to his feet and a screaming halt.

He immediately turned towards the assembly beacon in the valley and took a count of his troops. The whole group of Reapers were on the ground and, despite exiting after him, were already bounding for the beacon.

Tommy started to shake his head and quelled the reaction, setting his suit to max-run instead and heading down the hill. He had a lot of catching up to do.

Mike threw the full power of his inertial compensators and half-flew, half-bounced from his position on the shoulder of Oakey Mountain to the battalion staff assembly beacon at the intersection of Black Creek and Silver Branch. It was a point of pride to be the first out and the first assembled, even if he did have farther to go.

"Scouts out," he snapped as his foot touched down. "Two teams south, three teams north." He looked around and then went flat into the streambed. Bravery was all well and good but there was plenty of time to get killed on this mission.

"Boss," Stewart said, checking the intelligence schematic that collected sensor data from all the suits in the battalion. "I'd strongly suggest the last team up Rocky Knob. I'm getting some readings from up that a'way."

"Concur," Mike answered. He looked around at the battalion spreading through the bowl and took a deep breath as the first shuttle came under fire in the distance. "Bring in the fuel shuttles and make sure we're covered on the south."

❖   ❖   ❖

"And you want us to go into *that*?" Shari said, cradling Kelly under her body as the last shock wave shuddered away into stillness.

The sky to the east was still purple with fading plasma and a massive, complex, mushroom cloud glowed high into the air. Much of it was lost in the incoming cold front, but even that was momentarily shaken by man-made plasma.

"Well," Mosovich replied, cradling one of the shivering children. "We've already given up our coats and our blankets and these kids are still going into hypothermia. So unless you have another suggestion?"

"What about radiation?" Wendy said carefully. She had killed Posleen, had seen them overrun her town, had fought her way out of an underground rat trap, but the towering mushroom clouds were a wholly new experience and she suddenly felt as if none of the previous battles had occurred, like a rank newbie. It was an odd and unsettling feeling.

If Mosovich was unsettled by the change in style of warfare, it wasn't showing. "AID, radiation patterns."

"Given the placement of the rounds, there should be no persistent radiologicals in the area of the O'Neal farm. All of the rounds were air-burst and any incidental fallout from irradiated casing or ground material should drift with the prevailing winds to the east. However, I have a secondary ability to sense harmful radiation and will warn you if we begin to experience any radiation high enough to be harmful to humans."

"We're going," Elgars said, standing up. "We can argue all night and all that will happen is the children will die."

"As if you care?" Shari snapped.

"I see it as my mission to get them to a place of safety," the captain said, coldly. "Whether I like them or not is unimportant to the mission. And Cache Four is both hidden and strongly made. It is the best location to move to, despite being near the current fighting."

"I'd like to find out about Papa O'Neal," Wendy said. "And Cally."

"All right," Shari replied, staggering to her feet. Even with the enhancements they had gotten, it had been a long day and night. She was cold, tired, hungry and most of all tired. It felt as if she couldn't put one foot in front of the other, especially while carrying Kelly. But she did it. And then another.

Elgars watched until she was moving and then took a position directly behind Mosovich.

All of them avoided looking to the east.

Cally picked herself up and looked around the interior of the cache. Several of the heavy ammunition and storage lockers had been tossed off their pallets and several small chunks of rock had fallen. But the Old Man had known what he was doing; a concrete arch and "plug" at the rear of the cache supported the only portion of the rock that wasn't solid North Georgia granite.

"Fuck me," she said quietly, wiping a little blood off her lip; her nose had taken the fall badly. It was a hell of a choice. Sit here and hope the shelter held or head out into who knew what. That had been the first nuclear blast in over a day, but that didn't mean it would be the last.

Really, it wasn't much of a choice. If the battle ran over her location she would probably die. But as long as the nukes stayed over by the Gap, and so far they had, and they weren't *too* large, whatever that meant in terms of nuclear weapons, she should survive.

If she went outside, though, all bets were off.

"Fuck me," she said again, louder, and started taking off her gear.

"I know there's a pack of playing cards around here somewhere," she commented, starting to pile boxes into a second shelter, under the concrete arch, just large enough for one. "Time to play some solitaire. I don't think trying to build houses with them would work." After a moment she picked up her helmet from where she had dropped it and put it back on.

"Blatt, pick up that ammo pack," Sunday said, pounding past the Reaper. "We're going to need all the ammo we can load."

"Yes, sir," the specialist said, grabbing the bulbous plastic sack. He heaved it over his left shoulder and clamped it on then stumbled slightly as it threw off even the suit's massive gyros. "Gonna be hell to move with."

"You're doing fine," the officer replied, scanning up and to the left. "If you don't keep up, the Posleen will eat you. McEvoy, take your squad and pick up the spare gun packs; I'm thinking we're gonna need 'em."

"Gotcha," the specialist said. "When are we gonna rock and roll?"

Sunday looked around the smoking landscape and shivered. "Soon enough."

"UP! Up the hill!" Gamataraal called. "Sweep down upon them."

"The shuttles!" Aalansar said. His second in command gestured to the east. "We're supposed to wait for their shuttles."

"They send scouts up the hill," the oolt'ondai snapped. "In a moment we'll be under fire; we can't wait."

"Hey, we gots company, boss," Stewart called. "I make it a lesser oolt'ondai, heavy on weaponry. And it's right up in the gap on Rocky Knob."

"Now ain't that interesting," Duncan said. "I got no fire support, boss. The nukes are shot out and we're out of range of everybody else."

"And the Reapers are all loaded for anti-lander," Mike said. "Battalion grenade fire; we need to suppress these guys quick."

"Call off the shuttles?" Duncan asked.

"Negative," the commander replied. "Calculated risk; we need to move out, they need to come in. Spread 'em out, though."

"By teams!" Captain Slight called. "Grenades, my target, mark!"

"We're out of it," Blatt cursed trying to swing the huge bag to a better position as he trotted to the northeast.

"Not quite," Sunday said calmly. "Lamprey emanations over Black Rock Mountain. Platoon: Target!"

"Battalion, fire!" Mike called and watched the flight of the grenades to their targets. The suits mounted dual launchers and carried 138 of the 20mm balls in onboard storage. Each of the balls had a range of just over three thousand meters and an effective kill radius of thirty-five meters. So the battalion fire mission dropped across the oncoming oolt'ondar like the wrath of God, the grenades detonating at one meter above ground height and flailing the air with shrapnel.

"Check fire," O'Neal called, noting that most of the enemy had been swept away by the fire mission. "Prepare to receive landers."

The enemy landing craft were designed for space combat but their secondary weapons could reach down and destroy the spread-out battalion if allowed to engage without resistance. Unfortunately, the battalion had limited resources to take them on. "All Reapers, engage Lamprey targets west."

"This is getting a tad hot," Duncan remarked, dialing in the grenade targets.

"Yes, what," Stewart said. "Scouts are reporting a movement up the valley. If we don't get the hell out of here we're going to be walled up."

"It's all a matter of timing," Mike replied. "Battalion, rifle fire on the hills; suppress Posleen fire for incoming shuttles. All things considered, though," he continued, switching back to the staff frequency, "it might have been better to bring them in with us."

"Yeah, but we weren't expecting an ambush," Duncan noted. "Now, did they have *every* LZ covered I wonder?"

"Yeah, I wonder," Stewart said. "I'm putting that in the intel folder with a high-priority mark. I think we were set up, sir."

"But they bit off more than they could chew," Mike noted as the battalion fire started to sweep the charging Posleen off the ridgeline. However, he could see trooper icons dropping as well; the force on the hill was as heavily armed as any he had ever seen. "I hope."

"We are getting slaughtered," Aalansar said bitterly.

"The way the Path has taken us," Gamataraal said as another of the dismounted Kessentai was removed from the Path. "We close, and we kill. As long as they are unable to move, we are well off."

"Shuttle coming in to the south," his second noted. "But we have no targeting systems." The superior Posleen antiaircraft fire depended upon the sensors and motors of the saucerlike vehicles the God Kings normally rode. However, they also made the God Kings easy targets.

"The Path is never an easy one," the commander said. "Fire everything at it. Ignore the threshkreen."

"Oh, damn," Gunny Pappas noted. He had just come back from checking out the battalion as it tried to fight its way out of the pocket and the incoming shuttle couldn't have been timed worse. And the reaction of the Posleen wasn't all that peachy either.

"Now, why would they do that?" O'Neal asked as every single Posleen that was still under God King control turned their fire away from the suits and onto the shuttle.

"I dunno, but I think it's gonna work," Duncan noted, digging his head into the streambed. "Don't you?"

"Yeah, probably," Mike noted calmly. "Bank the other shuttle behind Oakey Mountain. Battalion: INCOMING!"

The oolt'ondai was armed with three-millimeter railguns, plasma guns and hypervelocity missiles. The shuttle crested the south shoulder of Oakey Mountain and headed down Stillhouse Branch, accelerating past Mach Four and preparing for a hot inertial drop along Black Creek. It turned out to be hotter than anticipated.

Most of the fire went behind or to either side, but the targeting systems of the God King's weapons were still good enough to lead the craft, and a hurricane of railgun and plasma rounds hammered the shuttle as it rocketed down the stream. In a blink of an eye it started to come apart, scattering its highly volatile cargo into the fire.

Class Five Antimatter Reactors, the system installed on shuttles, were designed for combat and to withstand the occasional misdirected round. They were *not*, however, designed to be hit by a storm of plasma fire. In less than a millisecond the containment was pierced and all hell broke loose.

"ASS TO THE BLAST!" Mueller yelled, dropping to his face then pulling the shrieking children on his back around to cover them. The flash of white had been so bright, like a flashbulb on megaoverdrive, that he could still see the trees and bodies ahead of him even after he shut his eyes.

All of the adults dropped, grabbing any child still standing, and waited for the blast wave. By luck they were on a relatively flat hill, so when the ground shock hit they merely slid a short distance down the muddy slope then stopped. Shortly after, the outer layer of the overpressure wave hit, but at the distance they were from the explosion it amounted to not much more than a strong wind that shook the brown leaves from the surrounding trees and dropped streams of frigid water onto their backs.

Slowly most of the screaming dropped to sniffles. No one had been looking at the burst and the distance was far enough that there hadn't been any flash-blindness or thermal pulse burns.

"This is insane," Shari said, getting to her feet. "Insane."

"Insane or not, we have to keep going," Wendy replied, tiredly. She hugged Amber to her as the child shivered uncontrollably. "We have to get them out of the wet."

"Just put one foot in front of the other," Mosovich said, picking up Nathan and perching him on top of his rucksack. "We either make it, or we don't. I'm glad we're not in it, though."

CHAPTER THREE

Rabun Gap, United States of America, Sol III
0257 EDT Monday September 28, 2009 AD

For Tommy it felt like being repeatedly hit by a giant hand while lying face down on a trampoline. The ground came up and slapped him up in the air, then he got slapped down again and up and down and up and down. It was not painful so much as extremely disheartening; he had never felt so completely out of control. He might survive a nuclear blast, was apparently going to survive this one, but he would never, ever, underestimate the power of one again.

After one more lift in the air, which he later surmised was the rising mushroom cloud, he dropped to the ground in a swirl of dust, totally blind.

There was no vision possible; virtually every single sensor was off-line from the chaos around him. His external temperature sensors showed an incredible two thousand degrees Celsius and he had to wonder what in the hell was keeping him alive until he saw the power gauge on his suit visibly dropping. The suits were able to keep a person alive in conditions that many considered flatly impossible, but it was at the cost of using nearly as much power as was being thrown at them.

Finally the external conditions stabilized enough that he could discern items around him and beacons started coming up. As they did, so did His Master's Voice.

Mike bounded to his feet as the sensors started to go live. "Up and at 'em!" he called. "What the hell are you doing on your faces? We've got Posleen to kill! Reapers, we've still got Lampreys coming in to the west! All units, form perimeter on the remaining shuttle and KEEP IT ALIVE."

He yanked Stewart to his feet and started to charge to the north.

"The good news," Stewart said, "is that this has cleared off the welcoming party."

"The bad news is that we're out half our power," Duncan noted, shifting over a battalion power graph. "And we just used up a day's worth in that one event."

"And there will be more to come," Mike noted. "Come to Papa, baby. Bring it right into the cloud. Bring it in fast and hard."

"These things aren't rated to fly through a thousand-degree mushroom cloud, Major," Duncan pointed out.

"No, but the *power packs* will survive."

The second shuttle, on orders, entered the still growing mushroom cloud. The shuttles were armored, but not well enough to survive that impact and it quickly started to fly apart, its load of much more heavily armored power packs and ammo boxes scattering at random across the LZ. Inevitably, accidents happened.

McEvoy let out a yell of anger as he was slammed in the back by a heavy weight. Rolling on his side, he looked at the anti-matter pack that had hit him in the back and let out another yell of fear.

"Now *that* was elegant," Sunday said.

"Where in the *Hell* did that come from?" the Reaper said, getting to his feet and backing away from it as if it were a giant spider. Or a potentially lethal nuclear weapon.

"Oh, pick it up, you big baby," the lieutenant said with a grin in his voice. "The Old Man flew the shuttle into the mushroom cloud. That masked it from fire—even the Posleen can't see through one of those—and dropped the power packs at the same time."

"That's *nuts!*" Blatt said, trotting past. "I keep telling everybody, the Old Man is *nuts!*"

"He's crazy all right," Sunday said. "Crazy like a fox. Those things are armored against point-blank plasma fire; they weren't going to explode from a little accident like that. Now never mind about the pack, although you might want to step away from it a bit. Reapers, drop your loads and take my mark: The Bear's Comin' O'er the Mountain."

"We've got three surviving lances," Duncan noted. "Do we use them?"

"Not immediately," O'Neal said. "What happened to the other one?"

"The launcher sympathetically detonated," Stewart answered. "It's headed for Atlanta."

"I'll have to bring that up with the manufacturing clan," O'Neal said seriously. "A little thing like a two-hundred-kiloton explosion shouldn't have damaged them!"

"Somehow I suspect you will," Stewart laughed. "But why are we saving them? We've got Lampreys on the way in."

"Lampreys can't point their anti-ship weaponry down," Mike pointed out. "We'll save them for C-Decs."

"Most of the packs are gathered," Duncan noted. "Some of them were gathered by Reapers, though, and they are preparing to receive cavalry."

"Have them deployed to the rifle units in jig time," Mike snapped. "Everyone but the Reapers make a run for the Wall. Reapers can follow but they need to be prepared to engage the big boys."

"It's moments like this that I live for," Blatt said as the rest of the battalion took off at a dead run.

"We're going, we're going," McEvoy said.

"Not fast enough, in my opinion," the specialist noted.

"We still need to recover the weapons pack," Sunday said. "We're going to need those special weapons once we get in place."

"Sir, I think they're toast," McEvoy replied. "The nearest pack is halfway up Oakey Mountain; they don't have our systems keeping them close to home in a blast."

"Fuck me," Tommy noted. "Okay, we'll pick 'em up later."

"Well, one of them seems to have gotten blown to the other side of Black Rock Mountain, sir," Blatt said. "We might be able to recover that someday."

"Your job, Blatt," Sunday said. "As soon as we get in place."

"You're joking, right?" the Reaper asked.

"Negative," the lieutenant replied. "Once we deal with the first wave of landers, we're useless without those mortars and shot-cannons. Recovering them is our number two priority. The number one being engaging landers."

"Speaking of which," McEvoy said as the first Lamprey crested the shoulder of Black Rock Mountain.

"Indeed," Tommy said, targeting one of the secondaries on the side. "Engage."

The long-barreled M-283 grav-cannons had additional acceleration ability over standard systems. In addition, the rounds contained an antimatter driven inertial accelerator and an antimatter "rocket" system similar to that used in the antimatter lances and Space Falcon fighters.

Thus the 75-millimeter round was accelerated to over a thousand kilometers per second by the time it struck the wall of the ship.

To survive the flight to the ship the round needed to be made of sturdy stuff and it was, a composite of gadolinium and mono-molecular iron with a carbon ablative coating. But when one struck the armor of the Lamprey, it turned into an expanding hemisphere of boiling white plasma; even the enormous energy of one of the penetrator rounds was no match for Posleen armor.

Of one round.

But there were twelve Reapers firing at the Lamprey, pounding five rounds per second into a contact patch the size of a human hand.

In addition, the aiming system on the penetrators was far more effective. It designated a particular *point* on the side of the lander, chosen from a database of lander weaknesses, and directed all the weapons in the area to fire on that point.

Thus, when the twelve Reapers paused and opened fire, twelve hundred rounds hit a single weapons pod on the side of the Lamprey, boring a hole into the interior and detonating the feed mechanism of the plasma gun. The rest began flailing around the interior.

As silver and red fire belched out of its side, the lander attempted to escape, reversing course and rotating its configuration to move the damaged portion away from the fire. But the God King at the controls must not have been one of their more elite pilots, as he proved by ramming the ship into the flank of Black Rock mountain just south of the radio tower.

The other Lamprey had engaged the main body of the battalion, and was now heading to the southwest and the Wall in long, swooping strides. But seeing the fire that had taken down its companion, the ship changed targets and began a careful manual rotation to reduce its damage.

"Begin evasive movement," the lieutenant said, putting orders to words as he started a slow trot to the southeast.

The manual fire from the Lampreys was, fortunately, not as accurate as their automatic fire. But it was heavy; the side of the lander sported over twelve medium weapons emplacements. So the ground around the Reapers was torn by fire as they began their move. And some of it was on target.

"Fuck me," Blatt said softly as a line of craters from a heavy plasma gun walked across the ground and onto his position. He attempted to dodge them but with all the other fire there was no place to run.

"Shit," McEvoy said as Blatt's suit of armor came apart in a ball of silver fire. "Motherfucker!"

"We're not getting this one," Sunday said angrily. The rounds were destroying many of the surface emplacements and putting pockmarks all over the face of the Lamprey but with it rotating as it was there was no way to bore into it. And the fire was getting heavier.

"What I wouldn't do for a SheVa gun about now," Tommy muttered.

✧   ✧   ✧

SheVa Nine, or Bun-Bun as its crew called it, was still faintly smoking when the first blimp appeared over the horizon.

SheVas were the sort of bastard weapon that only occur in the midst of really terrible wars. Early on in the battles against the Posleen one of humanity's greatest weaknesses was the inability to destroy the Posleen ships when they were used for close support of the alien infantry. The event was fortunately rare—the Posleen were not good at combined arms—but when it occurred it was devastating. Many weapons systems were created to try to destroy the Posleen landers, but with the exception of the Galactic-crafted heavy weapons, which were in short supply, only one system had proven effective. And it was monstrous in every meaning of the word.

During the fighting around Fredericksburg the battleship *North Carolina* had managed to tag a Posleen lander with its sixteen-inch guns and when nine sixteen-inch rounds hit, the alien ship more or less disappeared. So, obviously, sixteen-inch rounds would work. But there were many problems associated with that simple fact. The first was that battleship turrets were not designed for antiaircraft work; the shot had been luck as much as skill and improvisation. The second was that the engagement envelope, how high and far the guns would reach, was very small. The third was that battleships had a very hard time getting to, say, Knoxville, Tennessee.

The answer was to create a new class of guns, superficially similar to the battleship guns. They were sixteen inches in diameter but at that point the resemblance stopped. Like modern tank guns, they were smoothbore and very high velocity. The guns used an electroplasma propellant, extended barrels and secondary firing chambers to accelerate a depleted uranium dart as thick as a treetrunk to twenty-five-hundred meters per second. Firing a single penetrator round, the weapon designed to destroy a Posleen lander, was the recoil equivalent of firing *six* standard battleship cannons.

Because of the enormous energies involved, a tremendous recoil system had to be designed including shock absorbers the size of small submarines. While it was, relatively, easy to install in the few fixed fortifications that received the guns, the real necessity was for a mobile gun platform.

Most development groups despaired when faced with the challenge, but the Shenandoah Valley Industrial Planning Commission simply accepted that the platform had to be larger than anyone was willing to admit. Thus was born the SheVa gun.

SheVas were four-hundred feet long and three hundred wide, with huge tracks surmounted by a "turret" that looked like a metal factory building. At the rear, concealed in the turret, was a heavily armored magazine for its eight main gun rounds, each of which looked like a cross between a rifle cartridge and an ICBM. The cantilevered gun, massive against any other backdrop, stuck out of the turret like a giant telescope and was so small in comparison it looked like an accidental add-on.

The gun consisted of three main portions, the gun itself and its supporting structures, the monstrous "weather shield" turret that created the gun room, and the drive system.

The gun was a two-hundred-foot-long, multi-chambered "Bull" gun. The basic propellant was an electro-plasma system that used an electrical charge to excite material and provide propulsion far beyond that available with any normal chemical propellant. However, due to power drop-off over distance, the barrel had secondary firing chambers down its side that added their own propulsion to the gigantic projectile. The combination permitted penetrator rounds, discarding sabot rounds with an outer disposable-plastic "sabot" and an inner uranium penetrator, to reach a velocity of nearly twenty-five-hundred meters per second, an unheard of speed prior to the SheVa gun.

It was mounted on a pivoting turret and elevation system that permitted it to fire from just below zero degrees to just beyond "straight up." It was, after all, designed as an anti-"aircraft" gun.

Instead of the normal "bag and round" system of most artillery, where the actual "bullet" was first loaded and then bags of powder rammed in behind, the gun used enormous cartridges that looked like nothing so much as a cross between a rifle cartridge and an ICBM; eight of the rounds were stored in a heavily reinforced magazine at the rear of the turret. Damage to the turret was to be avoided: depending upon whether the system was loaded for "penetrator" or "area of effect" there would be from eighty kilotons to eight *hundred* kilotons of explosive riding around in a SheVa. For that reason, among others, regular units tried to give them a wide berth.

To protect all of this machinery, some of which was not particularly weatherproof, the gun was encased in a gigantic "turret," actually a simple weather shield, that was a major engineering feat in itself. The shield was a hundred-foot-wide cube that mounted to the turret ring at the base of the gun so that it rotated at the same time as the weapon. The exterior of the shield was six-inch steel plate, not for any armoring reasons but simply because any lesser material buckled whenever the gun fired. The interior, on the other hand, was mostly empty, a vast space of soaring girders and curved braces that held the shield in place.

At the center top of the exterior of the shield was a crane, much better supported than the rest of the structure, that served to move around the humongous equipment necessary for even the simplest repairs to the gun.

To drive all of this structure required more than a little power. That was supplied by four Johannes/Cummings pebble-bed reactors. The core of the reactors were the "pebbles" themselves, tiny "onions" with layers of graphite and silicon wrapped around a fleck of uranium at the center. Due to the layering the uranium itself could never reach "melting temperature" and, therefore, the reactors were immune to run-away reactions. Furthermore, the helium coolant system prevented any radiation leakage; helium was unable to transmit radiation and thus even in a full coolant loss situation the reactor wasn't going to do anything but sit there.

Admittedly there were . . . issues with the reactors. Despite careful use of Galactic heat regeneration techniques, the drive room was hot as the hinges of hell. And if the reactor took a direct hit, as had happened from time to time, the tiny "pebbles" became one heck of a radioactive nuisance. But the power that the reactors provided more than made up for those little shortcomings. And reactor breaches were what clean-up crews lived for.

The drive system for the tank was just as revolutionary, using induction motors on all the drive wheels to provide direct power. Thus the SheVa could lose one or more drive wheels and still continue moving.

Despite their size SheVas were remarkably fragile; they were mobile gun platforms not tanks, a reality that had been proven again and again in the last few days. But despite that, SheVa Nine had fought its way on a long, slow, painful retreat and survived mostly intact.

Only its crew, and especially its engineer Warrant Officer Sheila Indy, realized just how shot up it was. Although the smoke pouring out through the numerous orifices created by hostile plasma fire gave some clue.

"Now that's a sight," Pruitt said. The gunner of SheVa Nine was a short, dark male, stocky but not fat, and he looked about ten years older than he had just two days before. His clothing stunk of ozone and sweat as he looked up at the tower of metal above him.

The SheVa was called "Bun-Bun" mostly because of the gunner, who had hooked the rest of the crew on an addictive webcomic called "Sluggy Freelance" and had personally painted the two-story cartoon of a switchblade wielding rabbit on the front carapace. Most of the picture had been blasted away in the previous day's battle but the motto "LET'S ROCK, POSLEEN BOY!" was still faintly evident.

"Bun-Bun or the blimps?" Indy replied wearily. The engineer was raven haired, firm breasted and on the near edge of beautiful, but it was hard to tell at present. She, too, stunk of ozone and sweat and her coveralls were covered in grease and blood, hers and others. The blood was beginning to rot and the smell hung around her like a cloud.

"Either," Pruitt answered. "Both. What's the damage?"

"Two reactors off-line," Indy replied. "One of 'em's got a *hole* in it; thank God for helium coolant systems. Struts shot out, two tracks severed, damage to the feed mechanism, damage on the magazine wall, electrical damage . . . all over the place."

"I don't think we're getting out of here any time soon," Pruitt said. "Good, I can get some sleep."

"There's a Colonel Garcia coming in on the first blimp," Colonel Robert Mitchell said, walking up behind them. The SheVa commander was a rejuv, so he looked superficially like he was about eighteen. But he had trained as a young armor officer to stop the Soviet forces that might one day pour through the Fulda Gap and that training, to shoot and scoot, had permitted him, and his crew, to survive where others had died. He and his crew had fought a slow, delaying action from the Rabun Valley to their present position near Balsam Gap and they had taken a fair bag of Posleen landers along the way. Now it was his unhappy duty to tell his troops that the party wasn't over.

"He says he can get her up and running in twelve hours."

"Impossible," Indy snapped. "He'd better have at least two reactors with him!"

The SheVa's power source was pebble-bed/helium reactors. They were remarkably stable—even with total loss of coolant they would not go into melt down—but the ones on SheVa Nine *had* suffered total loss of coolant and weren't going to be going on line short of a full overhaul.

"He's got *six* reactors with him," Mitchell said. "*And* a suite of add-on armor. Along with a brigade of repair techs. There are *nine* blimps on the way."

"Jesus!" Pruitt whispered. "That was fast."

"Garcia seems like an efficient character," Mitchell replied. "He's also got some engineering whiz-kid with him who's going to look us over and do some upgrades." He looked up as the blimp maneuvered into the limited flat area not occupied by the SheVa. "When the repair crew takes over I want you both to rack out. When we get going again, it's going to get interesting. Especially since as soon as we're back on line we've got orders to retake Rabun Gap. At all costs."

"Well, sir," McEvoy said, trying to avoid the Lamprey's fire. "It would be nice to have a SheVa, but we ain't got one."

"No, we don't," Tommy agreed grimly as another round from the lander caught one of the Charlie company Reapers. "Major O'Neal?"

✧   ✧   ✧

"You're getting hammered, Sunday," Mike replied. The majority of the battalion had just turned the corner on the hill and was closing on the remains of the Wall. The Wall had once been a six-story-high monstrosity of guns and concrete. Now the area looked like it had been assaulted by gophers determined to smooth it flat; with the exception of a small channel for the creek, the whole pass had been leveled.

"Yes, sir," the former NCO replied calmly. "We're also low on ammo. But I think we can take this guy with support. I'd like the whole battalion's on-call fire, if I may."

"More is better?" the battalion commander replied dryly. "I see what you mean, though." He checked his intelligence schematic and there were no forces within sight of the battalion; it made sense for everyone to fire on the Lamprey. "Turning over controls: Now."

"He must really like this guy," Duncan said as a priority targeting karat flashed into view. The karat was behind him and he spun in place and dropped to one knee as the entire battalion opened fire on one point on the lander.

"The Lamprey?" Stewart asked. "I'd target that fucker too, if for no other reason than to kill a smart God King."

"No, Sunday," Duncan replied. "How many times has he turned over full battalion fire to somebody else?"

"Not often," the intel officer admitted. "On the other hand, it's working."

The three hundred rifles of the battalion, when added to the Reapers, had the desired effect. As the continually rotating point passed over one of the weapons positions the armored hard point first vaporized under the fire of the Reapers then belched outward as the grav-guns penetrated into its magazines.

The lander quickly jinked to the south, throwing off the point of aim as it began to fire towards both the main battalion and the Reapers. But the damage was already done; even as it began a movement to the south it first rose then lowered abruptly, finally falling out of the sky, slamming into the side of the mountain and rolling out of sight.

"Okay, I don't know why everybody is just standing around looking at it," O'Neal said. "Change in plan. Charlie, face north. Bravo, face south. Cigar perimeter with the Reapers, wounded, command and staff in the middle. Scouts, figure out how that oolt'ondar got on the mountain; if there's a path destroy it."

He looked around at the still apparently frozen battalion and sighed. "Move, people."

"I do not like this O'Neal fellow," Tulo'stenaloor said, reading the logs of the AID communications. "He thinks altogether too fast for my comfort."

"Yes he does, estanaar," the intelligence officer said uncomfortably.

"What?" the commander asked. He could tell that there was something the S-2 was not saying.

"I was exploring his record," the officer replied, bringing up a file on the human commander. "He has an impressive history in defending many areas since the landings began on this planet. His unit has been more effective, for less casualties, than any of the other metal threshkreen, the 'ACS.' However, his fame among the humans dates from before the landings on this world."

"Oh," Tulo'stenaloor said, turning to look at the information the officer had brought up. "Where *does* it come from?"

"He was instrumental in the success of the humans on Aradan Five," the intel officer said.

"Oh." The warleader paused and carefully lowered his fluttering crest. "How was he 'instrumental'?" he asked softly.

"It was . . ." the intelligence officer paused. "It was his unit of metal threshkreen which rose out of the sea in the boulevard. Furthermore, it was he, personally, that destroyed Az'al'endai by setting off a nuclear charge on the side of the oolt'ondai's craft. By hand."

"How is he not dead?" the estanaar hissed thinly.

"He was near the center of the blast that destroyed the oolt'poslenar," the officer said with a flap of his crest. "It is believed that a plasma toroid formed around his suit and protected it. It blew him miles out to sea, but yet he lived."

"Impossible!" Tulo'stenaloor said. "Not even metal threshkreen could withstand a weapon that gutted the ship of Az'al'endai!"

"Nonetheless," the officer replied. "Records such as this rarely lie. The humans believe he is invincible, unkillable."

"We will just have to disabuse them of that notion," Tulo'-stenaloor said, fingering a crest ornament. "Essthree, push a force of the local levies up the route that Gamataraal used and begin loading oolt Po'osol with oolt; we'll fly them around and land them behind this force to continue the drive."

"Yes, estanaar," the operations officer said. "But I thought that you said that the greatest fault in this war was throwing in a hasty attack."

"It's all a balance," Tulo'stenaloor answered. "If we succeed, it will clear the road quickly. If we fail, what have we lost but a few disposable units? Ensure, though, that the way is not led with scout units; their weapons won't scratch metal threshkreen."

"Yes, estanaar. It will be done."

"And prepare an oolt'poslenar," the warleader added. "We'll just have to see who surrounds whom."

"We lost Captain Holder," Gunny Pappas noted. In the background there was the faint *thump* of a digging charge going off.

"I noticed," Mike answered. "*We* lost a total of twenty-two. Frankly, we got hammered."

"They were waiting for us," Stewart said. "It's the only thing that fits all the evidence. Not only for us, but they knew which shuttles had our fuel pods in them."

"We're okay on that, by the way," Duncan said. "We're cycling personnel through the chargers that we have. We recovered five pods including two from the first shuttle. And there are several beacons on the hills; we might still recover those. Using this shit ammo will drain the power fast if we have to maintain sustained fire."

"We'll either have enough or we won't," Mike noted. "There's some possibilities in terms of resupply; we'll see what happens. Stewart, start working on ways they could have known where and when; don't fixate on one, explore all the possibilities."

"All I can come up with right now is a mole of some sort," Stewart admitted. "Nothing else makes much sense."

"Like I said," Mike repeated with a grin in his tone. "Don't fixate; use that febrile mind for good. Pappas, we need the defenses finished quick; we can expect a thorough-going attack soon. I want slit trenches, bunkers and movement trenches. Continuous construction until we get hit and when we reconsolidate."

"Yes, sir," the sergeant major said. "We're on rock; once we get dug into it we're going to be hard to dig out."

"That's why I'll expect a fast attack," Mike said. "He'll try to push us out while we're digging in. So get out there now."

"'He'?" Stewart asked. "You holding back on your intel officer?"

"Always," Mike said with an unseen grin. "But in this case it's a surmise. This has all the marks of a real planned operation, one that has been planned for a while, for that matter. Look at those flying tanks and the close cooperation of the landers. There is one very smart God King out there who was smart enough to gather *other* smart Posleen. That's our real enemy. See if you can dig into the Darhel intel files; sometimes they know one Posleen from another. I want to know who I'm facing. I want that very much indeed."

"The hell with intel," Pappas muttered. "I want some fire support."

CHAPTER FOUR

They do not preach that their God will rouse them a
  little before the nuts work loose.
They do not teach that His Pity allows them to drop
  their job when they dam'-well choose.
As in the thronged and the lighted ways, so in the dark
  and the desert they stand,
Wary and watchful all their days that their brethren's
  day may be long in the land.

—Rudyard Kipling
"The Sons of Martha"

Near Willits, NC, United States of America, Sol III
0318 EDT Monday September 28, 2009 AD

The blimp, nearly two hundred meters in length, had a giant container attached to the bottom of it. As soon as the skids on the container touched the ground the blimp released it and bounced into the air, heading back over the mountains. One Posleen in the wrong place would take it out in a second, but the nuclear fire from the SheVa had apparently cleared out the entire

49

valley and as long as the blimps stayed low they were out of direct line of sight.

The rear of the container dropped open and by the glare of Klieg lights a line of heavy equipment and troops in black coveralls came pouring out. About half of the group headed for the SheVa as the rest began widening the landing zone.

At the head of the column was a figure riding an ATV. He rapidly crossed the distance to the SheVa crew and pulled the vehicle to a skidding stop.

"Maj . . . Lieutenant Colonel Robert Mitchell," Mitchell said, saluting.

"Colonel William Garcia," the colonel replied. He was wearing black coveralls like the rest of his unit, with a large patch on the shoulder, HC4, indicating that he was part of "Heavy Construction Brigade Four." The colonel returned the salute snappily then reached into the bellows pocket of his coveralls and tossed Mitchell a small package. "Let me be the first to congratulate you on your promotion. Those are $6.50. You can pay me if you survive."

"Thanks," Mitchell said, looking at the package of lieutenant colonel's silver leaves. "What now?"

"My crew is going to do a complete survey," Garcia said, turning to Indy. "You're the engineer?"

"Yes, sir," she replied. "I have a preliminary survey," she continued, holding out her PDA.

"Thanks." He took the proffered device and transferred the data. "Are those *MetalStorm* packs on top of this thing?"

MetalStorm anti-lander systems were among the less successful devices tried over the years. MetalStorm was a device for firing thousands of rounds in a very short period of time. It basically consisted of a gun barrel filled with bullets. Each of the bullets was fired, in turn, by an electrical charge. The highest rate of fire available was something over a million rounds per minute.

MetalStorm anti-lander systems were a 105mm, twelve-barrel device mounted on an Abrams tank chassis. Each of the barrels was loaded with one hundred rounds. The rounds were the same type as had originally been carried by the Abrams as an anti-tank round, but with the MetalStorm system all twelve hundred rounds could be fired in under twenty seconds. Firing all the rounds in one ripple fire was extremely unpleasant for the crew; it had been described as being put in a barrel and shaken by a giant. Despite that, the system was fairly ineffective at killing landers.

"Yes, sir," Mitchell said uncomfortably. "The chassis were . . . expended by my order."

"I'm sure there's a fascinating story there somewhere," Garcia said with a dry smile. "You haven't been firing them from up there, have you?"

"No sir," Pruitt replied. "They're just chained down."

"Okay, we'll pull them off and lift them out with one of the blimps," Garcia said.

"Hey, boss, let's rethink that." The person rounding the SheVa was apparently a civilian. He was a tall young male, heavily muscled and movie star gorgeous with long blond hair, wearing a black trenchcoat and gold sunglasses, his hands tucked deep in the pockets. He glanced up at the top of the SheVa and shrugged. "There's better stuff to do with them than just fly them out."

"What are you thinking, Paul?" Garcia asked. "Oh, pardon me. Ladies and gentlemen, this is Paul Kilzer. He was one of the original SheVa designers and agreed to come along as a consultant."

Pruitt was staring at the apparition with his mouth hanging open. "Riff?" he asked with a gasp.

"No, my name's Paul," the civilian answered with a frown. "Do I know you?"

"Uh . . . no," Pruitt responded. "But . . . what are you thinking of doing with the Storms?"

"Do we have crews?" the civilian asked.

"They're scattered through the SheVa, racked out," Mitchell responded. "Why?"

"Well, I think I know where we can get some turret rings," Paul said. "Running power to them won't be hard. Run some commo and you've got really cool firepower. You'll need some additional juice, but we've got six reactors along with us. We can upgun this thing along with the armor add-ons. That should help. A bit."

"Dude," Pruitt whispered.

"Do you have a specific plan?" Garcia asked.

"I think I did some planning a while back," Paul said, pulling a book out of his right jacket pocket. "Let me check my notes."

Indy checked a hysterical laugh and looked around at the group. "Sorry."

Garcia looked at his PDA and nodded. "The survey team confirms all your damage reports, Warrant. Why don't you guys go get some rest and we'll get to work on this thing."

"Works for me," Mitchell said, fatigue causing him to sway. "The Storm commander is Major Chan. You'll need to consult with her. And her command, I suppose."

"They're all transferred to you as of now," Garcia said. "I'll handle the details, get some rest, Colonel."

Despite his fatigue, Pruitt found it impossible to sleep. He had taken half a Provigil less than two hours before the repair brigade had landed and until it wore off he was wide awake, if mentally slow. So he laboriously climbed the stairs to the top of the SheVa to get a better look at the activity.

The division of infantry that had been bottled up on the far side of Balsam Gap had finally started to flow through. Its APCs, trucks and tanks were now barreling down Highway 23 towards Dillsboro, probing for the Posleen in the distant valley and finding surviving bridges. Things had been tight, with nearly a million Posleen closing in on the trapped SheVa, until the President had released Bun-Bun to use nuclear fire. But three rounds of anti-matter "area effect" weapons had cleared out the main concentration. The division was now probing for the survivors and looking for where the aliens were reconsolidating. Not to mention trying to capture critical terrain features.

In the meantime the bulldozers and earthmovers of the SheVa brigade had opened up a larger landing area, permitting a continuous flow of blimps to drop their loads and pick up the empty containers, clearing the way for the next.

In addition to the earth movers, specialty heavy equipment had flowed in at a tremendous rate. One device, apparently made from a giant steam shovel, was an automated plasma cutter. The massive tracked system had driven directly from the container to the SheVa and begun cutting huge holes in the wall of the drive system. There were also three specialty track breakers which moved from damaged track to damaged track, removing the man-sized bolts that connected the tracks, pulling them off and replacing them with new. Some of the damaged tracks were on the underside; it would be interesting to see what the repair techs did about that.

As Pruitt watched, a massive forklift rolled out of one of the containers carrying a complete reactor pack. It drove from the container to one of the holes that had been cut and right into the interior of the SheVa. Pruitt hoped that any of the MetalStorm troops that had been sleeping in the engineering bay had been moved out of the way.

One whole load had been dropped directly in front of the SheVa. It was wrapped in plastic but appeared to be huge plates of some sort. He saw the civilian consultant pop up out of one of the hatches and painfully got to his feet to walk over.

"What are those?" he asked, pointing over the low railing on the top of the SheVa. They were nearly two hundred feet in the air so the view was somewhat disquieting.

If the height bothered Paul it wasn't apparent. "Add-on armor. We're going to throw it on the front of the track to cut down on damage."

"It looks . . . heavy," Pruitt said, thinking about some of the frankly insane maneuvers the SheVa had gone through in the previous battle. "It's not going to slow us down, is it?"

"Not after we add four reactors," Paul answered. "We're going to pull the two damaged ones and put in all six. Your top speed will stay the same, but your torque will go up, which should help in the mountains."

"What about the tracks?" Pruitt asked. Too much strain on the track connections could cause the entire track to blow free.

"Your driver had better be careful," Paul replied.

"Huh," Pruitt said, shivering in memory. "Did you hear how we got the MetalStorm turrets but not the chassis?"

"No."

"Good story. Got a second?"

Major Vickie Chan watched as the MetalStorm turret was lowered onto the freshly mounted turret ring. The blaze of light from underneath, where repair techs were welding in support struts, vanished as the turret settled onto the ring.

The major was a tall, pretty Eurasian whose calm demeanor was belied by her absolute intensity in combat. She had been a captain until the previous day, in command of a company of MetalStorm tracks. Her company had linked up with the SheVa during the retreat and had followed it the whole way, being carried for the last half. She had gotten used to an independent command. Since nobody knew quite what to do with her guns they had shuttled like gypsies from area to area, but after the loss of her chassis it was pretty clear that was going to end. If she was going to be tied into a larger command structure, a SheVa was probably a good choice. And Colonel Mitchell was a good commander: smart, capable and lucky.

So why did she feel like someone had just walked over her grave?

Maybe it was the speed with which things were changing. The dozen turret rings had appeared as if by magic, requisitioned from a tank repair depot in Asheville. Garcia apparently had a high and unquestioned priority for parts and equipment, but any situation in which Army Group commanders were giving orders for parts to be delivered on a priority basis meant that the situation was totally FUBARed. And, presumably, it was up to SheVa Nine, and its "secondary weapons commander" to unFUBAR it.

Joy.

She turned as the six-inch plate of the SheVa top deck rang to a set of bootheels and smiled at the repair brigade commander.

"That, sir, is something I never thought I'd see," she said, gesturing at the turret that was now being tested for true.

"It's a good basic idea," Garcia said. "As always, Paul's suggestions had to be tweaked for details, but it should significantly aid in the counterattack. May I ask a question?"

"Shoot."

"What happened to the chassis?"

"Heh," she laughed softly. "I'm not sure what happened to them officially. Do you want to know what *really* happened?"

"Out of school."

"Okay," she said. "Out of school, we used them to unstick the SheVa."

"Errr," Garcia looked down at the massive structure. Next to it the D-9 bulldozers of the construction battalion looked like Tonka toys. "Even a dozen Abrams could barely budge one of these things. I know; I've gotten three unstuck. It generally requires about a week."

"We didn't have a week," Chan said wearily, running fingers through her greasy hair then looking at them in distaste. "Mitchell, the crazy bastard, took us across Betty Gap, which doesn't even have a road. Or it *didn't* have one. Anyway, on the way down the SheVa started to . . . slide. Most amazing thing I've ever seen, and the scariest. It just . . . skied down the mountainside and ended up jammed between two bluffs. It was under fire at the time I might add."

"What kind?" the colonel asked, fascinated.

"At first it was a group of dismounted Posleen," she said. "We hit them from the flank, though. But then a couple of landers came over the ridge. Pruitt took both of them out at under a thousand meters."

"But that's . . ." Garcia stopped. "If their rounds went through, or if the lander's tanks sympathetically detonated, they were going to be blown away along with the lander."

"They did," she grimaced. "Both rounds went off outside the landers. At that point, though, Pruitt had gotten good at missing the lander's antimatter containment, or hitting it if he preferred. He's *very* good. Anyway, one of the landers rolled down the hill and nearly hit them; he blew it off by firing under it and turning it with the antimatter blast. That was at under five hundred meters."

"Shit."

"Yeah, very hairy. We got caught in both of the SheVa antimatter blasts. Anyway, at the end of it, the SheVa was stuck as hell. An engineer major happened to be in the area, retreating the same way. He suggested unloading the turrets and basically jamming the chassis under the SheVa like a bunch of boards. It worked but . . . well let's just say getting the crunched metal that we left behind is going to be an interesting exercise in salvage."

"Ouch." Garcia chuckled then shook his head. "Sorry about losing your tanks."

"Oh, I didn't really mind," she said. "You ever been in one of those things when it fires?"

"No."

"Let's just say that the crews cheered when the SheVa crushed them."

"Bad?"

"Indescribable," she said. "We'd just finished firing when one of the SheVa rounds went off. Ten kiloton explosion, maybe nine hundred meters away. You know what my gunner said?"

"No."

" 'What was that last bang?' " She chuckled grimly. "You know it's bad when a nuke going off is anticlimactic."

"I guess we'd better add some reinforcing."

"Yep. Better do that little thing. How's it going?"

"It's not the most shot up SheVa I've ever worked on," Garcia answered. "But it's close. We'll finish in time, though, or an hour or so over."

"How are we going to control the guns?" she asked.

"I'm putting in a secondary control area," Garcia answered. "Paul's design again. You'll be there along with the commo person that Mitchell picked up. You'll have commo with all your tracks but you'll have to draw your information from the SheVa's systems."

"That will work," she said.

"Paul's pouring out plans for a general upgrade on SheVas," Garcia said. "He wants to make them all bristle with secondary weapons. I pointed out that there's no way to control that much firepower without a large crew. He wants to use computer controls." Garcia grimaced.

"And the problem with that is?"

"You don't want to see Paul's idea of artificial intelligence," Garcia sighed. "He wants to rip some code out of a computer game. I've convinced him that that would be bad."

"Heh," Chan laughed. "Missile-armed kangaroos?"

"I've heard that story," Garcia sighed. "Something like that. I've got this image of the guns identifying Himmit as enemy Ghosts and Indowy as Protoss. For the time being, I think that it's better if your crews stay in the turrets controlling the fire."

"I'd better get with the commanders and start working on how to operate. Are they going to be scattered all along the rim?"

"More or less. Five at the front, three at the rear and two on each side. The outer one on each end will be able to support to the sides."

"Lots of firepower, but not much in the way of armor," Vickie pointed out.

"Plenty frontal," the commander said. "And Paul has a couple of additional concepts that he's working out. But if they get in close and swarm, you'll be in trouble."

"And if they do?"

"Well, Captain, that's going to be *your* job to prevent."

"You know, Stewie, this really sucks."

The battalion was crouched in a double line of mud-filled holes, some of them connected by the trench the unit had been constructing when the Posleen assault hit, with their grav-rifles on extensions, pouring fire into the oncoming waves of centaurs.

The M-300 grav-rifle was attached to the suit by a sinuous organic-looking extender over the right shoulder. The extender included a feed tube that was supplied from the ammunition lockers within the suit. In battle the firing suit could crouch within a hole, or around a corner, and extend the rifle out to engage oncoming targets; the rifle had its own sighting system that led back to the suit control systems.

There had been suggestion that the suits have *two* rifles attached, but the limit of the guns was not firepower but ammunition availability. The suits had six separate ammunition storage lockers, each with their own blow-out panel, but even so, and despite the fact that the actual "bullets" were nought more than uranium teardrops the size of the end of a pinkie, they could run through their entire on-board store of ammunition in three hours. Especially in what was called "a target-rich environment." And that description certainly met the current conditions.

The Posleen were coming on in good order, packed in like sardines and moving forward at a trot. Until they ran into the intersecting streams of depleted uranium grav-rounds. Where the streams of silver lightning hit the wall of bodies there was a continuous explosion of red fire and yellow blood. Each of the teardrop rounds of the ACS had the force of a small bomb and one that struck killed not only the target, but usually the centaur to either side. The resulting destruction built up a wall of flesh that the centaurs were beginning to find to be an obstacle. But still they kept coming. And if they kept it up for long enough, it might even work.

"We've got supply issues, boss." Duncan was in the line now, something that he had avoided for nearly five years. But with no resupply coming in, and no indirect fire support except the Reapers, and no way or reason to maneuver the battalion, he didn't have much else to do. And every round counted.

"Bullets we have aplenty . . ." Stewart said. "Power . . ."

Two troopers, a rifle troop that had had his grav-gun hit by a lucky HVM shot and a one-legged support troop, wearing a bulbous suit of armor that made him look like the Michelin Man, were crawling along a shallow trench from position to position, feeding power to the suits from the surviving antimatter power packs. The problem was not the power being drained by the suits, they were stationary and the trickle of power for their environment systems was no sort of drain, but from the rounds they were firing.

The bullets were accelerated to a small percentage of the speed of light before they left the barrel of the rifles. This gave them a tremendous, really an overkill, punch at the end, which explained why a three-millimeter-wide, four-millimeter-long teardrop was causing explosions the size of artillery shells.

But that took power, lots of it. The bullets were fired in a stream, much faster than any conventional machine gun, with multiple rounds in the barrel at any one time. And power was power. To cause the effect of a hundred kilos of TNT required that much power be put into pushing them down the barrel.

The power was supposed to come from the rounds themselves. "Standard" rounds had a droplet of antimatter at the base, sufficient to power the round and even bleed a little over to the suits. But the humans didn't have the technology to create the ultraminiature containment system necessary. So since the blockade of Earth had shut off the flow of Galactic Technology, and as "standard" rounds become few and far between, the suits had fallen back on "emergency" procedures, using the power in their suits to drive their guns.

And *that* was a major power drain.

Mike watched for a moment as one of the suits topped up, and then he followed the crawling tech suit as it made its way laboriously to the next position. Even as the tech moved, the previous suit's power levels dropped noticeably. And the antimatter pack it was dragging showed yellow.

"I'm open to suggestions," Mike said, trying to keep the weariness out of his voice.

"We're already sniping the God Kings," Duncan replied.

The normals that made up the bulk of the Posleen assault were of subhuman intelligence, but the God King leaders made up for it. With the battalion nearly invisible in their holes, it was hard for the normals to even find a target. But whenever a God King saw the streams of silver it naturally tracked back to the starting point and targeted it. Whenever a God King engaged a target, all the normals around him, bonded and unbonded, tended to aim at the same target. And when those storms of projectiles came in, suits, or at least the extended weapons systems, died.

To reduce the problem, they had sent the scout suits—which used a lower velocity projectile that was nearly undetectable in a battle—up the slopes on either side to target the leaders in the horde.

The problem with that was that spotting God Kings who were off their tenar was hard. They had crests, but if they didn't lift the crests, which laid down against the long Posleen neck, they were almost indistinguishable from their troops.

On the other hand, God Kings tended to raise their crests under stress.

"We're selecting for smart God Kings, you know," Mike said. "We have been for years."

"I suppose we have," Duncan replied.

"If this is what we get for it, I think it was a *bad* idea," Stewart said, then yelled.

"You okay?" Mike checked his monitors. Stewart's weapon was rated as destroyed.

"Well, I thought I'd seen it all," Stewart replied, slowly. "You know, it's really spectacular when a Posleen round goes in the barrel as one of ours is going out."

"You okay?"

"Well, my hand's still there." The command suits did not have extensors so the commanders and staff were firing their rifles by holding them up out of their holes.

"We've got about four more hours of power," Duncan said, getting the discussion back on track. The guns were firing almost on their own; killing Posleen was an easy multi-task for everyone in the battalion at this point.

"There's a local cache," Mike said, quietly. "It's even got a battalion load of standard rounds in it. And an antimatter pack."

"There *is*?" Duncan said. "It's not on the maps."

"That's because it's off the books."

"Oh."

"Yeah. And OH." Mike grimaced, unseen, inside his suit. "The problem, of course, is getting to it."

"Where is it?"

CHAPTER FIVE

Near Rabun Gap, GA, United States of America, Sol III
0518 EDT Monday September 28, 2009 AD

Mueller slid down the muddy slope and dropped to the ledge outside the cave, letting the muzzle of his rifle lead him in.

The cave that held what Papa O'Neal had referred to as "Cache Four" was on a nearly vertical, tree-covered slope. How the eldest O'Neal had gotten the dozens and dozens of large and heavy boxes into the cave was a mystery, one that on their previous trip Mueller and Mosovich had been careful to avoid questioning. But on that same trip they had also been attacked by a feral Posleen as they exited the cave. Thus Mueller's caution as he entered it.

The first change that he noted was that there was a heavy metal door in place; the cache had been open the last time they were there. All things considered, though, it was probably for the best, what with the occasional nuke round dropping in the pot.

The problem being that they needed what was on the other side of the door and there didn't seem to be any latches on this side.

That, on the other hand, seemed to indicate that someone or something was on the other side.

He was tired and the thoughts seemed to come slowly. He'd been using Provigil but all that really did was keep you awake; you still

61

got "tired stupid." Now he turned the gun around and banged on the door with the butt.

"Anyone home?"

Cally sat up at the bang and the muffled voice on the other side. It sounded like a human, but it was possible it was just a very smart Posleen.

She picked up her Steyr and went to the door. "*Who's there?*"

"*Cally?*"

"*Yeah, who's there?*"

"*Mueller! Open up.*"

She set the gun down and pulled the door back, composing her features as she did so.

Mueller just looked at her for a second then wrapped his arms around her in a bear hug.

"Jesus Christ! We were sure you were dead."

Cally wiped at the tears in her eyes as the rest descended the slope and slipped through door. She had to hug each in turn.

"Wendy, you made it!"

"Thanks to luck and some really weird shit," the girl replied, hugging back. "Papa?"

Cally just shook her head, wiping at the tears again and wondering at the frozen expression on the face of the unknown young woman who was last through the door.

Wendy turned and looked at her. "Shari..."

"Shari?" Cally asked. The woman in the doorway was about half the age of the woman who had come to visit their farm, and promptly fallen in love with her still older grandfather. But the face... "Shari?! Oh, God, Shari..."

"It's okay, dear," the woman replied, stone faced. "We all die somewhere."

"No, it's *not* okay!" Cally said, taking her hands. "We were... talking, just when the Posleen attacked. He, we, were really looking forward to you coming to live with us. I was, too. I...I'm so sorry!"

"I think I'm supposed to be comforting you," Shari said, starting to cry. "Not the other way around."

"We need to get the kids bedded down," Elgars said, stolidly. "We can talk about this later."

Cally showed them boxes with sleeping gear, both poncho liners and blankets, then started an electric space heater; the cave had been comfortable enough for her but the kids were obviously whipped. All of the children, even Billy, given reasonably dry clothes and a comfortable place to lie down, fell asleep almost before they were flat.

"How did you get here?" Cally asked.

"Walked," Mueller said, pulling off his boots with a groan. "The kids were about dead the last five miles; we had to carry them."

"There is plenty to tell," Wendy said. "But first, how did you get here and do you know what's going on?"

"When the attack got bad we moved to the bunker," Cally said slowly; it was obviously hard for her to tell the story. "We had Posleen moving up the valley and . . . things like flying saucers overhead. Then, when the lander came in sight, Papa told me to pull back. He was going follow right afterwards. Then there was a bright flash. I was in the doorway to the inner shelter and it sort of blew me in, I guess. I came to and the main passage had collapsed behind me. After I got my shit together I went out through the side passage; it had a cave-in on it, but I could wriggle through. The valley was . . . trashed. It had to be a nuke or something. The lander and Posleen were gone and the battle in the Gap seemed to have stopped, which I thought was pretty bad. I took a quick look around but everything was just . . . gone. Then I went to the bunker and found . . . Well, I could barely move the rubble but I found Papa's hand. It was cold." She stopped and shook her head.

"I will not bawl like a baby because my grandfather is d-dead," she half snarled, half sobbed. "Over five billion people on this miserable ball have died in the past years, I will not cry over one more!"

"Yes you will," Shari said, leaning forward and taking her in her arms. "You don't cry for him, you cry for yourself and that he is no longer there." Shari wiped her eyes on the top of the girl's head. "You cry for your loss."

"*I want him back!*" Cally shouted. "He wasn't supposed to *die*! I *needed* him!"

"I want him back, too," Shari said. "I do, too."

"The bastard just *left* me in the middle of a nuclear God-damned war," she said, sobbing.

"Well, that's one way to look at it," Mueller responded, stirring a pot of mushy, freeze-dried noodles and chicken.

"How?" Cally snapped.

"I always knew the old guy was tough and I was right; it took a nuke to take him out."

"Oh, Mueller," Cally said with a chuckling sob.

"We'll go down and check on the body," Wendy said, sitting up.

"Why?" Elgars replied. "The environment is incredibly hostile; going to recover a body that the Posleen have probably already eaten doesn't strike me as a good tactical action."

Shari turned on the captain with a snarl, but Mosovich leaned forward and laid a hand on her arm. "Captain, it's not good tactics but it *is* good in other ways. Most of the best units refuse to leave anyone behind, living or dead. It's a fifteen-minute walk. It will also permit us to get a good look at the valley. Recon *is* part of our job description."

Elgars frowned then nodded. "Okay, approved. If the security conditions permit. But somebody has to stay here to guard the fort and watch the children; we're not taking them with us."

"I'll do that," Shari said.

"I see you're carrying," Cally said, wiping her eyes and deliberately changing the subject from the loss of her grandfather. "And doing so like you know how. I guess you guys saw some action on the way?"

"The Sub-Urb is gone," Wendy said by way of reply. "We got out through an Indowy facility in the basement, in the agricultural section actually. It had some . . . weird facilities." She gestured at Shari.

"And part of the secret of my miraculous rebirth was explained," Elgars said dryly. "It was apparently that facility that 'rebuilt' me."

"And you, too?" Cally asked Shari.

"I got hit, bad, on the way out," Shari replied.

"Needle round right through her spine and mid-section," Wendy expanded. "Back to front. Very bloody."

"I woke up in a purple chamber," Shari continued. "Looking like this." She gestured at her body.

"You look . . . good," Cally said, starting to tear up again.

"What?"

"I was just thinking . . . how much Papa would like to see you like that," Cally said, regaining her composure.

"Oh, he liked me well enough the other way," Shari said with a shake of her head. "Amazingly enough."

"I never got it," Mueller said shaking his head in turn. "Oldest guy in the group and he gets the girl. Now there's, what?, four women in this here cave and *I'm* the one doing the cooking!"

"Oh, shut up you old fogie," Cally said with a laugh. "Where did you pick up these two parasites?" she asked Wendy.

"Near Coweta Hydrological," she said with a laugh. "I'd just fallen in a river. There I was in a sopping wet shirt, trying to hold my weapon out of the water; I looked like a 'Packed and Stacked' girl. Which Mueller, of course, was happy to agree with."

"We'd been tasked with reconnaissance of the Posleen movement," Mosovich said. "But they moved faster than we could and the routes north got cut. I was thinking that if we could get some stuff from here we could follow the Tennessee Divide across North Georgia and find one of the other passes that was holding out, then maybe get some transportation back to friendly territory."

"By the time we realized how hot the area was we were too close to go back," Wendy continued, making a motion like a mushroom cloud. "And the kids needed stuff to keep them alive in the weather; it's turning nasty out there."

"Well, there's plenty here," Cally replied. "Food, blankets, even rucksacks. As well as ammo and demo, but no guns."

"Guns we've got," Mosovich said. "We've even got about as much ammo as we can reasonably carry. Food and snivel-gear we're short on."

"So are we going to move out of here?" Cally asked.

"We probably need to," Jake replied with a nod. "There's an ACS unit holding down the Gap, your dad's by the way, but . . . I don't know how long they can hold and even if they *do* hold I don't see who there is to relieve them. There's an infantry unit all the way up by Dillsboro and a shot-up SheVa gun up there. But nothing short of there." He paused and shrugged his shoulders. "I think your dad's unit's not going to be much but a spoiling attack."

Cally nodded her head in thought but then shook it. "Dad I refuse to worry about. He has been in more 'impossible' situations than any other person in the world, I think, and he always comes out alive. Nobody *else* in his unit might, but he does. I guess he *could* die there, but I wouldn't bet . . . I was going to say I wouldn't bet the farm but if anyone wants four hundred acres of radioactive wasteland . . ."

"Um, speaking of which," Mueller said. "We've got AIDs. Do . . . You could talk to him if you want."

"That's an interesting idea," Cally said. "But I don't want to joggle his elbow." Even in the concrete reinforced cave the slam of distant explosions could be more felt than heard. "Just . . . let him know that I'm alive."

"Major O'Neal?"

Mike's arm was actually getting tired. It was mostly supported by the armor, but just holding it over his head for this long was getting hard. And not only was power going down like a waterfall, even the ammunition supply was starting to take a hit. The teardrops rounds were *tiny* and, unlike the power packs, most of the resupply had survived. But the battle had already expended over sixty *million* rounds; suits had had to reload onboard ammunition at least once, in one case twice. But that didn't mean the Posleen were running out of bodies.

"Yes," he asked tiredly. "What horrible news or emergency is it now?"

"Not horrible at all, sir, more mixed. Cally O'Neal is alive. She is in contact with Sergeant Major Mosovich from Fleet Strike Long Range Recon and they and some other refugees are in a shelter near your father's farm."

"And Dad?" Mike asked, suspecting why the news was mixed.

"Your father is presumed dead, sir," the AID said tonelessly.

Mike wrinkled his head at the tone and the wording. "Presumed?"

"Yes, sir, he was last seen in a bunker near the explosion of a lander."

Again, that toneless reply. Mike had noted that AIDs got all toneless when he hit a security baulk, at which point they became *non*-communication devices with remarkable alacrity.

Mike thought about a couple of things he'd like to say but skipped them all. "How many able bodies at that shelter? And is there any ground transportation?" was what he asked.

"Five adults and no, everything was destroyed by the blast."

"Hmm . . ." He looked at the power graph and shook his head. "Give me General Horner."

"Jack, it's Mike."

The major and the general went back farther than either of them cared to remember, but the casual familiarity was a sign of insult, not respect; Mike O'Neal had not yet forgiven the general for sending him on what was looking more and more like a forlorn hope.

"Yes, Major?" Jack Horner was a tall spare, man with cold blue eyes that belied his apparent age. He keyed the AID to throw up a hologram of the battle around Rabun Gap and shook his head; the image showed a solid tide of red going out of sight.

"We've got a little problem," Mike said.

"I can see that."

"Oh, it's not the Posleen, per se. After trying a few fancy tricks, they're coming at us in the same old way and we're stopping them in the same old way. We're taking casualties, but mostly to weapons-systems. No, the problem is we've got about three hours' worth of power left."

"What?"

"I blame it on Gunny Thompson," Mike said lightly.

It took Jack a moment to remember who Mike was talking about. Gunny Thompson had been on the design team for the ACS weapons system, along with a recently recalled web designer named Michael O'Neal and General Jack Horner.

"Why Gunny Thompson, who the last time I heard was on Barwhon?"

"Well," Mike said with a sigh. "He wanted a ray gun and the best I could do with the technology that was offered was a gravgun that shot fast enough it *looked* like a ray gun. The problem of course being that that meant it was a power-hog."

"Your guns are being used *that* much?" Jack asked. Even in the hottest battles the Posleen could only take an hour or so of being turned into offal; then they retreated.

"No artillery to slow them down, Jack," Mike responded. "They're just piling themselves up, literally. And they're not really going *forward*, just piling. It's . . . it's insane, even for the Posleen."

"Maybe not," Horner replied. "Maybe . . ."

"Maybe they *know* we have a power problem?" Mike asked. "Is there something you're not telling me?"

"Well, I got an intelligence report recently that suggested the Posleen *might*, I say again *might* be able to penetrate the AID network."

"So . . . they're listening to *this* conversation?" Mike said. "That explains the ambush."

"What ambush?"

"When we landed the Posleen seemed to be laying for us, but they concentrated their fire on the support shuttles. That's when most of our spare power went away."

"Another datum," Jack replied, running his hands through his hair. It had been white, then, after rejuvenation, black again. Now it was turning white at the temples. And he was still a physical age of about twenty. Command was hell.

"So if they can listen in to the AID network, what in the hell are we going to do? I can't disconnect my AID, it runs my damned *suit!*"

"I'll think about it. Tell me what your answer to the power problem is in the meantime."

"There's a cache near here, one that's not on the network, come to think of it," Mike replied. "It's got ammunition and a powerpack, *standard* ammo with its own power."

"From when you were laying down caches?" Horner asked.

"Correct. Here's my question, are there *any* more heavy weapons available? Can the SheVa range?"

"Do you *want* a direct answer?" the general replied.

"Yes."

"I don't know. The SheVa is out of range and it will be for some hours yet. I don't *know* of anything else." Horner smiled broadly, a sure sign that he was angry about something. "What I *normally* would do is ask my AID, which gives me the impression our enemies might know more about our capability than *we* do."

"*If* we're penetrated," Mike replied.

"Yes." Horner looked around the temporary headquarters and suddenly realized the AID could see everything that he could. The human senior officers had come to depend upon the systems, which was suddenly starting to look like a bad dependency.

"So who's coming to relieve us?" Mike asked, bitterly. "I seem to remember you promising that the Ten Thousand would be on their way in a jiffy. But I notice they're still up in Virginia."

Horner smiled thinly. "I've got forces on the way. We've got penetrations all up and down the East Coast, Major. This is *not* the only emergency on my plate. I had to divert the Ten Thousand to handle a major incursion in the Shenandoah. I know that you think your battalion comes first, but when I've got a big thrust headed right for six SheVas that are almost finished construction and two Sub-Urbs I have to decide where to allocate my assets. And in this case, the Ten Thousand is allocated to hold between the Posleen and the Sub-Urbs, Major. There is one spot of bright news; I've been informed that a reconnaissance force has been detached from the Barwhon fleet. I don't know how large it is, or what its priorities will be, but we might get some support from them."

"So, what *do* you have on the way, General? For sure? Not pie in the sky 'reconnaissance forces' that are probably one frigate and a drone."

"You can read your AID, *Major.*"

"You've got one *loser* division tasked. It couldn't even take Balsam

Gap from the *easy* side. And a SheVa gun that's rated as minimum time to repair of five days. So would you like to tell me who's going to play cavalry? General?!"

"They'll be there," Horner ground out. "No more than twenty-four hours from when the SheVa is repaired. And that will be sometime tomorrow . . . today. Soon."

"Glad to hear that, General, but 'sometime tomorrow' is going to be way too late. Here's the deal. In about three hours I'm going to have to perform a break-out and leave this position."

"You can't do that, Major," Horner said furiously.

"I can and I will. In three hours we'll be down to throwing rocks. I've thrown rocks at the Posleen in my time, but never as a primary assault method. As far as my scouts can tell, there is no practical end to the Posleen forces. If we can recover the cache, a big if, and if *you* can find some fire support, a big if, we can retake the Gap. And with the materials we'll have we'll be able to hold for another, oh, twelve hours or so. At our current kill ratio we'll be able to kill approximately six million Posleen before we become combat ineffective and get overrun. Which I think would be enough even for you."

"If you *can't* recover the cache, because the Posleen pour over the position, or if you *can't* retake the pass, the whole eastern seaboard will be turned."

"Yep, so you'd better go find us some more fire support, hadn't you, General?"

"Major O'Neal has disconnected," the AID informed him.

Horner just nodded, smiling broadly. The headquarters had gotten remarkably quiet during the conversation, which had been fully audible, and now it kept quiet, since everyone knew exactly what that expression meant.

"Colonel Nix," Horner called.

"Yes, sir." The man was slight, bespectacled and balding since he still hadn't hit the age that had been specified for rejuvenation. His uniform was somewhat rumpled and he had a pen sticking out of the corner of one pocket while all his blouse pockets bulged with materials. Anyone looking at him would have pegged him immediately as a geek. And they would have been right except solely for the "degree" of geekiness. Colonel Nix wasn't just a geek, he was an ubergeek.

His official title was "Special Assistant to the CONARC for Information Security." He had been the first to determine that the Tenth Corps had been hacked, how it had occurred and what to do to correct it. Since then Horner had ensured he was always at arms reach and on more than one occasion Nix had either foiled additional hacking attacks or detected them before they became a threat. Horner's abilities stopped at being able to compose a document and he both trusted and liked his ubergeek.

"Tell me why *you* think the AID net has been compromised," Horner said, smiling and without looking away from the wall.

"As I said, sir, there were some indications going all the way back to the battles with the Eleventh ACS division in Nebraska that the Posleen were either omniscient or reading the Eleventh's mail," the colonel replied. "The Darhel *guarantee* that the AID communications are unbreakable, and as far as I know no human group has broken them. But they also *guaranteed* that we would be materially supported. They've made a lot of guarantees that didn't stand up. I have *no* hard data, sir. It's more a gut call than anything, sir, but . . ."

"O'Neal's forces were apparently ambushed on landing," Horner replied. "They specifically targeted the supply shuttles."

"Pretty nice datum, sir," the colonel said with a frown as he looked at the device around the general's wrist. "Uh, sir . . ."

"I'm aware of the fact that they're probably aware of the fact, Colonel," the general replied with a frown. That meant he found the point humorous. "That they know that we know that they know."

"Yes, sir."

"It probably won't work to reduce emissions, but we'll do that. Get rid of this thing," he continued, handing over the device. "Put it in a safe someplace far away and get me a telephone. I need to make some phone calls.'"

"What are we going to do about the ACS, sir?" Nix asked. Everyone had heard the conversation.

"We're *not* going to discuss what we're going to do about the ACS in front of an AID," Horner said with a tight, angry smile. "That's the *first* thing we're going to do for the ACS."

"Yes, sir." Nix paused. "Is there a second thing?"

"Call the SheVa."

"Rise and shine, Pruitt."

Pruitt had been new to SheVa guns when the crew had taken over SheVa Nine, but he had quickly noted one defect in the design. While the crew quarters were more than adequate, nearly sybaritic compared to the conditions of "grunt" infantry or regular tankers, they were located half way across the turret. That meant a mad dash down a thirty-meter hallway and climbing two sets of ladders before anyone could be at their positions. While that wasn't a big deal most of the time, in the sort of conditions they had just been through, two days of hard fighting, with Posleen ships appearing at any time, it was a recipe for disaster.

And it wasn't like he could rack out in his chair. For whatever reason, the U.S. Ground Forces hadn't considered the rudimentary capability of reclining the chairs. He had heard rumors that some people had switched them out, but he'd had neither the time nor the inclination. He had a better idea.

Stopping by one of the numerous "military supply" stores that popped up around every base had actually been difficult; Ground Force was in a real rush to get the SheVa back in commission. But he had managed and picked up a few items he thought might be of use. One of which he was currently using.

Pruitt rolled over in the survival hammock and groaned. "Go 'way."

"Come on, Pruitt." Indy jabbed him hard in the ribs. "Posleen landers on the horizon."

It was as if she had hit him with a cattle prod; Pruitt was out of the sack and halfway up the single set of stairs between him and the command center before he even noticed that he was up. Or the laughter behind him.

"I was *joking* sleepyhead," Indy laughed. "But we do have to get going."

"What now?" he looked at his watch and shook his head muzzily. "Six hours? Are the repairs done yet?"

"Not all of them, but that's not going to matter if we don't get going."

"Why?"

"Let's just say that it sucks to be ACS."

"Okay, General Keeton woke me up, too." Major Mitchell looked as if he hadn't gotten any sleep at all. In fact, he'd gotten nearly three hours. However, on top of two days continuous combat ops, that was like *saying* none at all. All it had done was make him logier.

The meeting to discuss an operations plan for the SheVa's side of the counterattack was taking place in the command center; it was one of the only places large enough, there were projection screens for laying out the plan, and it had enough chairs and ledges for everyone to sit.

Besides the SheVa crew there was Captain Chan, her senior NCO and Mr. Kilzer. All but Kilzer looked half asleep. He, on the other hand, was bouncing around like a ferret on a sugar high.

Mitchell yawned and gestured at the projected map. "The ACS got chewed up on landing and they're running short on power. In a couple of hours they are going to have to pull out of the Gap and get a resupply. After *that* they're going to have to *retake* the Gap, put the plug back in the bottle.

"To retake the Gap, they need nukes. Guess who has the only nukes within five hundred miles?"

Reeves raised his hand. "Major, even if there weren't Posleen in the way . . ."

"There are an estimated one point two million . . ."

The normally taciturn driver gulped and nodded his head. "Yes, sir, but even if there weren't we couldn't *drive* that far in, what?"

"We have to be to Franklin in . . ." He glanced at his watch. "Six and a half hours."

"Im-possible," Pruitt snapped. "It took us . . . what . . . ? Nearly a day to get from Franklin to here." After a moment he appended: "Sir."

"Nonetheless . . ." Mitchell gave a thin smile to the group in the command center. "Has anyone ever heard the traditional punishment for a good job?"

"Fine, sir," Indy said. "The difficult we do immediately. Thanks to Mr. Kilzer," she nodded at the designer who gave her a short, choppy nod back, " . . . and the brigade we're nearly repaired and significantly rearmed. But the impossible takes time. We have to get across either the Rocky Knob Gap or Betty—God help us if it's Betty—to get to the fighting. And we can't exactly *zip* up and down those slopes."

"Well, I understand you have some experience at skiing them," the designer said with a grin.

"Puh-leeze," Pruitt snapped. "You weren't there or you wouldn't laugh. And, sir, there *is* the *minor* matter of one point two million Posleen."

"We still have full nuclear release," Major Mitchell said solemnly. "And we've been given extra reloads."

"Fine, we can hit concentrations that are not in contact with human forces, sir," Pruitt said reasonably. "What about the ones that *are*?" He gestured at the map where a line of blue and red met halfway to Rocky Knob Gap. "We can't exactly nuke *those* Posleen."

"No, but we can assault them," Kilzer interrupted.

"Oh, yeah, now *there's* a good idea!"

"No, seriously. That was the point of the upgrade. You have more frontal armor, now, than an M-1A4; from the front you're practically invulnerable to plasma cannon fire and will even shrug off most HVM hits . . ."

" 'Practically'?" Indy interrupted. " 'Most'?"

"In addition there's the squirt-gun," the designer continued. "That should give you at least ten percent more likelihood of survival . . ."

" 'Practically'?" Pruitt said, goggle-eyed.

"Oh, quit being a baby," Paul said. "You're the most heavily armored thing on earth; act that way!"

Mitchell grabbed Pruitt's collar as he lunged out of the chair but the civilian apparently had no idea what he had said. "Mr.

Kilzer, we've just wracked up more kills on this retreat than any SheVa in-toto, much less in a single engagement. So if one of us is 'being a baby' it is probably for good reason."

"I'm not saying going in there with guns blazing," Paul argued. "Although . . ."

"No," Indy snapped.

"Okay, okay, but what we'll do is provide fire support to the division already in contact, neutralize the forces moving through Rocky Knob Gap and then move forward in bounds with the division. If we get shot up too badly to move, they've got most of the brigade forming in ground mobile units and they'll come up behind you to repair."

"And Rocky Knob?"

"I was doing some mapping while you were asleep," the civilian said, bring up a three-D schematic of the mountains in the area. "You can't cross Rocky Knob; we need the road for movement of the support and combat forces . . ."

"We refer to them all as 'crunchies,'" Pruitt interjected.

"Heh, heh. Okay, we need the road for the crunchies. You'll have to cross Betty Gap again."

"No," Reeves said, standing up. "I'll quit first. I'll desert!"

"It won't be like the last time," Paul said. "I've got a few ideas that will help and I'll iron them out on the way."

"I'm not going up there," Pruitt said. "I'm not going SheVa skiing again."

"I'll work it out," Paul said, sharply. "I'm good at figuring out answers to problems. I do that, you shoot Posleen ships. Or maybe you figure out the answers and we switch; I'm a pretty good gunner when it comes to it. And we *can't* use Rocky Knob."

"Any *other* ideas how we're going to get to Franklin in time?" Mitchell looked around the room at the glum faces then shook his head. "I'll get with General Keeton so we can coordinate with the crunchies down the road. Are there any other comments, questions or concerns?"

"Just one," Pruitt said, suspiciously. "I think Mr. Kilzer has a pronoun problem. He keeps saying 'we.'"

"Oh, I'm going with you," Paul said. "All these systems are totally experimental. If anything goes wrong I want to be here to fix it."

"Oh, hell."

CHAPTER SIX

Tommy looked up from his ammunition readouts as the major slid over the side of the Reapers' fighting position.

The Reaper position was about a hundred meters behind the primary defense line, not far from the battalion headquarters hole. Like the battalion position, the Reapers had just shoveled out an area about six meters across. In their case there were two different levels, with the shallower being at the rear.

The Reapers, if they had any ammunition, could engage with a variety of heavy weapons. They had 75mm automortars for indirect fire and heavy flechette cannons for close-in work, both of these besides their anti-lander systems.

Unfortunately, in the last nine hours they had shot through every bit of ammo they carried in, gone out and scrounged up most of the additional packs and shot all of them off. They had moved forward to the line twice to support with flechettes, engaged additional landers and fired off mortars until the position was mostly protected by empty ammo boxes.

But at this point, they were pretty much flat. Tommy had about two dozen magazines left, but they weren't compatible with any of the Reaper systems and two dozen mags weren't going to stop the Posleen. That was not a particularly comfortable thought as he watched not only his own ammo but the rest of the battalion's going down like a waterfall.

"Lieutenant," Mike said as he slid into the mud in the bottom of the hole. The light rain had dropped off but it had lasted long enough to saturate everything in sight and fill all the holes with a few inches of slippery orange clay, the infamous "Georgia red clay" for which the region was unjustly famous. One of the areas that the battalion's energy was flowing away to was simply keeping the suits from sinking into the bog.

"Major," Tommy replied. If O'Neal wanted to go with monosyllables, fine by him.

"You been watching the battalion's readouts?" the commander asked.

"Ayup," the lieutenant replied.

"There is one possible way we can continue the mission. Sort of."

"And that would be, sir?"

"You're sounding rather cynical, Lieutenant," the major said.

It was impossible to get anything like body language through the suits, but Tommy would swear O'Neal was amused.

"Well, sir, I like killing Posleen. Not having them kill me because I'm out of ammo. That sort of situation always *annoys* me."

"Good news then; you and your troops are in position to save the day."

"Ah, great. Sir. Does this involve killing Posleen?"

"Possibly. But mostly it involves being pack mules. Your team has been using standard ammo, so you're at the top of the power levels in the battalion. And you're out of ammo. So I'm sending you to go pick up some. And some power."

Tommy raised his hands palms upward. "They also serve who simply fetch ammo. Are they sending in resupply birds?"

"No, but, coincidentally, there's a rather large cache of ACS materials nearby."

"Ah."

"One that's off the books. So until we started discussing it the Posleen shouldn't have known about it."

Tommy worked his face inside the gel in lieu of shaking his head. "Off the books?"

"Well, I'd have preferred that nobody find out, but if it's a choice of facing a court of inquiry for putting a cache at your family farm or having my battalion wiped out, I know which way I'll hop."

"Oh."

"More good news. Sort of. Your girlfriend is at the farm with a mixed group of civilians and military personnel. You can enlist her as a pack mule."

Tommy's jaw worked inside the armor and he counted to ten. "You want me to bring *Wendy* up here!? What in the hell is she doing *anywhere* near this *shit*?"

"The same thing my daughter is, surviving," O'Neal said with a smile in his voice.

"Your *daughter*?"

"She apparently survived the nuke that killed my father," Mike answered and gestured to the northwest. "They're about six miles that way. That's where I grew up."

"Oh, holy shit, sir. I'm . . ."

"Don't worry about it," Mike said, waving a hand. "Let's just say that we both have good reason to hold this position. And to survive doing so." He paused for a moment then gestured helplessly. "But . . . even if we can retake the pass after we pull out, we're probably not going to walk out. Or, hell, even be carried out . . ."

"They're sending the SheVa, sir. . . ."

"Yeah. One SheVa, about a million Posleen. I'm sorry, but, no offense, I wouldn't even expect the Ten Thousand to make it. Much less one unsupported SheVa. The point is . . . when you see my daughter . . . Just tell her I love her. Okay?"

"Okay, sir." Tommy started to reply then stopped at a raised hand.

"I've given your AID all the information it needs about the cache and the link-up point," O'Neal continued. "We're critically short on time so I want you to pull out right away, even before the rest of the battalion. Despite the time issue, you should take some R and R time when you meet up with the group. And your lady-friend." O'Neal waved vaguely again then tapped the knee of the lieutenant's suit. "Take what you can while you can get it, Tommy. There's only so much that God gives us in life." With that he rolled back out of the hole and crawled towards the battalion position.

"Boss, there's a little problem here." Sergeant Major Ernie Pappas still preferred the term "Gunny." He'd retired as a Marine Gunnery Sergeant long before aliens were anything more than science fiction. But as one of the early rejuvs he had been either training or in the frontlines since the first landings. And he knew a screwed up tactical situation when he saw one.

"Sure is," O'Neal replied. "Pulling out is going to be a stone cold bitch."

The battalion was laying down a continuous curtain of fire but the Posleen seemed to be limitless. They had slowed down in their advance, and all the forces to the north had pulled out, but they still were in continuous contact. When the battalion pulled out, it had basically two choices. It could pull out fast, above ground, or it could dig backwards. But in neither case could it maintain fire. And some of the suits, despite refills, were reaching red zone on power again.

"We're *going* to get chewed up when we exit," he continued. "Shit happens."

"We're not just going to get chewed up," the Gunny said. "We're going to get hammered."

"What if they pursue us?" Stewart asked. "I have to take their side, here."

"We'll go up Black Rock Mountain," O'Neal said. "They're going to find pursuit tough."

"They're hearing all of this, you know," Duncan interjected.

"Yeah, but I don't think their attacks can coordinate this fast," Mike said. "Otherwise they'd be all over us. We've been hit hard, what, five or six times? If whoever was running the show over there could hit us hard now, he would."

"Traffic control must be a beast," Stewart pointed out. "So we should get while they're limited?"

"Except we're still going to get hammered," Gunny Pappas said.

"You keep saying that, Gunny. I know."

"We'll get less hammered if somebody stays back to suppress them."

O'Neal turned his body towards the veteran NCO. "You've got to be joking."

"I can run a simulation, sir," the Gunny replied formally. "We're looking at nearly fifty percent casualties if we just pop out of the holes and run. We're out of grenades, we're out of mortars, we're out of anything we can use to knock them back. We're getting five to six God Kings on the line at a time, now. Unless they're engaged they'll *hammer* us even under holograms."

"I know, Gunny, but that doesn't mean I'm going to sacrifice some pawns to save the king," O'Neal said quietly. "Or a knight. We're all going out, as fast as we can. We only have to get around the corner of the ridge. Fifteen, twenty seconds *tops* in view."

"With every Posleen in sight hammering us from the rear," Duncan pointed out. "Which is our most lightly armored spot. Except on you."

"Thanks," Mike replied coldly.

"We've got a few troops that are . . . mobility challenged anyway," Pappas said grimly. "Nagel and Towbridge both lost a leg. Others have been hit. Leave me behind with a group of the worst off. Lowest on power, shot up, the sick, lame and lazy. We'll provide cover fire as you unass."

"We can fall back by fire and maneuver . . ." Stewart said. "Except I'm not an idiot and I know the Posleen just walk right into it. Christ, Top!"

Mike looked at the ground as the other suits turned to look at him. Finally he spoke.

"Fifteen. That's enough to suppress their fire as we retreat. I'll dump a list." He paused and switched over to a private frequency. "Top, I forgave you for First Washington a long time ago."

"I know you did, boss," the sergeant major replied gruffly. "You want to stay, but you know you can't. The battalion will just . . . go away if you buy it. You need Duncan and Stewart to watch out for the details. I can hold the . . . I can hold for long enough."

Mosovich led the way up the slope and over the hill. At this point, between the continuing rain and the heavy traffic into and out of the cache, there was a noticeable, and slippery, trail into the cave. The wet and the slope were not the only obstacles with which they had to contend; the hills were littered with fallen trees.

The area had suffered repeated multi-kiloton strikes and while none of them had been on the near side of the hill the ground shock and pressure wave had still dropped trees and caused small landslides.

They moved carefully, crawling over individual fallen trees, detouring around tangles from slides, the wet leaves slipping and slithering under their feet, until they reached a point just below the crest of the ridge. Then Mosovich halted the group and leopard crawled up to the ridgeline.

He had seen the valleys below only a few weeks before and the devastation that greeted his eyes required a moment's adjustment.

The western end of the main valley of the Gap was just visible from his position. The Gap was a narrow, but low, north-south crack in the wall of the Tennessee Divide; a crack from which the continuous racket of battle resounded. Mosovich wasn't sure what the situation was at the moment, but there was no question the ACS were hotly engaged.

Just to the north of the Gap the valley widened out to the east and west. This valley was both low and fertile and had once provided a significant fraction of the produce necessary to run the defending corps. When Jake and Mueller had passed through only a week before it had been busy with the movement of the corps and tan and yellow with the corn, barley and pumpkins ready to harvest. Now it was a barren wasteland. The only sign that there had ever been defenders there was a pile of melted metal that Jake suspected used to be an artillery battery. The ground itself was black and gray with some patches that looked shiny as if they had been turned to glass. The tree-clad slopes that had surrounded it were now covered in fallen, leaf-stripped trunks that looked like nothing so much as scattered matchsticks.

The O'Neal farmstead was in a small pocket or "hollow" on the north side of the main valley and about two hundred feet higher. It was roughly diamond shaped with the entrance pointing slightly southwest rather than directly south. The entrance ran up the gully created by O'Neal Creek and made several twists. Given that the hollow was settled in the early 1800s it appeared that the O'Neal paranoia was probably hereditary.

The holler had not suffered as severely as the main valley but it was badly damaged. The far side of the holler was totally destroyed with all the trees down and a center zone that was scoured down to the bare rock; the lander must not have been very high. The house was splinters and the heavy sandbag and concrete bunker to the side, which had been hidden in a hedge, was a smashed ruin. It was in the latter ruin that Cally said O'Neal had last been seen.

The near side slope was not as badly hit, but it was still going to take quite a while to pick their way down the hillside. There had been a path but it was nearly invisible for all the fallen timber. The one good piece of news was that the most probable avenue of approach, up the road which had apparently been ground zero, was completely covered in trees and rockslides.

Mueller led the way down, occasionally moving the more accessible trees and rocks. Despite his care he slipped twice on the wet hillside, once very nearly breaking a leg.

"At least the Posleen were going to have trouble getting in," Mosovich said, when he caught the far larger NCO on the second fall.

"Which just means we get to dig out his body," Mueller said quietly. "Even if he was alive, and it didn't sound like he was, he's not going to have survived the night."

"We'll see," Mosovich said. He slid over the bole of an oak that must have been growing there during the Civil War and then down the relatively open bluff beyond. Over the last few years he had humped up and down these mountains to the point that he considered most obstacles to be pretty easy stuff. But this tangle of fallen trees was a pain in the butt.

The last slither, though, dropped him into a narrow strip of ground behind one wing of the O'Neal house which was relatively free of debris. There was a fair amount from the house itself, including scattered clothing that they really ought to collect up for the refugees. But his attention was centered on the bunker. Most of the house was backed onto the hillside and the bunker was on the far side.

"Sergeant Major Mosovich," his AID chimed. "Be aware that there is a slight increase in radiation in this zone."

"Bad?"

"Not really. It won't reach clinically challenging levels for another six to eight hours. And the isotopes that I'm detecting are of a type to decay quickly; the radiation will reduce faster than you're absorbing it."

"Okay, we still don't want to stick around," he said, waving the group around the house.

He moved cautiously. Despite the fact that the area looked clear it was possible that the odd Posleen might be moving around or even waiting in ambush. Most Posleen normals were bonded to individual God Kings. However, when their master was killed, the normals tended to become "unbonded." Thereafter, until picked up by another God King, they wandered more or less as wild animals. These "ferals" were an increasing problem not only along the frontier areas but in the interior. Posleen reproduced at a phenomenal rate and tended to survive infancy even without care. So a single feral could pump out multiple young in just a few years, each of which reached maturity in eighteen months. Thus, in areas where they were not kept in check they occupied a primary carnivore niche in the food chain.

Jake Mosovich was not about to enter that food chain if he could avoid it.

The area appeared clear, however, and he slipped around the stump of the house to the front, carefully sweeping his rifle from side to side as the rest of the group closed up behind him.

He could see the bunker clearly now and he could see a very man-shaped hole where something wasn't.

"Cally?" he called, walking over to the bunker as he lowered the barrel on his rifle.

The bunker had reinforced concrete walls with a sandbag and

steel top. It was clearly designed to survive heavy-duty direct fire. The nuke, however, had ripped most of the sandbags off the top and smashed in one side of the concrete wall, dropping shattered concrete and bent steel I-beams into the interior.

Despite that Papa O'Neal might have survived. Overpressure blasts from nukes did more destruction to items that had an "inside" and an "outside" than the rather homogenous character of the human body. Jake remembered about a thousand years ago taking a class on nuclear warfare that covered that fact. Houses tended to be ripped to shreds in conditions where humans survived just fine. The heat and the radiation might kill them. But not the overpressure unless they were at ground zero or picked up and "tossed" by it.

Only two problems. Papa O'Neal had been inside the bunker when it collapsed. The debris was *likely* to have killed him. Second problem being that he wasn't there. It was pretty evident that something or someone had come along and dug a body out of the rubble.

"He was right there," Cally said quietly.

"Yep." Jake squatted and looked into the interior of the bunker. The rear was down as well, but a doorway was faintly visible at the rear. "Is that how you got out?"

"Yeah," Cally said, bending down to peer into the rubble. "He was right *there*, Sergeant Major!"

"He's gone now, Cally," Jake said gently, straightening up. "Let's take a quick look around to see if there's anything worth salvaging then get back to the cache before whatever took him comes back."

"Posleen?" Mueller asked, looking at the ground. Most of the grass had been flash-burned by the blast but there should have been tracks. Posleen made very definitive tracks with their claws.

"Probably," Mosovich said after a moment's pause. "I don't see any tracks *at all*. But the most probable explanation is the Posties got the body."

"Fuck," Cally said. "Fuck, fuck, fuck, god damn, cock-SUCKER! He really didn't want to get eaten. He really, really didn't."

"I'm sorry," Wendy said, wrapping her arm around the teenager. "I'm so sorry."

"Shit," Cally replied, wiping rain-mixed tears out of her eyes. "Shari is not going to be happy."

Wendy snorted and hugged her to her. "No, she's not. None of us are."

Elgars was sweeping back and forth around the fallen bunker but after a moment she came back shaking her head. "I find track of Cally. No other." Her voice sounded odd. Low pitched and singsong.

Mosovich looked at her side-long but Wendy just shrugged. "Annie, you're channeling again." Ever since they had met, the Six Hundred captain occasionally would seem to manifest personalities of other people. In the very few cases where the personalities were obvious, and known, they were *dead* people. It especially seemed to occur when she used a new skill, such as tracking.

The captain looked up at the sky and sniffed. "Yes." She sniffed again, deeply then looked toward the road. "Take cover. Someone come."

As Mosovich faded backward into the shadow of the ruined house his AID chirped again. "Sergeant Major, incoming message from Lieutenant Thomas Sunday, Fleet Strike ACS."

"Well, we have the pass," Tulo'stenaloor muttered. He had moved forward from the protected bunkers and factories around Clarkesville and now watched the streams of oolt'ondar moving up to the pass. "It only took two hundred thousand oolt'os and uncountable Kessentai. And we only have it because they *gave* it to us. And the ground is torn to ribbons, which will require repair before we can push through effectively. But we *have* the pass."

"But they will be back," Goloswin said. "They intend to fill it with fire again."

The Kessentai was that oddest of individuals among the Posleen; a known warrior who had quit the strife, settled down and been bitten by the bug of a hobby. In Goloswin's case the bug was tinkering. There was nothing that he loved more than getting a piece of equipment, human, Indowy, Posleen or Aldenata, and taking it apart to figure out how it worked.

Tulo'stenaloor had tracked him down on a planet a dozen systems away and lured him to Earth with the promise of puzzles to drive him mad. As it had turned out, every puzzle that had been thrown at him, from dissecting human sensor systems to breaking into the ultra-secure AID net, had been apparent nestling play.

However, he was still having a fine time. All this and the promise of riches beyond measure in addition; what could be better?

"Yes, but they will have trouble doing that," Tulo'stenaloor said.

"Will you pursue?" the technician asked carefully. He was well aware that his understanding of the new methods of the estanaar were spotty. Most Posleen oolt'ondar would latch on and chase the humans to their deaths. Like the Tinkerer, Tulo'stenaloor had found a new way to do business. But in the case of Tulo'stenaloor, that business was gathering the finest minds he could and then hammering the humans into so much thresh.

"No," Tulo'stenaloor said after a moment. "The route they took is difficult enough for them; trying to pursue them with oolt'os would be nearly impossible. We'll just have to let them go. But I will see what I can do about this resupply mission. What news on their efforts to arrange for . . . *fire-support?*" It was a human term that he had readily adopted.

"Their General Horner is no longer using his AIDs and the AID network is beginning to attempt to counter my infiltration. But at last word the only hope was still the SheVa gun they call 'Bun-Bun.' It is under repair and is being upgraded near Sylva."

"Then something must be done about that infernal contraption." The warleader sighed. He touched a control on his tenar and waited until it picked the signature of Orostan out of the mass of other Kessentai. "Orostan?"

The senior oolt'ondar looked down at the town of Franklin and the gathering lake to the west with distaste. He recalled the first major check to their advance when over a hundred thousand of the host had been trapped in the collapse of the Sub-Urb. Now they were being pushed back to it, and it looked no better than on the way through. Very little in the way of loot, hardly any decent land that had not been torn to shreds. Basically nothing but a useless dot on one of the human's "maps." Such a useless place to fight and die over.

"Estanaar?" he replied. He had hitched his star to Tulo'stenaloor all the way back at the Great Gathering. Most of his fellow oolt'ondar thought him mad; Tulo'stenaloor had been badly defeated on Aradan Five and his "New Way" was heretical in the extreme. But Orostan had been picking out all the information he could about these humans and it was apparent that the usual method of the host, of the Path, to charge ahead trying to use mass to overcome the enemy, was a quick route to suicide. Tulo'stenaloor's attempt to use human tactics against them had been at least partially successful. *Would* have been successful had the damned suits not taken the pass and the demon shit *SheVa* gun not fought so hard in the retreat. All the highly trained pilots of tenaral and oolt'pos had been destroyed by the gun or mischance, and most of the elite oolt'ondar had been lost in the assault, leaving them with nothing but to fall back on "charge and die."

Not for the first time, but for the first time so clearly, he felt a wave of depression. Such a waste, such an incredible *waste*. Fine Kessentai, young Posleen that he had trained with his own talons, nothing but thresh to be gathered and distributed to the host. There *had* to be a better way than this.

"The suits are preparing to pull out of the Gap," the warleader said. "Unfortunately, they have a distressingly good plan for doing so; they intend to leave a sacrificial rear guard."

"That's unusual for the suits," Orostan said. He had not fought the armored combat suits of the humans, but he had studied all that he could of them. And they rarely sacrificed even one suit, much less a detachment.

"Agreed, but they intend to return. They are awaiting the SheVa gun getting to the vicinity of Franklin, where it will be in range to reach the Gap. If it gets there, all will be over. We might as well throw the Staff."

"I understand," he replied. He did understand. But understanding and knowing what to do about it was two different things. "I'm getting reports from the front. The SheVa has been significantly enhanced. We couldn't stop it on the way in; I'm not sure we'll be able to stop it on the way back."

"I have somewhat more data," Tulo'stenaloor said. "It has been armored and heavy weapons added to it. But it is only armored on the front."

"Ah," Orostan snorted. "Not on the sides?"

"Only for plasma fire on the sides, and only under certain conditions. If you . . . *ambush* it . . ." the warleader used the human term; the Posleen had no equivalent.

"I will do what I can, estanaar," the oolt'ondar replied. "I will do what I can." He looked to the northeast and was just in time to watch the first fireball. The image was seared on his retina for a moment; the flash of white directly above the main concentration of forces that were lining up to take the road through Rocky Knob Gap.

He closed his eyes against the glare as his pupils and internal filters automatically darkened against the damaging light. "Well," he muttered, pulling his crest down against his neck in anger. "Now we know which way they are coming."

CHAPTER SEVEN

So 'ere's to you, Fuzzy-Wuzzy, at your 'ome in
   the Soudan;
You're a pore benighted 'eathen but a first-class
   fightin' man;
We gives you your certificate, an' if you want it signed
We'll come an' 'ave a romp with you whenever
   you're inclined.

—Rudyard Kipling
"Fuzzy-Wuzzy" (Sudan Expeditionary Force)

Near Persimmon, GA, United States of America, Sol III
1324 EDT Monday September 28, 2009 AD

Cholosta'an remembered the nests.

It was how every Posleen started life, dumped in a pen with nonsentient age mates, struggling to survive every moment. When food was scarce, or when one of the nestlings faltered, the nests turned on the weaker members and then there was nothing but scattered bones.

Kessentai were no different than oolt'os in the nests. No bigger, no stronger, no smarter, just another young animal, struggling to survive. And then the Change hit.

For the oolt'os it was not so great a change. Skills began to emerge in their brain, rudimentary communication developed. But they were still much the same: larger, stronger animals.

For the Kessentai it was different. Suddenly, their mind was flickering and flashing with not only new thoughts but entire new classes of thought. Skills appeared but with them came a deeper understanding of the theory behind them. Not just rudimentary language but the full, rich flower of the Posleen tongue developed in their brains like a sculpture from within the stone. Philosophy, tactics, engineering skills and star-piloting skills, often for beings who had never seen a star.

For the oolt'os it was much the same. They fought for food, they fought for survival, they fought to survive. But the poor Kessentai could find themselves having an existentialist moment in the midst of a full-up battle for survival.

It was not until they developed crests, and at about the same time began to develop their greater bulk and the various cues that to the oolt'os proclaimed that they were their lords, that the Kessentai could feel secure.

And then they were plucked from the pens, given their first oolt and sent forth to die.

It was times like this that Cholosta'an longed to be back in the pens.

This was the third debacle that Cholosta'an had survived. In the case of the first two he had limped back to his home settlement with hardly any remaining oolt'os and no supplies. You could only return to the well so many times; if it happened again he knew that he would be denounced as Kenstain.

There were only two types of God Kings: Kessentai and Kenstain. All debts, rewards and obligations, by ancient custom, were controlled and distributed by the Net. The Net judged the actions of each Kessentai and determined what rewards they should receive and Kessentai traded materials, information and allegiances through the Net.

Kennelai were different. Kennelai could not *own* anything. They were of Kessentai material but had either failed in the Path or turned away from it. Some refused to enter the path and took the way of Kenstain from the beginning. Kennelai were mainly used to run things in the absence of the Kessentai who actually owned them, but they were considered the bottom of the barrel in the Posleen hierarchy, in some ways lower than high quality oolt'os.

This attack was in some ways better and in some ways worse. In the other two he had been part of huge hosts that had hit the defenses of the damned humans and been slaughtered. The bad news was that in those conditions there was nothing to loot, all you could do was run and not bother to pick anything up. The good news was that at least you were close to the point that you could be safe from their demon spawned "artillery."

In this attack the beginning had been a dream. The tactics of Orostan and Tulo'stenaloor had permitted the host to cut through the humans like a tan blade against steel. And they had struck deep, almost to the point that the humans would have been unable to recover.

But that was almost. Then the humans had changed the rules of the game, again, and started using antimatter weapons and closed the Gap with their nearly invulnerable battle suits.

As soon as the first antimatter weapon detonated, destroying half the host in one terrible fury of light and fire, Cholosta'an had seen the future and it did *not* include an eventual victory. He had started to the rear with what remained of his oolt and never looked back.

The up side was that he had picked up enough loot, and thresh, that he would not have to return to his nest and be forced into Kenstain. The bad side was that he was pretty much back where he had started and unless he found a real treasure trove, he was never going to be anything but a bottom rank Kessentai, always first to battle and last to the loot. Always looking over his shoulder at the threat of failure.

It was really getting to be a drag.

"Cholosta'an."

He looked at his communicator and flinched; the indicator was for the estanaar, Tulo'stenaloor. He really did *not* want to talk to Tulo'stenaloor right now. Or ever again. So he ignored it.

"Cholosta'an, this is Tulo'stenaloor. I have a mission for you."

Tulo'stenaloor looked at the indicators and flapped his crest. The young abat must have fled immediately after the SheVa fired its first rounds to have made it so far back; he was practically to Highway 64 and obviously heading to "safe" territory. The demonshit little coward.

"Cholosta'an, you have retreated from the Path."

The Kessentai hissed, wanting to strike out at something, wanting to push his tenar to a higher rate of movement, but that would mean abandoning his few remaining oolt'os. So he had to fight this with words.

"Your attack has *failed*, estanaar," Cholosta'an snarled. "You took the flower of the host and fed it into a meat grinder. When an attack has failed, it is permissible to withdraw."

"But others still fight," the distant warleader said coldly. "You are one of the few who is withdrawing."

"And why did Orostan choose me as one of his elite? Because I'm *smart*! I know when the humans, may the gods of the sky eat their souls, have *won*. All that you are doing is throwing more bodies away in a futile attempt to cover your own failure! And I will *not* be one of them!"

Tulo'stenaloor took a deep breath and flapped his crest. He was, unfortunately, coming to the same conclusion. It was certainly the case that it would be . . . harder if the suits were resupplied. But he could not get a force to cut the resupply team off in time, not through the havoc of the lower valley. Cholosta'an was the only one in a position to do so.

Thus he had to be convinced.

"I have a mission for you. You chose to follow in this attack. If you refuse to attempt this extremely *simple* mission, I will gather a conclave of oolt'ondar and have you declared Kenstain."

Which was what Cholosta'an *knew* was coming.

Some days it just didn't pay to polish your crest.

"What is the mission?"

✧   ✧   ✧

Jake silently watched as the line of suits made their way up the road. They had salvaged Posleen boma blades and were using them to clear the trees off the road. The monomolecular-edged blades, especially in the hands of an armored combat suit, sliced through the thickest trunks as if they were tissue paper and then the suit troopers picked up the sections of trunk and tossed them aside.

But he had to wonder, given the fact that the trees were more of a nuisance to the Posleen than to the humans, why they were doing it.

Finally, the suit unit had the road cleared to its satisfaction and bounded over to the ruins of the house. Four of the suits were what Mosovich recognized as Reaper suits, specialized heavy weapons suits. By the design of the suit and the weapon he was carrying, the fifth was apparently an officer; command suits were a little slimmer and sleeker than the Reapers or the standard Marauder suits.

"Sergeant Major Jacob Mosovich," he said, saluting the ACS officer as the suit skidded to a stop. "What can I do for you, sir?"

"Hello, Sergeant Major," the officer said, taking off his helmet. "I understand you've been dallying with my girlfriend."

Wendy let out a howl and bolted across the ruined yard, throwing herself onto the suit. She grabbed his shoulders and wrapped her arms and legs around him in a full-body hug.

"Tommy?" she gasped, kissing him on the head and neck. "Is that really you?"

"It'd better be," he muttered. "Or some guy in a suit is in trouble."

"Uh, sir?" McEvoy said. "I . . . uh . . ."

"Wendy, meet McEvoy, the most incompetent Reaper in the whole wide world," Tommy said, kissing her back and then gently prying her off. "We'll have a minute or two, but I need to talk to the sergeant major. And I understand there's a captain around here?"

"That would be me," Elgars said, stepping out of the shadow of the house. "I recognize you from Wendy's picture."

"So do I," Mueller said, wandering over. "She uses it like a cross to keep guys away."

"Now, Wendy," Tommy said, thumping her with his arm. "That's not very friendly."

"I'm only friendly with people I *want* to be friendly with," she answered, taking his hand. "Okay, business first. What in the *hell* are you doing here?"

"You're Cally," Tommy said, pointing at the teenager. "Right?"

"Right," Cally replied. She'd taken a position halfway around the wall of the house, where she could peer around but back out if necessary.

"She's a frigging tiger when she's cornered," Wendy said, quietly. "But she's shy around strangers."

"You're okay, right? Your dad asked me to make sure."

"I'm fine," Cally said. "What are you doing here?"

Tommy looked around the group and ran his fingers over the stubble on his head. "That's . . . complicated."

Tommy looked at the back of the cache for a moment and then drove his hand forward.

The group had moved back to the cache and then gotten the children, who were at last mostly functional, outside on the dripping hillside. Tommy had been warned that opening up the *real* cache would be somewhat energetic.

His arm punched through about a foot of reinforced concrete and into an opening. With a wrench and a twist he pulled out a large chunk, then reached in and started ripping out the rebar. As he worked at it, it became apparent that the cache was not a small cave, but a much larger opening into the mountain.

"Major O'Neal told me that his family has been slowly mining this mountain for almost a century," Tommy said. "Half of it is mine shafts. That's what this is."

"How far does it go in?" Mosovich asked, looking through the growing hole.

"I don't know," Tommy replied. "Not too far. It gets blocked off again." With that he pulled a large segment of wall out and the light from the Coleman lantern finally penetrated into the interior of the tunnel. Five feet farther in the tunnel was blocked again. This time by a wall of GalTech plasteel.

"Curiouser and curiouser," Mueller said, pulling at some of the concrete himself. "And how many people knew that Major O'Neal had installed a Galactic weapons container on his father's farm?"

"Apparently not many," the lieutenant replied tonelessly.

"Is Dad in trouble?" Cally asked.

"Well, I'm not sure," Tommy answered truthfully. "First of all, I'm not sure what the *Galactic* regulations on something like this are, especially when you throw in all of your dad's secondary ranks like his Indowy rank. Second of all, as I understand it he was tasked with setting up caches along the eastern seaboard...."

"He was," Cally said. "I remember. We ... took a vacation just before the first landing. He spent some of the time planting power systems and ammo boxes." She looked at the structure through the hole that was now almost completely clear. "This is ... bigger though."

"I guess he wanted to make sure that Rabun Gap was never out of power," Mueller said dryly. "Shit!"

"What?" Mosovich asked.

"Where'd O'Neal's power come from?" the master sergeant said in a disgusted tone. "What a fuckin' idiot! Hardly anyone in the mountains has power anymore, nobody to maintain the lines. But *his* house *always* had power."

"No lines," Mosovich said, shaking his head. "I should have guessed."

"And I noticed an Indowy storage box when we were here," Mueller continued. "I figured that O'Neal had just given an empty to his dad. But those things are worth their weight in gold; they're armored like a tank and climate controlled; you don't just give them away."

"What?" Elgars asked. "What's the importance of no line?"

"No power lines," Mueller expanded. "When we came up here for dinner, I noticed that there weren't any power lines coming into the house. So where was he getting electricity from? Areas like this are getting to where electricity is pretty damned scarce, but Papa O'Neal had enough to run all his appliances and security systems. I dismissed it as a generator."

"And it was one," Tommy said. "An antimatter generator at a guess." He pulled a last bit of concrete away and put his palm on the lock of the plasteel door, which obediently opened.

"Jesus Christ," Mosovich muttered, looking into the tunnel. The walls were gray plasteel; from the exterior view they were at least six inches thick, which about equalled the armor of a space cruiser. The cache was about eight meters deep by four wide and the the interior was filled from floor to ceiling with Indowy storage boxes. Most of them were marked with the complex woven pattern, resembling a Celtic brooch, that indicated antimatter containment systems. There was enough raw antimatter in the cache to wipe out Georgia.

"Woo," Mueller whistled. "No wonder this thing is armored like a fortress."

"Are those all ammunition?" Cally asked quietly.

"Yep," Tommy said, yanking the top box down and opening it up. "This here is the motherlode; standard grav-gun ammo with antimatter teardrop initiators. If one of these went up, there wouldn't be any more mountain." He looked at the thousands of reloads in the box and shook his head. "McEvoy, get your ass over here and let's find out what we've got."

The cache had been partially emptied into the outer cave and the materials sorted out by order of preference. First priority were the three antimatter power packs. Each was rated to resupply one company of ACS for four full days of use in standard terrain. Excepting the power to drive the guns, they should last the remaining suits about six days in the current conditions.

Second priority was standard rifle ammunition. This was "the good stuff," Indowy manufacture complete with their own anti-matter power system on each round, which meant the suits wouldn't have to draw power to run the guns.

Last priority was Reaper ammunition. The Reapers were flat out but, like the MetalStorms, they ran through enormous quantities of material in firing.

Tommy determined that with clamps the three suits could carry all three of the antimatter packs (about the size of a large suitcase, mostly due to the armoring) and a couple of ammunition packs each. The unarmored humans could probably carry one ammo pack apiece for a total of twenty. He decided to make it eighteen standard packs and two of the Reaper packs, both flechettes.

In addition there was one oversized box that indicated a weapon. He looked at it and smiled inside his suit.

"W . . . AID?" he said.

"Yes, Tommy?" the AID answered in Wendy's voice.

"Can you . . . delete some of the information about this cache? Or modify the information about what we're going to carry?"

"I *can*," the AID answered. "But I've already uploaded the data."

Tommy frowned and worked his face in the gel. "Okay, correct your inventory of what we're carrying. I don't want *this* item on the inventory. Substitute a case of Reaper ammunition."

"Very well, Tommy," the AID replied sweetly. "Care to tell me why?"

"Because I don't want the Posleen to know that we're carrying it back," he grinned, ferally. "And make sure that the *other* AIDs don't show it."

"I'll try," the AID said.

"McEvoy, I've got a special job for you," Sunday said. . . .

"Okay," the lieutenant finally said, "McEvoy, you and Pickersgill move the packs to the top of the hill. Just clamp them together in a chain and haul them up."

He turned to the refugee group as the two troopers got to work and raised his hands. "I need each of the adults to carry a pack."

"We can do that," Elgars replied. "Where?"

"It's going to be a bit of a hump," Sunday admitted. "We need to get them across the valley and up the side of Lookout Mountain." He generated a map and put a pinpoint on the spot.

"I take it you're not talking about the one in Tennessee," Shari said sharply.

"No, it's a pretty common name for mountains," Tommy replied, equanimably. "You're uncomfortable leaving the kids?"

"Very," Shari said. "I didn't pull them out of a madhouse then drag them across the mountains just to have them killed by some passing Posleen."

"Shari, they'd have to get through me," Cally said. "I'm strong, but not strong enough to carry one of those boxes. So I'll be staying." She reached down and tapped Billy on the shoulder and grinned. "And Billy will be here to protect me."

The boy shook his head and grinned back. He had developed a severe speech blockage right after the first Posleen landing way back in Fredericksburg. Lately, it had started to clear up. But he still didn't talk if he didn't have to.

"I'm glad that you'll be here, but . . ."

"Shari," Wendy interrupted. "I was there the whole time, too. I don't want anything to happen to the kids, either. But if I had the choice of leaving you or leaving Cally . . ."

"You'd leave Cally," Shari said. "I understand that. But I don't think Cally is *enough*. What if the Posleen *do* come. I want Mueller or Mosovich to stay."

"Ma'am, I understand," Tommy said. "But we need to get this stuff to the battalion. And we need to do it as soon as possible." He stepped aside as the line of gray boxes started snaking out of the cave, dropping a load of wet soil onto the ledge outside the entrance. "And we need all that we can get; there are a sh . . . a *bunch* of Posleen to kill." He paused and waved his hands around wildly. "If we don't stop them, it doesn't matter *what* cave you hide in, they'll still come . . ."

"Hiding was good enough in Fredericksburg," Shari said.

"Only because the ACS came along and dragged us out," Wendy corrected. "The same unit, come to think of it, that's in the Gap."

"And if that don't beat all for coincidence," Mueller said with a grin. "Shari . . . we can't stay. And you're not going to be a hell of an addition to having Cally here. We need you to carry boxes and quit fighting it."

She sighed and looked at the children. They had started to move around and she and Wendy had gotten them fed. But even with children's usual ability to bounce back they weren't going to be up to another trip real soon.

"Okay, I'll quit complaining," she said, looking at Tommy. "But if one hair on their heads is harmed . . ."

"It won't be," Cally said, quietly. "I'll make sure of that Shari. I promise."

"I've had lots of promises in my life." The woman sighed again. "I know you'll *try*. That's not the same thing as succeeding."

"And victory doesn't always mean you survive," Cally said with a shrug. "I'll get it done."

CHAPTER EIGHT

Here's health to you and to our Corps
Which we are proud to serve;
In many a strife we've fought for life
And never lost our nerve;
If the Army and the Navy
Ever look on Heaven's scenes;
They will find the streets are guarded by
UNITED STATES MARINES.

—*Marine Hymn*

Rabun Gap, GA, United States of America, Sol III
1453 EDT Monday September 28, 2009 AD

Gunny Pappas slid into the fighting position and looked around. The front of the position was partially dug away where a lucky HVM round had taken out the trooper who had dug the pit. The trooper's armor was somewhere to the rear, piled into a hole with the rest of the luckless troopers who had died this day.

Pappas didn't think he'd make it to the pit.

"Battalion, mass fire."

The Posleen were still pouring through the narrow gap but at a slower pace and the battalion had reduced fire to conserve ammunition and power. But now every rifle on the line opened up with a full weight of fire, filling the narrow pass with lines of silver.

The Posleen had already built a wall of their dead, towering man high in places, over which they struggled to get to grips with the awful suits. They had also been nibbling at it from behind, dragging out functioning weapons and tearing out bits of flesh to deliver to the waiting forces as rations. Now they quit in those efforts as it became obvious something was happening and every Posleen in reach began scrambling over the mound, trying to drive forward to the line of suits.

The ACS was having none of it. The lines of silver picked out the God Kings and then swept from side to side across their assigned sectors, wiping the line from the top of the mound and adding to it as the dismembered bodies of the aliens scattered to lie amongst their brethren.

As the assault faltered again, Pappas heard the second command.

"Mobile personnel, retreat and regroup."

Pappas slid another magazine in his weapon and continued fire as the green dots of the retreating group moved backward on the tactical schematic. They moved fast, leaping out of their holes and running in quick, low leaps to the rear. But despite that, and despite the fire of the fifteen troopers still remaining on the line, he saw one suit go red. Then two, five. That was the last, though, as the remainder of the battalion made it around the curve of the mountain and disappeared off his screen.

The Posleen had not been idle. The forces backed up behind the wall of flesh, at the first cries that the suits were retreating, redoubled their efforts to close with the battalion, scrambling over the mound and through the lower patches.

They were met with fire but not enough. Despite the interlocking fires of the remaining suits, some of the Posleen drove forward, then more and more.

"Hmm, da dum," Pappas muttered, pulling another magazine out and slipping it into the well as the empty dropped out. "If the Army and the Navy, ever look on heaven's scene . . ." The

Posleen were pushing forward hard; a solid block of them were across the wall of bodies. Most of them had dispensed with shotguns and railguns and missile launchers and were dragging out their boma blades even as the fire of the remaining suits piled up windrows of bodies. But each windrow was closer and closer. Fifty meters, thirty, ten, five.

"If the Army and the Navy ever look on Heaven's scene," he half hummed, half sang as the first normal reached his hole. He blew it apart with a blast of silver fire, but there was another and then another behind it, all around, and his magazine dropped out. " . . . they will find the streets are guarded, by United States Marines."

Tommy had managed to get Wendy aside for a moment as the two Reapers assembled the boxes on the top of the hill. It had required, among other things, climbing around the shoulder of the ridge. But with the preparations to carry the gear over to Black Rock Mountain well underway, he could take a moment of private time.

He ended up carrying Wendy the last few meters as the side of the mountain got vertical; with ample power he could apply his full anti-grav system and simply fly around the precipice.

"Now that was exciting," she said as they landed on a relatively flat patch. It was a narrow ledge, mostly granite with some moss and twisted saplings growing out of the rocks. Under the rising moon it was an inhospitable and airy place that seemed to speak of sylphs and elementals, a place where lichen struggled to grab a gray foothold.

"So, Superman, what's the big secret?"

"Not a secret, really," he said, taking off his helmet so he could see her with his own eyes. "It's just . . . we don't have much more time." He paused and looked to the south. There was a strong, cold breeze from the north and their aerie was exposed to it, but he still could hear occasional sounds from the Gap where the Posleen hordes were pouring through. "When we go back . . . there's not going to be much we can really do. Just . . . dig in and hold on. And there's not anything really coming that's going to get here . . ."

"So you're saying that when you go, you're not coming back?" Wendy asked pushing her hair back behind her ear. The wind was hitting the ledge and being deflected upwards. The zephyrs yanked her blond hair back out from where she had futilely tucked it and streamed it out and upwards.

"I . . . I think so, sweet." Tommy toggled on a white light and looked her in the eye. Her eyes were a deep, magnetic blue. It had been so long he'd almost forgotten how blue. "It's been bad before. And there was always the chance of catching a round. But this time . . ."

"So you brought me here to tell me you're going to leave me?" she asked, quietly, stroking his face again. The suit undergel took care of all personal hygiene needs, including depilation. His chin was normally rough with a beard; he had to shave twice a day. But under the care of the suit it was as smooth as a baby's.

"Maybe, a little," he answered. "And . . . you know we're in a rush. We don't have much time. But . . ."

"Tommy?" she said, pulling her shirt over her head and starting to undo her bra. "Shut up and get that goddamned armor off."

Mosovich tried not to smile as the lieutenant and his "lady" joined them on the hilltop; if he'd had the opportunity he probably would have taken it as well.

"Well, Lieutenant, nice to see you back," Mueller said with a chuckle.

Tommy had the grace to look a bit shamefaced but Wendy just smiled languidly. "I guess it's time to port and carry, huh? I hope we can rig it so it doesn't hit my bruises."

Mueller coughed as Shari chuckled wickedly. "That sounds like a self-inflicted wound to me."

"Oh, it took two," Wendy said with a wink.

"If we're ready to leave," Sunday said, looking at the boxes, then at McEvoy. "Time to load up."

He lifted one of the boxes onto the side of the Reaper's suit and locked it in place with a gravity clamp, then added one to the other side. It took a moment to figure out but he finally found a place to add a third, and that seemed about the maximum that would fit. He did the same with Pickersgill then had them load him up with one of the power packs, an ammo box and the weapons box, now covered in cloth. Finally the three suits were ready, looking very much like some odd species of worm that preferred to camouflage itself in boxes.

With difficulty Tommy and the Reapers helped the unarmored group to each load up a box. The cases were heavy, running nearly a hundred and fifty pounds, and didn't have carrying straps. But by strapping them onto empty rucksack frames they finally got them on their backs. They were terribly unwieldy, but marginally portable.

"Let's go," Elgars said, leaning forward to try to get the box balanced.

"Take care of the kids," Shari said, shifting the weight to try to get it comfortable. But, really, there was no way to do that; she could feel the straps cutting into her back, and her legs already felt wobbly.

"I will," Cally said, looking over at Wendy and Tommy. "You guys take care, okay?"

"We will," Mosovich said. "Keep your head down."

"Will do."

Sunday looked around at the group, then at Elgars. "Captain, if you're ready."

"Cally, get back to the cache," Elgars said. "Let's move out."

With that she took a step down the trail, placing her feet carefully. One slip with these damned boxes on their backs and they'd end up in a broken pile of bones.

"I remember filling this out on my list of future employment," Mosovich said, shifting the weight again and trying to move his AIW into a better position.

"What's that?" Mueller asked. Of all the group he was the one who seemed the least bothered by the weight.

"Sherpa," the sergeant major said with a laugh. "I always wanted to tote somebody else's luggage over hill and dale."

"You know, there's got to be a better way to run a war," Mueller said.

✦   ✦   ✦

Dr. Miguel "Mickey" Castanuelo was a fanatic.

Miguel A. Castanuelo had first seen the United States from the bow of a pitching, overloaded boat. And if there was anything more lovely than that faint shred of land of the horizon, it was the Coast Guard cutter that had appeared just as it seemed the leaky boat was finally going to sink.

The boat was one of the last "official" refugee boats from Castro's Cuba; within a month all transport would be forbidden. Miguel's father, Jose Castanuelo, was a medical doctor who was the victim of one of the favorite post-revolution games: catch the Batistist.

Dr. Jose Castanuelo had not been involved in the Batista government. But when a colleague fingered him as a Batistist, he knew it was only a matter of time until he would be incarcerated in a "reeducation camp." Instead, he took his family out on a rickety boat towards freedom.

However, a degree of doctoral medicine in Cuba was nothing more than an interesting piece of paper in the United States. Jose never let that stop him, though. He found a sponsoring family in Atlanta, Georgia, and moved his family there. Then he and his wife, who was from a prominent family and had never before known a day of real work in her life, found jobs in a restaurant. He went to night school at Georgia State University and then Emory while his children, though donations from the parish, attended first Christ the King Elementary School and then Pope Pius X High School.

In time, Jose graduated from Emory (*cum laude*) in a pre-med track and entered medical school. After the first year his professors determined that what they had in their midst was not a student, but a very knowledgeable colleague who was stuck in a bureaucratic nightmare. The rest of med school was remarkably smooth. He attained his (second) doctor of medicine degree, stayed at Emory and eventually became a full professor. His wife, in the meantime, had opened a prominent and successful Cuban restaurant. Their combined income had finally caught back up to what they had lost nearly ten years before.

Miguel Castanuelo, in the meantime, had become totally Americanized. The Hispanic community in Atlanta in the 1960s and '70s was infinitesimal and his father had no intention of raising his child as a "separate but equal" citizen. Miguel quickly became Mickey, using Spanish rarely at home and never in public. He played American football and was indistinguishable from the Chads and Tommies and Blakes around him, until an announcer had to try to pronounce his last name. But his senior year at St. Pius, it had become a game. Whenever the announcer at some away game stumbled, the entire Pius side would resound: "Cast-a-new-Way!-lo!"

He had decided that on graduation he would enter the Army, much to the dismay of his parents. But Mickey had become more than Americanized, he was a fervent patriot. He knew that everything in life that really mattered was represented by that Coast Guard cutter that had risked stormy seas to save him and his family, by the sponsorship families who had welcomed them with open arms and the society that had let his father have that all-too-rare second chance. He felt that he had to give something back. And if that meant a tour in the Army before he went to college, so be it.

However, in his junior year of high school, a father of one of his classmates made a presentation to the physics class. The father was a senior officer in the United States Navy, stationed at the eminently land-locked Georgia Institute of Technology. What the father discussed was the opportunities open to bright young men (and women) who would be willing to give a few years to the U.S. Navy. The Navy was always desperate for anyone who could pass the rigorous academic challenges involved in nuclear power generation. And Georgia Tech had one of the premier schools in that subject. The Navy would pay for the education of eligible men (and women) who were willing to give six years of their life to the Navy.

Miguel practically broke an arm signing up.

He was easily accepted at Georgia Tech since his SAT score had been 1527 and his GPA was 3.98 (he'd gotten a B in Latin one year) and graduated in four years with a BS in Nuclear Power Generation. He then went to the Navy's nuclear power school "where we'll *really* teach you about generation" and then into service with the active fleet, working in nuclear "boomers," where he developed his long-term love of elaborate practical jokes.

Unfortunately, after one tour of duty he was beached with a

previously undetected heart murmur. Unsure what to do with himself, he went back to Georgia Tech and got the rest of a Ph.D. in nuclear physics. From there he went to the Department of Energy, but at Tech the second time his focus had changed from generation technology to weapons tech.

He ended up at Oak Ridge, which was no longer in the weapons building business but was involved in basic research. From Oak Ridge he moved to the University of Tennessee, to which he officially transferred his football allegiance when Georgia Tech started a business school. UT was pretty much right next door and had a long and fruitful revolving door policy with the government facility. He then spent a decade cycling from one facility to the other, with his theoretical research becoming more and more esoteric over time. Or so, at least, it seemed.

When the news of the Posleen invasion had come, he thought he was going to be going back into a blue suit; the conditions of space-board battle were similar enough to subs that submariners were at a premium in the Fleet. Instead, he had stayed at the University and Oak Ridge because it was there he could make the greater contribution. Because the "theoretical" research he had been involved in at Oak Ridge was the manufacture, capture and management of antimatter.

Mickey was just a tad on the "Green" side. He recognized that fossil fuels were both limited and an environmental nightmare. Not so much from the much overblown "greenhouse effect," which was clearly junk science, but from the extraction and distribution end. Not to mention traffic of which Knoxville, Tennessee, had more than its fair share. But he also was a realist and knew that to replace fossil fuels you had to have something equivalent or better. Petroleum, at its theoretical base, was a means of transporting energy. Hundreds of millions of years before, tiny marine algae (*not* dinosaurs) had gathered the energy of the sun and then died. They were overlaid with limestone and compressed, resulting in petroleum. It was relatively easy and cheap to extract and transport.

From Mickey's perspective, the only viable answer was antimatter. It could be produced in remote locations using nuclear power and transported easily and cheaply. An amount of antimatter the size of a thumbnail sliver would power a car (or even a flying car, which would help out the traffic no end) for a reasonable lifetime. Of course, if the containment was destroyed the car would become a nuclear fireball. But that was just engineering.

The real problem, which his colleagues were happy to point out, was making the antimatter in the first place. Until there was a way to make it in quantity, and control it, he was researching science fiction.

With the coming of the Posleen, and the Indowy, and the Darhel, and the Tchpth, it was apparent that his "wild ideas" were anything *but* science fiction. The Indowy could make antimatter like there was no tomorrow and microencapsulate it for safety. Suddenly, all the planet's problems, excepting only that it was about to be invaded by cannibalistic aliens, were solved.

As it turned out, the Indowy technique for making antimatter was trivial; it was one of the few things that human theory could comprehend about the new technologies. And they could contain it. The latter was important. Antimatter that contacted "regular" matter converted all of its mass to energy. It was that energy release that made it so alluring. Best of all, it could be contained in *very* small amounts. That way if some of the encapsulation failed, there wouldn't be a massive nuclear fireball. Microencapsulating it, though, or even containing it, turned out to be tricky. The Indowy knew how, but nobody else did.

But Mickey was a fanatic. Whatever it was he put his mind to, he threw himself at fully. The theory of manufacture was easy. And the Indowy could microencapsulate. It was only a matter of reverse engineering.

Unfortunately, that was not the case. After studying Indowy techniques (to the extent that they would allow) for nearly a year, he came away a frustrated man. The Indowy defied the laws of probability and that was just not fair.

All quantum mechanics, all chemistry, all metallurgy, comes down to probabilities. When two chemicals are mixed, there are several ways that they can recombine. But only one way is "probable." Therefore, almost all of the molecules combine in that way, with a scattered handful combining in others.

Often the "alternate" combinations are more useful. But they are also hysterically unlikely. The Indowy got the alternate combinations every single time. It was like hitting Lotto not once, but Every. Single. Time. What a rip.

It was the answer to all the problems. Not just microencapsulation but their armor, their drives, their energy and gravity technologies. All of them depended on hitting the Lotto, consistently and dependably. He didn't understand how they did it and they couldn't, apparently, explain it in terms that made sense. They just "prayed" and it happened.

Well, he was a good Catholic but he didn't believe in that kind of prayer. It was an advanced technology, that was all. But one that he couldn't, for the life of him, figure out how to replicate. So it was back to the drawing board.

Microencapsulation was the key. If he could microencapsulate, instead of using fossil fuels, the entire world (what was left of it at this point) could convert to antimatter. Now that production was fixed, microencapsulation was the Holy Grail.

There was one theory of microencapsulation that might work. There was a material called "fullerene," after Buckminster Fuller the inventor of the geodesic dome, which was a spherical molecule of carbon. Since each of the carbon atoms generated a "repulsion zone," any molecule or atom trapped in the center was automatically held away from contact not only with the carbon atoms but with the rest of the universe.

After exhausting every other theory, Mickey threw himself into the chemistry and physics of bucky balls. There was an existing knowledge base of how to produce them, and even how to wrap them around another atom. But wrapping them around antihydrogen, without it coming into contact with them, was a whole nother ball of fullerene.

It took time. And the process was not without its failures. But if Tennessee had anything it had miners (to dig holes in mountains to build the remote-controlled experimental facilities) and mountains. And it had only taken three mountains to find a way to perform microencapsulation safely. (Well, relatively safely. They weren't going to move it out of mountain four and into the middle of a city any time soon.) In the process he even got a minimal understanding of how the Indowy were warping physics to their own ends. Unfortunately what he got was useless for his purposes.

Fullerene was tough stuff. To get the energy out of the encapsulated hydrogen required "breaking" the fullerene first. And breaking it took nearly as much energy as was recovered from the explosion. It worked better setting up a chain reaction, putting a quantity of the "hyperfullerene" into a vessel and forcing the destruction of a small amount (usually by injecting anti-protons) which then broke up the rest.

Unfortunately, gauging the exact amount was difficult. After the first such difficulty, and at the request of the University of Tennessee regents, they moved the new lab into another mountain until the building was rebuilt. And somehow he couldn't see GM buying into a "chain reaction drive." What he basically had was a handful of black dust that was darned near impossible to get to explode. But when it did, look out.

He had an explosive, not a fuel. And had he mentioned the radiation problem?

When the initial carbon atoms were reacted, they were not fully consumed and they released a blast of alpha and beta particles along with a bit of gamma rays ("The Castanuelo radioactive chain reaction drive?" No, GM would not be happy.) The violence, at the atomic level, of the explosion also tended to cause some of the surrounding carbon atoms to chaotically fuse. The result was a spray of very "hot" radioactive material, more deadly than, if not as long lasting as, standard nuclear fallout.

Well, the Posleen had arrived at this point. And they seemed exactly the sort of people that deserved a very hot, radioactive, antimatter-driven, reception. Unfortunately, the President of the U.S. did not agree. So he was left with this remarkably stable stuff that in a nanosecond could turn half the eastern U.S. (he saw no point once the process was perfected in shutting down the production facility) into a radioactive wasteland. Although it was only *really* hot for a day or two. On a theoretical level it seemed like the perfect area denial weapon.

And, as has been mentioned, Miguel was a fanatic.

"You've got a *what*?" Jack Horner rarely shouted so it was that much more surprising when he did.

"We can range to the Gap." Gerald Carson, the President of the University of Tennessee, was not happy about the call. But he had been asked a question so he was answering the question. Calmly, politely and with sweat pouring down his face.

"We've got a gun project," he continued to the general's nod. Since the Posleen apparently couldn't hit ballistic projectiles, practically every school with an engineering program did. "It's able to range. It lofted a fifty-pound package into a low temporary orbit last month. It's a modified Super-Bull, three hundred millimeter. And we've also got this professor in the nuclear program, Mickey Castanuelo. He's a . . . he was considered a bit of a tenured nut before First Contact because he's been crazy about antimatter. Since First Contact he's been crazy about production and containment, which is why he's been getting a blank check from Ground Force R and D. He was working on energy systems."

"So we paid for this?" Jack asked.

"I don't know exactly *what* he was *supposed* to be researching," the president frowned furiously, "but he finally figured out a way to microencapsulate. Unfortunately, it was useless from an energy standpoint. But he's been from nuke energy to weapons and back so I guess he went back again. And he apparently got the specs for the Supergun so what he went and built was an antimatter cluster bomb . . ."

Cally walked out of the cache and sat down on the exterior ledge, looking down at the long slope to the distant valley. She'd never really looked over the terrain on this side of the mountain before and now seemed like as good a time as any; the adults weren't going to be back for a while.

To the north there was another ridge that flanked the narrow valley before her. The valley curved to the east, then back to the south before it reached Rabun Valley just west of the Rabun–Nacoochee School; the stream in the valley twisted its way through the former school property before reaching the headwaters of the Tennessee.

To the west there was another line of ridges that at the head of the valley, just below her position, were practically a knife-edge. There were some trees even there, but with the recent winds the leaves had mostly been stipped away. There was a red-tailed hawk flying just above the trees in the valley about a hundred feet below her and she watched it circle down and back until it disappeared around the shoulder of the ridge.

As the hawk crested the north ridge she noticed a movement among the trees and pulled up her binoculars for a closer look. At first the figures appeared to be a line of deer heading for the bisecting ridgeline but then her eyes adjusted to the perspective. And deer only carried weapons in cartoons.

"Oh, shit," she muttered.

It was a short company of Posleen with a God King, dismounted from his saucer. If she drew back, the group would probably pass right by the cache. But there hadn't been a Posleen group in the area since the first attack and this one was in a really odd place; the Posleen generally tried to stay *off* of ridges. So there had to be a reason they were here.

And the only really viable target in the area was the resupply team.

The Posleen weren't all that fast on the ridges, but as soon as they got down in the valley they'd be able to really speed up. And with all the guys loaded down with those huge frigging boxes, there was no way that the guys were going to be able to outrun them, even if they knew they were coming. Which they didn't.

She stood up and walked back into the cache, looking around at the kids. After a moment she came to a decision. It wasn't a *happy* decision, but it was the only one that made sense. Sometimes you just had to be an O'Neal, even if you were a thirteen-year-old girl.

"Billy, I'm going for a walk," she said, picking up her armor and throwing it on.

"I thought you were supposed to stay here," the boy replied, watching as she loaded up.

"Well, I've got something I have to do," Cally said with a frown. "Girl stuff."

"Oh." Billy frowned in turn as she locked and loaded her weapon. "Girl stuff. Okay."

"I'll be back before the grown-ups," Cally added. "If anybody comes by, get in the GalTech cache and close the door. Nothing can get through that."

"Will do," Billy replied.

"Bye," she finished, stepping out onto the ledge. The Posleen were halfway across the ridge. If she was going to get into a good position she had better hustle.

Whistling quietly, she started off along the narrow ledge. She didn't know the name of the song that she whistled, but if her grandfather was around to hear it he would have recognized it immediately.

"Fight the horde," she sang, sliding down the slope towards the lower ridgeline, "sing and cry, Valhalla I am *coming.*"

"The system consists of fifty-five sub-projectiles with an Indowy initiator in each," Dr. Castanuelo said, pointing at the diagram on the screen. "After firing, the system reaches its target point and begins to spread projectiles. It doesn't just drop them, which would cause massive overlap, but lays them down during its flight. Each projectile has slowing fins. These have been shown to not "trip" Posleen defensive systems. This system lets all the projectiles attain complimentary altitudes. At a preprogrammed height above ground, which is determined by radar altimeters in each sub-projectile, the Indowy containment field releases a burst of anti-protons into the fullerene matrix which then sustains a rapid chain reaction."

Jack looked at the presentation as the projectiles fell out of the back of an imaginary artillery shell and scattered across a wide area. The effect looked similar to a cluster bomb until you realized that what looked like gullies and small hills in the background was a backdrop of the Rocky Mountains.

"What's the footprint?" Horner asked. He had commandeered a shuttle and flown down to the university as soon as he got the word. He still didn't know if he had the answer to a maiden's prayer or the worst nightmare since the word of the invasion.

Dr. Castanuelo cleared his throat nervously. "Thirty-five miles deep, fifteen miles across. It's the equivalent of a one hundred and ten megaton bomb, but with significantly different gross effects. For example the thermal pulse is equivalent to a two megaton."

"And you built this on your own?" Jack asked quietly. "Without authorization? Or even mentioning it? One hundred and ten *megatons*?"

"Well, I had the hyperfullerene and the initiators just sitting there," Dr. Castanuelo said hotly. "I thought it might come in handy."

"You thought it might come in handy. Just how *much* of this . . . hyperfullerene did you make?"

"Well, once we got the production model worked out it seemed reasonable to continue production," Dr. Castanuelo said defensively. "I mean, we had the power plant and the materials. After that it was easy."

"How much?" the general asked smiling faintly. The question was nearly a whisper.

"Well, as of yesterday, excepting the material in the bomb, approximately one hundred and forty kilos."

"Of hyperfullerene?" Jack asked, taking a deep breath.

"No, we generally refer to it in terms of anti-hydrogen atomic mass rather than the . . ."

"You have one hundred and forty kilos of antimatter sitting around on *my planet*????"

"I thought it would come in handy," the doctor said lamely.

"Sure, for fueling Ninth Fleet!" Jack shouted. "Tell me about the radioactive effects of this bomb."

"Very hot, unfortunately," the scientist sighed. "It's one of the reasons it's useless for an energy source. But very short-lived as well. In a day or two the area is down to high background and in a month it would require sophisticated sensors to tell it has been hit. But not the sort of thing you want running your car. Fortunately, it's readily detectable."

"Sure, with a Geiger counter!" President Carson said.

"Oh, no, there's a visual chemical cue," the professor said. "It was the suggestion of one of my grad students and it made sense. The truly 'hot' areas will be readily detectable visually and the cue will fade as the radiation does."

"But the entire system has not been tested," Carson pointed out with the sort of quiet calm used when an emergency happens during brain surgery.

"We fired a mockup with transmitters in duplicate Indowy containment fields," the scientist said. "They all survived. If they survived, the containment works. And hyperfullerene has been tested against every kind of shock imaginable. Unfortunately, the problem is not it detonating prematurely but getting it to detonate at all."

"And it is armed," Carson said, accusingly.

"Well, yes, that follows."

"Positive action locks?" Jack asked.

"Not yet," Castanuelo admitted. In other words, the bomb could be detonated by anyone with rudimentary technical skills.

"Guards? Electronic security? Vault safety?" the general asked furiously.

"Well, we've got it in one of our mines," the professor said with a shrug. "And I've got a couple of students watching it. Look, it was a crash project!"

Jack glanced at his wrist where his AID used to be and then at his aide. "Jackson, get on the phone. I want an outside expert in here, one on antimatter, one on Indowy containment systems and one on guns and submunitions. I want a company of regular troops around wherever this thing is in no more than an hour and I want them replaced by special operations guard units by the end of the day."

He looked at the scientist and nodded. "Dr. Castanuelo, you're right, we did need it. I'm pretty sure that that is going to keep your bacon out of the fire. As long as it works. If it doesn't . . ."

"Sir, if it doesn't, I'll never know it," Castanuelo said. "If it, for example, detonates on launch, there won't be a Knoxville left."

"And if the *rest* of your material sympathetically detonates, say goodbye to *Tennessee!*"

CHAPTER NINE

Rabun Gap, GA, United States of America, Sol III
1522 EDT Monday September 28, 2009 AD

Mike didn't have to look at his readouts to see how bad off the battalion was. Most of the suits were laid out flat on the log-covered hillside. Part of that was fatigue—even with the suits, being in combat was murderously tiresome—but the greater part of it was experienced troopers trying to conserve every erg of power. Some of the suits were down to one percent power and when it dropped to zero the suit would pop open and "decant" the Protoplasmic Intelligence System out onto the cold, wet ground. Not a happy prospect.

Together with the loss of Gunny Pappas, it was a pretty bleak and depressing situation.

There were other problems. He still had nearly two companies of troops, but he had lost Captain Holder in the landing and Charlie Company was looking pretty ragged as a result. And he was short on officers except on staff, where they were doing less and less good. At this point he didn't really need an intelligence officer. The Posleen were right *there* and *there* and *there* and . . . On the other hand, he also didn't need an operations officer. The Posleen were going to come on in the same old way and they would

119

fight them in the same old way. Hell, this battalion didn't even need a *commander*.

Stewart would probably be the best choice for a company commander. He was naturally charismatic, he had a good feel for tactical, and, hell, operational maneuver, and he didn't have Duncan's . . . problems.

So why did he keep thinking he should put Duncan in command of Charlie Company?

He took off his helmet and spit his dip out on the ground, looking around at the suits. The whole battalion was simply fragged. Half of the personnel had gone to sleep where they dropped, Provigil be damned. He wasn't much better, which was why he was considering putting a combat-shocked officer in command of a company.

Duncan, along with Stewart and Pappas, had been with him for years, since his first company command. But before that Duncan had also been on Diess and then was transferred to Barwhon. Something about the fighting on Barwhon had just . . . snapped him. He was fine calling in fire and coming up with really elegant ways to manage complicated battles, but put him in the line and he just . . . closed down.

Duncan had a responsibility streak a mile wide, though. Putting him in charge of Charlie Company would do one of two things. It would either break him out of it or shut him down permanently.

And, frankly, if *he* went down, that would leave *Stewart* in place to take over battalion command. Which just might save everyone's butts.

"Duncan," he said finally. "I need you over here for a second."

"This really sucks," Shari said as she stumbled over another piece of debris.

The suits had cleared a path up the road to the house, but there wasn't much they could do in the valley; it was just too torn up.

The Rabun Gap Valley had once been a rather pleasant place, its hillsides lined with trees and the valley itself filled with a mix of light industrial plants and cropland. But repeated nuclear-class explosions had changed all that.

The trees on the hillsides had not only been knocked down but in many cases thrown around, some of them out into the valley. Along with them were the remains of the corps that had died there, shattered hulks of tanks, howitzers flipped end for end and sticking out of the ground, bits and pieces of trucks, buildings and people scattered across the ground in a crazy quilt. Added to this were ripples of soil and craters thrown up by the explosions, some of which had happened low enough to dig into the ground to the bedrock.

Through this nuclear nightmare the suits and the unarmored humans stumbled with their massive loads. The suits had it fairly easy; with unlimited power they could practically float over obstacles. The humans, though, had to struggle under, over and around them.

"Don't knock it," Tommy said nervously, looking to the east. "I think we'd have had company before now if it wasn't for all of this."

"The Posleen should be able to plow through this," Mueller said then cursed as he fell when one leg plunged into a hole. The weight of the battlebox on his back pushed him face down in the ground and for a moment he couldn't get the angle to straighten up. "Shit."

"No lying out, Master Sergeant," Tommy said with a chuckle. He set down one of the boxes he was carrying and pulled the massive NCO out of the hole like a cork out of a bottle.

"You know, Lieutenant, you could positively get on a guy's nerves," Mueller said with a rueful grin.

"When we started across we came from down valley," Sunday continued. "There's a . . . pile, sort of ripple, of dirt and debris down the end of the valley. I looked at it from up on the hill and it looks like a lander must have just about been grounded when it blew up. Anyway, between that ridge and the fallen trees on all the slopes they're going to have a hell of a time getting up here for a while."

"Hmm," Mosovich said. "So unless they come from the west, the cache should be okay."

"Or from the north," Mueller said. "There's a road up there, too."

"They'd have to be pretty lost," Wendy chuckled. "That's a lousy road."

" 'S' truth," Mosovich said. "And good news." He let out a hiss as a ridge of soil slipped out from under his feet. He looked up at the mountain they were supposed to ascend—it was covered in fallen trees—and sighed. "I'm getting too old for this shit."

"Sergeant Major, thank you for helping us get this gear up here."

Mosovich had never met the famous Mike O'Neal and wasn't particularly impressed with what he saw. The suit was . . . weird, with some sort of demon hologram on the front. And the major's unit was sprawled across the back side of Black Mountain like they weren't going to be going anywhere soon; most of the suits were flat on their backs. After humping all this shit up the hill, the sight of all the armored combat suits apparently crapped out was not particularly pleasing.

"Yes, sir," Mosovich replied correctly. "I'm not actually in command, Captain Elgars is."

"Sort of," Elgars said, dumping the battlebox she had carried up the hill. "What's the situation, Major?"

"As soon as we can get the suits powered back up, we'll be ready to move back into the Gap." As he was speaking, a team of technician suits was connecting power leads to the antimatter generators. "Since this is standard ammo, as long as it holds out we shouldn't have nearly as much need for power. And with the additional AM packs we'll be able to fight for at least two days. Assuming we survive, of course."

The suit was a blank image, but something about the body posture bespoke irony.

"I'm glad we could be of service, sir," Mosovich commented, dryly.

"I know it looks sort of stupid to have a company of ACS flaked out on a hill," O'Neal said, removing his helmet. "But we had to carry some of the suits the last hundred meters. We were *that* out of power. If I thought *I* could have gone, I would have. But Sunday and his Reapers were the only ones with enough power left to get to the cache. Again, thank you for your help."

Mosovich watched as some of the suit gel slid off the major's hair and arched out to drop into the open helmet. The officer was younger than he'd expected. He was a rejuv, of course, but something about him told Mosovich that he also was *young*, comparatively speaking. And tired.

"You gotten any rest lately, sir?" the NCO said, gruffly.

"That is what Provigil is for, Sergeant Major," O'Neal answered with a frown as he looked out at the valley. "You know I grew up here, I suppose."

"Yes, sir," Mosovich hesitated for a moment. "I . . . knew your father. We had friends in common. I went up to the farm."

"I understand his body was missing," Mike said, reaching into an armored pouch and extracting a can of Skoal. "Dip?"

"No, sir, thank you," the sergeant major replied. "Yes. Cally said that she had found his body at the bunker. But when we got there it was gone."

"Well, at least Cally is okay," Mike replied. "You need to get going. We're going to rearm and fuel fast. And then we're going to call in the mother of all nuclear strikes on this . . . situation. The inner cache is made out of plasteel armor and should hold out, but you may get buried. I'll inform Fleet where you are so . . . when we retake this area you can get dug out."

"How bad can it be?" Elgars asked. "The outer cache took, what, two blasts already?"

"I did say 'the mother of all nuclear strikes,' right?" O'Neal said with a lopsided grin. "How about one hundred and ten megatons."

"*Holy shit!*" Mosovich gasped. "Nothing is going to stand up to that!"

"It's going to be spread out," the major said. "Individual areas will get something around a two-megaton blast. It will be airburst. That cache will more than hold. But you have to be *in* it, and so does my daughter."

"Yes, sir," Elgars said. "We left Cally holding the fort. We should get back." She straightened her back and gave him a snappy salute.

O'Neal nodded at her and then slowly raised his hand in return. "We'll see you when we see you, folks. Good luck."

"Wendy," Tommy said and stopped.

"It's okay," she answered, reaching up to stroke the face of the armor. It was a simple, blank facet, not a face, but somehow it felt right to be touching it.

"I'll be okay," she said, flexing her jaw. "And I don't care what they say, you're coming back to me. Do you understand that? We've got a wedding to attend."

"I understand," he said, the voice echoing hollowly from the suit. "I'll be there."

"Promise?"

"I promise."

"If you don't show up," she said, wiping at his face again. "I'll cap you with your own Glock." She tapped the front of the armor for emphasis then started back down the trail to the valley.

"Nice girl. I can see why you want to get married."

Tommy hadn't noticed the major come up behind him. Now he turned and looked down at the shorter figure.

"Yes, sir," he replied. He paused then raised his hands, palms up. "I really love her. High school heartthrob. The whole bit."

"I understand. I met Sharon in college and when I realized she saw anything in me . . . I thought I'd died and gone to heaven."

"She's . . . dead, sir?" he asked, cautiously.

"Very. She was outside her ship working on a stuck clamp when a B-Dec came out of hyper. The ship attempted to launch from the system she was working on. The missiles, the clamp, the ship and my wife all disappeared in a cloud of radiation and light. That would be just about the same time you were burying yourself under Fredericksburg, by the way." He paused then tapped Tommy on the back. "That's why I told you to get what you can while you can get it, son. There's no guarantee she's always going to be there for you. And no guarantee that you're going to be there for her."

"Will she be okay?" Sunday asked. "That's . . . it's a big fucking weapon they're firing, pardon my French, sir."

"That safe the gear was in will stand up to just about anything," O'Neal replied. "She'll be fine. They close the door, take their Hiberzine and go to sleep until somebody comes to dig them out. You've been there and done that, right?"

"Yes," Tommy said. "And what about us?"

"I thought you lived for killing Posleen," O'Neal said with a snort. "Good news, it's a target-rich environment."

"I *live* for killing Posleen," Tommy replied. "I can't kill them if I'm dead."

"Well, we're rearmed. And powered up. And the Reapers have more rounds. So we'll go back and do what we always do; hold on until relieved."

"For how long?" Tommy asked, quietly.

"How long indeed. Let's just say I hope that goddamned SheVa gun puts the pedal to the metal."

Cally snuggled the rifle into her shoulder and took a breath.

The weapon was a Steyr AUG II, a 7.62x59 version of the venerable AUG Bullpup. The weapon had been fielded as a replacement just before the first major landings and a few had turned up with special operations troops in the United States just before the Posleen landings stopped all normal commerce. Her father had managed to snag one for her through connections and she was glad he did. The weapon was smaller and shorter than most of the 7.62 weapons out there and it was easier for her to handle with her lighter build. And the built-in buffer reduced the recoil to something along the lines of a 9mm carbine. So she was pretty accurate with it. Especially with a 3–9x variable-power scope. The problem was she didn't have a target.

She knew from talking to her dad and granddad that the most important thing to take out in a Posleen company was the God King. The God King had all the sensors so once you got him, the company was down to Mark One Eyeball. Also, after the initial, violent, reaction to the death of their God, the normals tended to get really disorganized and a bunch of them would just wander off to become ferals. So the God King had to be the first target.

The other side of that story was that Posleen were *tough*; if you hit one in an artery they just shunted to secondary systems and kept going. To kill one, quickly, required either hitting the heart or the brain.

The problem was that *this* God King had apparently learned

the concept of Posleen shields and he was surrounded by his normals. So there wasn't, ever, a close shot at the heart. And their heads, which held their brains just like humans, were on the end of long, mobile necks. So targeting a head was tough as hell.

Unfortunately, that seemed to be the only viable target. So she let the breath out slowly and stroked her trigger.

Cholosta'an was watching his sensors nervously. The sensors indicated that there was an electronic device somewhere on the ridge above him. That might just mean one of the randomly scattered sensors that permitted the humans to keep track of Posleen movement. And, if so, it was no bother; there weren't many humans around to react.

But it also might mean a human or humans that had active electronics, like a radio or night-vision systems.

Unfortunately, the sensors couldn't quite pin down the location; it was just beyond their sensory range. He kept glancing up the hill, though, trying to spot any target. Thus he wasn't at all surprised when his sensors screamed a warning of an incoming round just as the oolt'os to his left grunted from the impact of a round on his neck.

The target was clear on the sensors now, an armed human with a chemical rifle. He swung his plasma gun onto the vector and fired, knowing that the rest of the oolt would follow his lead.

Cally flattened herself into the narrow crack in the rock and muttered curses under her breath. She had *heard* about the way that Posleen reacted to being fired on but hearing about it and being the target of it were two different things.

But she had thought the shot out carefully and the rocks around here were solid. Of course, they were now smoking and cracked from stray rounds. Fortunately, most of the fire was off target, down and to her left. She didn't know what had kept the Posleen from being their normal accurate selves, but whatever it was, it had saved her ass. And for that she was thankful.

Not so thankful as to fire from this position again, though. As the fire slackened she shimmied backwards, concealed by the ghillie cloak she had donned before firing, and scooted around one of the rocks out of direct line of the Posleen fire.

Time to go find another point.

Cholosta'an sent one of the oolt'os up the hill to see if there was any sign of the sniper but before the normal was half way up the hill there was another shot and another one of his oolt was hit, dropping to the ground this time with a round straight through the heart.

"This is really getting annoying," Cholosta'an muttered as he, again, targeted the sniper. He didn't know why he was missing the gadfly but he intended to track it down and destroy it.

"Up the hill," he shouted, pointing towards the targeting icon. "After it!"

This was one human that was not getting away; best to kill it before it started calling in artillery.

Aatrenadar snarled as another volley of artillery scythed thought his oolt'ondar. The human positions were dug in deep, so even with the massed fire of thousands of Posleen the defenders were holding out, laying down murderous direct machine-gun and rifle fire while their blasted "artillery" hammered from above.

What was worse was the situation the Posleen found themselves in. The humans had reacted quickly to the nuclear fire that had reduced the bulk of the host, then had driven forward in a mass tenaral charge, cutting down all the remaining Posleen in their path. Many of the Posleen were so shaken they had never even seen the human tanks and personnel carriers until they were upon them.

This push had pressed the remnant of the host into a pocket just south of the town of Green's Creek. There was very little room to open out and get a mass of fire upon the humans since the humans had taken the high ground in the defile. Furthermore, the narrow, twisty road behind, while packed with oolt'os and Kessentai from a milling mass on the far side of the gap, barely fed enough through to sustain their losses. Add in the artillery fire that was dropping deeper in the pass and the Posleen, for once, were able to use the term "beleaguered" to describe *their* situation.

The only bright spot was that while the host could not advance, neither could the humans. If they came out of their holes they would be slaughtered and if there was no way for the Posleen to maneuver there, equally, was no way for the humans to maneuver large forces. It was a battle of attrition and as soon as the combat suit defenders in the southern pass were cleared out, it would be a battle of attrition the humans could not win.

Of course, *he* would not see the eventual victory, but the Path was a path of pain and death. As well here as anywhere. If he could just sink his teeth into one more human.

"Forward!" he cried. The oolt'os would fight like the simple beasts they were but the younger Kessentai needed encouragement. "Forward for the host! Forward for the Path! Blood and loot at the end!"

He toggled his tenar forward as the line jolted towards the humans, then froze it at a light like a giant flashbulb behind him. After a moment there was another great flash, then another and another. For a moment his shadow, stark and white on the backs of the oolt'os in front of him, was fixed on his vision, then it was as if the sun had darkened. But his enhanced vision quickly adjusted to all the changes in lighting and he thus had a clear view of the mass of metal, like a rolling mountain, that appeared around the shoulder of a distant hill.

"Third round away, sir," Pruitt said. "I'm not happy with the accuracy at this range; we have to fire the damned things practically straight up and we have no solid data on winds aloft."

"Is it going to drift to this side of the Gap?" Mitchell asked.

"No, sir, if anything it will be a bit far out."

"Then I'll live with it," he said, tapping his map controls. "Okay, Pruitt, reload with anti-lander rounds, Major Chan, you're just about up, Reeves, follow the vector I've laid in." He took a look around the room and shook his head. "Let's Rock."

The monstrosity was as big as an oolt Po'osol and nothing that large should be able to crawl along the ground. It appeared around the side of a hill, leaning at an angle that, given its height, should have rolled it over on its side. But it didn't fall. It just kept rolling forward, the fire, it seemed, of all the oolt'os and Kessentai in view sparking off its front carapace. Yet, still, with lines of plasma carving the picture on its face, with hypervelocity missiles sparking off of it like fireflies in the night, it kept coming.

Then it disappeared in a wall of water.

"Excuse me," Colonel Mitchell said, looking into his suddenly blank monitor. The SheVa had lurched downward, indicating that they were descending into the valley of Sutton Branch, which should reduce some of the murderous fire they had been taking. But losing all visual references in the middle of a battle was . . . not good. "What in the hell just happened?"

"Colonel?" Chan called. "There's a big . . . fountain of water up here. It's all over the place! We can't see shit, pardon me."

"Negative visual, negative radar, negative lidar," Pruitt sang out. "What in the hell just *happened.*"

"Darn," Kilzer said. "Let me check my notes . . ."

"Mr. Kilzer!" the colonel shouted across the compartment. "Is this *your* doing?"

"Well, yeah," the tech rep replied. "It's an experimental anti-plasma defense. We mounted a fifty-thousand-gallon water tank in the front of the turret and . . ."

"Well, before you check your notes, kindly *shut it off!* We're driving into the rear of an embattled division! Running over their headquarters, for example, would be a really *big* mistake!"

"HQ's way back near Dillsboro, boss," Pruitt pointed out. "But it would be nice to see so we can shoot."

"Okay, okay," the civilian muttered, toggling off a switch. "It wasn't like anybody got *killed* . . ."

"Hold it here, Reeves," Mitchell called, surprised how far forward they had traveled. They were already across the stream and on their way up the flank of the next hill. In fact, looking in his monitor he saw that the church that used to occupy the hilltop itself had just disappeared under a track and the primary power lines that had once been there were now scattered across Bun-Bun's carapace.

"Oh, no, there goes Tokyo!" Kilzer said.

"Gojira!" Reeves shouted as the main support began to tumble down the hill.

"It's one of those eternal questions." Pruitt laughed. "Who would win in a fight, Bun-Bun or Godzilla?"

"Depends on the Bun-Bun," Pruitt pointed out. "Maj . . . I mean *Colonel*, we're in range of the Posleen, I think." His comment was punctuated with the *bong* of another HVM round hitting the frontal plate.

"Major Chan, are you in range?"

"Yes, sir," the MetalStorm commander replied. "We don't really have much of a target, but we're in range."

"Put it on the road," Mitchell replied. "They seem to be running right up it. After your initial volley, spread it to either side, arching it over the divisional positions."

"Yes, sir," Chan replied. "Whenever you're ready."

Mitchell opened his mouth and raised one finger just as Kilzer lifted his hand in a halting motion.

"Colonel, this isn't strictly necessary, but I heartily recommend it," Paul said, tapping a control. Over the intercom came a thump of drums, then the sound of bagpipes.

Mitchell paused to listen to the music for a moment, then grinned as the lyrics started.

"Oh, *yeah*," he said, his raised finger starting to thump the time in the air. "What is that?"

"March of Cambreath."

"You're right. Works for me. *Major* Chan!"

"Sir!" the MetalStorm commander replied, nodding her head to the beat.

"*Open fire!*"

CHAPTER TEN

Axes flash, broadswords swing,
Shining armour's piercing ring
Horses run with polished shield,
Fight Those Bastards till They Yield
Midnight mare and blood red roan,
Fight to Keep this Land Your Own
Sound the horn and call the cry,
How Many of Them Can We Make Die!

Follow orders as you're told,
Make Their Yellow Blood Run Cold
Fight until you die or drop,
A Force Like Ours is Hard to Stop
Close your mind to stress and pain,
Fight till You're No Longer Sane
Let not one damn cur pass by,
How Many of Them Can We Make Die!

—Heather Alexander
"March of Cambreath"

Green's Creek, NC, United States of America, Sol III
1648 EDT Monday September 28, 2009 AD

"Lord it's nice to shoot light stuff again." Specialist Cindy Glenn was a female, like her commander. Unlike her commander, she did not consider anything about the Army to be a career, especially not in *this* job.

The basic theory of the MetalStorm system was conceived shortly before First Contact. The idea was simplicity in itself, like most interesting inventions. Instead of putting bullets in a complicated feeding system, load them all into the barrel, one stacked on top of another, with the propellant packed in between. Detonated electronically the device produced an awesome amount of firepower as literally hundreds of bullets spewed out of the barrel in bare seconds; one device had shown a theoretical rate of one million rounds per minute.

It was the "theoretical" part that was the sticking point. Since the barrel was also the bullet supply, "reloading" involved replacing the entire barrel. Furthermore, the "bullet to weight" ratio of the system was just astronomical; it could never be considered a reasonable system for infantrymen who were always overloaded anyway.

But it had certain benefits. After the coming of the Posleen, MetalStorm was used widely as an "area denial" system, laying down masses of bullets that could best be described as a "rain of lead." When stopping Posleen wave assaults, more was always better when it came to firepower. And there wasn't much "more" than MetalStorm.

It was also used for some specialty systems, one of which was the "MetalStorm Anti-Lander Enhanced Firepower Armor Combination." The weapons system consisted of an Abrams tank chassis with a twelve-barrel MetalStorm pack mounted on top. The caliber of the barrels was 105mm and each had one hundred rounds of anti-armor discarding sabot loaded into it. At the touch of a button the system could spew out twelve hundred rounds in under a minute. It was hoped that this storm of depleted uranium, the same type and caliber of round that had originally been designed for the Abrams to defeat Soviet armor, would be capable of penetrating and destroying the Posleen landers that often played havoc on defenses. Unfortunately, it did not quite live up to its design potential.

The designers had been trying to get everyone to call it "Malefic" but they failed miserably. The system *was* malefic, but only to its crew. The Abrams had been designed with the 105 round in mind. And it had successfully upgraded to the 120mm round, a significant increase in firepower that it nonetheless managed smoothly. However, firing twelve hundred 105mm anti-armor discarding sabot rounds in less than a minute turned out to be . . . one of the few situations where "more power" was not necessarily the best thing. Crews normally screamed as they fired. Many crew members deserted or deliberately maimed themselves to avoid duty in MetalStorm tracks. Because when those twelve barrels began spewing depleted uranium, the sixty-ton tanks would shake like an out-of-balance blender. Broken bones were commonplace as the crews were slammed from side to side in the vehicles. Most of them likened it to being rolled in a barrel of gravel.

Despite the firepower, however, Malefic turned out to be unsuited to its primary role. The armor on Posleen landers was thick, the ships were large and they did not, unfortunately, approach on the ground. While the MetalStorm tracks could get penetration at short ranges, say down to fifteen hundred meters or so, they seemed unable to do any significant damage at anything other than point-blank range. And at that range, attempting to kill a lander was suicidal.

However, the military had designed the weapons at enormous cost and even fielded a few companies of them. So rather than simply take the turrets off and use the chassis for replacement parts, the powers-that-be decided to use them at the few things they were good at. Notably, area denial.

However, to do that required different weapons systems. The 105mm "twelve-pack" was poorly suited to killing vast numbers of Posleen. The rounds overkilled rather excessively but there were, for a MetalStorm system, relatively few of them.

But since the MetalStorm system replaced not just the ammunition in firing, but the barrel as well, there was no reason that the track was locked in to using 105mm. And a similar pack, even larger, was designed and fielded in 40mm.

The design used the basic 40mm grenade, the same projectile as was found in the venerable Mk-19 Mod 4. It fired a "bullet"-shaped projectile with a three-thousand-meter range that was just under a pound and a half of wrapped explosives and wire. On contact the projectile exploded, sending out a hail of notched wire that killed or injured anything in a five-meter radius.

Each of the MetalStorm "40 Packs" contained twenty thousand projectiles.

Instead of twelve barrels there were one hundred, ten across and ten down in a square block of metal that actually weighed more than the "heavy" pack. And instead of one hundred rounds packed into each barrel, there were two hundred.

A mass of Posleen were visible trying to push through the gap against the heavy fire of the human infantry. They were getting slaughtered, to the point that the following ranks were having to scramble over the bodies of the slain, but they were still inching down the road.

That was about to stop.

Glenn laid her targeting reticle on the front of the column and opened fire.

What spewed from the rectangular packet on a U-shaped mount on the tank looked like nothing so much as a continuous vomit of fire. One in five rounds was a tracer and with the rounds hammering out at such a high rate the tracers were not only continuous but overlapping. It was a wall of fire a meter and a half wide which, when it touched anything, exploded.

The Posleen touched by the wall of flame literally disappeared as dozens of rounds hit each individual centaur. As soon as it was clear the advance had stopped, Glenn started to walk the rounds up the road, toggling the gun from side to side to ensure she got all of the oncoming horde. It was less like a weapon than some flaming broom, that both killed the Posleen and ripped them into nothing larger than hand-sized chunks until what was left behind looked as if some angry god had put it through a meat-grinder.

Unfortunately, even two hundred thousand rounds could be expended in a short period of time. Which was why after only four seconds Turret One fell silent. After a moment Glenn hit the eject button and the massive steel firing pod was ejected backwards to lie on top of the SheVa.

"I'm out, ma'am," the gunner said, flipping on the reload winch. "I'll be up shortly, though."

Chan had seen the effect of the 40 packs often enough, but never in such a concentrated location and it took her a moment to react. "That's fine. Not a problem. Turret Two?"

"Two."

"Continue engagement. Three, when two goes dry . . ."

"Three, gotcha."

Chan flipped off of the company frequency and down to the SheVa intercom. "Major Mitchell, we're going to be out of targets soon."

Mitchell shook his head at the blood bath on the roadway. The road-cuts to either side of the narrow gap were *splashed* with yellow nearly to their tops. And you didn't often see *that*.

"When the opening is clear arc your fire over the ridgeline. We don't have much maneuvering room here; the crunchies are in the way."

"Understand, sir. I'd like to get us up on the next ridgeline. My map says it opens up on the other side. I think we could do good works up there."

Mitchell chuckled and nodded his head, unseen. "Concur, and we're probably in trouble for running over the church. I'll get on the horn to the division and see if they can clear out a few of their crunchies."

"Yes, sir." There was a pause. "We're shot out on turrets one through six and twelve. The others don't have the angularity."

"How long to reload?" Mitchell asked, turning his head sideways as the tech rep waved one arm in his direction.

"About another three minutes, sir," Chan said awkwardly. "We fire this stuff off way faster than we reload."

"Hold on a second," Mitchell replied, cutting the intercom audio and furrowing his brow at Kilzer's gestures. "Yes?"

"Rotate the turret," Kilzer said.

"She *did*," Mitchell replied acidly then stopped. "Oh. Jesus."

"Don't worry about it," Kilzer said, waving his hand. "I've been thinking about this stuff longer than you have."

"So, boss, you want I should rotate the turret?" Pruitt said with a chuckle.

"Major Chan," Mitchell said, keying the intercom again. "We're going to rotate the turret to bring the rest of your guns into action."

There was another pause and he smiled. "If you're pounding your head on the TC controls, it's okay. So am I."

"Thank you, sir," Chan called back as Pruitt keyed the controls.

"Hold it there, Pruitt," Chan said, flipping to the company frequency. "Number Five, you're up. Everybody watch where the previous turret has fired," she continued as the blast of fire arched over the nearby ridgeline. "I want to try to saturate the area on the other side of the ridge."

She nodded as the SheVa turret began to rotate. Pruitt apparently could feel the MetalStorm fire even in the heavily armored control room and had rotated automatically when five had finished its shot. And he did it again when six was done. So she could quit worrying about it.

Time to find something else to worry about.

She popped her head out of the TC's hatch and watched as Glenn manipulated the loader. There were four packs, three 40s and a 105, connected to the SheVa's top directly behind the turret. The loader was a multi-angularity forklift that connected to special points on the bottom of the packs. Once it was connected, which was the most ticklish part, all that Glenn had to do was hit the "Load Sequence" button and the multi-ton pack was lifted through three dimensions and carefully dropped into the gun-cradle. Once in place the gun system inserted the pintle and trunnions making the whole system ready to fire.

Simple. So simple that they'd be reloaded before Nine's turn to fire came up. And so would Nine. The question was whether to continue the fire-mission.

There were packs stashed in the interior. But to get to those would require the crane and someone, Pruitt probably, who was qualified to operate it. Which meant an hour or so to replace all her ready-packs. Which meant she really didn't want to shoot off all her reloads blind.

"Colonel Mitchell," she said, switching back over to intercom. "I recommend we give them one stonk from here and then either move forward to the ridgeline or begin our movement towards Franklin."

Mitchell was regretting releasing Kitteket. The specialist had been dumped on them by accident during the retreat, but having someone to handle all the communications had turned out to useful. SheVas, by and large, did not do a lot of communicating. They mostly stayed in place or were moved by careful coordination of the local force commanders, who "owned" the SheVas as attachments. Operations orders, movement orders and communications were laid out days in advance. Otherwise they tended to run over such unimportant obstacles as front-lines, headquarters or, in one particularly unpleasant accident, the entire logistics "tail" of divisions. There was a reason that SheVa crewmen referred to everything other than SheVas, including "lesser" armor, as "crunchies."

But the battle for the Tennessee Valley had been a wild scramble and, as far as Mitchell knew, he was an independent command under Army headquarters. Which meant that he wasn't in the decision loop of the local division. Furthermore, the entire battle both in retreat and advance had been, of necessity, much more fluid than most battles that involved something the size of the Great Pyramids. And then there were the MetalStorms.

All of that meant far more communication load than was normal for a SheVa commander.

Which was Mitchell's problem at the moment.

"Wait one, Vickie," he said, switching back to another frequency. "Whiskey Five Echo Six-Four, this is SheVa Nine, over."

"SheVa Nine, you are not authorized on this net."

"Great, Echo Six-Four. I'm glad you have such great commo security. The point is that we're about to make a movement forward and unless we can coordinate it, we'll run over about two companies of your troops, over." He was on the division command net and he knew he was supposed to be on a support net, probably a dedicated one. That was how they usually ran SheVas. But he didn't *have* a correct frequency. All he had was a hastily scribbled note that said "Local Division" and a frequency.

Welcome to the Real and the Nasty, boys.

"SheVa Nine, authenticate Victor Foxtrot."

"Look, first of all the damned net is compromised in case you hadn't been told. Including the current SOI. Second of all, I don't *have* your SOI. So, I'm sorry, I can't authenticate. Look, we're this great big metal thing on a ridge near Green's Creek. If you look closely, we have 'U.S. Defense Force SheVa Nine' on our side and we have a great big picture of a mini-lop rabbit on the front. And we're getting ready to roll over one of your battalions. So can we quit the commo games?!"

"SheVa Nine, this is Grizzly Six, over." The voice was gruff with a slight accent. It fit the name.

"Grizzly Six, this is SheVa Nine, over." Six meant a commander. Hopefully the commander of the unit they were about to run over so that *maybe* the crunchies would get out of the way.

"You're right, the SOI is compromised. But that doesn't mean you're you. Rotate your turret back and forth."

"Hang one, Grizzly, we're completing a stonk." Mitchell unkeyed the radio and looked over at Pruitt. "Pruitt, where we at?"

"That was eight. We're done. Vickie wants to hold onto her ready ammo."

"Okay, rotate the turret back and forth a bit. And don't you *ever* call her Vickie around me again."

"Will do, boss," the gunner replied, with a shrug. He tapped the controls back and forth. "What was that in aid of?"

"No idea," the commander replied. "But at least we're talking to the locals again." He keyed the microphone and took a breath. "Grizzly Six, have complied."

"Roger, welcome to the net," the commander said. "It will take me at least ten minutes to get those troops prepared to move. Where do you want to go?"

"There's a saddle on the ridge, directly across from the Savannah Baptist Church. UTM looks to be . . . North 391111 East 293868."

Mitchell no longer considered the odd nature of reply. Grid coordinates worked off of imaginary "lines" on maps and depending on the number of digits used, the accuracy of the location got higher and higher. At eight digits the accuracy of the location was less than a meter. So what he had just done was give a location that was accurate to the millimeter. For a "tank" that was a hundred meters wide.

Often he got asked about it. Normally in the military, when someone was just reading a map, they would use, at most, six digits for a location coordinate. So when he gave locations in twelve digit coordinates, it occasioned comment. His answer was fairly simple: The location tracker in the SheVa guns read out in twelve-digit coordinates.

He didn't *know* why it did; maybe he ought to ask Kilzer. But it gave twelve numbers. When faced with the numbers, he had one of two choices. He could figure out how to round them off to a six-digit coordinate, which would be normal, or he could just read them off the screen. Rounding them off wasn't *hard,* it just took a few seconds, was prone to error and distracted you, often in the middle of a fire-fight. Abstract thought in combat was a good way to end up a hole in the ground and so was taking a few seconds on a nonessential task. So he just read the damned things off the screen.

"Understood, SheVa," the commander replied after a moment. "I'll call you when the movement is approved, do not make the movement until I call."

"Roger, be aware that it is my intention after firing from that position to move backwards and then do a movement out of this zone of control. I prefer not to discuss that over open channels. Please advise the appropriate people. Over."

"Concur. After your fire, we'll do lunch."

"Roger, Grizzly."

"Grizzly Six, out."

"Whew," Mitchell said. "Anybody know if that was the battalion commander or what?"

"The unit in this area is the 147th Infantry Division," Kilzer replied not looking up from where he was doodling in his notebook. "Its logo is a grizzly bear."

"Oh, shit," Mitchell moaned. "That was the *division* commander?"

✦   ✦   ✦

Arkady Simosin was learning about second chances.

Not many corps commanders that lost eighty percent of their corps got a second chance. Most of them never commanded so much as a mess-kit repair company. So he supposed he should be happy.

After First Washington he had been relieved and demoted to colonel. The only reason he hadn't been kicked out of the Army entirely was that the board of inquiry noted that the hacking of his corps artillery system had been impossible to anticipate or prevent and that there was a critical shortage of officers trained in modern techniques. So he found himself a colonel, again, working in the Third Army Group J-3 office of Plans and Training.

In time he had even stood for brigadier, again. Three times. The first two had been blackballs; one or more members of the flag officer promotion board had felt him unacceptable as a general officer. The third time, though, he had been passed. In the old days you only had one pass at flag rank, but with the war continuing and even generals occasionally becoming Posleen fodder, the rules had been loosened. Slightly.

He'd stayed in Army J-3 then transferred to the Asheville Corps when it became obvious the only "plans" they had were survival.

Asheville was a tough case. The five divisions in its Line had all sustained hundreds of days of combat. With the exception of some of the fortress cities on the plains, Asheville had probably had the toughest fight of all. There were at least three "easy" approaches to the city and the Posleen had hit it, hard, after each of the main landing waves. Landers, C-Decs and Lampreys, had managed to brave the Planetary Defense Center and even land *inside* the defenses. Probing attacks, really just the odd God King that either didn't know any better or got a scale up its butt, were a constant problem.

So the units that were actually *in* the line, usually three of the five divisions, got very little rest and virtually no training. And the two divisions that were *out* of the line tended to take that fact as permission to just fuck off. That was *part* of the rationale for replacement and two thirds of the time away from the line was specifically designated as "refit and refresh." But what they were supposed to do with the *rest* of their time was train. Improve the individual skills of the personnel, run the officers through "tactical exercises without troops" and do small unit tactical training.

What they did, instead, *all* of the divisions, was fill in the blocks on their paperwork and let their units fuck off.

This had become obvious at least a year before when a small Posleen force had taken a position on Butler Mountain and used it for intermittent harassing fire on the support forces. First a battalion, then a brigade, and finally an entire division of the "rest and refit" units had been sent forward to try to dislodge the Posleen force that was not much larger than a company. The God King in charge was tenacious and smart, to the point of rebuilding the defense positions and occupying them, but it shouldn't have taken a *division* to dislodge him. And if any of the *other* Posleen in the area had conceived of *reinforcing* him, Asheville might have fallen.

The problem was that the Line units had become specialists at running their automated guns and had forgotten everything else. Or never been taught it.

The Corps G-3 and commander were relieved and the incoming G-3 had asked for Arkady. So he had found himself in charge of "evaluating" individual unit training.

What he'd found was even worse than anticipated. There were entire units that had never even zeroed their individual weapons or boresighted their heavy weapons. There was an armor storage site with sufficient tracks for two brigades, but none of the brigades had trained on them in three years.

The first thing that he did was cut the "rest and refit" to one third of the "rear area" period. He knew it wasn't enough time, that units would go back into the line insufficiently rested, but until they learned how to be soldiers again rest would have to wait.

Then, with the concurrence of the G-3, he began finding out which of the blocks were "real" and which ones were in the imagination of the unit commanders. There were a few of those who were relieved and others whose feelings were going to be hurt for a long time. Oh. Well. It was about making sure the soldiers were ready to fight, not just sit in their positions and let the Posleen impale themselves on their weapons.

Physical training, weapons training, tactical training, small unit tactics and mechanized infantry, all of it was crammed in. Along with testing to ensure proficiency on their basic job of, yes, maintaining the automated weapons of the Wall.

Slowly, by cajoling and checking and running around at least eighteen hours per day for the better part of a year and a half, he got *some* of the units to the point that they could find their ass with two hands. One of the ones that *couldn't* was the 147th.

It was never their fault, of course. It seemed that every time they fell back for refit, they had taken massive casualties on the Wall. Where other units would sustain five or ten percent wounded and killed in a mass attack, the 147th ended up taking thirty, forty even *fifty* percent casualties. So they had a constant need for new recruits. And the recruits always arrived half trained.

After the second time the 147th came through the rest, train and refit cycle, Arkady took a trip up to the Wall when they were returned. The unit had left the rear-area training cycle with, as he well knew, the recruits barely familiar with maintaining and rearming their weapons. But instead of starting a vigorous training series up on the Wall, the division had proceeded to squat in place like so many units of slugs. The few recruits that he talked to all knew they didn't know how to fight the Posleen even from such heavily fortified positions. But their officers and NCOs rebuffed their requests for advanced training. And in the case of the "veterans" the opinion seemed to be that it was pointless training newbies. Most of them were going to get killed in the first attack, anyway. Why bother?

Of course it was never their fault.

One of the few military aphorisms that Arkady firmly believed was inviolable was "there are no bad regiments, just bad officers." His brief was specifically for rear area retrain and refit but a word in the G-3's ear was enough for the "ongoing training" officer to start paying special attention to the 147th's methods, just in time for the next attack.

If anyone had figured out how to read the Posleen mind, it surely wasn't the Asheville Corps G-2. Marshall was a decent guy but the Posleen were just *beyond* him, or his analysts. Arkady had been in the daily "dog and pony show," to watch his briefer deliver their daily sermon. He turned up from time to time, just to make sure "his" major didn't decide to start speaking in tongues or anything. "Trust but verify" was a decent statement for leadership as well as nuclear diplomacy.

The young lieutenant colonel from G-2—they all looked like kids these days with rejuv but you could tell this guy *was* a kid, no more than thirty five, maybe forty—had *just* finished his presentation, in which he had concluded that "only two out of thirty-five indices call for a major Posleen attack in the next week." In other words, everybody could kick back and relax. *Just* finished, and the Corps Arty guy was about halfway through his daily delivery of Valium in the form of innumerable columns of more or less incomprehensible numbers:

"Average tube wear rate per battery per day has been trending downward for the last month and a half while consumption versus resupply of standard ammunition types has, happily, been trending upwards. Based upon G-2 analysis of probable future Posleen intentions it is likely that we can begin getting ahead of the tube-wear power curve in no more than three more months. The last quarter has seen significant increases in trunnion stress analysis training among the second-tier maintenance personnel." All delivered in a deadly dry monotone. It was always the same briefer from Corps Arty and it was one reason that the daily dog and pony show was a *must* avoid for most of the senior officers that might otherwise attend.

Arkady had *just* started to drift off, the previous day had been another long one, when the Corps chief of staff, who had to attend this thing *every day,* it was a wonder the man hadn't shot the redleg by now, stood up and, with a decidedly ambiguous expression, stopped the presentation.

"Thanks, Jack, that was just great, as usual, but the 193rd is reporting a heavy attack on the I-40 Wall. I think we all need to get back to our sections and earn our pay."

A serious Posleen attack would mean thousands of casualties by nightfall and if it was tough enough it might mean hell and blood for days on end or, if they did their jobs wrong, the fall of the city and millions of civilian casualties. Serious attacks in the past had come close. But it was pretty clear that everyone else in the room was trying to stop themselves from cheering. They'd managed to avoid the rest of the Corps Artillery presentation! Hooray!

The 193rd got hit in the first attack and then the second attack hit the 147th. Which promptly, for all practical purposes, went away. It sustained over fifty percent casualties in the assault and if it hadn't been for one of the reserve divisions relieving it the Wall would have fallen.

Which meant that something had to be done.

As soon as it was recruited back up to strength, Arkady had scrapped the original training schedule, which emphasized a range of skills, and concentrated on getting the recruits up to proficiency in their basic combat duties. The division commander had protested that the training regime was contrary to Ground Force policy and he was right. But the choice seemed to be an entirely unprepared division or one that could at least survive in a fixed position.

He had been in the midst of the retraining program when the Posleen assault on Rabun Gap, and *another* major assault on Asheville, had hit.

The assault had immediately forced the 193rd, which was also in its rest phase, to be moved into the Line. And the 147th would have followed. But then the Posleen took Rabun Gap and started charging up the back hallway to Asheville.

With Posleen at both doors, and more coming knocking through the undefended back, the corps commander had no choice but to deploy the 147th to try to stop the Posleen coming up from Rabun. The Rabun Corps had been well and truly trashed by the unexpected nature of the assault and several nuclear detonations from a trashed SheVa gun and some landers its mate had potted on the retreat. The simple fact was that the entire unit would have to be either replaced or rebuilt.

In the meantime the *Asheville* Corps was, "in addition to its other duties" to start pushing the Posleen back out of the bottle. Pushing them back through narrow mountain valleys and passes. Pushing nearly a million of them out of the valley and away from the narrow lifeline of I-40 that was the only thing keeping Asheville alive.

A tall order for any force. And the 147th got the job.

It was a job for the Ten Thousand, for the Armored Combat suits. It was a job for an elite mechanized infantry unit with heavy artillery backing.

And the 147th got the job.

The division had been incredibly slow to get off the stick. So slow that a Posleen mobile force had taken the critical Balsam Pass and cut off not only the vast majority of the Rabun Corps, but the only SheVa left that could support the counterattack.

Eventually the 147th had tried to assault the pass. And tried. And tried. It wasn't taking many casualties in trying and yet it was still taking too many for the results.

Since, with the withdrawal of the last refit unit, Arkady didn't have much to do, the corps commander sent him up to figure out what was going on. And it was pretty much what he expected. Highway 74 up to Balsam Pass was a long line of vehicles, just stopped, with troops marching up the side of the road in a double line. None of the vehicles were in defensive perimeters. None of the soldiers seemed to know what they were doing, where they were going, or much to care. They were all sullen and unhappy at having been pulled out of their comfortable barracks. And none of them seemed to have a clue how to do their job in a mobile combat situation.

The division headquarters was worse. He remembered reading a description of the British Expeditionary Force in the first battle of France. Something about "generals wandering around the head-quarters tent looking for string." He'd thought it was a joke until he saw the division commander of the 147th wandering around asking everyone if they had a sharpened pencil. The man had a pen sticking out of his pocket.

The "front" wasn't much better. A battalion had been tasked with retaking the pass but they were stymied by Posleen roadblocks. The Posleen force had sent some of its "normals" down the road and placed them in cover to stop the humans.

The initial assault hadn't even had a scouting element and the first few trucks full of troops had run straight into what was effectively an ambush. Even if the alien on the other end of a gun was a semi-moron. It had killed no more than a platoon or so of troops, but suddenly to all the units the Posleen could be *anywhere*!

The battalion commander was dithering, the S-3 was blithering and the XO was having a nervous breakdown. They had been stopped by what appeared to be a single Posleen. Orders to the companies in the advance to move forward were ignored; the company commanders couldn't get their troops up off their bellies. Calls for fire to the artillery section led to fire everywhere but on the target, everywhere including some of the front-rank soldiers. Finally, the lone Posleen was taken out by a mortar section and some of the troops were induced to crawl forward. But it was nearly four thousand meters to the pass, and crawling wasn't going to get them there any time soon.

Arkady had returned to the corps headquarters and given a short and somewhat profane description of the situation at the pass. After a moment the corps commander dictated a short note.

"Major General (brevet) Arkady Simosin appointed commander of the 147th Infantry Division vice General Wilson Moser. General Wilson Moser relieved."

"Arkady, you've got twenty-four hours to make it to Rabun Gap," the commander said.

"It's going to be ugly."

"I don't care. Make it to Rabun, or even close, and those won't be brevet stars."

He had his second chance. What he was learning was that no matter how hard the first chance might have been, the second chance was harder.

At the division headquarters he had handed the note to General Moser then read himself in. After that he gave the chief of staff a few orders.

"Get this clusterfuck under control. When I return if I hear one hysterical voice, I will shoot it. If I see one officer running I will shoot him. If the maps are not updated I will shoot *you*. You're all on probation. We are going to Rabun Gap. If I get there with a platoon left it will at least be a platoon that knows what in the hell it is doing."

He'd then gone up to the front. The lead company was stalled, again, by another Posleen outpost.

The company commander was belly down off the side of the road when he walked up.

"Get down, General!" the captain had shouted. From up the road there was a crackle of railgun fire and Arkady could hear it going by overhead.

"Captain, are any of your men dying around you?"

"No, sir?"

"*That* is when you get down on your belly, Captain."

The company was hunkered down to either side of the road, still in a tactical roadmarch position. As far as he could determine there was no attempt being made to move forward.

He spotted the company sniper by the side of the road, clutching his Barrett .50 caliber rifle to his chest.

"Son, do you know how to fire that thing?"

"Sort of . . ."

"Give." He took the rifle, and the sniper's ghillie blanket, then slid down the embankment.

The company was huddled behind a curve in the road. There was a sharp road cut and a ditch on the left-hand side and a nearly vertical cliff leading down to a stream on the right. At the turn itself there was a small hillock through which the road was cut. He slid down the embankment, nearly breaking an ankle, then puffed up the hill on the right. At the top he realized how out of shape eighteen-hour days and no PT can make you. But he flipped the ghillie blanket up and slithered forward anyway.

The Posleen was in a similar position about five hundred meters up the road and Simosin was damned if he could spot it. He looked but since everyone was out of sight the damned thing wasn't firing. The Posleen were not supposed to use snipers; in a way it wasn't fair.

"Commander!" he yelled down the hill. "Have one of your men stand up!"

"What?!"

"I need to see where the Posleen is. Have one of your men stand up in view of it."

"I . . ." There was a pause. "I don't think they will!"

"Okay," the general replied and put a round into the wall by the head of the point. "You! Walk out into the road. As soon as the Posleen fires, you can go hide again."

He could see the point's face clearly. The kid was probably about seventeen and terrified. He looked over towards the hill the general was on and shook his head. "No!"

Arkady took a breath and put a round through his body. The fifty caliber bullet caromed off the wall behind the private and blew back out through his gut in a welter of gore.

"You! Behind him! Step out into the road. *Now!*"

And he did. And Arkady finally spotted the Posleen. One round was all it took.

When he got back to the company CP, he could see his sergeant major standing behind the company commander with a leveled rifle.

"If you had been doing your job, that kid would still be alive," the general said coldly. "If your men don't move, you have to make them move. If they don't obey orders, you have to *make* them obey orders. I'm giving you a second chance. I want you up that road. If you can't do it, I'll get someone who will. And if I have to relieve you, it might just be in a bodybag."

He turned to the sniper and hurled the thirty-five pound rifle at him. "Learn to use this. If you think you can use it on me, give it your best shot."

The word got around quick.

After a nuke round took out most of the Posleen, and an attack had hit the survivors from the Rabun side, they had made it to the pass. And on the other side, things started to move. He'd ended up relieving quite a few people, and the people he put in place relieved a few others, but the division had finally started to click. And he'd heard there'd been a couple of other "friendly fire" incidents, at least one of them from the front to the rear rather than vice versa. But he didn't care. As soon as they had the pass cleared he had sent a battalion of Abrams and Bradleys, with scouts out, barreling down the road past the smoking SheVa. They had taken Dillsboro after light resistance and then barreled up the road to Green's Creek under increasing fire. The replacement for his artillery officer had finally found people who could hit the broad side of a barn and the replacement for his logistics officer had figured out how to move trucks. All it had taken was explaining that they had *better* remember old lessons or they would get new ones.

He didn't *like* being a son of a bitch. And he *really* hadn't liked killing that poor, lonely private. But that one round had gotten the division off the stick better than two months of training or even killing every tenth man.

But at Green's Creek they were stopped again and it was a fair stop. The lead elements had been so into the chase, or so afraid of what was behind them, that they had gotten chopped to hamburger trying to push the Posleen out of position in the Savannah Valley. And the next brigade had taken more casualties grabbing the high-ground. But they had it. The only problem was, instead of scattered Posleen shell-shocked from the nuke rounds they were faced with apparently unlimited fresh forces pouring down from Rocky Knob pass. He was bleeding troops like water and there seemed no end to the Posleen when the SheVa finally showed up.

He'd worked around them a couple of times but he'd never seen one tricked up like this. It had what looked like MetalStorm 105s on top of its turret and the front was some sort of add-on armor. And the water fountain had been spectacularly visible for miles around. Obviously they'd been doing more than a hasty battlefield repair up Scott's Creek.

If the thing could take direct fire, and it looked as if it could, and if it could fire into the valley, together with an assault from their present positions he might be able to push the Posleen all the way to the end of the Savannah Valley. The terrain there was even better for stopping the Posleen and together with the nuke rounds the SheVa had fired up towards the gap they might be able to push through.

If, but, might.

Time was awastin'.

"Son, drive up to second battalion," he said. He had taken to driving around the battle in a Humvee and the word had already gotten out that no matter *where* you were, The General, two capitals, might show up at any time. "Let's see if we can find the battalion TOC."

"Yes, sir." The battalion commanders had taken to getting right up on the front lines. It was the only way to be sure that most of what you ordered was getting done. And since you were likely to see the general there, too, hiding back in a rear-area CP was just not done.

Which meant that he was going to have to go drive a friggin' Humvee into the teeth of Posleen fire. Again.

But he wasn't about to tell this cold, angry officer "no."

Better to take on the Posleen with a pocket knife.

CHAPTER ELEVEN

Green's Creek, NC, United States of America, Sol III
1725 EDT Monday September 28, 2009 AD

"We got a crunchy walking around right by the left track," Reeves snarled. The terrain he had to cross was bad enough, worrying about a crunchy was not what he wanted on his mind.

The direct route from their current position to where Colonel Roberts wanted the SheVa was not much farther than the SheVa was long. But it might as well have been on the moon for all he could just drive there. If he went straight he was going to end up nose down in what anyone else would call a valley and a SheVa considered a ditch.

So first he had to slowly go down the easier slope to the west then make a *hard* turn to the left, hoping that the tracks would dig through one of the cliffs rather than get stuck, and then drive up the slope. Simple. Sure. It was like parallel parking a Suburban with two inches to spare in either direction.

And if the crunchy stayed where he was when Reeves reached the bottom, he was going to get turned into stew.

Colonel Mitchell glanced at the monitor and frowned. "I think he's headed for the personnel door." He looked around and spotted the civilian. "Mr. Kilzer, can you find . . ."

"I *designed* it, Colonel," Paul said, getting to his feet with a grin.

It was a general, all right, dragging an oversized briefcase, what used to be called a sample case, and accompanied by a female captain. The general seemed below normal height, but Mitchell realized when he stood up that that was due to his broad bulk. He was probably about five-ten, but seemed damned near as broad across; his BDUs were filled out enough to strain the seams. Some of it was fat, but most of it just looked like muscle.

The captain was fairly short, maybe five foot max, with brown hair and green eyes. What was most notable, however, was that the front of her BDUs were swelled out to an incredible degree. Either she had a sleeping bag tied to her chest or she was stacked like a brick shit house. After a moment Mitchell tore his eyes away and met hers only to realize that plain as she looked, other than her chest, her eyes were even more arresting than her figure. After another moment he tore his eyes away from the entire encounter and saluted the general.

"That's a long damned walk for an old man," the general commented, returning the salutes of the crew. "Arkady Simosin. For the time being, I'm the commander of the 147th."

"General, you didn't have to come up here! If I'd known it was you down there I would have come down myself."

"Not a problem, Colonel, you've got a better briefing area in your hold than we could have gotten anywhere else." He gestured at the officer with him. "Captain LeBlanc is the local battalion commander."

"Captain?" he said. "The battalion commander? She's MI!"

"There has been a rash of reliefs lately," she said coldly. Her voice was quiet so that he had to strain to hear it, which for some reason added emphasis.

"And a few deaths," the general added. "Captain LeBlanc ended up in temporary command and it turned out she was the best choice for the job."

"Repeat that if we pull this off," the captain said. "So, I understand you want to run over some of my men, Colonel?"

"Not if we can help it," Mitchell said, calling the local area map up on the main viewscreen. "We need to get up on this ridge," he continued, highlighting the point. "We're going down off this hill to the southwest then up the ridge." He used a light pen to draw in the projected movement.

"Nice gear," she commented. "I'm glad you got with me; you would have run right over my forward TOC." She thought about it for a moment then shook her head. "All my companies along that ridge are in heavy contact. I *can't* pull them out; they'll get shot to shit. Even if I bring up their APCs."

Mitchell removed his helmet and scratched his head for a moment then shrugged. "We can lay down denial fire just ahead of their retreat. We . . . might tag a few of your troops. But at that point you'll be out of contact. Once we get up on the ridge we'll be in control of the situation."

"If they don't flank you," General Simosin pointed out. "And if they don't eat through your armor. You're not invulnerable, you know."

"Darn near, frontally," Kilzer pointed out. "Sides though?" He shrugged then looked at the captain. "Has anyone ever told you you have magnificent breasts?"

"Yes," she snapped. "Just before I dragged their testicles out through their nose." She turned back to Mitchell and shrugged. "You really think you can stop the Posties before they eat my guys?"

"General, what sort of artillery can we call?" Mitchell temporized.

"Everything," the general said. "I'll redirect it. If you can push up that ridge then lay down heavy fire on the far valley, we can push forward again."

He turned to the captain and shrugged. "You've got all the tracks. Can you pull out and then counterattack. I mean, just like that?'"

"I'll try," LeBlanc said with a shrug. "I've got the tank platoon in reserve anyway. They'll take the gap while the rest are reassembling. I need to get a good op-order out, though; this won't work with a frag. How long do I have?"

"Thirty minutes," Simosin said. "No more."

"Thirty minutes to get the order out, *sir*?" she snapped. "Or thirty minutes to effect the movement?"

"No more than thirty minutes for each," Simosin replied.

"It'll have to be a frag order!" she argued. "And a short one at that! Half my company commanders are lieutenants! I've got one company 'commanded' by a *staff* sergeant! I don't think it's possible. Seriously."

"It has to be," Simosin ground out. "Do it."

"Shit," she snarled. "Yes, *sir!*" She turned around and dropped into the exit hatch then stopped. "And, *Kilzer*, my face is up *here*," she snapped, pointing towards it. Then she was gone.

"I suppose saying 'va-va-va-voom!' would be out of line?" Paul asked.

"Yes, it would," the general snapped. "Okay, one hour. Be ready to move."

"Sir, it's going to take more time than that . . ." Mitchell said, quietly. "She's got to move her TOC among other things."

"It's four Humvees parked in a yard," the general said, equanimously. "I'll give her a bit more than an hour. What I *really* should do is turn over the tracks to another battalion and let them perform the assault."

"And what's wrong with that, sir?" Mitchell asked.

"She's the one that carried the lead battalion this far. Or, rather, she's the one that ended *up* carrying it this far," the general said with a sigh. "I've got more colonels relieved than still in command and the ones that are in command . . . I'm going to end up relieving most of them."

"So she gets to carry the spear some more?" Mitchell said doubtfully. "It's your division, General."

"It's my division if I can get to the Gap in time," the general corrected. "And I intend to do that. Not only to keep the division, but because that's my mission. Now, how are *we* going to get there?"

"As I said, sir," Mitchell replied carefully. "After we assist your unit in clearing this valley, we're going to have to go over the mountains." He pointed to the west and shrugged. "That won't be easy, but we'll get it done. At that point, however, we'll be out of contact for all practical purposes; the trail we leave won't be traversable by most of your division. We'll be especially cut off since we don't have secure communications."

"As to that." The general opened up the sample case and extracted a small folder. "This is your Communications and

Electronics Operating Instructions for communicating with my units. Actually, it's only good for communicating with the division headquarters. I'll *try* to get you a CEOI for Glennis' battalion before you go into action. But in the meantime use this to maintain commo."

"Sir," the colonel said delicately. "We don't know how far into our commo security the Posleen have dug . . ."

Simosin smiled thinly and shook his head. "This isn't 'our' commo security, by which I mean it's not from Ground Forces. I've carried that around since shortly after Fredericksburg. An officer in General's Horner's staff wrote the code but I ran the program on my own computer, one never connected to a network." He tapped the briefcase again and chuckled grimly. "Most people just thought I was crazy, but I always knew there would be a day that it would come in handy."

Mitchell looked at the sheets in his hand and shrugged. "So this is clean?"

"As clean as human technology can make it," the general replied. "I want you ready to move in forty-five minutes. I think it will take Captain LeBlanc a little longer than an hour to get ready, but not much. I'll signal you when the time comes."

"We'll be there," Mitchell said.

"Once more unto the breach, dear friends," Pruitt said with a chuckle. "Once more unto the breach."

Elgars raised her head at the racket of fire from the ridgeline. "Problems."

"No shit," Mueller replied, breaking into a run. The fire was coming from well off the line to the cache. "Who is that?"

"Cally," Wendy said, trotting right behind him. "It has to be."

"That's not where the children are, though," Shari said, her face strained. They had crossed the open area around the former farmstead and were up into the fallen timber behind. In the two passages through the area, and with the help of Sunday's team, they had partially cleared a path. But it was tortuous and slow going.

"The big problem is that she's way the fuck over there," Mosovich said, gesturing to the west. "And that bomb is coming in any minute."

They reached the ridgeline and Mosovich tried to get some idea where the firing was coming from. But it had died down and in the hills with the echoes he could get no sure direction.

"Shit. AID, get me Major O'Neal." He looked at Elgars and shook his head. "We have to get that nuke stopped. Or at least slowed down."

"No."

Mosovich stared at the AID for a moment in shock. "Sir, we're talking about *Cally*." He looked around the outer cache and shook his head. "We can find her and retrieve her in no more than an hour or so."

"Sergeant Major, have you taken a look at the operational situation on the eastern seaboard?" O'Neal asked.

"No, sir, I haven't," Mosovich replied angrily. "But we're talking about Rabun Gap."

"So am I, Sergeant Major. There's now an incursion headed for Sylva. That has the division that is coming in to support us cut off. I don't know how they got through the defenses up that way but with everything *else* going on I'm not surprised. There are incursions over the Blue Ridge in Virginia as well; Staunton is toast and so are the SheVas that were under construction around it. The Ten Thousand is getting pushed back into a pocket. We're talking about a full-scale breakout in the Shenandoah. Horner *should* be using this nuke there, but he's chosen to use it here. Care to consider why?"

"Because if you can hold out for another few hours, the SheVa will get here," Mosovich said, expanding his tactical map. "But not if it's got heavy opposition."

"Bingo," Mike replied. "If the SheVa can plug the gap, and it will do it by demolishing it and then *parking* if it has to, *we* can fly out to *another* hopeless battle. But we can't do that if we don't have *this* nuke, *here* and while we can still catch most of the Posleen before they deploy against the SheVa. Once it reaches Franklin it's in range and it can scratch our backs all the way in. But we need this nuke, *now*, actually about an hour ago. So, no, I'm not going to stop it for another hour, or forty-five minutes, or even *five* minutes while you go look for one singular refugee civilian."

"Who is your *daughter*," Mosovich said, coldly.

"No shit Sherlock," O'Neal replied, furiously. "I would very much like to care about what happens to my daughter, Sergeant Major, but I have a fucking *world* to save. And if that means that Cally dies, then Cally *dies*," he finished.

His reply had been cold and furious, but Mosovich heard the anguish buried in it and lowered his head into his hands. "Yes, sir."

"Get in the cache, Sergeant Major, close the door. Twenty minutes."

"He's just writing her off?" Shari asked. "He can't *do* that!"

"He just did," Mueller said, pushing the door closed.

"We can't just sit out in this one, boss," Stewart said.

"I know," O'Neal replied, looking around at the remnants of the battalion. "So we dig." He bent down and started pulling dirt up out of the side of the mountain. "Bury the resupply then dig as far as you can, and fill it in behind you. What the hell, keep digging until the rounds hit."

In moments the entire battalion was busy burying itself in the earth.

"Billy, you have to take the Hiberzine," Shari said softly.

"I won't!" the boy said, backing up to the cache wall. "I'm not going to do that again!"

"Son, we all do," Mosovich said reasonably. All of the other children, Wendy, Elgars and Mueller were already out, laid on mattresses across the spread-out remaining boxes. The biggest fear was that something would fall on them; if the walls of the cache failed nothing would save them anyway. And if anyone remained out of hibernation in the room the oxygen would quickly be used up; already Mosovich felt the air getting close and fetid. "There's not enough air in here for us to stay awake."

"I'm not going to do it," the boy said stubbornly, shaking his head.

Shari's face was strained and tired but just as determined.

"Everyone's going under this time, Billy. Even me." She shifted to the side and spread her empty hands wide. "You just have to trust me. Somebody will come."

"I don't want to," Billy repeated, trying not to whine. "I *can't*."

Mosovich waited until he was outside the boy's peripheral vision and then struck like a viper, injecting him in the side of the neck. He caught him as he twisted and started to fall, laying him out carefully on the boxes.

"Just us," he said.

"I guess so," Shari said, lying down and taking Billy and Susie in her arms. "I don't like this any more than he did," she added, her face pinched.

"Like any of us do," Mosovich muttered, injecting her in the neck and watching as her face slackened. He replaced the disposable container in the injector then lay down next to Elgars, looking at the injector and then at his watch.

"Oh, well, here goes nothing."

In another moment the cache was still.

"Well, Dr. Castanuelo, you're *sure* this thing isn't going to blow?"

The control center for the experimental cannon looked like NASA. There were at least fifteen operators in the center, all of them busy monitoring various aspects of the gun. The weapon itself was mounted in a building the size of a large observatory placed at the edge of the UT campus and surrounded by fences keeping out the curious and suicidal. It had finally been loaded and now, with the ACS battalion resupplied, it was time to find out if Knoxville was going to disappear, or North Georgia.

"Yes, sir," the academic said. "Almost definitely."

"How reassuring," President Carson said. "General, if you give us another hour we can have most of the region evacuated."

"In another hour one hundred thousand Posleen are going to pour through the Gap, Mr. Carson," Horner replied. "Dr. Castanuelo, are you sure enough to push the firing button?"

"Yes, sir," Mickey replied.

"Then do it."

Mickey flipped up the cover of the firing mechanism and

sounded the preparatory warning. "Preparing to fire," he announced over the intercom. He hit the controls to begin the liquid propellant cycling then turned the key activating system. Last he hovered his hand over the actual firing button. Then he screwed up his eyes and stabbed downward.

Horner was amused to watch the reaction. He, himself, simply turned to the video cameras monitoring the event and watched it eyes open. He figured that if it was a screw-up, he'd never know it.

The gap they were crossing was not much larger than the SheVa was long so they ended up straddling the road, nearly three meters in the air.

"This is not good for the frame," Indy commented idly as the SheVa creaked and groaned its way from one hill to the next.

"It'll take it," Kilzer replied. "We ran it through trials on things like this."

They all realized that they were just avoiding the thought of what they were about to do. The light of plasma and HVM fire could be seen sparkling all along the ridgeline and it was clear that, despite the fire of the MetalStorms and a hurricane of artillery, the Posleen were heavily massed on the other side of the slope. As soon as they crested the ridge, they would be the biggest target in sight.

"Sir, I can't get us hull down on this one," Reeves said. "The slope's wrong."

"Do what you can," Mitchell replied.

Reeves nodded his head and gunned the giant platform up the side of the ridge. As he did he could see the infantry pulling out of the defensive positions along the top. Some of them had trenches connecting them but mostly they were just foxholes and the defenders had to crawl out into fire to retreat. Some of them weren't making it. And it was apparent that the Posleen were now firing from close range.

"This is going to be tricky," Mitchell muttered as the first MetalStorm opened up on the ridgeline. There was the usual storm of fire, but in this case most of it was clearing the ridgeline and dropping into the dead ground on the far side. "Crap, I was afraid of that."

Because of their height, the 40mm rounds had about a four-thousand-meter range. And they would arm within fifty meters. But the guns could only depress a few degrees below the horizon. Therefore the SheVa had a large zone around it in which the guns could not engage, depending on the MetalStorm and the angle at which the SheVa was at, that could range anywhere from five hundred to a thousand meters.

The problem in taking the ridge was, therefore, two-fold. They would be a target to every Posleen in sight. But even worse, the ones that were close would have a free shot.

"Colonel, this is Chan." The MetalStorm commander had the toneless voice of the well trained who were in a very bad situation. "I can't get the close ones and we can see them coming up the hill. The valley is . . . Look, sir, we're talking Twenty-Third Psalm here. This is definitely the Valley of the Shadow of Death."

"Don't worry," Kilzer muttered as the top of the SheVa crested the hill and the first plasma and HVM rounds began to ring on the armor. "Got it covered. For Bun-Bun *is* the baddest mother-fucker in the valley."

"What?" Pruitt asked. For the first time he felt completely useless. His only job was managing the main gun, and there was nothing he could fire at in these circumstances.

"Let them get in close," the tech rep said. "I can't do anything out at range, but in close we're covered."

Finally the main gun, and the visual systems associated with it, crested the top of the hill and the view on the other side became apparent. And the comparative frenzy on the MetalStorm channels made sense.

The artillery had shifted to create a curtain barrage all along the front. The sun had begun to set behind the mountains to the west and the purple flashes of variable-time artillery were a continuous ripple along the base of the ridge. But in the dying light the valley seemed to heave and ripple, as if covered in cockroaches. After a moment it was apparent that what it was covered in, from slope-edge to slope-edge, was Posleen. Thousands of them, tens, hundreds of thousands of them, all pressing forward to try to force their way over the ridges and through the Gap. And an increasing number of them were firing at the SheVa.

As Mitchell watched another swath of destruction was cut by the MetalStorms. But as fast as the Posleen were cut down, the gaps were filled by the pressure from behind. And he could see the surviving centaurs picking up scraps of meat from their deceased fellows, and heavy weapons that had survived, and either storing them on their backs or passing them to the rear.

"We're not killing them, we're just filling their larder," he muttered.

Another storm of fire came in and more of it was striking from the side, passing through the relatively light metal along the edge of the turret. Time to rethink and regroup.

"Major Chan, maintain maximum sustainable fire on all targets in view," he said. "Reeves, back us off the ridge. We need to get most of the hull and turret somewhere along here where the MetalStorms have an angle of direct fire but the rest of the gun is down."

"I'll try," the driver said, putting the tank in reverse with a glance at the map. "But I don't see a good spot."

"Well, keep loo—" Mitchell flinched as a massive boom echoed through the gun. "What the hell?"

"Posties close!" Pruitt called as more bangs and booms echoed through the hull. "Left side front. A full company. I don't know where they came from."

"Back us up, Reeve!"

"Hang on, Colonel," Kilzer said, touching a button. Another boom, much more massive than the first, shook the hull. "Problem solved."

"Holy *shit*!" Pruitt said, looking at the monitor. Mostly what could be seen was dust. But what was visible of the Posleen company looked like someone had pounded it with a giant meat mallet. "What in the hell was *that*?"

"Claymore," Kilzer replied. "There's two on the front, two on the back and three on each side. It's got six shots."

"Cool."

"That's still not going to keep us alive down there," Mitchell replied.

"Sir, I've got an idea," Reeves said, stopping the tank and spinning it in place.

"Ouch," Pruitt said with a laugh. "Did it hurt?"

"Fuck you, Pru," the driver, who was not noted for his intelligence, replied. He locked one track then threw the other into full drive, spinning up a roostertail of dirt and rocking the seven-thousand-ton gun sideways down the hill.

"Ah, I know what you're doing," Kilzer said with a grin. "Watch it, though. You can get yourself stuck as hell."

"Okay, I'll bite," Mitchell said in a bemused voice. "What *are* you doing?"

"He's trying to dig in a fighting position," Kilzer explained for the driver, who was repositioning the tank. "Dig out the upper side of the position by spinning the track in place."

And it appeared to be working. The friable stone of the hillside was shattering under the weight and power of the SheVa's tracks and with each spin the upper side of the SheVa sank lower. After a moment Reeves spun the monstrous vehicle in place and moved some of the dirt over to create a wider spot, then went back to work.

"Colonel, this is Chan," the MetalStorm commander called. "We've got another group of leakers coming in along the eastern edge of the ridge. The infantry has reconsolidated on the far hill and is engaging them at long range, but they seem to be planning on closing with us. And they're under my angle of fire."

"Let them close," Mitchell replied. "Mr. Kilzer will be waiting for them."

"Yes, sir," the major replied in a puzzled tone.

"I'll explain later," Mitchell said. "How's it looking from your angle?"

"Smelly," the major replied. "Glenn just threw up all over the compartment."

"How's the angle of *fire*," Mitchell replied with a grimace. Being on top of the SheVa when it went through these gyrations would not be fun.

"Well if Reeves is looking for an excuse to stop putting us through this, I'll give him one. We can see to fire and most of the turret is hull-down."

"Okay, Reeves, get a good position and hold it," the colonel said. "Major Chan, concentrate fire on the zone from directly in front of us to the road. We want to keep them off of us but also open up a situation where the infantry can stage a breakout." They still had monitors where they could see the valley and he shook his head. "Although I think that we might be being optimistic about that one."

"What do you want me to do?" Pruitt asked.

"Get up to the crane and start hauling out MetalStorm packs," Mitchell replied. "I think we're going to need them."

"I'm going to go survey the damage we took from those hits," Indy said, unsnapping and standing up to follow the gunner. "I didn't like the feel of that last engagement."

"Don't go out and kick the tracks," Mitchell said. "I don't know when we're going to move."

He went back to watching the monitors and after a few minutes nodded his head. The antimatter "area denial" rounds they had fired up the road had to have wiped out a good collection of what would be reinforcements for the forces in the valley. And the combination of artillery, which was now shifting out into the main mass, and the MetalStorm fire was now opening up patches of ground. The Posleen *looked* unlimited, but they weren't. And the heavy firepower that was now pounding the valley was whittling them away. And doing so rather fast, all things considered. He glanced at his watch and realized that it had been less than fifteen minutes since they had left the hilltop opposite; it seemed like hours. Somewhere to the south, the ACS was getting ready to retake the Gap. Somewhere near Knoxville a true hell-weapon was about to fire. But there was only one and for the ACS to survive, and the plug in the Gap to be maintained, it was necessary to clear out this plug of Posleen and drive on with the mission. Fifteen minutes was starting to sound like a long time.

"Ask me for anything but time."

CHAPTER TWELVE

Now, first of the foemen of Boh Da Thone
Was Captain O'Neil of the "Black Tyrone,"
And his was a Company, seventy strong,
Who hustled that dissolute Chief along.

There were lads from Galway and Louth and Meath
Who went to their death with a joke in their teeth,
And worshipped with fluency, fervour, and zeal
The mud on the boot-heels of "Crook" O'Neil.

But ever a blight on their labours lay,
And ever their quarry would vanish away,
Till the sun-dried boys of the Black Tyrone
Took a brotherly interest in Boh Da Thone:

And, sooth, if pursuit in possession ends,
The Boh and his trackers were best of friends.

—Rudyard Kipling
"The Ballad of Boh Da Thone"

165

Clarkesville, GA, United States of America, Sol III
1905 EDT Monday September 28, 2009 AD

Tulo'stenaloor glanced at his sensors then tugged at his earring; he had better things to do than learn skills that others had.

"How much time do we have?"

"Not much," Goloswin replied thoughtfully. "They are preparing to fire."

The estanaar looked at the bloody read oval on the schematic and sighed. He had spent *years* learning to understand maps and now he wished he hadn't. He could well imagine the results of this hell-weapon.

"And the radiation?"

"Bad," the technician admitted. "The zone that will be hit directly by the weapon will extend up the valley almost to the town of Dillard. The primary isotope will be carbon 13, which has a high ionization rate and will induce thermal damage on uptake. My model estimates twenty percent casualties for oolt passing through the zone in the first hour with about a one percent decrease per hour thereafter. Humans, of course, are relatively fragile; unprotected humans will not be able to enter the zone for at least ten days." He fluttered his crest and snapped his mouth in humor. "It's actually a very . . . what is that human term? It is a very *elegant* weapon in its way. The power is frightful, of course, but it also denies territory for some time. However, the ground is fully cleared in a month or two, at least sufficient for life. Elegant."

"Horrible," Tulo'stenaloor replied. He turned to his operations officer with a snarl. "Pull all estanaral forces out that can be withdrawn; send only the local forces into this madness. Begin working on a plan to control the movement after the attack; we have been hitting these humans in waves which gives them time to recover. Use the estanaral forces to put gaps between blocks of the locals so that we hit the humans in a continuous stream."

The operations officer nodded and tapped at the controls on his sensor unit. "Most of the estanaral were prepared for an exploitation attack, so they are back from the area where the weapon will hit. Should I stop the flow for a while? We're actually getting low on local units."

"No," Tulo'stenaloor said after a moment. "We won't know exactly where the weapon hits until it does. Some of them will survive. It is enough." He flapped his crest again and keyed his communicator. "Orostan."

Orostan looked up the hill at the gap and snarled as his communicator lit up. "Yes, estanaar."

"The humans are going to fire a hell-weapon into the Gap." Tulo'stenaloor gave him a brief précis of the situation and then waited.

Orostan flapped his crest in agitation and snarled. "How many of my reinforcements am I going to *lose*?"

"About half," the warleader admitted.

"Too much," the forward leader muttered. "That hellish SheVa gun has been reinforced, strengthened and given many weapons instead of just the one. It has taken a position near Savannah valley and is eating oolt as if they were *abat*."

"The idea was to stop it," Tulo'stenaloor noted. "Not have it stop *you*."

"I'm *trying*," Orostan snapped. "I have teams waiting for it to come through the pass. I think it is vulnerable on the flanks. When it comes through we will destroy its wheels and tracks. That will stop it. Short of where it can fire at the pass. But *you* were supposed to take and *hold* the pass, estanaar. And with the resistance that I am facing from these hell-spit humans, may the demons eat their souls, I need more *forces*."

"I'm working on it," Tulo'stenaloor said. "But the situation, as the humans say, truly sucks."

"This really sucks," Cally whispered. "I'm *way* too young to die."

She had managed to break contact with the Posleen but they had stayed on her trail like bloodhounds. Now they were spread out on either side of her hide, beating up the hill. She had thought she could lie low and avoid them but it seemed no such luck.

"Papa wouldn't have gotten trapped this way," she muttered,

checking her rounds. Out of grenades, two magazines left, one partially empty. One full magazine in the well. Posleen to the right so if she tried to sneak out they would have her there. Ditto on the left. Solid wall up behind her. What was that old saw? *"There I was, this is no shit ... Was I afraid, sure, I was afraid one of them would get away."*

She just wished they would *go* away.

There was a rustle in the bushes below and she lined up on where a Posleen would be bound and determined to come in view. "Well, time to get one more," she sighed, snuggling her cheek into the stock. As the yellow-brown snout nosed around the bushes she took up trigger slack. It was the God King.

Even if she couldn't destroy all the Posleen in the world, she could destroy this one.

The team leader paused and raised one fist, sinking into a crouch. Ahead of them through the trees there was a shot from a rifle and a crackle of railgun fire with the occasional thump of a plasma rifle.

Major Alejandro Levi had been a Cyberpunk for more years than he cared to remember. He had been recruited right out of high school, something about being a Westinghouse Scholarship Finalist *and* the quarterback of the football team. And over the ... okay *decades* would be the best way to put it, he'd been in a lot of hairy missions. But wandering around in the middle of a nuclear battlefield scattered with Posleen, potentially hostile humans and potentially hostile "others," pretty much took the cake.

He looked to his rear then to his side and stepped to the left. Suddenly, he reached out with his left hand and sank it into what appeared to be naked air.

"What do we have here?" he whispered, getting a grip with the other hand as a Himmit shifted camouflage and wrapped three of its hands onto his body. "Spying on us, were you?"

"Spying for you," the Himmit whistled in passable English. The creature was almost man-sized but lighter than humans and resembled nothing so much as a symmetric frog. It had four "arms" set at opposite ends of its body and a sensory cluster near the center of the body. On each side of the sensory cluster it had a pair of eyes. It appeared as if you could split it down the middle and easily have two "half Himmit."

Alejandro had it by the cranial cavity, at the center of the delicate sensory area; a twitch of the human's strong hands would crush his primary sensors, a possibly fatal wound. "You're here for the same reason I am!"

"How do I know that?" the Cyber said, loosening his grip lightly.

"You're here to retrieve Cally O'Neal and Michael O'Neal, Senior," the alien replied. "And you're *late*."

"The traffic was terrible," Alejandro replied, dryly. "Where are they?"

"Michael O'Neal, Senior, was caught in the pressure wave from a lander detonation and sustained mortal injuries. Cally O'Neal is the one doing the firing right now. She has been in a running battle with a group of Posleen. I believe she is now trapped."

"O'Neal's dead?" the team leader asked, shaking his head.

"Dead is such a definitive term," the Himmit replied. "He is in my craft at the moment. I do not know his current state of reality."

"Wha . . . never mind," Alejandro said, shaking his head. If he asked an open-ended question the Himmit would go on all day. He was lucky this hadn't taken longer; the Himmit was clearly out of sorts to be this abrupt. Maybe it was having fingers jabbed into the Himmit equivalent of a nose. "How many Posleen?"

"Less than when she started; she is a remarkable sub-human," the Himmit said. "She initiated the ambush with—"

"How many and where?" Levi asked, tightening the pressure ever so slightly.

"Fourteen, seventy-five meters," the Himmit replied, pointing. "Spread out. She is in cover up the slope, but if she moves . . ."

"God King?"

"There is one Kessentai, plasma rifle, using portable sensors. He is not using them very effectively; he appears used to having his guns aimed for him."

The Cyber straightened and made a series of gestures indicating that the team should spread out, prepare to engage the enemy and turn off all electronic devices. The last was a pain, but the God King's sensors could pick up the slightest emission, even background.

He watched as the team seemed to appear from nowhere, a bit of leaf mold, the bark of a tree, a bush. The Cyberpunks had trained in the days before the war against the Posleen to enter enemy territory and corrupt battlefield systems that could not be "hacked" from a distance. They were trained to be ghosts, shadows, on the battlefield.

But they were also trained to be the deadliest ghosts on earth. Time to see if they were the *fastest*.

The Himmit watched them as they disappeared into the woods then followed at the fastest rate consonant with remaining concealed.

He wouldn't miss this for worlds. What a tale.

Cholosta'an stepped forward cautiously. His sensors said that the human had last been *somewhere* on this ridge. But since she had cut off her last electronic device, he had lost her. It was possible she had fled over the ridge, but the steep, open slope meant that they probably would have spotted her. She was likely hiding in the bushes along the base of the bluff. If so, they would have her soon.

He had only gotten glimpses of her before, enough to determine that it was a human female, as Tulo'stenaloor had said.

His last thought at the sight over the barrel of the human rifle was "A *nestling*?"

Tulo'stenaloor flapped his crest as the datum appeared.

"So much for Cholosta'an," his operations officer muttered.

"So much indeed," the estanaar replied. "And so much for stopping the resupply of the threshkreen unit. Or even hitting them from behind, given that all the other forces in the valley are gathering to stop the SheVa.

"It's a simple solution set," he continued. "If we destroy the threshkreen in the pass, we can pour enough forces through the Gap to destroy the SheVa, no matter what. If, on the other hand, we can destroy the SheVa, we can eventually wear away the threshkreen. If we do neither . . . then we have failed."

"So far we are doing neither," the essthree opined.

"Agreed," the estanaar replied. "And we have done no better at it than Orostan. It is our job to destroy the threshkreen in the pass. Part of that is pressure. When we begin moving forces back into the battle, we must have them moving steadily. We were hitting them in fits and starts, in waves. This gives them time to recover."

"Yes, estanaar," the lesser oolt'ondai said doubtfully. "The question is 'how.' Any time you have a line of oolt, they . . . move unsteadily, sometimes fast, sometimes slow. It is that which is causing the gaps to occur."

"We'll spread them out," Tulo'stenaloor said after a moment. "Have elite oolt'ondai station their oolt along the route. Create gaps between the oolt that are marching into the battle. Thus, when one hits the fire of the threshkreen and is destroyed another will step into place immediately. This will give us the constant pressure we seek."

"As soon as the hell-weapon detonates, estanaar."

"Oh, yes, after that," Tulo'stenaloor snarled. "Why waste more oolt'os than we must?"

Cally checked fire as the yellow skull disintegrated under the hammer of the 7.62 rounds and tracked right to where she thought the closest Posleen might be. But as she took up the trigger slack again there was a muffled series of pops and a wild flail from a railgun that bounced ricochets off the rocks above her head.

As far as she knew, the nearest humans (that would be fighting) was her dad's battalion or maybe the rest of the gang. But none of them had been using silenced weapons. So who was out there? Friend or foe?

An assassin had been sent to kill Papa O'Neal years before and had only been stopped because he discounted the skills of an eight-year-old girl. But that didn't mean that more wouldn't be sent. Admittedly, sending assassins in in the middle of a nuclear fire-fight seemed to be overkill, but it wasn't paranoia if people really *were* out to get you.

She heard a rustle from below, not even what a deer would make, more like a field mouse. Then there was a human standing over the dead Posleen.

It was a special operations troop, no question. He, probably he, was wearing Mar-Cam and a ghillie net over his back. As she looked he took a step to the side and seemed to just vanish. She squinted for a moment and realized that he now looked for all the world like a bush alongside one of the poplar trees. He was *good*, better than Papa, probably.

She watched as he stepped forward, slowly, testing each bit of ground, and then stopped again.

Alejandro stopped as he caught a faint whiff of human scent. He would have detected it, should have, before but the stench from the dead Posleen had overridden it.

The thing about scent is that it's only mildly directional. There wasn't any real wind under the hill and the air was wet, cold and still. But somewhere there was a human lying very still. But sweating as if . . . *she* had been in a hard run.

He looked around but, remarkably, couldn't see anything. As close as she was she should have stood out like a mountain. Either he was getting old or she was going to *smoke* the advanced recon course.

"Cally O'Neal?" he whispered.

"Breathe wrong and you're history," Cally said in more of a sigh than a whisper.

Alejandro sighed and looked over at where the sound came from. The girl was under a ghillie net covered in leaves. He wondered how she hadn't displaced her surroundings and then realized that she had shaken the small birch bush over her to aid in the camouflage. Clever.

"I was sent to extract you," he said, straightening but keeping his MP-5 pointed to the side.

"Sure you were, pull the other one, it's got bells on." Cally heard another faint sound of movement to the side and realized that she was bracketed. Again. "And if your buddy gets any closer we'll just have to see how many of you I can take out. Starting with you."

"I think we're at an imps arse," Alejandro said. "You won't trust me and I have no way of convincing you to."

"Not quite," a voice whispered from above.

Cally froze as a Himmit appeared out of mid-air and lowered itself to the ground.

"Miss O'Neal, we are here for your protection," the Himmit whistled. "We have no proof of that, but I give you my word as a member of the Fos Clan, that you will come to no harm. However, there is a nuclear attack incoming in less than fifteen minutes . . ."

"WHAT?" Cally shouted. But she was drowned out by the Cyberpunk.

"Rally!" Alejandro shouted. "Where is it aimed at?"

"It is *aimed* at the Gap, Major Levi," the Himmit said, shifting back into camouflage. The voice seemed to be moving away. "But the coverage area is . . . extensive. Consider this spot to be ground zero for a two megaton blast."

"Wait!" Alejandro said. "Can your craft lift us out of here?"

"Ah, so *now* you trust me," the Himmit said, from higher in the trees. "Head due west for six hundred meters. I'll meet you there."

"Well, Miss O'Neal," the Cyber said, turning to the west. "You can come with us or not. Up to you."

"Out of my way, commando dude," Cally said, scrambling to her feet and glancing at her compass. "You move too slow."

"Over here."

The Himmit had again appeared as if out of thin air, its skin shifting from the color and pattern of tree-bark to its apparently "normal" purple-green. It gestured towards a crack in the ground and flowed rapidly downward and into the hole.

Cally stopped, panting and shook her head. "Hiding in a hole isn't going to keep us alive in a nuclear explosion!" she shouted.

"You may come or stay," the Himmit said, sticking the "rear" half of its froglike body out of the hole. "I was requested to retrieve you and the Cyber team. It was not a requirement of debt, however. And *I* am not going to stay here and be turned into radioactive dust! Four minutes." With that it disappeared downwards.

"Shit," she muttered, glancing at Alejandro. "Cybers, huh?" she said, then bent over and slithered into the crack.

It was wider than it looked but not easy to negotiate, even for her; she wasn't sure if the Cyber team would be able to make it. She crawled and slithered downward at about a twenty-degree angle through a series of turns. It quickly got dark but she crawled onward, wondering what would await her. Probably a Himmit butt, not that they had butts. She had just begun to wonder if the damned thing was simply a Stygian route to hell when she noticed a purple light. Rounding another corner she saw the open hatch of a Himmit ship and a compartment beyond. She quickly crawled through and then moved to the far end to see if the Cybers could make it.

The Himmit was nowhere in sight.

She had heard about Himmit stealth ships but never really expected to see the interior of one. It was . . . odd. Definitely alien in a way that was hard to define. The compartment was about three meters across with a set of seats on either side. While it was high enough for *her,* she suspected it would be cramped for the Cybers. The light was just *wrong* and the seats, while they appeared to be made to fit human-sized creatures, clearly were made wrong for *humans.* She sat in one to try it out. The seat back was too low and the seat itself too narrow; it was uncomfortable for her and she suspected that the longer-legged Cybers would find it torture after a short while. She supposed that it would be equally difficult for a human to make something comfortable for a Himmit.

The smell in the compartment was acrid, like a leak at a chemical plant that occasionally dealt in garbage and there were odd squeaks and groans in the background. All in all, it was a pretty unpleasant place.

She had just come to that conclusion when the first Cyber clambered out of the narrow passageway and stooped his way into the compartment. He quickly moved to the seat across from her and leaned back, taking off his camouflage hood.

"Himmits," the guy muttered. "Why'd it have to be Himmits?"

"I take it you've been on one of these before?" Cally said, wondering what response she'd get.

"It's how we got here," the Cyber replied, looking to the entrance. "We were supposed to walk out and link up with vehicles. I'd rather walk a hundred miles than spend fifteen minutes in one of these things."

"Well, any port in a storm," Cally said, philosophically, then frowned. "Not to bitch to a stranger, but this has been a lousy couple of days. My dog's dead, the horses are dead, my cat's dead and my grandfather's dead. My dad is in a fucking forlorn hope and will probably be gone by morning. Oh, and I've been in two nuclear bombardments. Being in a Himmit ship is starting to look pretty good."

She shook her head as the next Cyber entered the compartment, rapidly followed by the rest of the team; the team leader was the last through the hatch. As he stepped through it started to cycle shut. At almost the same time what appeared to be the "front" wall of the vessel dilated open and a young human stepped through.

All of the Cybers froze at the sight of the unknown visitor but Cally couldn't look away. Except for height, build and hair color he looked *a lot* like her father; it could have been a brother if Mike O'Neal had one.

On second glance that wasn't quite the case. The visitor's arms were longer, hanging almost to his knees, and his nose was much smaller than her dad's. Actually, except for his age, he looked like . . .

"Grandpa?"

CHAPTER THIRTEEN

Knoxville, TN, United States of America, Sol III
2200 EDT Monday September 28, 2009 AD

The massive cannon belched in flame and that was it. The shot had left too fast for the human eye to follow.

The main viewscreen, though, was slaved to a tracking camera that *could* manage a view of the projectile as it flew through the air, and everyone let out a sigh of relief at still being there. Next to the image was a shot clock that estimated exit of rounds and detonation. The round was "smart" in that it determined its location and height to lay down its lethal cargo precisely, and the only actual drop that was visible was the first. But after first sub-munition ejection a detonation clock started ticking.

"Seven, six . . ." Castanuelo said. "Damn, I wanted to be outside to watch this!"

"Could we see it?" President Carson asked.

"They'll see *this* in *Pennsylvania!*"

Horner suddenly opened a metal case and ripped out his AID. "O'Neal! Splash in . . . one second!"

At the warning O'Neal just shrugged as well as he could inside his armor. He had been tossed around by . . . Jesus, he'd lost count. At least five nukes in his time. Not to mention being buried in a building by a near-nuclear class explosion, run over by a SheVa gun—twice on that one—and had various and sundry other unpleasant items occur while he was in a suit. Then there was that poor bastard Buckley who had had a space cruiser fall on him.

Frankly, being buried five meters in the ground at the ground zero of a two megaton nuclear explosion wasn't anywhere *near* the bottom of his experiences. It was sort of comforting in a way.

"Gotcha," he said, flipping frequencies to internal. "Battalion, splash over."

There was a brief rumble, high frequency ground shocks, that preceded the impact, but in less than a second after the first shudder the ground began to spasm around his suit. The shocks went on for about five seconds, about as bad driving a jeep across rough ground, and then it was done.

"That's it?" someone queried on the general frequency.

"Grandpa?" Cally said softly, looking up at the stranger.

"Yeah, sweetie," he replied, stepping forward and ruffling her hair. "It's really me. Sort of. I guess."

"But you . . . I thought . . ."

"Dead?" he said with a snort.

"Um, yeah."

"Well, there's a Tch . . . Tph . . . a Crab around here that can explain it better. Basically, the Galactics sort of consider death to be not quite the is/isn't thing that humans perceive."

"So were you or weren't you?" Cally asked, angrily.

"Cally, *Princess Bride*?"

"Oh. So you were 'mostly dead.'"

"Bingo. I think I was flatlined, if that's what you mean. But the Himmit got to me in time to administer Hiberzine and then the Crab here . . . restarted me."

Cally looked at him again and shook her head. "So are you *you*?"

"I *think* so," Papa said, shrugging his shoulders. "I think there are some holes in my memory. I'm younger though. Strong. It feels . . . amazingly good."

"Hah, you're not the only one!" Cally said. "You should see Shari. You'd pop your shorts."

"Shari?"

"Long story, I didn't understand all of it. But they survived and got out of the Urb."

Papa O'Neal nodded and then frowned. "Out of the Urb? Survived?"

"You didn't know the Franklin Urb was gone?" Cally asked. "Or that the Posleen are all down the Valley?"

"I've been out of it for the last few days. What's happening?" He looked around at the Cyber team who had started to stow their gear. "And are these white hats or black?"

"White, I think," Cally said. "And we're about to get hit with a nuke. . . ."

"Oh, shit," he said, shaking his head. "*Another* one?"

Something about the way he said it caused Cally to burst into giggles that led inevitably to a belly laugh and then she found herself crying and holding her sides, unable to stop laughing. "Yeah . . ." she gasped after nearly a minute, wiping her eyes and at the snot running out of her nose. "Another one." As she said it, the floor began to rumble.

Pruitt maneuvered the pack up out of the bowels of the gun and swung it over to MetalStorm Nine. Nine, for some reason, had done a double fire at some point and was flat out of packs. Getting more up, fast enough, would be tough.

The job wasn't particularly *fun*. The Posleen had noticed the MetalStorms and were trying, at very long range, to successfully engage them. So stray rounds, railgun, hypervelocity missiles and plasma fire, were flying by on a regular basis. But, on the other hand, at his height he was pretty sure he had the best view of any being in the battle. And it was one hell of a view; the battle was *intense*.

The infantry had moved back into position on both sides, although at a fair distance, and in the twilight their red tracers could be seen flickering through the darkness, striking, disappearing and bouncing off into the distance. And, of course, the continuous rain of artillery was fascinating. Then, at intervals, the MetalStorms would open up and spit liquid fire into the valley. And all the while the Posleen were filling the air with streams of plasma.

Really spectacular.

As he thought that, a bright flash to his right, over the mountains, caused him to look up from the monitors. Before his head could even come up, the entire horizon behind the mountains flashed bright white in a lightning ripple of strobes, as if klieg lights the size of a state had been flicked on and then off, lighting up the valley for almost four seconds as if it was bright daylight.

He threw his arm up against the light but it was too late to help. Each of the blasts was a nuclear fireball and in the continuous stream of flashes he could see mushroom clouds rising even as the last lightbulb winked out. It was as if the world to the south had been consumed by a sun and then gone back to black.

"Holy shit," he muttered, his eyes watering, as ground rumble caused the SheVa to sway back and forth. "I've got to redefine my definition of spectacular."

He sat shaking his head to try to get some night vision, hell *any* vision, back and then gave up.

"Holy shit."

Cally stopped laughing as the rumble died away and then grinned at her grandfather. "So, there any cards in this tub?"

"As if I need to lose money on top of everything else," Papa O'Neal said with an answering grin. "Damn, Granddaughter, it's good to see your face again."

Within the cache the impacts caused one corner of the container to buckle and Billy to slip out of Shari's arms. And then it returned to the silence of a tomb.

"UP AND AT 'EM!" O'Neal bellowed over the battalion frequency. "Head for the Gap."

He put actions to words, scrabbling at the dirt above him and pushing down with his feet. It was a bare fifteen feet to the surface but it still took time, time he was afraid they might not have. Finally he saw an opening above him and popped his head out to look around at total devastation.

As far as the eye could see, and from the edge of the mountain that was a fair distance, there was nothing but scrubbed dirt. Not a stick, not a house, not a scrap of vegetation survived; the very soil had been stripped off in the titanic fire.

He shook his head and checked his radiation monitors, blanching as he did. The suits were more than capable of handling four hundred rems per hour, but it would kill any human stone dead. Or, hell, most *cockroaches*.

The dust was starting to clear and the moon was breaking out to shine on the ground, but there was something odd about it. Under the moonlight, everything was gray, even under the enhancements of the suits that brought it to daytime ambient. It was bright, but still in shades of black and gray. But still, there was something . . .

He toggled a switch and a patch of white light shone down from his suit on the stripped granite at his feet and he swore. He swiveled the light around, then walked away from his hole, looking at the ground and swore again.

"General Horner, this is O'Neal."

"Glad to hear your voice, old friend," the general said. "How'd it go?"

"We were underground," O'Neal replied. Horner could almost hear the shrug over the communicator. "General, about this bomb that just detonated. *Where* did you say it came from?"

"Knoxville," Horner replied, puzzled. "Why?"

"I mean, where was it developed?"

"Oak Ridge," Horner said. "And the University of Tennessee. Why?"

"That figures." There was a pause. "I just thought that you should know that Rabun County is now orange."

"What?" Horner thought about that for a moment. "The soil in that area . . ."

"No, General. The soil, the rocks, the fucking mountains. It's all *orange*. And not 'international distress' orange, boss. It's a redder orange than that."

Horner's face turned up in a gigantic smile as he looked over at Dr. Castanuelo. The good doctor had just pulled a can of dip out of his back pocket and was reading over the shoulder of one of the techs. He had on a University of Tennessee ballcap and a UT Volunteers windbreaker. Both of them bright orange.

"This is what you get for letting rednecks play with antimatter, boss," O'Neal said.

Horner didn't bother to point out an accident of birthplace. There was no question in his mind that the guy who had just painted half of north Georgia in the colors of one of their bitterest football rivals was well described as a "high-tech redneck."

"Dr. Castanuelo," he said sweetly, smiling from ear to ear, "could I have a moment of your time?"

Pruitt had gotten back to work pulling MetalStorm packs as soon as his vision returned. He had lights that he could use, including a big-ass spot that would have lit up the whole top like day. But all things considered he didn't want to be any more of a target than was strictly necessary.

Fortunately the loading system the SheVa repair guys had installed was simplicity in itself and the crane on Nine had an autograppler that *worked,* unlike the POS he had used in training. All he had to do was snatch the packs out of the hatch, swing the crane and drop them in the appropriate racks. He was even ahead of the way the Storms were running through them.

Finally he was done, and decided to take a good look around. The crane had a couple of good visual systems on it and slaves to the main monitors, so he started flipping through images.

The best view seemed to be from monitor seven. It was mounted high enough that it had a better view even than the crane and it had thermal imaging so sometimes he could pick out details that way.

In the distance he could see streams of Posleen still coming down the road from the Gap but they were more spread out and not moving *nearly* as fast. It looked as if there *was* a light at the end of the tunnel. OTOH, a few more area denial rounds couldn't hurt.

He swept the monitor to the left and noted that he could just see where East Branch came down from the mountains and opened out. He could see the tracks from where the SheVa had come through the last time and sighed. You should only have to take one of these things over the mountains *once* in your life.

"Over the mountains," he sung, swinging the monitor around, "take me across the sky . . ."

There was a cluster of Posleen on the ridge above East Branch and something about them made him sweep back for another look. He dialed up the magnification but it wasn't until he hit the thermal imaging system that he was sure what he was seeing.

"Colonel," he breathed after a moment. "You're going to want to take a look out of monitor seven."

Mitchell tapped the control and brought the monitor up on the main viewscreen. "What am I looking at, Pruitt?"

"Check out the group on the ridge to the left." Pruitt sounded dead, as if someone had just ripped his soul out.

"What's wrong?" the colonel asked, dialing up the magnification. "The ridge just above East Branch?"

"Yes, sir," Pruitt replied. "Switch to IR."

Mitchell did, then swore. "Those are . . . are they *human* figures?"

"Captain Chan, reload your guns," Mitchell said, coldly. "Prepare for close fire support. Reeves, back us off the hill. Pruitt, get your ass down to personnel entrance one."

"Yes, sir." The driver checked his monitors and then spun the gun in place, pulling back down the hill. Suspecting what the next drive order would be he pulled all the way back and pushed the rear up the Savannah Church hill. He could see the crunchies arrayed on the hill panicking as the giant mass of metal backed towards them but he had other things to worry about. Like, how much longer he was going to be alive.

"Romeo Eight-Six this is SheVa Nine," the colonel said on the division artillery net. "I need a brigade time on target box centered on UTM 29448 East, 39107 North. I want everything you've got."

"Uh, roger SheVa," the controller called back. "That will take a few minutes to effect. And, that's not our priority of fire."

"Do it," Mitchell said. "I don't care about your priority of fire, do it now."

"SheVa Nine, this is Quebec Four-Seven." It was Captain LeBlanc's voice. "What in the hell are you doing?"

"We're preparing to move forward to East Branch."

There was a pause while the local commander assessed this statement. "SheVa, that wasn't the plan."

"Plans change. There's a group of humans that are being used as a mobile feed lot for the Posleen. And we're going to get them."

Angela Dale had turned to look when the amazing series of flashes had occurred to the south. But since then she had dropped back into her own straitened world. It seemed they had been walking for days since the Posleen had captured her near Franklin. She had already lost track of her parents in the desperate retreat in front of the Posleen advance and she was pretty sure that, like everyone in the group who hadn't been able to keep up, they were dead. And probably eaten.

She couldn't remember, didn't want to remember, how many had died. The group had been much larger to begin with. Sometimes people were added. Once the group had been broken up and occasionally a group of confused refugees would join them, including a bunch of Indowy with massive packs and bundles on their backs.

She had spoken to the Indowy, a simple greeting she had been taught in school, and the little green aliens had apparently decided she was their best friend and huddled around her as far away from the Posleen, and other humans, as they could get. The leader spoke English, haltingly and with a strange accent, and he had told her that the Posleen had brought them from another world, apparently to do engineering for the invaders. They had built some bridges and then, when the centaurs were forced to retreat, they had been added to the group of humans, he used the Posleen term "thresh," as a mobile pantry. And so it was.

For, most of the time, instead of adding refugees one of the escorting Posleen at some unseen command would reach into the group and drag people out. Then the knives would descend. The humans in the group had been offered the food from time to time but even with their stomachs pressing against their backbones, no one had taken the dripping gobbets of flesh that had until moments before been one of their group.

Now, though, the Posleen seemed to have plenty of food; groups had come to the rear bearing masses of yellow flesh that could only be coming from the battle to the front.

Mostly, she didn't notice anymore. She had retreated into a warm mental place where nothing could touch her. Someday she would be warm again, safe again. Someday she would be happy again and all of this would be over. She knew that it was unlikely that place would be this side of heaven, but she really didn't care anymore. She just walked where she was pointed to walk and sat where she was pointed to sit.

So it took her a moment to notice that the artillery fire that covered the plains had stopped and that the fire from whatever had been laying down masses of red death had stopped as well. What went on in the battle didn't really matter. Nothing was going to save her short of death. And death was beginning to look pretty good. It was the being eaten that still seemed bad.

But after a moment the mutters of the people around her, and the agitation of the Posleen, cut through her fog. She was afraid it meant they were going to choose another and she edged to make sure she was near the center of the group. But quickly it became apparent that something else was going on. And she looked to the north just in time to see, by the light of the fires in the valley and the gibbous moon that had appeared in the east, a mass of metal crest the distant ridge just as the artillery started to fall again.

"Pedal to the metal, Reeves!" Mitchell shouted. The driver had gunned down Church Hill and back up the far ridge at maximum possible drive because this was the worst moment of all. For just a moment the vulnerable underside of the armored gun system was exposed to fire and if the Posleen poured fire into it they were dead. That was where the drive systems and reactors were. Much fire in that area would leave them stopped on the hill, a sitting target for at least fifty thousand Posleen.

But the combination of the artillery fire and the speed and

surprise of the assault seemed to work. Fire started almost immediately, but by then they were accelerating down the far side.

"Kilzer! Water curtain, Now!"

"Uh . . ." Paul looked over and shrugged. "I guess I forgot to mention: we're out. We've only got five minutes and we used it up before."

"Shit," Mitchell cursed. "Chan!" But the command was unnecessary as every MetalStorm opened fire as if for dear life. And it was.

The valley was still filled with Posleen and even those that were in close combat with the human defenders on the ridges turned to fire at the giant tank as it tore down the slope and up the road towards Savannah. A storm of fire licked out towards it but SheVa Nine was giving as good as it got.

Again the ribbons of red fire lashed out at the Posleen, jumping from remaining concentration to concentration. The artillery box had opened up a zone of more or less open space and into that space the SheVa rocketed, belching fire in every direction.

"Mitchell!" General Simosin seemed a little upset. "What in the hell are you doing?"

"You wanted a breakout, General," Mitchell said as rounds caromed through the interior of the SheVa. "You've got a breakout."

"You dumb son of a . . ."

"There's a group of humans by East Branch," Mitchell said. "We're going there and ain't nothin' gonna stop us."

Arkady Simosin looked at the radio for a moment and then shrugged. "We'll be right behind you."

He turned to the driver of the Bradley he was currently occupying and gestured. "Son, if you don't catch that SheVa before it's halfway across the valley I'll have you shot."

"Yes, sir!" the driver said, kicking the armored fighting vehicle into gear. "Not a *problem*," he added with a feral grin as the track commander cycled his guns. The Bradley was one of the scout systems equipped with double 7.62 Gatling guns; and it was getting ready to do some harvesting.

Simosin brushed his RTO aside and keyed the division command

frequency as the Brad lurched into gear. There was garbled conversation coming from half a dozen commanders but he overrode
them.

"All units, assault NOW, NOW, NOW. Follow the SheVa. Forget plans, forget frag orders. The order is FOLLOW THE SHEVA."

"Move it!" LeBlanc snarled as she climbed the steps of the tank.
And it was a *long* goddamned way up for a female who was just
five feet tall. Really, she should be in a Brad or a Humvee. More
radios and fewer distractions. On the other hand, if she wanted
to command her unit she had to *survive*.

"But what are we doing?" the commander of Bravo Company
called. The idiot was just standing by the Abrams looking around
in confusion.

"We're going to Savannah!" LeBlanc said, plugging into the
vehicle intercom system. She was about to order the driver
forward but he had already closed his hatch and started the tank
forward. It moved with the smooth oiliness that was the hall-
mark of the Abrams series and it seemed that nothing could stop
it. Of course, one plasma gun that hit just right would do just
fine. There had been improvements in the armor of the Abrams
series over the course of the war, but they could still be taken
out with plasma or HVM fire. If it hit right.

"Get back to your unit and get it moving!" she screamed at the
company commander then keyed the battalion command frequency.
"All units, general breakout! Follow the SheVa!" She looked out
of the TC hatch as the tank accelerated up the hillside and shook
her head. The 147th was a cock-up outfit. That was for sure and
for certain. But in the last day or two something had happened,
a new spirit had infected them. They might be cock-ups, but they
had led the charge from Balsam Pass to here, where other units
had failed. And they seemed to have caught the spirit of *winning*
against the Posleen, instead of just taking it on the chin.

Which was why she realized she didn't have to kick her useless company commanders in the ass. On either side, rising out
of their holes like an unstoppable tide, the men of the 147th were
rising. And running forward, screaming.

The Posleen were turning and running before the mass of the SheVa, and the troops of the 147th were going to get some.

"What a bloody mess," Mitchell muttered, looking in the monitors. He hadn't really expected support but he was by God getting it.

The troops of the division, in some cases it seemed *without* orders, had climbed out of the defensive positions they had occupied for the past several hours and were charging forward. Most of them weren't in vehicles so they were falling far behind the SheVa, but they were drawing fire away from it. And getting slaughtered themselves.

It didn't seem to matter, though. Mitchell saw one Bradley crest the ridge and drive right into a concentration of Posleen, running several of them over. For a moment the troops inside raved at the aliens with their mounted weaponry then the troop door opened and they poured out, taking positions around the fighting vehicle and pouring fire into the Posleen.

The aliens, used to throwing themselves onto human defenses, were reacting with shock and apparent fear. It must have seemed to them that the rabbits were attacking the wolves and it was happening *everywhere.*

The valley was an absolute madhouse. Groups of humans were running down the valley, some of them on the flats and others on the steep ridges along the sides, while a stream of armored fighting vehicles and tanks poured through the Gap. Other vehicles, tanks, Bradleys, Humvees and even some trucks, were coming over the ridges where they were negotiable and charging forward, sometimes stopping to pick up infantry but always moving forward.

The artillery had gotten totally confused and rounds seemed to be falling almost at random, some of them into the human troops. But even that didn't seem to be slowing them down.

"Are we all insane?" Mitchell asked, flipping back to monitor forward. He looked at the rippling waves of Posleen and the heavy fire coming from them and smiled maniacally. "Yep."

CHAPTER FOURTEEN

If, drunk with sight of power, we loose
Wild tongues that have not Thee in awe,
Such boastings as the Gentiles use,
Or lesser breeds without the Law—
Lord God of Hosts, be with us yet,
Lest we forget—lest we forget!

—Rudyard Kipling
"Recessional"

Green's Creek, NC, United States of America, Sol III
2238 EDT Monday September 28, 2009 AD

Paul Kilzer grinned as he tapped the controls for the close-in defense systems and a ripple of fire tore out from the SheVa. Reeves had apparently been anticipating this because he had driven right into a mass of Posleen and the millions of ball-bearings tore through the group like a mechanical thresher.

"It's good to be the king." Kilzer chuckled as the SheVa's tracks ground the aliens. "I think I remember something about 'use their guts for track grease'?"

"Patton," Pruitt said over the intercom. "'Why I almost feel sorry for those poor Kraut bastards.' I've often wondered what he would have done with the Posleen."

"Seen how many of them he could make die," Mitchell growled

LeBlanc stared at the CEOI for a second and then shook her head. "Alpha, this is battalion, what's your situation?"

She waited a moment then keyed the radio again as the Abrams hit the bottom of the slope and pitched her around like a marionette. "Bravo!" she coughed. "Charlie! Anybody this net, dammit!"

"This is . . . oh, hell, this is Captain Hutchinson's RTO, ma'am," the radio operator for the Alpha company commander panted. "The company just . . . got up and started charging after the SheVa, ma'am! The captain's trying to get them stopped."

"Stopped, hell!" she shouted. "All stations this net, you will move forward and *aggressively* engage the Posleen! Support the SheVa! Move *forward*! Any company commander who doesn't keep up with his company is going to be *relieved*. And the last company to Savannah is on extra duty for a *month*. Don't stop them, *push* them."

She flipped frequencies and snarled as the tank dropped into a streambed and shook her around again. "This is no way to run a railroad," she muttered. "Scouts!" she snapped, keying the mike.

"Alpha Six-Seven, over." She remembered that the Scout Platoon commander was a graduate of VMI, a regular of sorts. And apparently he could keep up with the damned CEOI even in the middle of a battle. Although that would be easy if he was still sitting back at Church Hill.

"Where are you?" she snapped.

"About four hundred meters behind the SheVa, ma'am," the platoon leader said calmly. In the background she could hear the snarl of a Gatling gun. "It's a pretty exciting place to be at the moment."

She popped up through the TC hatch and looked around. "We're coming up behind you, about a klick back and catching up," she said then paused. "Be advised there's a Posleen group to your left rear." She grabbed the pintle-mounted Gatling gun and sent a stream of fire into the mass as she keyed the intercom. "Gunner! Target ten o'clock!"

✧   ✧   ✧

Otinanderal couldn't decide where to turn. The humans, who normally fought like abat, were everywhere. His oolt had poured fire into the massive human tank but it was as if they were scratching the sides of an oolt'pos. Now the human tanks were flying forward all around him and he couldn't decide where to target his fire. But when one of them started firing at *him* it was pretty plain.

"For what we are about to receive..." Glennis muttered as she hit the seat switch and dropped into the belly of the tank. The vehicle shuddered and the temperature jumped noticeably as a plasma round glanced off the front glacis plate. A moment later an HVM round ripped her hatch cover away into the night and filled the interior with reflected searing white light and heat. But by then the gunner had slewed the main gun on target and opened up with main and coaxial.

The Abrams Main Battle Tank was originally designed for the sole purpose of killing other tanks, almost assuredly Soviet and ex-Soviet designs. It had advanced composite armor, a quick-firing, stabilized 120mm main gun, sophisticated targeting systems, nuclear, biological and chemical protection and an amazing turn of speed supplied by its Lycomings jet-turbine engine. Furthermore, on battlefields across the globe, it had proven itself the finest machine in the world for that task, able to both out-fight *and* outmaneuver any other tank on the planet, seventy plus tons of fast-rolling incredibly deadly meanness. But with the coming of the Posleen, changes in design were inevitable; the Posleen didn't really have anything worth hitting with a 120mm depleted uranium dart. Or, if they did, it was too large to *care* about being scratched by an Abrams.

However, the base tank was the finest piece of war machinery ever designed and it seemed a shame to simply throw all that engineering away. At first, when they turned out to be highly vulnerable to plasma and even 3mm railgun fire, the tanks seemed doomed. But technology came to their aid in the form of new, and lighter, armor materials. The M-1A4's turret and primary frontal armor was a layer of battle-steel, room-temperature superconductor, nano-tube composite and synthetic sapphire threading. The combination meant that frontally it could shed off the fire of anything but a direct and unlucky HVM hit.

From the side it was not so well armored but if the Posleen were on your flank you were screwing up anyway.

To reduce the possibility of being flanked, and to deal with the main problem of the Posleen, the fact that there were just way too many of them, the gunnery of the tanks was modified. On either side of the turret "add-on" weapons were installed. These were 25mm cannons like the main gun of a Bradley, but where a Bradley had one gun the Abrams were mounted with first two, one on either side, then four and finally eight. The .50 caliber TC gun was replaced with a 7.62 Gatling gun capable of hurling 8000 rounds a minute and the "coaxial" 7.62 machine gun mounted alongside the main gun was switched out for another. Even excepting their main gun, the "A4" Abrams could hurl an amazing mass of lead.

The main gun, however, remained a problem. It seemed a shame to pull the weapon, since it was about as good as it got from a cannon perspective. Finally, it was decided to leave the cannon in place and simply change the ammo mix. The ammo bin still carried a few "silver bullets" for old time's sake, but the majority of the rounds stored in an A4 were canister.

Unlike the complex depleted uranium or High Explosive Anti-Tank rounds, canister was simplicity in itself; in effect it was a giant shotgun shell. Each round held 2000 flechettes packed in ahead of a powerful firing charge.

As Glennis' seat hit the bottom of its elevation and another plasma round glanced off the armored front plate, the gunner laid his reticle on the company of Posleen, toggled his joystick to "All" and hit the firing button.

The Abrams didn't fire quite as many rounds, or as quickly, as the MetalStorm but the effect was similar. There was a blast of what looked like liquid fire and then the Posleen company started to come apart. The fire had only put one round of canister down-range but it had taken out the center third of the company by itself and as the gunner swept the tank's "secondary" weapons from side to side the rest ceased to exist.

"And that's what we call balling the jack," the gunner muttered as the loader slammed in another round of canister. The entire engagement had taken less than four seconds.

"Good job," LeBlanc said, keying her microphone. "SheVa Nine, this is Captain LeBlanc. We're closing on your six. What's your situation?"

Mitchell grimaced and looked over at Indy's panels; half the systems were yellow and there were an increasing number of red lights. "Well, we *were* getting the shit shot out of us, but other than that . . ." He looked around and realized that fire had started to fall off. "Is it just me or . . . ?"

"Major, I personally don't believe it, but it looks like we're *clearing* this valley," the battalion commander replied with a grin that could be heard over the radio.

Mitchell looked at his monitors and snorted. The largest remaining group of Posleen were those around the humans, which he intentionally had not engaged. And it was less than a company. Other than those, and a few leakers in the side valleys, the way was totally cleared. He snorted again and then began to laugh hysterically.

"Major?" Reeves called. They were alone in the compartment but Mitchell had shut off his radio and was rolling around in his chair laughing as if he couldn't stop. "Sir?!"

"Oh!" The major gasped, getting some control over his laughter. "Oh! Oh, shit. Sorry, Reeves. Shit!"

"What's so funny, sir?" the driver yelled. "I mean, we still have to get those guys out of there!"

"I know," Mitchell said, wiping his eyes. "Oh. It's just what went through my mind. I was looking around and all I could think . . ." He started laughing again until he was heaving.

"What?"

"I was just thinking: 'Ka-CLICK!' "

Simosin's driver had clearly taken him at his word. Either that or the boy was just insane. They hit the slope for Deere Creek so fast the Bradley was momentarily airborne and then slammed into the far slope.

The general pulled himself upright and waved at the TC. "Tell him he doesn't have to go *that* fast!" he shouted, pulling himself around to look out one of the vision blocks. There wasn't much that could be seen that way so he waved at the TC again and forced him out of his hatch.

When the general finally got up where he could see, it took him a moment to get his bearings. For just a second he was afraid that they had gotten out ahead of the SheVa or that the division was just *gone*. But he quickly noted the light fire going on to either side and the somewhat heavier fire, including the occasional blossom of a plasma gun, at the end of the valley. The problem to either side was the lack of fire. And the reason for the lack of fire was a lack of targets; the Bradley was lurching over a carpet of centauroid corpses.

He gestured for the TC to give up his crewman's helmet and plugged it into the intercom. "Son, don't worry about getting shot. Forget the SheVa for a second and get me up on a hill. I've got to get a look around."

The Bradley obediently made a hard left and headed up the nearest slope. There was a house at the top, or had been—it was a shattered shell now—and the Bradley driver added insult to injury tearing up the driveway and into the yard. But it was a hell of a view.

Simosin had snuck up to the fighting positions during the battle and had seen the valley rippling with Posleen. What it was filled with now was . . . bodies. Human and Posleen, but mainly Posleen. Here and there a fighting vehicle smoked, but looking at the results by the light of the fires and the moon, he was convinced that they had charged across the entire valley at the cost of *maybe* a half a battalion of troops. And they had been taking that every few hours during the *defense*.

"Holy Mary Mother of God," he muttered. "Holy . . ." He looked down at the TC and shook his head. "Get a squad out on security, get the RTO to contact headquarters and get me a relay to General Horner. Tell them to pass on that we've taken Savannah and are preparing to continue the advance."

✧   ✧   ✧

Angela shuddered as the giant tank rolled up the hill towards them. Other tanks, much smaller, were spreading out to either side and there were other vehicles underneath it.

The Posleen that had been guarding them weren't firing; they seemed as shocked by the situation as the human captives. The hundreds of thousands of Posleen in the valley were just *gone*, with the last few survivors being hunted down ruthlessly. And now the tanks were driving up *their* hill and surrounding *their* position.

The giant tank, it must be one of the *SheVa* guns she had seen on TV, ground up to within a few dozen yards of the Posleen and then just stopped. It sat there for what seemed like forever and then a door opened in the base, flooding white light down onto the ground. An elevator dropped out of the door and all the way to the ground then opened and a single human stepped out. He was wearing a trenchcoat and sunglasses and had a plasma rifle cradled in his arms, muzzle down.

He put a hand in his pocket and walked up the slope, looking around at the humans and Posleen as a massive spotlight turned on at the top of the SheVa. The spotlight swung around for a moment and then bathed the group in white light, flooding out the sight of the massed tanks. But in the darkness the sound of opening doors, squeaking turrets and pounding feet made it clear what was going on.

The single human walked up to the group and looked around until he spotted the God King on his saucer. He walked over to the alien, looked him up and down and then said one word:

"Leave."

Angela looked at the leader of their tormentors and wondered what would happen. If it came to fighting, she was going to hit the ground and hope for the best. She suspected that there were riflemen out there, now, but in a fight if one of the tanks opened fire it would be all over for the humans.

She wasn't sure if the Posleen could understand English or not. She'd heard that some could. But they never spoke it, just gestured. Usually for a person to put their head down to be cut off.

Now the God King looked down at the human and slowly

fluttered his crest. He had to know more or less what was being demanded of it. And what the penalty would be for refusal.

Finally he raised his crest to its full height, lifted his plasma cannon, slowly, and turned his saucer around. In seconds, all the Posleen had faded into the night.

Angela looked up at the giant tank, the SheVa, and wondered for a moment why there was a picture of a rabbit on the front. Then she passed out.

Mitchell lowered the stairs of the personnel door and waved a hand in the general direction of his head at General Simosin. The general, who was sitting on the troop ramp of a Bradley, just grunted and went back to spooning down MRE beef stew. He had taken off his helmet and LBE and all of it was piled on the tail of the track.

"I just talked to Keeton," the general said after another bite. He wiped up a bit on his chin then wiped it off his hands onto his filthy BDUs. "He kept trying to get me to say that I was back at Green's Creek. Especially when I told him my lead element was reporting from halfway to Rocky Knob."

"I'm beginning to wish I still was, sir," the colonel replied, looking up at the SheVa. It didn't look too bad from the back, but he knew the sides looked like Swiss cheese. "There's going to be one hell of a bill for this repair."

"Oh, don't be that way," the general grunted. "You're the hero of the piece. Do you know how rare it is to recover Posleen captives? If it wasn't for me controlling the traffic, and, of course, the Posleen still being all over the place, why we'd be crawling with reporters."

"Ah, fame." Mitchell snorted and then sat down on the perforated metal stairs. They dug into his butt, but since he ached from head to toe it wasn't really noticeable. "That and a few billion credits will get this SheVa running again. We're not exactly dead in the water, General, but we're going to need some repairs before we're fully combat effective again. Among other things we lost the main power bus for the MetalStorms right at the end. And we need more MetalStorm packs; I don't know if there are any more around."

"Yep." Simosin glanced up at the wall of metal and then shrugged. "Your repair battalion's got priority of movement and there's a full battalion of MetalStorm supply trucks headed down the road from Asheville. I'll tell the division to map out a spot down valley for you guys to do your repairs. You're still planning on going over Green's Pass?"

"It's easier to access on both sides, sir," Mitchell said with a nod and a yawn.

"You're going to be swinging in the breeze over in the Tennessee Valley," the general noted. "I've got all I can handle pushing up this way. And I can't move behind you to support you, not with a whole division. You do too much damage to the roads."

"Breaks of the game, sir," the colonel replied. "We *can't* get across Rocky Knob, not and leave anything you can use as a road. And even going up to Betty will tear things up. More than they are, that is."

"Hmm." Simosin looked around and smiled as an Abrams pulled to a stop beside his Bradley. "I think this is about the right cue."

Mitchell watched Captain LeBlanc hoist herself out of the turret and chuckled. "Big tank, little lady. I think there's something Freudian there."

"I *know* why you're thinking of Freud," the general replied with a snort. "And I think it's Freudian. I was thinking 'big *gun*, little lady.' "

"You sent for me, General?" the captain said, saluting. After the general returned the salute she nodded at Mitchell. "Colonel."

"Captain," Mitchell replied soberly. "I'd like to thank you for all your support. We wouldn't be here without your unit."

"True," she said immodestly. "But it wasn't just my battalion or we *both* would be dead. I remember reading somewhere, Keegan or *On Killing*, I don't recall which, that the purpose of tanks is not, as it is generally believed, to break the lines by shock, but to get themselves so entrapped by the enemy that it triggers in the infantry a 'rescue' reaction. 'Oh, look, those stupid tankers are way the hell over there and if we don't go get them they're going to get kilt.' I thought about that, from both sides, while we were riding to Balaclava."

Mitchell found himself giggling again and got it under control quickly. "There is probably some truth to that, Captain. 'Onward, onward rode the six hundred . . .' "

"Major," the general corrected. He reached into his cargo pocket and rummaged around until he found a pair of major's leaves. "Before you know it you'll have enough rank to actually be in command, Major."

"But I'll still be MI," the major said, pinning on first one leaf and then the other. "And a female. Two strikes against commanding an infantry battalion."

"That, my dear, is why there are waivers," the general said loftily. "There will be orders and awards to go along with that later— I've told both the corps commander and General Keeton about your performance on this drive—but for now we're not done. What was your damage?"

"I'm down about twenty percent," the commander replied, abruptly sitting down on the ground. "But body count doesn't cover all of that and I'm missing at least one company commander. Some of them might still be mixed in with other units but I think a few did the bug-out boogie."

"If so the MPs will round them up." Simosin pulled out a notebook and made a notation. "I'm going to give you two companies from the Second Brigade; one of 'em's a mech team, the other is motorized. They were in the lead for the first assault and have done some reconsolidation since then so at least they're not green. Consolidate what you have got into three companies. That will make you overstrength in each, but I'm sure that will take care of itself."

"Yes, sir," LeBlanc replied. "What then?"

"Get refueled and rearmed," he continued with a sigh. "That may take some doing; my inherited staff has not yet grasped the basic concepts of maneuver warfare such as forward deploying logistics elements . . ." He looked at her face quizzically. "Why the smile?"

"Ah, well," she laughed. "Refuel and rearm will not be that much of a problem, General. I sent one of my NCOs out to find our supply trucks. And he did."

"*Your* fuel trucks?" the general asked.

"Close enough. Somebody's. Might as well be mine. And when he pointed out that he had two fully armed Bradleys, with crews, and all they had were some dinky fifty calibers, they got amenable to reason. Alpha and HHC are all refueled and rearmed and the rest of the unit is pulling maintenance."

The general shook his head and sighed again. "Maybe I should make you my chief of staff. No, forget I said that, I don't want to explain to General Keeton why *other* divisions are out of fuel and supplies."

"Speaking of other divisions," Mitchell said, "isn't this about the time that somebody else is supposed to pass through while you reconsolidate?"

"It would be, if there was anyone else to pass through." Simosin grimaced. "There's a division coming down from Knoxville but it's green and short a brigade. I'll probably get it, in which case I'm going to mix it in by battalions and use them carefully. So it's just us."

He looked over at LeBlanc and smiled grimly. "Which was why my operations officer thought I was nuts to send my main mechanized unit off on detached duty."

"Oh?" the major queried then looked up at the SheVa. "I don't *think* so!"

"Major LeBlanc, you and your reinforced battalion are detached to duty in support of SheVa Nine as it makes a flanking maneuver through the Tennessee Valley," the general said formally.

"Oh, shit," the major said, shaking her head. "We're fucked."

"I need you alive and at Franklin," Simosin said to Mitchell's raised eyebrow. "I don't need a smoking wreck sitting in the lower Tennessee."

"Yes, sir," the colonel replied then shrugged. "What the hell, if we get stuck again Abrams are jim-dandy field-expedient unstickers." He turned to the major and grinned. "We're going where eagles get nosebleeds, you understand?"

"Oh, yeah," the major replied bitterly. "But, what the hell, if that big old bastard can make it, so can we. I hope."

"I'll see you both in Franklin," Simosin said, scooping up the last of his stew and climbing laboriously to his feet. "SheVa supported," he said, licking the spoon and dropping it in his cargo pocket as he tossed the empty MRE packet to the side, "fuel getting to tanks, troops moving forward, now I have to go back and straighten out that cluster-fuck of a headquarters I inherited."

"Drop a bomb on it, sir," LeBlanc replied. "It's the only way to be sure."

"Nah, think of the paperwork. I've got enough headaches."

"Move, move, move, move, MOVE!" O'Neal shouted, bouncing down the scorched side of Black Rock Mountain.

It was a race against time. Somewhere to the south there were undoubtedly Posleen racing to reach the Mountain City line before the ACS. But the suits needed to not just reach the gap before them, but to have enough time to get dug in and set. If they were caught in the open by the advancing Posleen, they might as well slit their own throats.

"Bastards," Stewart muttered. "They filled in all our positions!"

The Posleen had driven a road through the former defenses of the battalion and all but the outermost holes had been filled in. In addition, all the laboriously constructed communications trenches were gone.

The spare ammunition and power packs had been distributed to the platoons of the battalion but they were with individual suits. If they didn't get a way to move the ammo around it was going to be cut off as soon as the Posleen arrived and created a "no movement zone" above ground.

"Back to work," O'Neal said. "Bravo, Charlie, start digging in. Reapers and tech suits, make yourself some holes then start digging trenches. Everyone get below ground level as fast as possible."

Duncan looked at the area designated for his company and began detailing platoon sectors. "Marauders on the line, command suits to the rear," he said, detailing individual zones for the platoons. "Move people!"

He reached a point halfway between the designated area for the battalion command team and dropped a digging charge on the ground, glancing down the defile as he did so. There was still no sign of the Posleen, and that bothered him.

"Stewie, scouts?" he asked on a discrete channel to the battalion S-2.

"I've only got two left," Stewart said, irritably. "I was going to move them up the flanks."

"Be nice to know when the boys were coming to tea," the company commander said.

"Agreed," Stewart replied.

Sunday waited until all his Reapers were dug in and then dropped three more digging charges, opening up the area and connecting a couple of the holes to the consternation of the occupants.

"That was a little close, sir!" Pickersgill called; the charge had blown the side of his hole in on him.

"I could have dropped it *on* you and it wouldn't have mattered," Sunday replied, dropping into the middle of the combined Reaper section. He had carried the disguised box down the hill and now opened it up, pulling out the weapon inside. It was in three pieces and he carefully assembled them below ground level, ensuring that none of the other suits saw what he had concealed in the over-sized hole.

"Get started on the trenches," he said when the suits had finished opening out and finishing their holes. "I'll be here."

"What are you fiddling with, sir?" McEvoy asked, looking up over the side of his hole.

"Don't you worry about that," Tommy said with an unseen grin. "I'll show you when you get back."

Stewart looked at the take from the scout that had just reached the top of Hogsback and frowned.

"Hey, boss, we've got *zero* additional fire support, right?" he asked, jokingly.

"Yep," O'Neal replied. There was a pause as he was obviously checking the raw take as well. "Well, things are going to be interesting."

"I'd say fifteen more minutes until they round the corner," Stewart commented.

"That's enough time and more," O'Neal said with a quizzical tone.

"They're not moving as fast as usual," Stewart admitted, "but can you see what's between the blocks?"

"Gaps," O'Neal responded. "And look right on the edge of the picture," he continued. There was another pause. "They're spacing out their battalions."

"So they hit in a solid stream?" Stewart mused. "I don't like smart Posleen, boss, I don't like them at all."

"Well, they may be smart but they're slower. Let's use the time as well as we can." He looked up to the mountains on either side and frowned. "And let's hope they don't figure out how to climb."

CHAPTER FIFTEEN

Green's Gap, NC, United States of America, Sol III
0037 EDT Tuesday September 29, 2009 AD

Pruitt looked at the tree-covered mountains filling the main viewscreen and laughed. "Bun-Bun's a rabbit, not a monkey!"

The repairs on the SheVa had been expedited with remarkable speed, since the SheVa brigade was already in place. By the time the gun got to them, Kilzer and Indy, between them, had worked up a full survey of the damage. After the welders and electricians were done, and some new antipersonnel defenses were installed, it was time to roll. This time with an escort of Abrams and Bradleys, spread out like Chihuahuas herding an elephant.

They had headed up Brushy Fork creek, the Bradleys, Abrams and six-wheel-drive trucks struggling with the torn path left by the SheVa; where the SheVa passed, the rougher parts were laid flat but the weight of the gun turned granite to dust a meter thick. It was, however, the SheVa path or nothing; the narrow dirt road would have been impassable to the tanks even without the damage the giant gun system was doing to it.

They had eventually made their way to their current stopping place, the shoulder of a ridge at the head of Brushy Fork about three thousand meters across a couple of narrow valleys from

203

Green's Gap. The smaller vehicles had arrayed themselves on other ridges, with a few of the tanks down in the gullies of the creek; there was room for only the SheVa on the hilltop.

The tank crews were up in their hatches looking at the route and shaking their heads in the cold. The sun was long gone, taking with it any warmth. The nearly vertical mountains glittered, frosty under the moon.

"Okay, I for one vote that we turn around," LeBlanc's voice crackled over the radio.

"O ye of little faith," Kilzer said. He had a multicolored three-dimensional view of the terrain up on his display and now tapped a control to bring sections of it up on Pruitt's targeting system. "Okay, Pruitt, load up a penetrator."

Pruitt looked at the screen and shuddered. "You're joking, right?"

"Nope," Kilzer said, tapping his keyboard again and bringing up a set of fifteen target points on the mountainside. "Okay, it's going to be an expensive road. But we'll *have* a road. And I won't have to go skiing with you."

Pruitt looked over at the colonel, who had a pensive expression on his face. "Colonel?"

"Is this going to *work*, Kilzer?" the officer temporized. "The rounds aren't that big . . ."

Kilzer's laugh was deep and infectious. "Oh, Lord, that's a good one, sir!" he chuckled. "You've obviously been in SheVa combat too long, sir. They're TEN KILOTON rounds! That's the equivalent of *ten thousand tons* of TNT, sir. *Twenty million* pounds of explosives!"

"Hmm . . ." After a moment Mitchell grinned and chuckled in return. "You're right. My version of what is a 'small' explosion has gotten sort of skewed. Go on."

"Each of them is going to vaporize a big chunk of North Carolina rock, sir," the tech rep pointed out. "And the rock around it is going to settle in rubble. Fifteen shots, by my calculations, will reduce the ridgeline by only two hundred feet or so. But that two hundred feet is going to take out the steepest portions and lay down a ramp—a steep ramp, admittedly—on both sides."

"Pruitt?" Mitchell said.

"I dunno, sir," the gunner admitted. "I mean, one side of me says 'hey, it's *Bun-Bun*. No problemo.' And then the rational side of me says 'It's a frigging *mountain*.'" He rubbed under his helmet for a moment then grinned. "What the hell, sir. If fifteen doesn't do it . . . Hey, how many *do* we have in reserve?"

"There's more coming from the Asheville reserves," Mitchell said. "We'll have two full loads of penetrator and six area denial after we shoot fifteen."

"Colonel, this is your add-ons. What's the situation?" Major Chan could not hear the conversation and thus was getting curious.

"We're just discussing some engineering details," Mitchell replied over the group net. "Okay, Pruitt. Do it." He keyed his mike again and sighed. "Okay, everybody, stand by for big noise."

Major LeBlanc had never seen a SheVa fire and she had to admit that even for someone who crewed Abrams tanks it was impressive. The sixteen-inch smoothbore belched fire with a blast of sound that was like the bellow of a giant. The round itself was, essentially, an enlarged version of the Abrams main anti-tank round, a depleted uranium dart. The main difference being that the SheVa round had a dollop of antimatter at its core.

But like the Abrams "silver bullet" rounds, and the teardrops of the ACS grav-guns, the depleted uranium penetrator and its tungsten stabilization fins left a streak of silver light behind. The light went directly into the shoulder of the right-hand mountain and vanished. There was a flash of light out of the hole, quickly extinguished, and a muted rumble through the ground.

"I hope the next one is a little more impressive," one of the tank crews said. The shot might as well have been a pebble dropped in the ocean for all the mountains seemed to care.

Pruitt methodically fired all eight of his onboard rounds. Each of them disappeared virtually without a trace.

"We're not making any impression that I can see, Kilzer," Mitchell said.

"We will, sir," the tech rep replied. But he looked a tad nervous.

Pruitt waited while the reload process went on. Each of the

reload trucks, specially fitted HMETT vehicles, had to pull up to the back of the SheVa and load one round at a time. Then the rounds were transported up to the turret armory. It took quite some time and by the end of the exercise the tank crews had gotten out and were walking around, talking, joking and smoking. Some of them were lighting fires to heat up their rations.

"Colonel, you might want the crews in their vehicles," Kilzer noted as Pruitt loaded the next round.

Feeling like a bit of a martinet, Mitchell passed the order on to LeBlanc who slowly collected her crews. Finally everyone was loaded back up and Mitchell gave Pruitt permission to fire.

The first set of eight rounds had been in a flattened U, following the line of the gap and about two hundred feet below the actual ridgeline. The ninth and tenth rounds were at the center of the U and had the same effect as the others, precisely none.

"Are we going to see any result soon, Kilzer?" Mitchell asked impatiently.

"I thought that last one would have shifted something," Kilzer said with a frown. "Let me check my notes. . . ."

"What the hell," Pruitt said, lining up the next shot. "I've got rounds to spare." He aimed at the next target point, on the shoulder of the first hill about sixty feet above the first shot and fired.

Each of the previous rounds had, in fact, made a very solid impression. The antimatter explosion had vaporized a sizable chunk of rock, a sphere ranging from fifty to a hundred meters in diameter. But the refractory material above the explosions had managed to survive and each of the explosions was widely enough spaced that there were ersatz "pillars" between the newly wrought, extremely hot, slightly glowing, caves in the pass's heart.

The eleventh round, however, penetrated rock that had already been fractured by previous rounds and the impact of the ten kiloton blast propagated along the lightly supported bridge of rock across the top of the pass. With, literally, earthshattering results.

"Holy shit!" LeBlanc muttered, looking up as the entire pass began to move. Down. "Back us up!" She watched helplessly as a section of mountain larger than the SheVa slowly turned to rubble and began sliding towards three of her tanks. She noted in passing that all of the personnel had dropped into the belly of the vehicles and that they were just getting into motion when her own tank suddenly revved and reversed, slamming her into the coaming. She bounced back into the slag where the hatch used to be, banging her back and tearing a hole in the back of her uniform then howled like a banshee as first one and then two of the tanks disappeared in the avalanche.

"Ah," Kilzer said. "Now we're getting somewhere . . ."

"It's okay, Major," the colonel said as soothingly he could manage. It had taken a while to get the battalion, and their commander, calmed down enough to have any sort of conversation. Fortunately, most of the tanks weren't loaded with anything that could really harm a SheVa. Otherwise, it might have come to blows. "Their gun tubes are still exposed. We can hook up to them on our way up the slope and pull them out."

"You're going to make more shots!" LeBlanc snapped. "They're going to get *buried.*"

"Oh, probably not," Kilzer said. "Most of the rest of the rubble should go onto the other side. That shot was just designed to lay down a ramp."

"*Lay down a ramp!?*" the major shouted. "You just buried two of my *crews!*"

"It's not like they're *dead,*" the tech rep replied. "I mean, they *were* in their vehicles when the avalanche hit, right?"

"I am going to come over there—"

"No, you're not," Mitchell said. "Kilzer, shut up and go check your notes or something. Look, Gl . . . Major, we can *get them out. After* we finish the shots and open up the pass. As long as we can get a chain around *anything,* the SheVa will yank them out like a cork."

"I *knew* it was a bad idea coming along on this trip."

Pruitt picked up a largish rock and banged on the only bit of metal visible on the turret, which was the edge of the hatch. "Anybody in there?" he called.

The response was muffled but somehow the profanity filtered through. Actually, from the sounds of it it was surprising it didn't *scorch* through.

"Okay!" he yelled. "We'll have you out in a second!"

The crew of the first Abrams to be yanked out of the rubble was scattered across the scarred surface of their tank, breathing real air and swearing like . . . well, soldiers that had been buried alive and then unceremoniously yanked out of the ground. The vehicle itself was fully functional—it took more than a multiton avalanche of granite to break an Abrams—but the company commander and the major were having a hard as hell time convincing them that they had to get back in and drive.

Pruitt checked the fit of the massive chain on the gun mantlet and then walked up the slope about a hundred meters. There was always the possibility that the chain could slip and he wanted to be far enough away that *any* possible reaction to that mishap would pass him by. He wasn't particularly worried about the chain breaking; it was the same design used to anchor aircraft carriers and had been adapted for SheVa recoveries. An Abrams tank, even covered in rubble, was not even in the same country much less league.

"Okay, Reeves, do it." He looked up at the SheVa as it began to inch up the slope. He could tell that the driver had applied less than ten percent power. Despite that, and despite going up a thirty-degree slope, the chain snapped taut for just a moment and then the seventy-two-ton tank came out of the ground like a racehorse out of the gate.

"Whoa there, big fella!" he called as the weight of the chain dragged the Abrams farther up the slope and then stopped. "And the next time you need roadside assistance . . ."

Mitchell walked over to where the battalion commander was checking on the crew of the second tank. They hadn't taken any damage in the avalanche but the TC had managed to break his nose when the vehicle was ripped out of the ground like a weed.

The colonel waited to the side until LeBlanc was done talking to the crew, then walked farther away as she strode over. The ground was rough, littered with rocks from boulders the size of small cars down to pebbles and dust, so he had to watch his step. In more ways than one.

"Well, we have a road," he said, gesturing at the pass. What had previously been a slight saddle with sharp cliffs on each side was now a deep and nearly flat U shape. "You have your tanks back and everybody's happy."

"They could have been killed," she muttered, but he could tell her heart wasn't in it. She turned to look up at the SheVa and shook her head. "That thing is just . . ."

"Amazing?"

"Dangerous," she answered, but after a second she grinned. "And amazing."

"Yeah, it is that," Mitchell said softly. "But when you've got a seven-thousand-ton vehicle on one side and a seventy-ton vehicle on the other, being able to tow it, or, hell, pull it out of set concrete, isn't that surprising. The bad part is, we haven't met up with what all that amazing design is made to fight. And if you think *this* has been bad, wait until we meet up with our first lander."

Getting the support forces across the gap turned out to be much harder than getting the mech over the ridge. In the end, the Abrams and the SheVa had been forced to tow the trucks over much of the rubble.

But they had finally made it down into the Cowee valley and the whole assemblage stopped just short of the intersection of Cowee and Caler creeks to work out their movement plan.

"We've got to get down the Tennessee Valley and link up with the division, probably near Watauga Creek." Colonel Mitchell shone a flashlight on the maps and then looked up at the surrounding hills. Most of the armored force was up on them, looking around for Posleen, with a few of the vehicles refueling at a time. None of the tracks were particularly low on fuel but this might be the last chance to stop for gas, and tankers hated running on anything other than a full tank.

So far the enemy had been staying out of sight, which was fine by him.

"Not a long drive but a pretty hard one. It's going to be a tight fit going through by Iotla. And there's probably going to be Posleen in front of us and behind. I don't know why there aren't any in this area. There were when we came through the first time, but they were behind us then. I'd, frankly, expected this valley to be crawling with the little bastards."

"I'll put a couple of recon squads of Brads out front," LeBlanc said. "Maybe three, four thousand meters out. In this country any further would be pointless and that way if they run into trouble we can snug up fast."

"Works for me," Mitchell said. "But we need to keep some support on the trucks."

"I'll put Charlie company in ass-end Charlie position," the mech force commander said, taking off her crewman's helmet and scratching her hair. "I'd say Bravo on point, then Alpha, then you, then the support vehicles and Charlie in trail. I'll ride with Alpha."

"Concur," the colonel replied, flicking off the light. "I figure I don't have to remind you to keep an eye out in every direction?"

"Nope," LeBlanc said with a tight smile. "But you can be sure I'll pass the word along."

LeBlanc scanned the commander's viewer around and shook her head. She had paused the company along the forward slope of the ridges south of Cowee Church as Bravo bounded forward. So far the enemy had yet to make an appearance, which just made no sense whatsoever.

There were high ridges to both sides and the Tennessee River snuggled the ridges to the west. It flowed northward from the wide valley near Franklin, then passed through a narrow gap which opened up into the valley they were currently in. The terrain was extremely broken, with a mixture of farms and woodland. The area was actually well suited to defense, against either humans or Posleen. The problem being that they were in a movement to contact and if they made contact they would have to assault through. The terrain was *not* well suited to assault.

She swung the viewer to the southwest at the lower hills across the river. Posleen, by and large, were not very good at reading maps but they had a certain logic to their movement. They wanted big targets, towns, factories and cities, so they tended to stick to large roads, making the generally valid assumption that they would lead to the best targets. But they occasionally branched off on small roads and there was a network of those across the river. She took another look at the map and shrugged, keying her microphone.

"Juliet Six-One, this is Alpha Six-One, over." Time to send some screening forces across the river.

"Juliet Six-One, over."

Well, at least Lieutenant Wolf, the new Bravo company commander, was awake. He'd been the Bravo executive officer until Savannah, when the former commander had turned up among the missing. She'd found out after the battle that the XO had ended up leading the charge and immediately put him in command.

"Find a ford and send a platoon to make sure we don't have any visitors across the river, over."

"Roger, out."

She waited a moment until she saw a force of three Bradleys and an Abrams nosing down towards the river then looked to the south again.

"Charlie Six-One, what's your position, over?"

"Getting ready to stop just west of Buzzard Ridge; recon elements are just short of Iotla. Be aware that we're basically in road march formation; there's no room to spread out and there's no way to cross the river around here."

"I can see that," LeBlanc called. "Push it a little closer to Iotla; we can redeploy to the east there if we have to."

"Roger, I'll push the scouts up to the edge of the Franklin Valley as well."

"Can they see the Iotla Bridge, over?"

"Stand by."

She waited in the cold, wondering where the platoon from Bravo had gotten to and wondering when the movement to contact would become "contact."

"Negative, Alpha. Sending them forward to the bridge at this time."

"Roger, move up and spread out, get ready for Juliet to pass through your position."

"Roger, out."

She switched over to intercom and ordered the tank to move forward. It was only as it rocked back into motion that she wondered if she should contact Mitchell.

"She's good," Mitchell muttered.

"What's that, sir?" Pruitt asked. The two of them were nearly alone in the compartment. Reeves' position was forward and a level down, so unless they used the intercom it was impossible for him to hear their conversation. And Indy and Kilzer were somewhere in the bowels of the SheVa. So Pruitt was the only one to hear the comment. He waited, wondering if the colonel would reply, and flipped from monitor seven to eight. He'd seen the platoon of tracks cross the river then disappear behind a range of hills, wondering if maybe that was enough to send.

"She's got good control of her units and she's got pretty good subordinates," Mitchell replied after a moment. "She's also not letting things get ahead of her, she's using her forces effectively and she's keeping control without micromanaging her sub-units. I'd probably push the scouts out farther than she has, but that's more a 'by the book' reaction on my part and it would mean overruling the company commander. Frankly, if I had a battalion of tanks I'd love to have her as a company commander."

"But she's a *battalion* commander, sir," Pruitt pointed out.

"Truth to tell, there's nothing wrong with her that a tour at Command and General Staff College wouldn't sort out," the commander said by way of reply.

"Except that she could never have gotten to that point other than by how she has, sir," Pruitt said with a shrug. "What happens if her tank has to crack track? Or if the loader gets taken out? She can't slam shell, she can't crack track. She's too small and too light. She can get through some of it by sheer mental discipline, but the reality is she can't fight tank anywhere but in the TC hatch."

"I dunno," Mitchell said with a shrug. "She can do *that* just fine and, by and large, company and battalion commanders don't pull maintenance on their tracks. Besides, *you* can't crack a SheVa track."

"Nobody can, sir," the gunner pointed out. "But virtually any *guy* could crack Abrams track. And they have to in combat. I mean, could she even lift a tow-cable?"

"Probably, but I take your point," Mitchell said with a shrug. "Fortunately, she *did* end up in command, though. Instead of some guy with big muscles and no brains."

"Yeah," Pruitt admitted, swiveling the monitor around to watch the tracks starting to move down the road. They were spread out as much as possible, but as he watched, first one platoon then the other dropped back into column march formation.

"As long as she can screen us to Franklin, I don't care if she pees standing up, sitting down or standing on her head," Mitchell said.

"Well, I hope like hell it isn't the latter, sir. 'Tisn't a pretty image."

Corporal Jerry Bazzett flopped to the ground and shimmied forward under the low screen of bushes thinking to himself that it was a damned cold night to be lying on the ground. He surveyed the terrain below the hill with his monocular then switched to the thermal imaging scope on his AIW. With the monocular, even with the moon descending in the west, not much had been visible; just broken country and darkness. But as soon as he switched to thermal he started picking out targets.

The valley below was packed with Posleen, most of them stationary as if awaiting a call. And all of them were looking to the east.

Mitchell looked at the updated information and keyed the radio. "Alpha Six-One, this is November Seven-Zero. Plan?"

"November this is Alpha, how does 'game called on account of lack of motivation' sound? We have an estimated thirty thousand in the flats and more on the hills. I was prepared to punch through light resistance but this doesn't meet my definition of 'light.' "

"We can try to sneak up Sanders' Town Road," Mitchell said, doubtfully.

"Somehow the words 'sneak' and 'SheVa' just don't work in my head." Even over the frequency-clipping radio the note of humor was clear.

"The alternative is back up and shoot them with an area effect round," Mitchell said. "Or . . . can we get artillery fire from the 147th yet?"

"Negative, they're still bottled up near the pass; artillery is firing from Savannah, which is *way* too far."

"These guys are *all* oriented to the east?" Mitchell said doubtfully.

"According to my scouts," LeBlanc answered. "The description is that they look like they're waiting for something."

"Time," Mitchell said, thinking of the ACS unit trapped in the pass.

"Agreed," LeBlanc replied with a sigh. "This is going to be ugly."

LeBlanc looked at the map again and frowned.

"November, can you cross the river?"

"Roger, over."

She frowned again and looked at the update from the Bravo platoon. The far side of the river was still clear and they had halted in place when the Posleen large-force had been spotted.

"I think I know how to handle this."

"We're going to be a major target," Kilzer said as the SheVa rumbled forward. "And a big one at that."

"You said we were practically invulnerable from the front," Pruitt said. "And it's been working out that way."

"Practically is not the same as entirely," Kilzer replied. "And we're not invulnerable at all from the sides. There's *a lot* of damage that hasn't been repaired already."

"We'll be fine," Pruitt said, slewing the view sideways to where Bravo had gathered just below the hilltop that was holding the bridgehead. So far the Posleen seemed entirely unaware of the presence of the armored force on their flank.

CHAPTER SIXTEEN

Then 'ere's to you, Fuzzy-Wuzzy, an' the missis and
   the kid;
Our orders was to break you, an' of course we went
   an' did.
We sloshed you with Martinis, an' it wasn't 'ardly fair;
But for all the odds agin' you, Fuzzy-Wuz, you broke
   the square.

—Rudyard Kipling
"Fuzzy-Wuzzy" (Sudan Expeditionary Force)

Iotla, NC, United States of America, Sol III
0317 EDT Tuesday September 29, 2009 AD

Alentracla looked around at the massed host and flapped his crest impatiently. The group had been gathered by the host leader for a very specific mission and he should be glad.

He had been grabbed more or less at random, separated from the stream of Po'oslena'ar headed towards the fighting around Rocky Knob. He and the others had given up their weapons, gladly, when told why. Then, as the host had passed, Kennelai from the warleaders had bartered for heavier weapons from passing forces. They had taken the shotguns and light railguns from Alentracla and his fellows and traded them for hypervelocity missile launchers, plasma cannons and three-millimeter railguns. All of them going to Alentracla and his fellows for *no debt*! It was amazing!

Not only had his oolt been reoutfitted with the most powerful weapons that were available, but it had also been held out of the blind slaughter occurring in the mountains ahead. The humans had continued to press forward and soon it was expected that they would be down onto the flats. There the Posleen would have many advantages and might even stop them, but in the meantime the host was being slaughtered by the human's artillery while the ground fighters moved forward relentlessly.

Better to be here, but it was annoying to wait.

He stepped off of his tenar and walked down the lines of his oolt, checking the oolt'os' weapons. All of them had the skills to handle the devices, but they had only recently been upgraded and he wished to ensure that all was well. Instead of the shotguns and light railguns they had sported only a day before, each of the oolt'os was armed with a plasma cannon or hypervelocity missile launcher. He had been surprised at the apparent generosity of the warleaders, but when he was told the reason it made sense.

If you're going to hunt big game, you need big guns.

He finished his inspection and was walking back to his tenar when he looked to the north and froze; a giant shadow was moving in the darkness under the mountains. As if one of the hills was cruising along the river.

"*Up!*" he shouted, pointing to the north. "*It comes! It comes!*"

Posleen had as much trouble with a flank attack as humans. The oolt'os could care less; they shot where they were told to shoot. But the Kessentai were as susceptible to surprise as humans, perhaps more so. And physically moving the aim-point of the oolt'os was *more* difficult than moving that of humans; when packed groups of oolt'os tried to turn, simultaneously, they actually tended to fall over.

In this case while Alentracla saw the SheVa's shadow, and recognized it for what it was, many of his fellow God Kings did not. Even after he opened fire.

But when the SheVa opened up all doubt was erased.

"Hoowah!" Pruitt shouted. "Look at those MetalStorms go!"

The crimson fans of forty millimeter fire were spreading across the mass, erasing whole battalions at a time. And in this case all the guns on the fore part of the turret as well as on the sides were firing simultaneously. For just a moment it seemed their fire would fully suppress the Posleen. But, unfortunately, there were only so many rounds in each pod. And then they had to reload.

Now it was the Posleen's turn.

"*Fire!*" Alentracla yelled, suiting action to words in fear of the distant mountain of metal. No wonder Orostan had offered such rich incentives to have it killed; it had just wiped out a third part of this host in one volley.

"Holy Jesus!" Pruitt shouted as the storm of fire hit the SheVa. Most Posleen units had a mixture of railguns, plasma cannons and HVMs, with the weight thrown, generally, in the direction of the railguns. And with the newer armors, even 3mm rounds generally bounced off. This force seemed to be composed of nothing but plasma cannons and HVMs. The MetalStorms had opened fire only a moment before the Posleen, but the red fans of their efforts were dwarfed by the return fire; the fire was so intense it lit the ground like daylight. It was not so much return fire as a wall of plasma striking the front of the SheVa. And they were firing . . . low.

"Back us out!" Mitchell said. "Now!"

"Doing it," Reeves said tightly. The SheVa suddenly gave a lurch that did not seem to have anything to do with the ground and the radiation alarms started screaming. "I just lost most of my control on the left side, sir!"

"*Indy!*"

"Holy Mary Mother of God," the engineer said as the left front of the reactor room seemed to open up to the night air. She actually *saw* the round that punched through the number six reactor. The black dust that suddenly filled the air was, fortunately, at the far end of the reactor compartment. And it wasn't dust, but the black, layered, less-than-a-millimeter-diameter radioactive beads that made up the "pebble" part of a pebble-bed reactor.

She turned and ran for it. There wasn't much else she could do.

"Reactor breach in the engine room!" she called over the radio. "It hit the pebbles! We're hot, sir!"

Major Chan involuntarily ducked as a storm of plasma and HVM hit the upper section of the SheVa. Most of the fire had been targeted at the base of the gun system but at least one God King was firing at the MetalStorms. They had engaged with all the forward deployable guns but with the inability to turn the main turret, they were in reload mode before they could significantly affect the mass of Posleen. They had killed a lot of them and cut the fire down somewhat. But not enough.

Now the Posleen were returning the favor.

"This is not fun," Glenn said as plasma rounds rang against the turret. It was upgraded just like the E4s but even room temperature superconductor could only handle so much heat and the interior of the turret was starting to feel like an oven. Suddenly she felt a lurch that seemed to come from the turret itself and an odd sliding feeling.

"What is that, ma'am?" Glenn said, turning around wide-eyed.

"I think the turret rings are cutting loose," Chan replied in a totally calm voice as the turret jolted forward again toward the two-hundred-foot drop.

"We've also got track damage on the left side," Mitchell replied as the SheVa finally backed around the corner of the hills, taking a last spiteful blow to the engine room as it exposed that side. The night was still alight with the glow of plasma from the far side of the hill, however, showing that the infantry company on the hillside was fully engaged. It was amazing they could hold out at all; the air above their positions must be reaching hundreds of degrees just from the plasma heat-bloom.

"I'm back in the reactor room," Indy said, her voice muffled by the GalTech radiation suit. "We took hits in two reactors. One is just vented but the other one scattered pebbles all over the room; it's hot as shit down here."

"This is Kilzer," the civilian said over the same circuit. "It's not track damage on the right side, it's in the motors; one of the wheel motors is fried. I've cut it out but we're going to be moving slow until it's fixed."

"Moving slow is a bad thing," Mitchell said. "Kilzer; Chan's turret has slipped out of the rings or the rings have been shot away. Something like that, I'm getting really confused reports. Get up there and see what you can do. Pruitt, rotate the turret to let the rear Storms fire over the hills. Reeves, park this thing behind Bravo Company. I hope they can hold."

Bazzett huddled in his scraped hasty fighting position and fired his AIW remotely. He had to stick his hand out into the fire but he could use the connection to his monocular to generally aim it at the approaching mass. Fortunately or unfortunately, there were so many of the centaurs they were hard to miss. The Brads were firing their 25mms in indirect mode from behind the hilltop and that was racking up some kills, and the Abrams had braved the hurricane of plasma to drive forward and engage direct. And, for that matter, the SheVa was still sending its own hell over the hill, wiping out masses of Posleen under the fans of MetalStorm rounds. But that didn't stop the almost continuous stream of plasma, railgun rounds and hypervelocity missiles coming at the hilltop.

In this case, "sticking his hand into the fire" felt literal; there was more plasma coming his way than he had ever seen in his life. And as he had found out before, while a near miss from an HVM was pretty unpleasant, a near miss from a plasma round was damn near the same as getting hit. The heat-bloom from a strike was lethal at four meters and fell off from there.

He was pretty sure he'd been in the "lethal" zone at least twice in the battle so far and he was starting to wonder if the dirt on his back was burning through his uniform. Fortunately the newer cold weather gear, including gloves, had an outer shell of Nomex, which was probably the only reason he wasn't a crispy critter already.

He heard the Barrett .50 caliber sniper rifle below in the next scrape and shook his head; Caprano just wouldn't quit.

"Cap, dude, you're gonna get yourself killed!" he yelled. There was no way to fire the big gun off-hand which meant the sniper was raising himself up out of the scrape. He looked over and could see the body rise up against the light.

"I can barely see in this shit!" the sniper called back. His rifle boomed and he ducked down as a plasma round hit just down the hill and covered them both in steaming soil. "Got the fucker anyway!"

"Just ride it out, man!" Bazzett yelled back, spotting some movement at the base of the hill and firing a few rounds in the general direction. With the monocular it was possible to see what the rifle was aiming at, but there was no way to get a decent shot off. It was sort of like looking through a straw. "Keep your ass down!"

"It's not my ass I'm worried about!" Caprano laughed back, lifting himself up, then screamed as the next bolt washed hot plasma over him.

Bazzett caught the edge of the blast as well and it felt as if his hand turned to cooked meat, but for Caprano it was infinitely worse. The sniper rose to his knees, shrieking in pain. The rifleman could see the sniper's face and it was a mass of red and black with screaming white teeth in the middle. As he started to drop back onto the smoking ground he was hit by the next blast from the approaching Posleen. What dropped into the hole was steaming legs and hips, with a few juts of bone sticking upward.

Bazzett screamed and fired an entire magazine down the hill in a bloody mixture of fear and rage.

The good news was that he wasn't cold anymore.

The bad news was that the Posleen were moving forward in

their usual suicidal charge mode and if somebody didn't do something about it they were going to be coming up the hill in just a second or two.

Kilzer hammered at the TC's hatch but it was welded as solid as if it was a continuation of the turret. He had already tried the gunner's hatch and found it the same way.

The turret was skewed at an angle on the top of the SheVa, leaning forward precariously with the front edge of the turret ring actually protruding *through* the front of the SheVa and into open air. The heat was like an oven even through the resistant rad suit. He could hear the environmental system in the turret trying to vent the enormous overload but it must have been nearly impossible.

He lifted up the wrench he'd brought with him and hammered on the metal.

"Anyone alive in there?"

There was an answering hammering which he took for a yes. But he knew that if he didn't get them out, and fast, they were all going to cook.

"Hold on!" He keyed his radio and looked up at the crane. This had better work.

"Colonel Mitchell, Chan is trapped in her turret. I need Pruitt up here on the double. Have him bring some explosives, some Nomex strips, heat-resistant glue and detonators."

The question was, of course, how solid a weld they were dealing with.

Pruitt watched from the crane control room as Kilzer laid the explosives around the rim of the hatch. He wasn't sure what they were for. There was no way the blocks of C-4 were going to cut through the turret and even if they did it would just kill the crew inside.

Kilzer waved at him and keyed his radio.

"Apply pressure," the civilian said, hooking the cable onto the hatch coaming. "Just pull up until you've got a good pressure on."

Pruitt engaged the transmission and watched as the cables came taut, then applied a touch more motor until he could hear the resistance singing in the system.

"That's as much as I can do," he called.

"Hold that then," Kilzer said, backing away from the turret. He walked to the base of the crane then tapped the remote detonator.

With a *clang* the C-4 flashed purple-orange and the hatch sprung open. The hook to the crane went flying upwards in a parabola and then back down as the engine whined in overdrive pulling it in.

Pruitt quickly disengaged the transmission then hurried out of the crane as the civilian pulled the crew out of the hatch and carried them across the top of the SheVa to a cooler spot.

"We need to get them below," Kilzer said. Glenn, the major's gunner, was already laid out on the cooler steel but it was obvious she needed some serious attention. She was nearly unconscious and her skin was dry as toast.

"There's an aid station just under the crane," Pruitt said then paused. "Of course, you *know* that, don't you."

"Yep," Kilzer replied, dragging Chan across the steel. "It's also shot full of holes. We need to get them transported back to the battalion aid station." He turned around to go back and get the last crewman.

"No," Chan whispered. "Just . . . find me an IV. I'll transfer to one of the other turrets."

"Pruitt," Mitchell called. "Get your ass back down here; we are leaving."

"Sir, we've got wounded up here!"

"Get them under control quick then, if we don't move Bravo is going under."

There was an elevator but that had been a pretty low repair priority and God only knew what damage it had taken in the last exchange. Just getting the crew down to the aid station, the *unprotected* aid station, was a two story trip.

Pruitt looked up as Kilzer came up dragging the last of the crew.

"Damn," the gunner muttered, yanking the major into a fireman's carry. "What we need about now is the cavalry to come riding to the rescue. But we *are* the cavalry."

"Hammer it, Nichols," Major LeBlanc snarled. She was out in front of most of the battalion but she could care less; if the rest of the unit didn't draw the Posleen off them, Bravo was going away.

The mass of tanks and Bradleys rounded the hills that had sheltered them from view and finally saw the solid wall of plasma and HVM fire striking the hills. It was as if the air was on fire, linking the valley and the hilltop.

"Holy Christ!" she heard over the radio. "What in the hell *are* these guys?"

"Quiet," she said. "Echelon left, forward by bounds, Charlie lead."

"Charlie, open fire!"

"Alpha, echelon left!"

Glennis suddenly felt a cold fire in her stomach, a strange sensation she couldn't quite place. It was almost sexual, almost orgasmic, and then she understood as the battalion opened out on the flats, the Abrams and Bradleys going to maximum speed on the outer flanks to present one almost continuous line. The maneuver was beautiful, almost flawless as the tanks, bellowing fire, descended on the flank of the Posleen force like an enraged metallic monster.

She had created this. She had planned it, she had planned how to sucker the Posleen into reacting to two separate flank attacks. And it was her battalion, her creation that would destroy this Posleen force, despite their superior weapons, despite their superior numbers.

Glennis grinned like a Celtic Goddess as the first rounds of white phosphorus from the battalion mortar platoon started to drop into the Posleen. The white phosphorus provided a smoke-screen for the forces engaged on the hill. And the fact that it threw burning bits of impossible-to-put-out metal all over the Posleen was just a benefit.

This was what *she* had wrought.

This was command.

"Open fire."

"Open fire," Mitchell said, controlling the MetalStorm tracks directly. "Lay a curtain of fire in front of Bravo Company."

He looked up as Pruitt slid into his gunner's seat. "Major Chan?"

"Bad dehydration," the specialist replied. "Same with the other two; Glenn started spasming on the way to the aid station. We've got IV's running in all three of them and Kilzer is rolling Glenn into a water pack. Other than that there's not much we can do until we can get them to a regular medical facility."

"With heat injuries generally just rehydrating will work," Mitchell said. "We're moving back into position."

"I noticed," the gunner said, keying his targeting screen.

"When we clear the hill I want you to fire across the Posleen force," Mitchell said. "As low an angle as you can manage."

Pruitt kicked on a map screen and zoomed it out. Then he shook his head.

"No target, sir. What in Sam Hill am I shooting at?"

"Nothing," the commander said with a faint grin. "Just remember, lowest angle you can manage."

The fire was getting heavy, the night was bright with the streams of plasma flying through the air and the impact flashes of hypervelocity missiles, but Glennis stayed with her head out of the TC's hatch, engaging with her Gatling gun and generally enjoying life. The battalion was cutting through the massed Posleen like a scythe to wheat, which was a fine difference from normal. Catch them *enough* off guard and they didn't react any better than humans. It was all a matter of maintaining dominance.

She looked to either side and frowned. The other necessity was having enough firepower to maintain dominance. Some of the Posleen were leaking around to the sides, despite her having spread the tracks out as widely as she dared. And they were starting to fire back; as she looked an Abrams on the flank was lit with silver fire and ground to smoking halt. She was going to have to do something fast or the whole battalion would get flanked. Possibly on both sides.

"Charlie, open it out a bit more to the left," she called. "Alpha, more echelon, battalion prepare to wheel right."

That would leave them open to the leakers on the east but Bravo was laying down a good base of fire out there and sooner or later the SheVa . . .

As she thought it, a tongue of flame a hundred meters long lashed across her vision.

"Beautiful!" Pruitt shouted as the backwash from the penetrator threw the Posleen to the front into disarray; while there was no way to use the penetrator itself the blast from the massive cannon was a weapon in itself. The impact hammered the center section to their knees or spun them through the air and even those outside the center of the wash were shocked into momentary immobility.

"Mr. Kilzer, forward antipersonnel systems if you will," the colonel said calmly. "Let's finish these visitors off. Maj—MetalStorms, fire at targets of opportunity. Be aware for friendlies to the east."

"I hate humans," Orostan said with a ripple of skin that was the Posleen equivalent of a sigh.

"Yes, oolt'ondar."

He looked over at the younger Kessentai and flapped his crest.

"You're tired of hearing this?"

"I, too, am tired of humans," the Kessentai admitted hastily.

"I took *hours* to set it up! I promised everything but my personal fiefs to its preparation! I made promises, the Net knows, I *cannot keep.* Those oolt'ondai were waiting to take *it* in the flank! They were supposed to ambush the *SheVa. Not the other way around!*"

"Yes, oolt'ondar."

"I am tired to death of them," the warleader snarled, looking at the fighting near Iotla. "Why, *why,* can't these *miserable, duosexual, hairy, two-legged, DEMON-SHIT, SONS-OF-GRAT* just *once* take the sensible path?!"

"I don't know, oolt'ondar."

The warleader watched as half of his barely controlled force at the base of the pass turned to regard the distant fighting. And then as the groups, all of them individuals under no discipline except the coercion of the Path and some minor bribery, turned in three different directions, one group moving towards the fighting by Iotla, one to face the main enemy coming down the pass and one to the rear where, surely, there were greener pastures. In no particular order. More or less simultaneously.

What was left was a devil's cauldron of angry Kessentai and confused oolt'os, many of whom were losing track of their Gods. This tended to make them touchy and that led to them taking it out on the other oolt'os around them.

"Herding cats," he snarled. "That is what humans call it. Herding *cats*!" he shouted as the first oolt'os lost its fragile grip on sentience and discipline and started to shoot its way through the group between it and its God. At which point things could only get worse. Especially as a new barrage of artillery started to fall.

"Herding cats. What the *hell* is a cat?"

Bazzett lifted himself up on his elbows as the fire started to slacken and shook his head; the front slope of the ridge was *glazed*.

But what was more important was that the Posleen weren't trying to fire at his position anymore. Some of them were directing their fire at the returning SheVa, which had just rumbled around the side of the hill. As he watched, the SheVa fired, killing a few thousand of the centaurs in front of it from the backwash of the gun; where the penetrator went was impossible to guess.

With the blast from the SheVa, the Posleen were starting to come apart. Some were trying to get reoriented to face the tanks rumbling down on their flank. And a fair number of them were streaming off to the south. There were a few still struggling up the slope of the hill but they were probably outnumbered by the company. And, really, they weren't all that dangerous one on one.

"Cowards!" he yelled, snugging the rifle into his shoulder and picking out targets for aimed fire. He shot off an entire magazine in single aimed shots, most of them hitting, then slipped in another. To either side he could hear other rifles barking and the stutter of one platoon machine gun. Interspersed he could hear the boom of one of the sniper rifles and see the occasional flare of silver-purple as one of them blew up a God King's saucer. Out of the corner of his eye he could see the red fans of fire from the SheVa as it ground forward into the river and up the far slope. Suddenly there was a titanic explosion from either side of the SheVa and he was afraid that it had blown up. But afterwards it just ground on and the ground to either side was an abattoir; the damned thing had giant claymores on the side!

Finally, unbelievably, there weren't any more targets and no more fire was coming their way. He stood up and looked around at the ghostlike figures around him, at the heat rising in waves off the slope and raised the rifle over his head in with a bellow.

"Take that!" he screamed. "Take that you yellow motherfuckers!"

"Quite a few of the yellow motherfuckers," Stewart commented.

"I think they're serious this time," O'Neal replied.

The Posleen had been coming in a solid stream for the last four hours, an unremitting tide of yellow bodies that had done little but create a massive pile of corpses.

However, unlike the earlier attacks, where they had come in waves permitting a moment's pause between assaults, this had been absolutely continuous. Any break in the line of fire, and there had been many as the occasional lucky shot had carried away weapon or dug into a hole deeply enough to destroy the suit within, had permitted the tide to push forward by increments.

The God Kings were using their saucers again, occasionally popping up above the bulk of the horde to spot and engage the human defenders. While they were easy prey under the conditions, especially since they were automatically designated for engagement by whatever suit had that sector of the line, they had caused damage disproportionate to their numbers. It was mostly the God Kings that had struck into the holes, killing another dozen of the suits, and it was the God Kings that moved the line forward, charging into the teeth of the fire in an attempt to reach the hated humans, or at least get one last clear shot.

The pile of corpses was now more of a broad wall, a wall that concealed both sides equally until the aliens presented themselves at the top of it, slipping and slithering in the body fluids of their brethren, and were swept away to form another layer. Over it all there was a bitter haze of steam rising from the slaughtered bodies and a mist of gaseous uranium so thick it had started to form a thin layer of silver on the ground.

But the rate of their advance could be distinguished by the slow creep of the bodies forward.

"This is annoying," Mike continued. "We were supposed to be *maneuver* forces, for God's sake. Sitting in place waiting to be slaughtered is for Line troops."

"We've tried maneuver," Stewart pointed out. "Not too survivable in these conditions. It's just a good thing we don't have to worry *too* much about barrel wear. I remember the old joke before the war about 'if you use up your bin of ammo you can consider it as having been a bad day and take a break.' The average trooper surviving has fired *four million* rounds in the last day."

"I know," the commander replied. "It's just so . . . so *asinine*. Eventually they'll force their way through. But we've killed, how many? A hundred thousand? Two hundred thousand? A *million*? And they just keep *coming*."

"They always do," Stewart pointed out, turning his suit to face the commander.

"Almost always," Mike replied. "This time I'm really surprised. Generally even the *Posleen* give up after a few million dead on one patch of ground."

"Well, I'm not coming up with any brilliant stratagems," Stewart replied, turning back to the battle. "You?"

"Nada," Mike grumped. "Just sit here and take it."

"Fortunately, neither are the Posleen."

"How many have we lost?" Tulo'stenaloor snarled. "Four million here and in the valley?"

"Four point three as of last count," the essthree replied.

"Four point three," the commander snapped. "Thank you!" He looked again at the human map and shook his head. "The road over the mountain is well and truly gone, but send at least six oolt'ondar up here on this hill called 'Hogsback' and tell them to try to climb over the mountain. Perhaps *that* will distract the humans."

He looked at his list of available assets and frowned. "And put out a call for anyone who wishes to try their hand with an oolt Po'osol as well. Usually humans would have retreated by now. We *will* figure out a way to destroy them!"

"Or else we're all doomed," the essthree muttered. But quietly so that the raging warleader wouldn't hear.

CHAPTER SEVENTEEN

Porter's Bend, NC, United States of America, Sol III
0442 EDT Tuesday September 29, 2009 AD

Indy pulled her arm out of the sleeve of the antiradiation suit, into the still-sealed interior, and used a paper towel to wipe condensation off her faceplate. It was a technique she had picked up while doing a short stint in high school working in a nitrogen chamber and it stood her in good stead today. Now if something else she had learned over the years would just permit her to come up with a miracle, they might even be able to fire again.

"I think we're pretty much doomed," she said to the engineering officer below.

Colonel Garcia looked up at the shock absorber of the SheVa's main gun and admitted privately that she might be right. The gun had been hit by something, with all the damage it was hard to tell what, but the weapon, an HVM or maybe a plasma bolt, had dug a half-meter hole in the side of the massive shock absorber, spraying the area with hydraulic fluid.

"We've got replacement fluid," he said doubtfully, thinking of the parts and supplies the repair brigade had with them. "But we don't have a replacement shock, short of bringing one in by blimp. And that's not going to happen. It kind of ticks me off;

we're engineers, we're supposed to be able to figure problems like this out!"

The SheVa was hull down behind a low line of hills, just south of Rocky Knob. The 147th had fought its way down to the valley and now was spreading out along a line roughly delineated by the Tennessee River and Oak Ridge. They had mostly cleared the Posleen on this side of the river, but the far side was still strongly held by scattered groups and any blimp coming over the mountain would be Public Target Number One to an estimated two hundred thousand remaining Posleen.

The line of hills was one of the anchors in the defenses and the SheVa, with its surviving supporters, had scuttled for cover behind it as soon as they made the turn around Rocky Knob. If "scuttled" could be used as a term for a four-hundred-foot mass of metal that had lost fifty percent of its power.

"I don't think a welded patch would work," Garcia continued as Kilzer walked out from under the gun. "The pressure on firing is too high. It would just blast it right off."

"There's welds and welds," Kilzer said, rubbing a smear of red hydraulic fluid off his suit. "You got any plate sections with you?"

Plate patches were not the standard six-inch steel but ranged from one to three inches.

Garcia looked up at the shock again and shrugged; the structure was the size of a mini-sub and the pressures were high enough that it was unlikely any sort of weld would hold.

"We've *got* them," he temporized.

"Okay, I need a section of replacement plate, three meters wide and exactly nine point four two three meters long."

"Exactly?" the colonel said with a grin and a raised eyebrow.

"Exactly. And, hmm, a track replacement vehicle, a hull cutter, two platoons of technicians in rad suits, an engineering officer, sixteen vertical work harnesses, four welding kits, two hundred kilos of C-4 and a cup of Kona coffee."

Garcia thought about it for a moment and shrugged. "I can do it all except the Kona."

"Damn the Posleen for cutting us off from our supplies!"

✧   ✧   ✧

Kilzer had exited the vehicle, still wearing his rad suit, and now walked around the section of hull plate, marking on the surface.

The plate had been cut into a long rectangle, exactly nine point four two three meters in length, by one of the hull-plate cutters. The devices used a chemical-pumped laser that had the ability, among other things, to cut to very precise depths and angles. Which was useful when, for example, a section of hull abutting a nuclear reactor had to be cut away.

After cutting the section of plate, the same vehicle had then opened up a six by six meter hole in the side of the SheVa, then wandered off to find other work. There was plenty to do.

While Kilzer and Indy worked to repair the damaged main gun, the rest of the brigade was busy at work on the "minor" items. There were no more reactors this side of Knoxville and no way to bring them in by blimp, so the gun was going to have to maneuver at half power. But there was more than enough other damage to occupy the brigade as it replaced damaged struts, patched holes in the hull plates, lifted off the destroyed MetalStorm turret and re-ran hundreds of cut electrical cables.

Paul looked up at the opening as one of the techs came out dragging the cable from the top-side crane.

"Three lifting shackles, here, here, here," he said to the welder, noting the points where the connections were to be made. Then he walked to the other end of the plate and showed another welder where to do the second set. "When you're both done, put a couple more near the centerline for control lines."

While that was going on, he led the other two welders into the interior and showed them the ragged hole in the shock absorber.

"Cut away the damaged metal, make a nice smooth hole."

One of the welders looked at the thin coating of hydraulic fluid on all the surfaces and waved his buddy away from the metal.

"Gotta call in a fire crew, sir," the technician said.

"Ah." Paul looked around at the hydraulic fluid and shook his head inside the bulbous suit. "I *knew* I was forgetting something."

He waited while the fire-suppression crew was called in and made notes. The crew consisted of two blower teams and a safety supervisor. Because the SheVa repair brigade often had to operate under pressure and in less than safe conditions they had developed techniques to handle things like welding around explosive materials.

As the laser welders cut through the materials, the fire team took care of secondary effects. The hydraulic fluid had a high vaporization temperature but with enough heat it would first vaporize and then combust. Generally these were small, smoky fires that were easily put out, but a few were larger and more energetic. The CO_2 extinguishers, however, were able to handle both types of fire with relative ease.

Setting up the cut had taken longer than the cutting itself. The two technicians were experienced enough to be something on the order of artists. They skillfully carved around the hole, creating a smooth exterior and a regular opening where before had been twisted metal.

After they were done Paul thanked the entire crew and waited until they had left to find other work. When they were gone he first cleaned the surface of the metal with carburetor cleaner, then applied a thin coating of what looked like double-sided tape to the top of the shock absorber.

"Okay, I get it, you're going to weld it onto the hole," Indy said, coming up behind him and looking over his shoulder. "And it's long enough to wrap around. What I don't get is how you're going to get it to hold; you can't weld from underneath and tape isn't going to work. And I don't get how you're going to wrap it since we don't have a press that's nearly large enough."

"There's ways," the civilian said cryptically.

By then the big section of hull plate was starting to slide into the interior. The SheVa techs had carefully wrapped the crane cables through control points so the cables weren't doing any damage to the interior, but the multiple turns and the length of the cable, not to mention the weight of the huge slab of steel, made for jerky movement.

"Get control lines on the sides," Garcia said, coming up from the reactor room. "And hook onto the rear with a dozer to stabilize it."

All three engineers watched as the hull-plate lifted up over the shock and stopped, swaying slightly.

"Don't drag it," Kilzer said to the two noncoms who were acting as eyes for the controllers on the far end of the lines. "Drop it straight down on the shock, slowly."

The plate began to inch down, swayed slightly as one of the side lines slipped, then tapped into place, leaning sideways and then finally coming into full contact with the top of the shock absorber, adjacent to the hole.

"Great," Kilzer said, taking a remote control out of his pocket. "Hold it there for just a second."

"Paul, what are you—?" Garcia asked as Kilzer's thumb dropped onto the red button. There was a resounding *clang!* and fire shot out from under the plate.

"Welding explosives!" Kilzer said over the ringing in his ears.

"You're supposed to shout 'Fire in the Hole' or something!" Indy yelled in reply, shaking her head and tapping her ears through the radiation suit. "That was bloody loud!"

"It's in place," Kilzer said. "What's the problem?"

"Paul, that wasn't a very safe way to do that," Garcia pointed out, carefully. "Somebody could have gotten hurt. And I'm pretty sure we all just sustained quite a bit of hearing damage."

"I didn't," Kilzer said, pulling his arms out of the sleeves and reaching up through the suit to pull out earplugs.

"You could have told *us!*" Indy shouted.

"Wonk, wonk, wonk," Paul replied, waving at the technicians dangling overhead on lowering harnesses. "Put the explosives in place!"

"More explosives?" Indy asked. "Oh, no . . ."

"Paul, are you sure about this?" Garcia asked.

"You asked for a press, Warrant Officer Indy," the civilian said with a smile. "Two hundred pounds of C-4 will do a fine job."

"Oh, shit," Stewart snapped. "Boss, we've got problems!"

O'Neal had been trying to figure out if he should suggest to Captain Slight that she reform her line a bit when the call came in. Bravo company had taken nearly two thirds of the casualties so far and there was a noticeable gap in second platoon. But at Stewart's words he glanced at the transferred data and sighed.

"Duncan," he said, shifting to a private mode. "I need . . . three of your troops."

"That's going to be tough, boss," the company commander said. "I'm already starting to get some additional leakers from the way we're sopping up casualties."

Mike tossed him the data and listened as the former S-3 swore.

"Boss . . ." he said and paused, looking at the icons of nearly four thousand Posleen struggling up the steep side of Hogsback. "Boss, I'm not sure they can make it."

"I'm sure they can't in the face of any sort of resistance," O'Neal said. "Slight's got even more casualties than you do."

"I know," Duncan replied pensively. "Major, I'm not doing anything here but sitting in a hole. I'll take *two* of my troops and head up the hill myself."

Mike thought about it for a moment and frowned in his suit. "The purpose of a commander, Captain . . ."

"Is to command, boss, which ain't the same thing as leading, I know the mantra. But in this case, I've got two platoon sergeants handling the company who can do it just as well as I, and if we're going to pull people out I'd rather it be as *few* people from the line as possible."

Mike frowned again, then sighed. "Accepted, Captain. Do it your way. Just get your ass up the hill."

"Roger, boss," Duncan replied. "And . . . thanks."

"Oh, gooder and gooder," Stewart said as Duncan broke off. "And now we have lander emanations."

"Why is it there's never a SheVa around when you need one?" Mike asked.

"I'm not sure I'm getting this."

Colonel Mitchell had just gotten off the radio with General Keeton. The ACS was taking heavy casualties and if the SheVa couldn't get them some covering fire soon the Gap was going to open up again. Mitchell knew that if the Posleen started pouring through the Gap with impunity there was no way that any number of antimatter rounds would stop them. Maybe if they had a couple more of the hell-rounds the university had developed it might work. But the SheVa's rounds just had too small a footprint; the Posleen would simply spread out.

So getting to Franklin before the ACS turned into a battalion of smoking holes in the ground was vital. Especially since even if they *could* push the Posleen back for enough time to retake the Gap, only the ACS could survive in the current conditions.

And getting the main gun up was all part of making that happen. Which was why he was sweating in a rad suit when he could have been checking on the progress of the rest of the repairs or even, God forbid, catching a cat-nap.

"We need the shock absorber functional," Colonel Garcia said. He had reluctantly come to the conclusion that Kilzer's plan, crazy as it was, might just work. But it was dangerous enough he felt the SheVa commander needed to know the possible consequences. And the SheVa's engineer was *not* happy about the plan.

"Exactly!" Indy interrupted. "We need it *functional*, not permanently crippled!"

"What Paul proposes," Garcia continued with a glare at the warrant officer, "is to wrap a piece of steel around it with the underside coated by welding explosives then set those off. He intends to do the wrapping by applying C-4 in a pattern to the outer side of the steel and setting *that* off. As the metal settles in place a detonator will trigger the weld.

"This will do one of two things. It will work, to an extent, giving the gun some shots, I'm not sure how many, or it will totally destroy the shock. It *could* neither work, nor destroy the shock. But the safe bet is on 'either or.'"

"Indy?"

"It's crazy," the warrant officer said quietly. "When the C-4 goes off it's going to crumple the shock like a tin-can. The sheet will be forced downward into it and the metal of the shock will fail. That's just physics."

"Colonel Garcia?"

"Paul?"

"Janet?" Kilzer said. "Never mind. That may seem like physics, Warrant Officer, but it's not high-energy physics. I'll start the explosion from the outer edge so that the plate has the maximum interest in bending and the minimum interest in pressing down-ward. It will wrap faster than the underlying metal can crumple. And weld explosives are low power; they won't cut the steel."

"Essentially correct," Colonel Garcia said with a shrug. "Part of the reason it might work is that the hole is in the side of the shock; there is a solid arc of metal at the top of the shock. In addition to that, yes, the hull plates are six-inch steel. But the metal of the shock is *three*-inch steel, which gives you an idea of the sort of pressures we're talking about. Which is why a simple weld is a ticket to failure. And it's not as if we can do *more* damage. Dead is dead and right now the main gun is *dead*. This might get it functional. It's stupid. But if it's stupid and it works . . ."

"It ain't stupid," Mitchell concluded. "Chance of success?"

"Honestly?" Garcia said. "Probably forty/sixty. Maybe thirty/seventy. But it's a *chance*. A normal weld won't hold. Period."

Mitchell looked around and rubbed at his face tiredly inside the suit. The faceplate had fogged up and it made everything look gray and unreal. Finally he shook his head.

"Do it," he said. "Down is down. It gives us a chance to be up again."

"One last problem," Indy said. "All this hydraulic fluid is going to catch on fire."

"Oh, I think that we can handle a little fire," Garcia said with a tired chuckle. "Some nice normal problem like a little fire would be nice for a change.

"Holy Toledo!" Paul yelled, waving the fire-extinguisher into every corner in reach; the entire interior of the firing room was engulfed in flames. "I think I should have checked my notes!"

After most of the brigade flooded the interior with extinguishers, nitrogen guns and finally blankets, the raging fires were finally put out. Many of them went out on their own; the hydraulic fluid was thinly spread and tended to flare and then die.

"It's a good thing we were shot so full of holes," Indy snapped as the commanders and Kilzer met back at the scene of the crime. "If we hadn't been, we probably would have blown up."

"Oh, get a grip," Kilzer snapped. "Hydraulic fluid has a very high vaporization temperature. We were hardly ever in danger of blowing up."

"Hardly ever," Indy giggled hysterically. "Hardy *ever.*"

"Oh, shut up."

Colonel Garcia had been examining the scorched metal wrapped around the shock. There was a slight indentation around the edge but it looked as if the unorthodox technique had worked.

"I think this will do," he said.

"It will probably leak like hell after the first shot," Kilzer noted. "But as long as Indy keeps it topped up, and as long as it doesn't blow off entirely, the gun should be functional."

"Indy's got a lot of other things on her plate," Mitchell noted.

"I think I'll call for a platoon of volunteers to accompany you on this ride," Garcia said. "There's still a lot of damage and you're going to sustain more. You could use the help."

"Amen," Indy muttered.

"Works for me," Mitchell said. "Where are we at otherwise?"

"All that can be done has been done," the SheVa repair commander replied. "We had to pull one wheel as too damaged to replace, but with your reduced speed that shouldn't matter. She's not exactly ship-shape and Bristol fashion, but she'll run."

"Okay, let's get ready to rumble."

"Orostan, I note that the SheVa is still coming on." The warleader looked at the maps and shook his head. "This is not a good thing."

"I expected it to follow the humans over the pass, or lead them," the oolt'ondai replied angrily. "Not come around on my flank. It was that which broke the defense at the base of the pass!"

"Humans are like that," Tulo'stenaloor said, rattling his crest. "Always turning up when you least expect it. But it has to be stopped."

"I'm trying."

"Yes." The warleader looked around and then clapped his lips in humor. "I have more oolt'poslenar than I have trustworthy pilots. But I think I'll send out some of them, good pilots or not. They're doing me no good here."

"This SheVa is incredibly lucky," Orostan pointed out. "I don't know how many of our ships it has destroyed, but it is many. And when it does..."

"Yes, problems, problems, problems," the estanaar replied. "I'll handle it on this end. You just mass your forces and *stop* that damned thing. Or we'll *both* end up as decorations on some human's wall!"

Duncan bounded up the hill and flopped to his belly, crawling forward the last few yards so as not to sky-line himself.

Getting out of the position had been harder than getting to the top of the hill. The Posleen fire was almost continuous over the battalion position so the only way out was through the connecting trenches. However, although the Reapers and technical suits had dug trenches to all the fighting positions and command holes, that was as far as they went. There hadn't been anywhere "else" to go, so the troops hadn't bothered digging their way out of the fire zone.

It had been up to Duncan and the two troops with him to dig their way to the rear and then around to the east until a projection of rock cut off the sight, and fire, of the advancing Posleen. It hadn't taken all that *much* time, but it had been time consuming. So as soon as they got out of the area he had hurried up the hill to the Wall.

The Long Wall had been laboriously constructed in the years between the first scattered landings and the last major wave. It traveled, more or less, the entire length of the eastern Continental Divide but in this little patch of hell it was a shambles. At passes and other areas that might be struck by heavy Posleen attacks it was built up into modern fortresses of concrete and steel bristling with weaponry. Everywhere else along its length it was about twenty feet high and made out of reinforced concrete with a reinforcing "foot" on the inner side. And, despite the protests of environmentalists, it had no openings. On the inside of the wall was a road, a track really, that had been carved across the entire eastern U.S. Along this wall, when there wasn't a murthering great battle going on, patrols would crawl along, looking over the wall from time to time to make sure the Posleen weren't sneaking up the far side.

However, where the UT hell-weapon had hit, the reinforced concrete had taken a bit of a battering. The wall along the top of Hogsback had already had problems, legacy of the first Posleen attack on the battalion when a small force had blasted holes in it to get through to the humans' landing zone. But the hell-weapon had done far more, smashing a good third of the wall in the area to the ground and truncating all that was left.

The *good* part to that was that the remaining stumps made dandy temporary fighting positions.

So it was that the company commander stuck his head over a bit of concrete and swore.

"Apparently good sense *is* contagious," he muttered; the Posleen were building a road.

It wasn't *much* of a road and they weren't going it very well. But they were clearing away rubble and digging into the hillside, cutting a serpentine path up the hills that, otherwise, were impossible for them to scale. They had barely started, though, so there was plenty of time to deal with it.

"Race, move down that way about thirty meters," Duncan said, gesturing to the east. "Poole, same distance to the west. Open fire when I do. Target the God Kings."

He waited until the two suits were in position and had lined up the distant targets. At the base of the hill, about two thousand meters away, was a cluster of concrete stumps that revealed little more than that there had once been buildings there. It was around those ruins that most of the God Kings were clumped but even two thousand meters was was a simple shot with AID targeting systems. He checked that they had designated their targets then lined up on his first and snuggled the rifle, unnecessarily, into his shoulder.

"On three. One, two, three."

Panoratar drifted his tenar back and forth as he watched his oolt struggle to clear the way up the hill. The majority of the dirt of the mountains had been stripped away by the titanic fire of the human weapon but what there was of it was being stripped even further down and then roughly smoothed to lay down something resembling a road.

It would have gone faster with human equipment, much less Posleen, but there was none locally—any that had existed had been destroyed by the recent blasts—and even if there were, there was not one of the local Kessentai who had the skills to use it. So they had to make the road the old fashioned, and slow, way. Fortunately there *were* some of the oolt'os who had that as a skill and they were leading the way, skillfully using the rubble from the hill to reinforce the low places and create a narrow path.

Given time, and a few skilled stone-worker oolt'os, they could create a road that would last for a thousand revolutions of the sun. But that would be unnecessary. All that the local force needed was enough breadth to run their oolt up the hill and then take the humans from the rear.

"And won't the humans be surprised," he grunted to Imarasar just before his tenar exploded.

The saucer-shaped craft of the Posleen God Kings used a crystal matrix power storage system that was highly efficient; it was, in fact, virtually identical to the system used in armored combat suits. But while it was capable of storing enormous power in a very small space, that power was also barely controlled; if the crystalline matrix was disturbed it started a chain-reaction uncontrolled energy release. Which is another way of saying "massive explosion." In the case of Panoratar's half-charged system, it was the equivalent of a couple of hundred pounds of TNT. And then there was the shrapnel from the disintegrating tenar.

The blast slapped outwards and smashed the surrounding God Kings, along with all their most elite normals, to the ground, killing most of them and rendering all the tenar out of commission.

And then more lines of silver lightning dropped among the force at the base of the hill.

"Nice *shot*, sir," Race called. The specialist ran a line of fire across the normals who were at the lead of the road-builders and watched as the depleted uranium teardrops blasted each of the normals into yellow gobbets. "I think those were the guys leading the build."

"Probably the ones with the skills," Poole said, targeting a God King at the edge of the massed group. "Darn."

"Missed the power box, huh?" Duncan said. "Your targeting systems won't pull those up. You have to specifically designate it."

"How do you do that?" Race asked as a storm of 3mm rounds slammed into the concrete behind which he was sheltering.

"Here, I'll show you," Duncan replied, activating a command so that Race could watch as he brought up the menu.

"Uh, if you could just tell me, sir?" Race said, sliding backwards down the hill and scrabbling sideways. "We're kind of busy."

"First you bring up the menu for secondary targeting parameter," Duncan replied, ignoring the private's response and a series of HVMs that hammered below his position. "Then choose 'power systems.' Once you have that you can see that the gun targeting karat *automatically* starts prioritizing not just the God Kings but the power crystals in their storage compartment *under* the God Kings. Then you just stroke the firing button," he finished, sending a needle burst of teardrops through the power system of an approaching Kessentai and detonating the God King's saucer. "You'll notice that it gives a pop-up reading of power *levels* as well, and if you have the time you can use those to fire on the better-charged saucers, giving you more bang for your buck."

There were six overturned tenar and a couple of disintegrated ones at the base of the hill now and if there were any God Kings they were lying low. Duncan nodded his hand and highlighted a couple of the tenar.

"This is a widely gathered force," he pointed out, bringing up the bows of the tenar in high relief. "Note the rounding. We've got two that are almost pointed, one that is rounded almost into a semicircle and one that is halfway in between. This sort of difference has been noted before in the saucers, called tenar by the Posleen, and in weapons design up to the design of the landers. There seem to be four or five broad styles."

Poole ducked down below the concrete and scuttled sideways again, trying not to giggle hysterically at the lecture. "You know, sir, this is *just* the right time for a lecture on distinctive Posleen styles in saucer design."

"What causes the style difference?" Race asked with a laugh.

"Nobody really knows," Duncan said. "But it's interesting to note that while our enemy *seems* like formless waves of one-ness, they *do* have some individual and group differences. Probably it's the difference between Ford and Chevy, but they *do* have differences. At least the leadership, the Kessentai."

He glanced down the hill again where most of the mass of normals was still trying to climb the hill.

"Not much you can do about these jokers, though," he sighed, starting to pour fire into the mass. "You just keep killing them until they stop trying to kill you."

Mitchell glanced up at the main viewscreen and shook his head; the whole valley beyond the river was peppered with red enemy indicators. Cresting the hill was going to be a "special" moment.

"Everybody ready?" he asked.

"We've got four minutes of water," Kilzer said. "We found a community water supply but it only had forty thousand gallons. After that's gone, we're open to plasma fire."

"We're still here," LeBlanc said. "We're rearmed and we've got enough replacements that we're at ninety percent strength. And the river *looks* fordable."

"We've got about fifty percent power," Reeves said. "When the MetalStorms are really going, cross-country speed is going to be cut by two-thirds."

"Storms are up, the ones that are left." Captain Chan sounded tired over the radio. Her crew had consumed half the IV's in the SheVa and Glenn had had to be evacced. But other than that they were fine. Exhausted, but fine. "Garcia redesigned the reloads so we could have six available each. But we're down to only fifty-three total reloads so I put six on each of the front systems and scattered the rest out. Once those are gone, the nearest are on the road from Knoxville. The *long* way. We need to shut these guys down *soon.*"

"Eight rounds loaded," Pruitt said. "Six anti-lander and two of the euphemistically entitled 'area of effect.' Also known as God's Lightbulb and The Big One. And behind us there's a string of tacitly avoided and spread-out vehicles filled with more hellfire and destruction just in case four ain't enough. We've got a half a pack of cigarettes, a tank of gas, it's ten miles to the FP and we've got sunglasses on."

"What??" "Are you crazy? It's pitch black out here!" "Pruitt, get off the radio . . ."

Mitchell shook his head. Even after all the fighting Pruitt was irrepressible.

"Okay," he continued, "I guess that will have to do."

"Yeah! though I WALK though the valley of the shadow of death, I will FEAR no evil!" Pruitt cried as he cycled the gun to "on" and checked the telltales. The hydraulics were still showing yellow, but what the hell. "For I *am* the baddest bunny in the valley!"

"The Lord is my Shepherd; I shall not want," Kilzer said quietly. "He maketh me to lie down in green pastures: He leadeth me beside the still waters. He restoreth my soul: He leadeth me in the paths of righteousness for His name's sake.

"Yea, though I walk through the valley of the shadow of death, I will fear no evil: For thou art with me; Thy rod and thy staff, they comfort me. Thou preparest a table before me in the presence of mine enemies; Thou annointest my head with oil; My cup runneth over.

"Surely goodness and mercy shall follow me all the days of my life, and I will dwell in the House of the Lord forever."

There was a moment's pause then Mitchell shook his head.

"Just this once, I think I prefer that version," he said quietly. "Okay, let's go do unto others before they do unto us. Roll it, Reeves."

As they crested the hill the world disappeared in water, but not before they saw the entire valley erupt in fire.

"Indy, we've already lost power to Turret Nine," Chan called as the SheVa shuddered from strike after strike.

"Mitchell, this is LeBlanc. There's concentrations everywhere. Fortunately, they're all shooting at you!"

"Colonel, we're getting hammered in here!" Indy said. "We're getting hit heavy on the right flank."

"Reeves, turn us ten degrees right," Mitchell said, looking at the map and estimating their current location. "Kilzer, kill the water, we need to see what we're doing."

As the waterfall dropped away, Mitchell could see fire coming from every hilltop. The terrain was extremely broken so there were probably more Posleen in the valleys, but the ones in view were more than enough to worry about.

"Major Chan, engage targets of opportunity," he said, looking at the terrain and trying to determine a good path that would keep them out of the majority of the fire. Most of the fire seemed to be coming from the flats over towards the airfield; the Posleen had apparently retaken that area already.

"Reeves, keep us down in the river valley," he finally said. "We'll head in towards Franklin just before the oxbow up ahead."

"Hammer it, Charlie," LeBlanc said. The river had appeared to be fordable to her scouts, but she had no solid numbers on depth or best crossing spots. That being the case, the best bet with an Abrams was just to charge the damned thing and hope that momentum carried them through. It was going to make one hell of a splash.

She thought about the water for a moment, and the cold of the night, and decided, as the bank approached, that discretion was the better part of tanker valor and dropped into the interior. She was probably still going to get soaked, since her hatch had been blown away by an unlucky round. But any little bit helped.

She steeled herself for the impact as the tank dropped off the bank and, just for a moment, hung in the air.

To the massive SheVa crossing the river had barely been noticeable. At least at the level of water depth.

"Colonel!" Indy called as the SheVa wallowed along the bank. "We've just gotten a spike on the radiation detectors! It's not just from the reactor breaches."

Glennis looked up at the screaming box over her head and had to think for a moment what kind of alarm it was. She realized the meaning just as a huge dollop of water dropped from the hatch onto her back.

"Son of a BITCH!" she screamed, tearing at her top. She was wearing Gortex cold weather clothing and most of the water had rolled off. But she could feel splashes all over her hair. And the radiation alarm was still squawking. "All vehicles! The river is *hot*! Radiation! Button up!"

The only good news was that the river was low and the Abrams had hardly been slowed by the crossing. It was already on the far bank and climbing the slope of the hill, following on the SheVa's right rear flank.

She got the Gortex off in the tight confines of the turret and followed it with her BDU top, rubbing at the hair that had escaped her helmet.

"Nichols, get something to mop that shit up," she said, gesturing at the spreading puddle on the floor. "We need to get all this stuff out of the turret as fast as possible."

"Yes, ma'am," the loader said, grabbing a wad of cleaning cloths and slipping out of his seat to slither to the floor of the turret. It was a tight fit and he slammed his arm into one of the innumerable protruding bits of metal as he did so. "This really sucks, ma'am."

"No shit," Glennis whispered. The rad alarm was screaming fit to wake the dead and she wondered how many rems she'd just picked up. "Colonel Mitchell," she said, keying her radio, "this is Major LeBlanc and we've got a problem, over."

"General Simosin, this is SheVa Nine," Mitchell called. "Be advised that the river is hot, probably from runoff from the blast upstream." Mitchell paused and checked the tactical readouts. For a wonder nobody was shooting at them at the moment. "Major LeBlanc got exposed, we don't know how badly. And all of her vehicles, and the SheVa, are hot."

"Understood," Simosin said, his voice clipped. "It should make fording interesting."

"I don't think fording is an option, General," Mitchell replied.

CHAPTER EIGHTEEN

If in some smothering dreams, you too could pace
Behind the wagon that we flung him in,
And watch the white eyes writhing in his face,
His hanging face, like a devil's sick of sin,
If you could hear, at every jolt, the blood
Come gargling from the froth-corrupted lungs
Bitter as the cud
Of vile, incurable sores on innocent tongues,—
My friend, you would not tell with such high zest
To children ardent for some desperate glory,
The old Lie: *Dulce et decorum est*
Pro patria mori.

—Wilfred Owens
"*Dulce et Decorum Est*"

Porter's Bend, NC, United States of America, Sol III
0523 EDT Tuesday September 29, 2009 AD

"Stop it right there," Kilzer said over the radio. He was back
in his rad suit to direct the vehicles into place.

Although the Posleen were on every side they were not in view of the small pocket below the hills surrounding the river. And for the moment, decontamination had to take precedence over assault.

LeBlanc looked at all her tracks snuggled up to the side of the SheVa and shook her head. She wondered if she really was starting to feel sick or if it was psychosomatic. She'd know in a few minutes.

"We're all here, Kilzer," she said over the radio. "Do it." The civilian had found a piece of steel about the right size to cover the hatch and now she slid it into place as a curtain of water fell on the vehicles.

"I hadn't even considered this possibility," Kilzer said over the radio as he watched the torrent dropping on the tracks. "What a great secondary use, though."

He looked up as the last trickle dripped from the spouts, then walked out, running a portable detector over the tanks and APCs.

"What's the word?" LeBlanc called from her track.

"You're still hot," he called back. "Not immediately life threatening. But we need to get you to a 'cold' area within a few hours. We dropped the output by at least half with the shower." He gestured at her to get down from the track.

She slid down the side, wondering how much more radiation she was picking up in the process. She noticed that, for once, he didn't seem to be noticing her chest. In a way it was nice to know he could focus in a crisis. On the other hand, the fact that it was enough of a crisis to distract him was frightening.

He waved the detector over her front and then gestured for her to turn, covering her back and sides as well.

"Part of the problem is the ground we're on is hot from the spills," Kilzer said in a distracted tone.

"How bad is it?" she asked, worriedly. He'd been waving a long, thin rod over her chest and hadn't even made a snappy comment. Things were definitely bad.

"Did you get splashed?"

"Yes." She wanted to grab him by his suit and shake him. "How. Bad. Is. It?"

"Bad." He answered shortly. "I'm trying to think what to do. You need a full decon, *fast*."

"Oh," she said, then thought about what that meant. "Shit. I can't even accuse you of coming up with an excuse to look at my tits, can I?"

"No," Kilzer said, keying his radio. "SheVa Nine, I need some help here."

"Move," Indy snapped, lifting the decon kit onto her shoulder as Pruitt followed with a tank of foam. "We have to get out of this mud; it's all hot." Both of the SheVa personnel were in rad suits and sweating up a storm despite the cold of the night.

"I'm giving you fifteen minutes," Mitchell said over the radio. "The battalion is spread out on the hills on overwatch but the Posleen aren't targeting them. They are, however, moving this way. So you don't have much time."

"We'll get it done," the engineer said, reaching the two figures standing in the moonlight. Without her Gortex and BDU top LeBlanc was shivering in the cold, her breath puffing silver in the night air. It was just going to get worse.

"Get the rest of the crew over here," Indy said to Kilzer. "That track is officially deadlined. And they don't need to be sitting around in a radioactive environment."

"I wish I could consider this fun," Pruitt said, slamming the foam pack to the ground and running back for more gear.

"We've moving all the tracks out of the mud; it's hot as hell," Indy said as the remaining APCs that had been snuggled to the SheVa's flanks rolled out.

"Not the Sh-SheVa?" the major asked, her teeth chattering.

"No," Indy said, throwing a rope up and across a limb of a handy oak. It dropped back down again, naturally, but she got it over on the second try. "It's already contaminated. But *we've* got gear to handle it. None of you guys do."

"Oversight on m-my part."

"I think, given when you took over your battalion, that nobody could complain," Indy said with a grin as Kilzer arrived with the three tank crewmen.

"Strip, all four of you," the warrant said, hooking a portable shower up to the rope and lifting it into place. "Kilzer, I need *light*."

"I'll see what I can do," he replied, hurrying to the SheVa with barely a backward glance.

LeBlanc sighed and pulled off her undershirt followed by her bra.

"All my stuff is hot," she muttered, looking at the latter article of clothing. "And I'm not going to be able to find one of these short of Asheville."

"Not that fits, anyway," Indy sighed, lifting her brush.

"I hope that wasn't envy," LeBlanc grumped.

"No, I've got enough back problems."

Kilzer dragged the last of the extension cord up the hill, hooked the drop light to a branch, turned it on and only then looked around at the tableau under the oak.

The Abrams' driver, his head already shaved as close as a cueball and nicked in places, was shaving the head of the loader while Pruitt was busy scrubbing down the already shorn gunner with decon foam and a bristle brush.

And Indy was doing the same to Major LeBlanc; she'd started on the major so fast she hadn't even stopped to shave her. As the light came on the major turned towards it and snarled, her lambent eyes seeming to spark like an angry leopardess caught in a spotlight. She was stark naked except for a patchy coating of yellowish-white decontamination foam.

"Shut up, Major Ma'am," Indy said, rubbing the officer behind an ear. "I need to see."

Kilzer stood frozen for just a moment, his eyes blinking rapidly; then he shut them and shook his head. "I have got other things I need to be doing," he said in a tone that was trying to sound definite and ending up sounding distracted. "I'm sorry, Major, my crisis override just got overridden."

"It's okay," the major said, tightly. "I'm more worried about dying of radiation poisoning than being ogled."

"Ma'am?" the gunner said and sputtered as some of the decon foam got in his mouth. "What about us?"

"You got less of a dose," Indy said. "Your hair may fall out and you may have some other symptoms, but you're unlikely to die.

We need to get you med-evacced soon, though. And all the ambulances are on the other side of the river."

"What about the major?" the loader said, pushing away the electric razor. "You can quit, now," he said to the driver.

"They've got good ways to fix this stuff these days," Indy said, but the doubt was clear in her voice.

Kilzer picked up the portable detector and waved it away from the group, checking the background conditions. Away from the contaminated material, the ground was clear of radiation, but when he swept it back across the clearing the detector immediately began climbing.

He turned off the audible alarms then swept the wand around the major. After a moment's look he shook his head.

"Still bad?" Indy asked.

"Not *as* bad," he said quietly, looking LeBlanc in the eye. "I'm sorry if I sort of froze there, Major. I have to tell you, though, you're a very pretty woman. Not to mention competent. It's an attractive combination. Especially covered in soft, slippery foam."

"Why thank you, Mr. Kilzer," the officer replied, dryly. "It's that bad, huh?"

"Yes, ma'am, it is," he said, holding out two gel-caps. "Rad-Off. It's not going to keep you alive, but it will stretch things out."

Glennis smiled tightly, her jaw working at the words. "Is *anything* going to keep me alive?"

"If we can get you air evac to a Galactic regen tank," Kilzer said. "I'm not an expert in this sort of thing, but from these readings I'd say in a couple more hours the damage will be pretty irreversible. And the nearest regen tank I know of is in Asheville, which, under current conditions, would take about three hours to reach."

"Oh . . ." Glennis smiled angrily again and shook her head. "That . . . really sucks."

"I know, Major," Kilzer said, looking at the ground and shrugging his shoulders.

"Christ, Major," the gunner said. "Can't we do *anything*?"

"Short of GalTech there's not much you can do for extreme radiation exposure," Indy sighed, lowering the brush. "If you decon fast enough, sometimes it helps. You guys are pretty okay. But . . ."

"Shit, why all the glum faces?" LeBlanc said, trying to smile. "Let's get this finished and get on the road. We have Posleen to kill!"

"You should head back to the division aid station, Major," Indy said shakily.

"Why? If I'm just going to die anyway?" The commander shrugged, flicking some of the foam off. "Might as well go out in a blaze of glory, right?"

Indy sniffed and started scrubbing her back again.

Pruitt had finished scrubbing down the Abrams gunner, who had needed it quite frankly, radiation or no radiation, and walked over to the tableau around the naked, shivering major. He touched her, lightly and carefully, on the shoulder and shook his head.

"I'm sorry too, ma'am," he said, carefully looking her in the eye and *nowhere* else.

"Thanks, but that doesn't get my people scrubbed down," she said, pointedly, with a gesture of her chin at the waiting loader and driver.

Pruitt nodded his head but walked over to Kilzer and looked at the readouts on the counter. He looked at them again then took the counter and waved it at the major's shoulders and back.

"I want to talk to Mr. Kilzer for a minute," he said, then put his arm companionably around the civilian's shoulders and walked him into the darkness.

"Okay, how far are you going to push this?" he asked, trying to keep from laughing. *Maybe they'll think I'm crying. God, I hope they think I'm crying.*

"What do you mean?" Kilzer frowned.

"You didn't realize you had the sensitivity on this thing cranked all the way to the bottom?" Pruitt asked. "I thought you just had a terrific dead-pan! I was waiting for you to make some silly comment about 'well, since you've only got another hour on earth . . .' or 'You don't want to die a virgin, do you?'"

"Oh, fuck," Kilzer said, snatching the device out of his hands and tapping controls. One adjustment and the radiation bar dropped by two-thirds. When he actually pulled up the recorded rem count, instead of looking at the bar readout, it was about as bad as sitting in an airplane during a solar storm. Major LeBlanc had not, by any stretch of the imagination, been exposed to a lethal dose of radiation. "Shit!"

"You are so fucked, man," Pruitt said, turning his back to the group under the lights and hoping like hell that his shaking shoulders would be taken for sobs rather than the belly laughs that were threatening to sneak out. "There's *no way* the river was that hot. Sure, it's going to set off alarms, the fuckers are so sensitive you can set them off with a watch face. But the damned blast was only a few hours ago. There's not enough *runoff* to kick up the rad count. And there's a dam between us and the fallout."

"Why didn't you *say* something!" Kilzer hissed, staring at the readout and wishing it would go away.

"I just figured it was a way to get Major LeBlanc naked, a goal not to be ignored. Worked like a charm, by the way. The decon foam was a nice touch. Really morale building. I can feel my morale *soaring!*"

"I'm so screwed! We didn't even have to decon them!"

"Yeah," Pruitt said with a shrug, "but we got to see *Major LeBlanc* covered in ice-cold, slippery foam with a serious case of nipples erecti. *And* we got to watch Indy washing her down. Sort of a two-fer. I kept trying to think of a way to get the warrant into a white tee-shirt but nothing came to mind. So keep that in mind as your last thoughts because she's gonna fuckin' tie you to the ground, strip you naked, paint you blue and run you over with one of her tanks. Probably from the groin up. Speaking of which, is the tank actually hot?"

"I dunno, it was pegging but with the counter set that low . . ." Kilzer said. "I'm so screwed!"

"Just shoot yourself now, dude," Pruitt said, finally breaking down into smothered laughter. "I'm so out of here," he snorted, putting the back of his hand over his mouth and heading for the SheVa's door. Maybe in there he'd be safe.

Indy watched as Kilzer walked back up the hill. He had the Geiger counter in one hand and the other one held protectively in the area of his groin.

"Where is Pruitt going?" she asked, standing in the cold air with the brush still upraised.

"He . . . had to go get something out of the SheVa," Kilzer said in a rush and then handed the counter to Indy. He pointed at the gain control and then turned around. "And I have to go help him!"

Indy looked at the device then at the gain control as Kilzer pounded down the hill. Then she swept it across Glennis' back and arms.

"Oh." She just stopped for a moment then looked into the darkness at the retreating civilian. "COWARDS!"

Glennis cocked her head to the side and shivered. "I am b-beginning to think I'm n-not going to die?"

"How's Major LeBlanc?" Mitchell asked as Indy slumped into her station chair.

"She's fine," the warrant replied wearily. She fumbled out a Provigil and took it without a chaser. "Angry, but fine. Amazing how fast a person can warm up in the jet-turbine exhaust from an Abrams." The engineer looked over at Pruitt and shook her head. "You realize that *you're* on her shit list, too."

"*Moi*, ma'am?" the gunner replied with a butter-wouldn't-melt-in-my-mouth expression. "What did *I* do?"

"Failure to point out something like gain fault is the same as *intending* to see a female battalion commander naked," the warrant said firmly. "Some officers would put you up for an Article Fifteen. I think I'll just let LeBlanc track you down."

"Oh, shit," the gunner muttered under his breath.

"I need an honest answer, Pruitt," Mitchell said, quietly. "When did you realize something was wrong?"

"Honestly, sir, it wasn't until I was scrubbing down the gunner," Pruitt replied. "I started thinking about how many rems they might have taken and I was wondering about the river. Then I had to think about the course it took, and where it would have gotten contaminated. All that didn't take long, no more than a few seconds once I started to think about it, but I all of a sudden realized that it, the river that is, shouldn't have been that hot. And I made a gain-control mistake in training one time; I caught it almost immediately, but I knew what could have happened. And with everybody running around like chickens with their heads cut off . . . So when I was finished scrubbing down the gunner I went and checked and, sure enough, Kilzer had the gain cranked all the way to the bottom. That's the default setting, because you want to catch low-level radiation and then work up to high level. He'd been using it in the SheVa, and the reactor room *is* high level, so he had the gain cranked way up and he was used to looking at the readouts and figuring it at that gain. I think he just forgot that the system resets when you turn it off. Honest mistake on his part and at least I *did* think of it." He looked over at the warrant officer pointedly.

"Instead of, for example, the local radiation expert?" Mitchell grinned.

"It's not funny!" Indy said. "Major LeBlanc was embarrassed, thought her life was about to end and, and . . ."

"Got covered in slippery foam?" Pruitt asked. "Look, her loader, her gunner and her driver were all out there, stripped naked and shivering along with her. If you want to play with the boys, you play the same game." The gunner shrugged and then snorted. "At least I didn't try to get you into a white tee-shirt. Now *that* would have been something to sell tickets for!"

"Enough, Pruitt," Mitchell replied as the warrant drew in a breath through her nose with a hiss. "And enough, Warrant Officer Indy. We have Posleen to kill. We'll worry about how to manage *accidental* sexually overtoned situations in a combat environment *after* we survive the combat environment. Agreed?"

"Agreed, sir," the warrant replied. "I . . . Never mind. We are still in bad shape physically, the SheVa that is."

"I'm aware of that," Mitchell said. "We're going to have to go with what we've got. Pruitt?"

"Hydraulics are still showing yellow," the gunner replied in his most professional voice. "All other systems are go."

"Then let's get this show on the road again." Mitchell keyed his microphone to the general frequency. "All SheVa attachments, same plan as before. Let's roll."

✧   ✧   ✧

The plan was for the SheVa to follow the river, with one set of tracks actually in the radioactive water, while the rest of the vehicles followed along on the near bank; despite the fact that they now knew the water wasn't dangerously hot, the scare from the crossing had made a lasting impression. Keeping up was no trouble, however, because with the loss of power from three reactors the SheVa was limited to a maximum speed of about forty kilometers per hour. Keeping out of the spray of *mildly* radioactive water and mud from its tracks was somewhat more difficult.

There was a narrow saddle between two of the hills near Porter's Bend. The only way for the SheVa to survive was to limit the number of Posleen that could engage it at any one time. Following the valley seemed like the best bet. The top of the SheVa might be in view over the hills, but beggars couldn't be choosers.

"Tango Eight-Nine this is Quebec Four-Six." With the passing of the previous day the CEOIs had rotated and everyone had to learn new names. Another one of the happy necessities of military training. Along with the thirty minutes or so after the switchover while everyone hunted for the correct frequencies and quite often settled on the wrong one.

"Quebec this is Tango-Papa, over."

LeBlanc frowned at the radio and wondered why Pruitt, whom she still hadn't forgiven, was answering for the colonel. But sometimes you had to deal with the RTO.

"I'm sending out a scout unit at this time," she replied. "And we'll move outward to screen your west flank."

"Thank you, Quebec." It was Mitchell replying instead of Pruitt. "The Mike unit reports no visuals on the enemy, over."

"Roger, we'll just have to go find out where they are."

"Unload!" the TC called as the troop door thumped to the ground in the gray moonlight.

The Bradley had stopped at the base of a wooded ridgeline; the maps said that there was an open area beyond and it was up to the dismounts to check that out.

Bazzett hefted his AIW and trotted out of the Bradley, fanning out to the left towards the woods. Somewhere to the west, maybe a klick, was Highway 28. For sure the Posleen were using it for movement; it was the job of the scouts to find out whether there was more than light forces in the area.

Since crossing the river and turning to the east they hadn't seen any of the horses. Generally the Posties got more spread out than was apparent in this area. Maybe that was because of the battle across the river where the rest of the 147th was apparently pounding them.

But the rest of the 147th *was* on the far side of the river and until a better crossing point than Iotla, where the Posleen appeared to be reconsolidating, was found, they were going to be *staying* on the far side of the river.

The specialist hit the cold ground again and wriggled forward as he came to the end of the light woods. The scrub ended abruptly at a line of fence. The sheep or cows that had once been in the field were gone, but at the far side of the valley he could see some movement in the shifting light. He didn't bother with his monocular this time, just raising the thermal sight on the rifle to his eyes and scanning the distant ridgeline.

"Fuck me," he muttered again. "Why does this keep happening to *me?*"

"Tango Eight-Nine this is Quebec Four-Six," LeBlanc said tiredly. She had taken a Provigil and even dropped a tab of meth but she was *still* tired. Why wouldn't the Goddess-damned horses just *go away?*

"Tango," Mitchell answered. He sounded tired, too.

"Scouts report a major concentration near Windy Gap Church," she replied. "I'm deploying my troops along the ridgeline to establish a base of fire and have contacted division for artillery support. They're still in movement so we only have a battery, but we have to pass through this gap. I can patch a visual. Over."

Mitchell glanced up at the screen and shook his head. There was a solid mass of Posleen moving down Highway 28 with a gathering on the hill occupied by the church. There was a good chance they were also using Windy Gap Road for transportation.

Which meant that even when the SheVa and the battalion took them under fire they would have, in effect, reserves ready to counterassault. He had discovered that the worst part of a battle was when the MetalStorms were reloading but that seemed to be the nature of the weapon's system. And he was down two Storms on his front plate, not to mention the plate itself being sort of shredded.

He was getting really tired of these damned skirmishes. Just once he would like to be able to skip to the end, smoking holes in the SheVa and all. He brought up the map and looked at it but that was no help. Right now the battalion, and the SheVa, were concealed by the ridge. Once they moved on towards their firing point they would be in view and all hell would cut loose. The best bet seemed to be to go with LeBlanc's implied plan; lay down a base of fire and then assault the Posleen with the tracks, tearing them up with direct and indirect fire.

That would leave a force at their back, though, and they'd still be taking fire as they moved forward. Shitty choices all around.

The Windy Gap Hill was relatively steep but covered in roads so the Posleen could move on it easily. And while it was in range, now, of the MetalStorms they couldn't direct accurate fire on it until it was in view.

On the other hand, it really stood out . . .

"Pruitt," he said thoughtfully. "You ever watch the movie *Raiders of the Lost Ark*?"

"A couple of times," the gunner replied. "Why?"

"You know that scene where the big bad guy comes out of the crowd and Indy shoots him?"

"Yes, sir?" the gunner asked.

CHAPTER NINETEEN

T'was sad I kissed away her tears
My fond arm round her flinging.
When a foe, man's shot burst on our ears
From out the wild woods ringing.
A bullet pierced my true love's side
In life's young spring so early.
And on my breast in blood she died
While soft winds shook the barley.

But blood for blood without remorse
I've ta'en at Oulart Hollow.
I've laid my true love's clay-cold corpse
Where I full soon must follow.
Around her grave I've wandered drear
Noon, night, and morning early.
with breaking heart when e'er I hear
The wind that shook the barley.

—Dr. Robert Dwyer Joyce
"The Wind That Shakes the Barley"

Porter's Bend, NC, United States of America, Sol III
0648 EDT Tuesday September 29, 2009 AD

Tenalasan looked to the north, waiting for the great tank, the
"SheVa" to appear. It had so far cut through two groups that were
supposed to stop it and was expected to come down the road at
any moment. But so far there had been no shooting from the north,
much less signs of the great beast.

The moon had set and the night would have been pitch black
to humans. It was quite dark to the host as well, but their eyes
expanded to drink in what light there was from the stars glitter-
ing overhead. The skies had cleared and the temperatures dropped,
but as with most physical conditions that was of little interest to
the Po'oslena'ar; they could survive temperatures that would kill
an unprotected human.

Snow was bad not so much for the cold or the way it slowed
them but because it meant little to forage. Away from their bases
the Po'oslena'ar generally depended upon forage for food. They
were designed for pure efficiency and could move for days on the
food that a human would need for one. Eventually this caught up
with them and they would have to feed, but in the meantime they
would keep going.

His oolt had not properly fed in two days and it would probably be another day before he let them rummage in their food bags.
They had been given a few scraps of flesh from the human thresh
and more lately from the battles over the mountains, but it was not
enough to build them back up. With luck the coming battle would
go to them and then there would be much thresh upon which to feed.

But until then they must wait.

"I hate waiting," Artenayard said. The younger Kessentai shifted
his tenar from side to side idly and flapped his crest. "We should
be moving out to find it."

"We agreed to obey the estanaar," Tenalasan replied. He had
been in enough fights against the humans to appreciate waiting
in ambush rather than throwing himself on their defenses. He
didn't *like* it, but it was better than dying.

"We should be moving with them," the Kessentai snarled,

gesturing at the solid line of Po'oslena'ar moving up the road. "They are taking the way to the riches! An untouched land is just over the mountains!"

"And if the SheVa reaches Franklin the entire advance will be cut off. So we wait."

"Human ways!"

"Ways that work," the older Kessentai replied. It was Artenayard's first battle and so far it had consisted of lining up to pass through the Gap and then walking through the night. He would learn soon enough that humans were no joke to fight.

"It's another ambush group," Pruitt said, adjusting the angle of his gun.

"Yep, they're learning," Mitchell mused. "But they forgot something that less control would have given them."

"What?"

"Flank security."

The ground was starting to rumble and Bazzett leaned into his rifle as the first flight of 40mm went overhead. Since it was near its maximum range the spread was wider than normal but in a way that was good; it spread though half the Posleen force, throwing them quickly into disarray. A disarray to which the hastily dug-in infantry began to add.

"Who needs a Barrett?" he whispered as he zoomed in his scope on one God King that was just beginning to move and stroked the trigger.

Tenalasan backed his tenar and gestured to the east as Artenayard's head exploded in yellow blood and brains.

"To the east!" he yelled, waving at his oolt'os as he began bonding Artenayard's. "Attack to the east!"

"Pretty," Mitchell said as the first monitor came in view of the Posleen. The force was splitting its fire between the SheVa and the troops on its flank, which was just fine by Mitchell. But that wouldn't last long.

"Major LeBlanc, tell your troops to withdraw to their vehicles. Now."

"Fall back!"

Bazzett looked over at the platoon sergeant and shook his head. "We're good!"

"Orders!" the sergeant called. He was only an E-5 but he was the senior remaining NCO in the platoon. And the hard-core fucker was serious.

"What the fuck?" the specialist called, slithering out of his hole. The trees were being stripped of their branches by the fire pouring into the wood but most of it was, fortunately, going high. He slung his rifle and did a leopard crawl to the rear as fast as he could, noting other gray shadows in the trees. The Brads had pulled right into the edge of the wood, pushing over the saplings at the edge; the L-T must have been serious about pulling out.

"Into the Brads!" Wolf was running down the line slapping at stragglers. "Do NOT look towards the Posleen!"

"Colonel, we're mostly loaded," LeBlanc called dubiously. "And the Posties are coming hell bent for leather."

"Works," the colonel said. "Button up and prepare to move. Pruitt, fire."

"Demon-shit!" Tenalasan shouted as the blast from the giant tank's fire flipped scores of oolt'os and Kessentai through the air. But that was the least of his problems. Because this time the penetrator dug itself into Windy Gap Hill and blew the top off.

Besides the human buildings, the hill had been surmounted by Posleen, oolts that were trying to get reestablished after the fire from the snipers and MetalStorm packs and the reinforcing units just cresting the hill. All of them disappeared with the hilltop which now was dished out in a rather nice reverse hemisphere.

The majority of the granite at its heart was pulped to dust but the outer sections came off in the form of fast-moving rock, from gravel to boulders the size of cars, all of which lifted into the air and began flying in every direction.

As the silver-cored avalanche blasted outwards, Tenalasan flapped his crest in momentary wonder at human ingenuity in the field of killing.

"Quebec Eight-Six, move forward to finish off the survivors then sweep south."

"Next stop, Franklin," Pruitt said, loading another penetrator.

Glennis twisted the controls on her TC's viewer and highlighted a group of Posleen that were still trying to move north on 28. It was pretty evident that the aliens hadn't seen the tanks as they nosed out of the woodline and she preferred to keep it that way.

"Target, Posleen company."

The battalion had moved through the remnants of the Posleen force then turned to the south, screening the SheVa and probing for resistance. There were still scattered forces both on the hills and moving up the road. But so far they hadn't hit anything that managed to return fire, much less do damage. For once the humans had the Posleen off balance and that was just the way she liked it.

The gunner slewed the combo guns onto the target and fired a burst, turning most of the oolt into dog-meat. A few got off rounds in their general direction but the tank was still outside their range of accurate fire so all of their fire flew high or wide. Another burst finished those off and the unit rolled out of the thin covering of scrub and on towards Franklin.

They were beginning to hit the fringe of the small city. Houses and buildings had been thickening as they approached and most of the open fields had been replaced with houses and light industrial buildings or facilities for the support of the local corps. There was a smattering of trees around the buildings but much of the area was still open fields or roads.

"Quebec Eight-Six, this is India Three-Niner."

LeBlanc keyed her microphone and glanced up the hill where a scout team of Bradleys had taken position; a small suburb occupied most of the hill and she guessed from the map that it had a view of the town of Franklin itself. Which was why she'd sent the Brads up there.

"Go."

"You probably want to come eyeball this, Major."

She looked up at the hill and shrugged her shoulders. They were probably right.

LeBlanc slid off the front of the tank and walked up through the backyard of the house to where two of the Charlie Company troopers were hunkered by a picket fence. The house was apparently deserted; the back door was torn from its frame and tossed into the yard and a brief view of the interior showed the sort of mess the Posleen normally left in their first pass through an area. As she passed the back patio she trod on a teddy bear, still fairly fresh despite the rains. She looked down at what had caused her ankle to turn and then walked on; after ten years of battle the pathetic tale told by the doll was an old and worn one.

"Morning, ma'am," the senior trooper, a specialist, said, handing her his thermal imaging scope. "Take a look at the town."

"Horse-dicks," she muttered after a glance through the scope. "Don't these guys know they're beat?" The town was swarming with Posleen and more seemed to be pouring in from the east and south. Furthermore, many of them were working on some sort of underground structure near the center of the town. It looked very much like they were "digging in."

"Apparently not, ma'am," the scout answered with a chuckle, taking the scope back. "What are we going to do this time?"

"My guess is blow up the town with the SheVa," she said after a moment's thought.

"What's that thing they're building, ma'am?" the junior trooper asked.

"At a guess it's a command bunker of some sort," LeBlanc answered. "No, I take it back," she said, thinking like an S-2 instead of a battalion commander. "Most of the Posleen infrastructure is underground. I'd say that's either a factory or a food processor. Maybe both."

"Like they're getting ready to move in?"

"Or they're trying to establish a logistics point," the major replied. "Whatever it is, it's about to receive a ten-kiloton retirement present."

✧ ✧ ✧

Orostan looked over at the Kenellai that was running the resupply effort. "How is the work progressing?"

"The tunnels will be completed soon, oolt'ondai. After that perhaps twelve hours to complete the basic factory."

"Too long," he growled, looking around at the massed oolt'os and Kessentai. "We'll be out of ammunition and thresh by then."

"It can progress no faster, oolt'ondai. But I will see what I can do."

"Oolt'ondai, the SheVa approaches." The operations officer gestured to the north. "And the forces with it. The force at Windy Gap . . ."

"Is gone, I know," the warleader growled. "Well, they cannot attack us the same way. Send two oolt'ondar out to engage the tracks around it and have the others spread out on this ridge; we will *not* allow it to reach its firing point."

"As you command, oolt'ondai."

The warleader looked to the north then keyed his communicator, waiting as it hunted for the distinct address of Tulo'stenaloor.

"Orostan, here," he said when it pinged acceptance.

"Orostan, how goes there?" Tulo'stenaloor asked.

"Like the Sky Demons were driving the war," the oolt'ondai said with a flap of his crest. "When I arrange forces to attack the SheVa from the side, it comes in on their flank. When I arrange them in front of it, it turns to the side. For something so large it is being infernally hard to pin down."

"Will it reach Franklin?" the estanaar replied.

The warleader thought for a moment then rippled his skin in a sigh. "Perhaps, estanaar. Perhaps. It is . . . difficult to stop. No . . . I *will* stop it before it reaches Franklin. But I don't know at what cost."

"The cost is no matter," Tulo'stenaloor said after a moment. "If you have to take it in a tenaral charge of the last of your forces, stop it. We will have the Gap back shortly. Then I can pour forces through. But you must *stop* it; we cannot take the Gap in the face of nuclear fire."

"I shall, estanaar," Orostan said. "I'll stop it."

"Do so," Tulo'stenaloor replied. "And then, we will *own* this world. Good luck."

"I *will* stop you," Orostan growled. "By the bones of the Alld'nt I will stop you."

"No can do," Pruitt said, shaking his head.

"Why?" Mitchell asked, glancing at the map.

"The other shot, the hill was pretty steep; there was a real target. This one, the hill is a long, winding slope on our side. Not a steep one, either. I can't put a round in unless I've got something like a bluff in the immediate area."

"That's a hell of a lot of Posleen," Mitchell said, pointing at the map. "And they're not just going to sit on their hands."

"I know, sir," the specialist replied. "But we don't have a shot. If we were on the *south* side we would, but I don't think you want to swing around to there, do you?"

"Not with the force structure in the area," the colonel replied. "Suggestions?"

"Hmm," Pruitt looked at his display and made some adjustments then did some measuring. "If we back up to our last FP . . ."

"Minimum distances of four thousand meters," the colonel said with a glance at the map. "We can make it, barely. What about drift?"

"That . . . will be a problem," the gunner admitted. "In general the winds aloft are from northwest to southeast. Who knows, we might have to fire twice!"

"We'll be firing practically straight up; if the damned round comes back on us we won't be firing ever again!"

"Quebec Eight-Six, pull your advanced units back. We're going to have to back all the way up to damned near our starting point. Please detach a sub-unit to cover us."

LeBlanc thought about the combination for a moment and shivered despite the heat pouring up from the interior of the tank.

"Am I to assume that your answer to this problem involves something that is danger close at four thousand meters."

"Roger, over."

"Even at our starting point, if we don't cross the river we'll be less than four thousand meters from the target, over."

"Roger. Recommend we back up and hunker down."

"This ain't gonna be good."

"No, it's not."

"You know the problem with the SheVa gun?" Utori said. "No damned finesse."

"What do you mean?" Bazzett replied, cutting open an MRE as the track lurched from side to side. If they were going to be stopped for a few minutes, might as well eat.

The battalion had rapidly backed up, retreating over ground they had captured at cost. Only a single Abrams had been left behind, hull down in a revetment, with all its electronics shut down and turned away from the blast. All of the troops had been pulled into their vehicles as well; if a Posleen force came through they were probably toast.

But it beat being out in the cold with a nuke going off over the next hill.

"Look at this thing. It's got a choice of nuclear annihilation or nothing." The Squad Automatic Weapon gunner had broken down his SAW and was brushing at the breech with a worn, green toothbrush.

"It's got the MetalStorms," Bazzett argued. Both of them were ignoring the fact that at any moment an antimatter round could land on their heads. Part of the reason for the four thousand meters minimum range of the SheVa area effect round was that it was notoriously inaccurate at short ranges. Because it was designed for a fifty-plus kilometer range, firing at short ranges meant firing practically straight up in the air. At that angle, it was practically a matter of luck where it would land.

"Sure, but they're just forty millimeters." Utori snapped his weapon back together and took a drink from his camelbak. "It needs some 105s with some small antimatter rounds. Like . . . I dunno a ten KT round, maybe. That would be enough to clear a hilltop. Not a fucking hundred KT, which requires clearing out the whole damned *county*."

"Maybe, but it wasn't *designed* for direct assault like this." Bazzett set his spoon down as the TC stuck his head into the crew compartment.

"The SheVa just fired."

"Shit, what's the time of flight?" Utori asked, grabbing his helmet and pulling on it as if he wanted to crawl up inside.

"Must be nearly a minute," the TC answered, crawling back up into his chair. "Hang the fuck on," he added, shutting down his radios and throwing all the breakers; the blast would have an unpleasant electromagnetic pulse that could damage the electronics of the track.

Bazzett raised the plastic and metal pouch to his mouth and squeezed out the last of the entree, beef and beans, then tossed the packet into the ammo can they used as a trash can. He washed it down with a swallow of water then put his fingers in his ears, bending over and opening his mouth. "This is gonna suck."

"Damn," Pruitt muttered, watching the shifting reticle of the estimated impact. The SheVa tracked the round on its upward flight and predicted its probable point of impact based on observed flight. "Not good."

"Where's it going?" Mitchell asked.

"Looks like it's veering northeast," the gunner replied. "If it doesn't veer back it'll land as close to LeBlanc's unit as it does to the Posleen. The only good point is that I set it for proximity impact. So as long as it lands on the Franklin side of the valley, they should be in the blast-shadow."

Mitchell just grunted; there was nothing anyone could do at this point.

Tulo'stenaloor looked at the report of a high ballistic fire and flapped his crest in agitation.

"Demons of sky and fire eat and defecate their *souls*," he snarled. "Orostan!"

But the oolt'ondai had already seen the belch of fire skyward. It was far away but he knew that it could only mean one thing.

"I'm sorry, estanaar," he said, without even looking at the communicator. "It's up to you now."

Then he turned his face to the sky and awaited the fire.

The 100-kiloton round was heavier than the penetrator. This was due to a carbon-uranium matrix that was designed to armor the potentially dangerous round against stray impacts. The armor, however, fell away after firing, and the round tracked upward and then over at apogee, after which the tracking system lost lock and the round became an unknown actor.

Fortunately for all the humans involved it caught one more blast of wind from the recently passed cold front and nosed a tad further south, angling in to land just south of the Franklin water tower. And at one hundred meters off the ground, just above the tank farm, it detonated.

The antimatter blast created a hemisphere of fire, the ground zero zone, in which everything but the most sturdy structure was destroyed. Directly at the center was a small patch, the toroid zone, in which many structures were, remarkably, virtually untouched.

Outward from ground zero a blast of plasma and debris from the detonation expanded in a circle, destroying everything in its path. It was this shock wave that did the majority of damage, sweeping over the Posleen gathered in the town center and, unfortunately, over the tank left at the top of the hill. The Abrams was rocked by the blast-wave and the terrific overpressure but all the seals, designed back in the 1970s for full-scale war against the long-defunct Soviet Union, held and the crew survived. They were shaken, but alive.

The blast spread outward, sweeping across the hilltop occupied by the city center and erasing the majority of the historic buildings that made up the previously idyllic town. As the circle of pressurized air increased in size it decreased in power until an equilibrium with the surrounding air was reached . . . and passed. Then the air rushed in to fill the vacuum at the center and a return wave collapsed inward destroying much of what had survived the outward wave. When the dual shock waves passed, the only thing that was recognizable on the hilltop was the basement and foundations of the courthouse and half of the gem-and-mineral museum.

Bazzett rocked to first one and then another blast-front, leaning back and forth in his crewman's seat, then started dancing in his seat.

"'If the Brad is a rockin' then don't come a knockin'...'" He looked over at Utori, who was just starting to look out from under his helmet, and shrugged. "I just noticed the track was rockin' to the beat." He lifted his AIW out of the rack and thumbed on the sight, going through an electronics check. "I'm gonna get me a tattoo. I always said, I'd never get a tattoo unless I was in a nuclear war. I think this counts. Even if it is our side that's shootin' at us."

"Fuckin' nuts, man," the SAW gunner muttered as the Bradley rumbled to life.

"Most of the tracks are up," the TC called. "We're making a speed run from here on out. Hang the fuck on."

"'If the track is a rockin' then don't come a knockin'.'"

"Tango Eight-Nine this is Quebec Four-Six," Glennis said. "I lost three tracks to the EMP; the shields on all the rest held. Also various and sundry electronics and shock damage."

"You're mobile, though, right?"

Glennis looked at the tanks and AFVs moving through the pre-dawn darkness and shook her head. "I guess you could call it that, Tango."

"Next stop firing point Omega, Quebec. Tango Eight-Nine out."

"Right, the mission is to get the SheVa to where it can support the ACS. Not to kill every Posleen in the valley." Glennis looked around at the devastated landscape, the smashed houses, tree trunks tossed hither and thither, the blackened ground, and shook her head. "Although..."

"Boss man," McEvoy called over the platoon circuit. "Posleen lander emissions. Three sources, one heavy two light. System says two Lampreys and a C-Dec. Should we head back and attach anti-lander systems?"

Since the suits had been detailed to resupply the Marauders,

Tommy had had them change out their heavy grav-guns for flechette cannons. If the shit hit the fan, it was much more likely that they would need to stop, or at least slow, an attack by the ground-pounder Posleen than that they would have to stop landers. It looked, to most of the battalion, as if the gamble had played out.

Tommy had been looking at the same indicators and now he grinned. "Nah, I'll take care of it."

The lieutenant left the puzzled suit to wonder what that meant and laid out two power packs as he prepared the item that he had kept under a blanket.

He turned as his sensors indicated a suit entering the hole and started to nod at the battalion commander. His head just sort of wallowed in the mush within the helmet and his vision swung wildly. But he corrected after a moment and saluted instead.

"So how, exactly, were you planning on taking out three landers, Lieutenant?" Mike said, returning the salute with a wave.

"With this, sir!" Tommy replied, removing the silvery cloth from the device in the hole. "Ta-da!"

"Hmmph," O'Neal grunted, looking at the terawatt laser. The weapons had been common in the early days of the war but had been dropped out of service within the first couple of years. They were, however, remarkable anti-lander systems, at least against Lampreys and unsuspecting C-Decs. So it would probably work in this instance. "And why were you keeping it a secret?"

"I figured if nobody else knew about it, neither would the Posleen, sir," Tommy said. "I hope that was all right."

"Your AID knew," Mike said thoughtfully.

"I asked it to modify the inventory it sent back," the lieutenant replied, carefully. "If *you* didn't get the word, then neither would the Posleen. Sorry about that, sir."

"Oh, it's okay," Mike waved. "Do you know *why* these were removed from service?" he asked.

"No, sir," Tommy said. "It never made any sense to me."

"Well, it won't affect anything in this battle," the battalion commander replied. "I'll just head back to the battalion hole. Good luck, Lieutenant. Good shooting."

"Yes, sir, thank you, sir."

✧   ✧   ✧

Mike slithered into the hole that had been dug out for the battalion headquarters just as the first lander crested the ridge.

"Why isn't he having his suits rearm?" Stewart snapped.

"Oh, he's got a better idea," Mike said with a chuckle. "I had
a terawatt laser in the cache."

"And he's going to *use* it?" the battalion S-2 said.

"Looks like it. Should be fun to watch. Preferably from a safe
distance."

"I think they're serious this time,"

SheVa Nine crawled forward slowly over the ruins of downtown
Franklin searching for a firing point.

The hill that had once held downtown Franklin, and all the
rolling hills in every direction as far as the eye could see, was
covered with detritus of the nuclear strike. There was rubble from
the houses as well as lighter debris scattered across the roads,
and in the neighborhoods around the city there were trees fallen
across the roads and fires smoldering from the intense heat of
the fireball. There was a fan of tracks out in front of them but
for once since its wounding the SheVa could make nearly as good
time as the Abrams and Bradleys; what they had to dodge, it
could crush underfoot.

Somewhere around Franklin they should reach a point in range
of the Gap. The problem was twofold: angularity—they had to be
able to fire *into* the Gap—and height—the Gap was slightly higher
than Franklin and since they had to use air-bursts they needed a
tad more range than a ground burst would require. The first and
best chance was the hill that Franklin had once occupied, even
though it would make them a better target. Failing that, they would
keep moving forward until they had a good and secure firing point.

Pruitt was watching the ballistic targeting reticle slowly creep
up the Rabun Valley, sometimes getting closer to the Gap, sometimes farther away, when the SheVa rocked in the shock wave from
a heavy plasma gun.

"Jesus!" the gunner yelled, slewing the turret as he kicked on
his long-range radar and lidar.

"Colonel! We've got four, no *six* C-Decs cresting the ridges! And they're *spread out*."

"Crap," Mitchell muttered, flipping up the terrain map. The SheVa had taken on more than six ships during the retreat, occasionally at the same time. But in that case they had had terrain to hide behind and "shoot and scoot." Unfortunately, the Franklin Valley was relatively open, at least for something on the scale of the SheVa: rolling hills with the occasional higher stony prominence. It offered some obscurement to the ground-mounted Posleen but it was as open as a putting green when taking on ships.

The sole and only chance they had was that Posleen gunnery was not all that great; the ship guns had to be manually aimed at ground targets like the SheVa and it had been apparent on the retreat that the concept of "training" was foreign to the invaders. So they didn't get really accurate until they were inside the firing range of the SheVa. But taking on six with nowhere to hide, especially with only four rounds of anti-lander left and a max speed of fifteen miles per hour, wasn't going to be particularly survivable.

"Better call the ACS and tell 'em we're gonna be a little late."

Tommy crouched behind the laser and targeted the first C-Dec cresting the ridge. This was going to be tight.

The holographic sight showed interior and exterior targets as well as the antimatter containment system. Tommy deliberately avoided that, firing the beam along a vector to penetrate on a weak point and enter the battlecruiser's engine room.

The weapon spat a beam of coherent purple light just as the C-Dec opened fire with the first weapon that bore, an anti-ship plasma weapon. The ship's fire missed the battalion, striking north of it on the graded roadbed laid down by the Posleen and digging out a crater the size of a house.

The weapon was a poorly controlled nuclear reaction that was captured between massive electromagnetic fields and converted to pure photons. The beam itself was rated in gigajoules per second and cut through the heavy armor of the Posleen ship like tissue paper. It lanced through interior bulkheads and into the engineering compartment, destroying the antigravity system and removing power to most of the external weaponry. Denied its antigravity support, the cruiser lurched and dropped through the air.

"Oh, crap," Duncan snorted, looking up. He had seen the cruiser drifting towards his position but the weapons of the three on the ridgeline would have been love-taps to the ship so he had just hunkered down and hoped it would find another target. But when the terawatt laser hit it in the side, it was just about directly over their position.

The cruiser staggered and then started to drop, fast, and he knew there was nothing he could do.

The ship fell straight down at thirty two feet per second per second and impacted on the top of the ridgeline, only fifteen meters from his position and, fortunately, on the Posleen side of the ridge. Then it started to roll.

The impact of the multiton ship had flipped all three suits into the air and they fell back with a couple of bounces. But Duncan was up on the ridge again almost immediately. This he wanted to see.

The dodecahedral ship was not the best item at rolling, but the slope was steep and it didn't really have much of a choice. Still randomly firing, with occasional blasts of fire and plasma jutting out of hatches and along weapons positions, the gigantic ship rolled down the hill, over the Posleen scrambling to find a purchase on the side and onto the roadbed below, partially blocking it.

"Damn, couldn't have planned that one better myself," Duncan muttered, looking over at the other two ships. They were Lampreys, far smaller and less dangerous than the C-Dec. But dangerous nonetheless. "Now if that damned laser will just hold together."

Tommy swung the laser onto the leftmost Lamprey, which was a tad higher and had a better shot at the battalion. It had already opened fire with one of the heavy lasers on one of its five facets and the line of fire was wiggling randomly across the ground but in the general direction of the battalion command post.

In this case Sunday didn't target quite so carefully; the ship was farther away and if the antimatter containment system detonated it wouldn't disturb things quite as much.

The purple laser flashed out again, digging into the side of the ship in a flash of silver fire and penetrating deep into its vitals. The shot missed the containment system but cut the feeds from it to the engine. Once again the ship stopped and dropped like a stone. Some of the Posleen in both ships would be alive but they were relatively unimportant compared to stopping the ships themselves.

He quickly rotated the weapon onto the third ship but in this case he was just a tad too late.

"Captain Slight!" Mike called, cursing. "Behind you!"

Karen Slight had survived innumerable battles and skirmishes in the five years since she had taken over as the Bravo Company commander. Sometimes she felt like a fugitive from the law of averages. But if so, they had just caught up.

She flipped her vision to the rear and leapt to her feet as she saw the line of flashes from a heavy HVM launcher closing on her position, but it was just a fraction of a moment too late. Before she, or First Sergeant Bogdanovich, could do more than stand up the weapons had hit their hole. And when it walked on there was nothing to be found but scattered armor.

"Shit," Tommy muttered, as he targeted the third ship. This ship had learned from its predecessors and tried to jink aside, spreading the fire. The terawatt laser was not, however, like the lighter gravguns. They had only a fraction of the power available to the laser. It scythed into the third ship, clawing through crew quarters and the command bridge. For that matter, the ship pilot had not had significant training in flight at such low levels. The Posleen ships, by and large, managed their operations on automatic, so manual flight was something for which very few Posleen were trained or prepared. And it was evident in this case as the ship, accelerating sideways to avoid the laser, slammed into Black Rock Mountain and bounced backwards, hard, into the very laser it was trying to avoid.

In this case it was unclear if it was the laser fire or the sudden impact, but the third ship stopped, droppped and rolled down the hill and impacted with the C-Dec, where the two of them almost entirely blocked the narrow pass.

Tommy watched the ship roll down the hill then extended the tripod on the laser to jut over the top of the fighting position to where it had a clear line of sight on the approaching Posleen. Down below they must be having a tough time forcing their way past the roadblock created by the two fallen ships but there was still a solid wall of them attacking the front ranks. And with the death of their first sergeant and company commander, Bravo company had started to slacken its fire, letting the Posleen drive forward against that side.

Tommy had a fix for that, however, and he opened fire at the approaching centaurs with a snarl of anger.

"Good job, Lieutenant," Mike said with an unheard sigh of relief. "But you might want to cease fire, now."

"With all due respect, sir, Bravo needs the support," Tommy replied, pouring laser fire into the line of Posleen. Already the beams of purple light, designed to destroy ships, had sliced deep into the Posleen ranks, cutting through six or seven of the centaurs at a time as he swung it from side to side.

"Yeah, but it has a little problem," Mike said. "Let me put it this way . . ."

The "little problem" with the terawatt laser had been discovered within a year of its actual fielding in combat. The weapon was, as previously noted, a poorly contained nuclear explosion. Anti-hydrogen was injected, in carefully measured doses, into a lasing chamber filled with argon gas. The anti-hydrogen, opposite of real matter, impacted with argon and immediately converted itself and some of the argon into pure energy.

This energy release was captured by *other* argon atoms and when they released the energy it was as photons of light. These photons were then captured and held until a peak pressure was reached when they were released.

All of this happened in a bare nanosecond, managed by vibrating magnetic fields that drew *their* power from the same reaction.

The same laser, to an extent, was used shipboard and in space fighters. In both cases it was a regarded with awe and respect, for the barely chained sun at its heart was as much a danger to the ship as to the enemy. And so, in the case of the ships and the fighters, massive secondary fields ensured that the slightest slip on the part of the primary fields meant that the system simply got out of alignment for a moment. Perhaps the weapon would "hiccup." But that was all.

On the ground-mount version, however, these secondary systems were unavailable. And thus, when in a brief moment of chaos the power levels in the lasing cavity peaked over the maximum rated, or posssible, containment levels of the magnetic fields, the highly excited argon, and a bit of still unconverted anti-hydrogen, escaped the confinement. And proceeded to destroy the weapon. Letting all the *rest* of the highly excited argon out in a manner that was quite catastrophic.

One second Tommy was firing the laser and the next moment he was flying through the air. Well, not "flying" so much as hurtling uncontrollably. Once again his sensors were overwelmed but what he managed to read in the maelstrom and under the G forces that were slipping through the compensators indicated that the external temperature, while dropping rapidly, was pretty similar to that found in the photosphere of a star.

There was one short, sharp shock and then he was no longer hurtling. As far as he could tell he was sliding. Probably down a mountain.

He noted that he wasn't thinking very well just about the time he passed out.

Mike looked up from the battalion command hole at the smoking atmosphere and sighed.

"I *told* him he'd better quit while he was ahead," he said. The air was still filled with incredibly hot gasses and dust but the systems were already starting to stabilize and it was clear they hadn't lost anyone to the detonation. In fact, it looked like the laser, which had blown up as usual, had actually cleared the Posleen off their position. Again.

"Nukes," he muttered. "We should have brought nukes."

"Oh," Stewart said, then laughed. "Yeah. Why hadn't we thought of that before?"

"I dunno, maybe because they were a no-no?" O'Neal muttered. "But some big damned bombs? Why have to ask other people to scratch our back?"

"Or maybe we should just have brought lasers." Stewart laughed. "Why didn't you tell him about the secondary 'issues,' as the manufacturer puts it?"

"Oh, well, experience is the best teacher," O'Neal answered. "And, hell, nobody *else* was going to fire the damned thing." He glanced at his telltales and gave an unseen half shrug. "He's alive. Out like a light but alive. And the ships are gone and so are the Posleen. Looks like he did a pretty good job to me."

"Same here," Stewart said, chuckling. Then he sobered. "We still lost Slight. Dammit."

"Yeah," Mike said. "I could give the company to Sunday, as soon as he regains consciousness, but I think I'll just turn it over to one of the platoon sergeants. They're down to about a platoon and a half anyway."

Stewart stood up and looked around in the clearing dust. "Time to go find out how they're doing."

"Yeah, and I'll call Duncan back down. Not much more to do up there."

O'Neal looked at the battlefield schematic. "I don't know that there's much more to do. Period."

"Well," Stewart said. "I suppose we *could* charge."

CHAPTER TWENTY

Let Bacchus' sons be not dismayed
But join with me, each jovial blade
Come, drink and sing and lend your aid
To help me with the chorus:

Chorus
Instead of spa, we'll drink brown ale
And pay the reckoning on the nail;
No man for debt shall go to jail
From Garryowen in glory.

We'll beat the bailiffs out of fun,
We'll make the mayor and sheriffs run
We are the boys no man dares dun
If he regards a whole skin.
Chorus

Our hearts so stout have got us fame
For soon 'tis known from whence we came
Where'er we go they fear the name
Of Garryowen in glory.
Chorus

—"Garryowen"
Traditional 7th Cavalry Air

Franklin, NC, United States of America, Sol III
0726 EDT Tuesday September 29, 2009 AD

"Quebec unit, follow me!" LeBlanc called over the battalion frequency then flipped to intercom. "Drummond, put your foot in it and head down the road!"

"Where are we going?"

Glennis pulled up her map screen and frowned; it was a good question. She scanned the map and finally found what she was looking for.

"Head down 28," she said, flipping back to the battalion. "All Quebec units. Order of march, Bravo, Alpha, Charlie. We're going to head to Highway 64 and get on the road embankment; if we get some elevation on the guns the Abrams might be able to engage the C-Decs."

"That's crazy, ma'am," the Abrams gunner said. "Our guns will barely scratch that thing!"

"The SheVa's only got four anti-lander rounds left," LeBlanc answered. "There are six ships."

"Yes, ma'am," the gunner replied. "Balenton, load a silver bullet."

"Aye, aye!" the loader said. "But if she starts singing 'Garryowen,' I'm outta here."

"Reeves, back us up, fast," Mitchell said, glancing at his map. "Head northwest. Major Chan! Switch out for one oh fives, it might come down to that!"

"What's northwest?" Pruitt asked, lining up the first of the targets. It was a real question; should he take the outside ones and work in or the inside ones and work out? Oh, what the hell, right to left. "Target C-Dec, twelve thirty."

"Confirm," Mitchell replied, flipping up the appropriate screen. The Posleen ship was just cresting Pendergrass Mountain, less than five miles away. Others were closer, though, and the SheVa rocked again to the slap of one of their heavy guns. "There's some hills over by Windy Gap. I don't think we can make it that far and if we do we'll probably run into ground mounts. But one problem at a time."

"On the waaay!" Pruitt called, visually tracking the round into

the ship. "Target!" he called as the hatches of the ship gouted silver
fire. The lander started to fall to earth and then exploded, but not
catastrophically. The remains pelted into Pendergrass Mountain and
rolled out of sight. "I think I must have gotten a magazine that
time," Pruitt muttered, tracking to the left. "Bun-Bun's on the WAR-
PATH!"

"Bloody hellfire!" Kilzer snapped as the back of his rad suit was
sprayed by liquid. He looked over at the giant shock absorber of
the SheVa gun and shook his head. "Colonel Mitchell, can we call
a time out?"

"Boss, I've got a red light on hydraulics!" Pruitt called.
"This is not good," Mitchell muttered. "Kilzer, Indy, talk to me.
How bad is it?"

"This is Indy," the warrant replied, climbing through the hatch
from the engineering deck. "We've got hydraulic fluid all over the
gun room, but I don't see a breach."
"There's not one," Kilzer said, rubbing his hands up the side
of the shock. "It just blew fluid through the seals. We should be
able to top it up and be back up shortly."
"*How* shortly?" Mitchell snapped, looking at the encroaching
C-Decs. "We're under *fire* here people!"
"Shortly," Indy said as she gestured one of the loaned SheVa techs
over with a hose. "No more than two minutes!"
"This isn't good," Pruitt muttered over the radio. The SheVa
shook to another near miss as if to counterpoint his statement.
"We're working on it." Indy said.
"Reeves, keep backing us away," Mitchell ordered. "They're not
coming on very fast."
"No, but they are coming on steady," Pruitt said. He had pulled
up a reservoir indicator on the hydraulics and watched as the level
reached yellow and then green. "Sir . . ."
"You're up," Indy interrupted over the radio. "There will be a
short lag between each firing while we top off. And God help us
if we run out of hydraulic fluid!"

"I'll get someone right on that," Mitchell replied. "Pruitt?"

"Target, C-Dec!"

"Fire at will," Mitchell replied. The SheVa suddenly lurched to a titanic *BOOM* through the structure. "Son of a BITCH!"

Indy ducked as a live cable swung overhead throwing sparks. The cable itself dropped onto one of the luckless SheVa techs, sending him spasming across the deck. Indy's flailing hand snatched a stanchion as the firing chamber filled with a rush of superheated air, and held on for dear life as it seemed the entire weather-shield, with its attached armor, was going to rip loose. The shaking finally stopped and the air cleared, too quickly; she looked up to see stars where four MetalStorm mounts had once been.

"Oh, my God," she muttered, keying her radio.

"Colonel, we're hit," Indy said, unnecessarily. "We just lost the upper left side of the gun cover. Along with three MetalStorm turrets."

Mitchell closed his eyes and shook his head. "Pruitt, are we up?"

"The gun reads as functional, sir."

"The gun wasn't hit," Indy interjected. "Just the side of the cover. But I don't think we can fire *any* of the Storms until we're sure of the structural integrity."

"Colonel Mitchell, this is Kilzer," the civilian said over the radio. "I'm looking at the damage, too. We might be able to fire the right, rear Storms. But all the others aren't going to have enough structure to withstand the shock of firing. And the frontal armor is . . . creaky. The hit slagged some of the supports on the left side and I can see support beams dangling. The whole place looks like a pretzel twister with an evil sense of humor got loose in the gun room. I think the combination of the heat and the shock probably broke the welds. And we've got a lot of electrical damage."

"We can still fire the main gun, right?" Mitchell pressed.

"As long as it lasts, sir," Indy replied, nervously.

"Pruitt, get as many as you can, while you can."

✦   ✦   ✦

The gunner slewed the turret and sought out the next target as the SheVa lumbered laboriously to the north. There was nowhere to hide; it was just a matter of shoot and hope like hell the Posties kept missing. So far they had.

Pruitt lined up the third C-Dec as another shot crackled overhead and one slammed into the ground, tearing up soil and leaving a smoking crater large enough to swallow an Abrams.

"On the way!" he called, then "Target!"

This time the target vanished in silver fire, and a mushroom cloud formed where it had been. However, although the nearest C-Dec rocked in the blast front, it neither was destroyed nor wavered in its course.

"Blast, they're too far apart!" Pruitt snarled. "Why did they have to get *smart*." He lined up the fourth ship and then paused. "I want it to get a little closer, sir."

"Okay," Mitchell replied. At least the fire had been halved and the third C-Dec had been the closest. Mitchell glanced at his map then at the external monitors. Most of them were down from the damage but a few on the right side were still functioning. "Reeves, to the right rear, see that gap?"

"Yes, sir," the driver replied, angling the SheVa slightly to the right. "Are we going to be hull down?"

"Close," the commander replied.

"Okay, they're closing," Pruitt said. "Hydraulics are up. On the way!" The round tracked straight and true "through the x ring" and the C-Dec rolled to the side, seeming momentarily to be under power, then dropped into the river before rolling out of sight.

At the tremendous splash, Pruitt sighed. "That's it, sir. Four rounds. We're out." He glanced at his indicators then at the targets. "Then again, maybe not. Sir, where are the lead elements of the division?"

"General Simosin, this is SheVa Nine, over!"

"Station on this net, identify!"

Mitchell frowned at the radio; every other time he had tried to call the general he had gotten the *general*. So who the hell was holding the radio this time?

"Look, this is SheVa Nine. I don't have *time* to identify because, in case you hadn't noticed, we've got Posleen landers on the way in. We're going to try to take out the last two, but there's a problem; what we're going to do will probably hit the division. Now, where are your lead elements?"

"I can't answer anything unless you identify yourself and I *certainly* can't give you the location of our units."

"Okay, well, in that case I hope like hell that they're all behind the line of hills around Wooten Mountain. If they're as far forward as East Franklin, tell them to duck and cover because it's about to get nasty. Out."

"Okay, Pruitt, whenever you're ready," the colonel said.

"Sir, are you sure about this?" the gunner said. He had keyed in the particulars and was just updating the target point now. "We *are* going to catch the division in this blast."

"I don't like it, but that's what we've got to do," Mitchell replied tiredly. "Fire."

"Roger, sir," Pruitt replied, looking straight into the rising sun. "On the way."

The area effect round tracked straight and true to a point two thousand meters above an imaginary line between the C-Decs and then detonated.

The ships were interstellar battle cruisers as well as transports for the Posleen. And under normal circumstances a 100 KT round detonating 2000 meters away would have been shrugged off. In vacuum. Between planets.

In this case, however, it was *not* in vacuum and it was *not* between planets except by the widest description thereof. And all of the differences came into play.

The shock wave from the explosion slapped downward, hurling the ships aside. If the violent acceleration from the nuclear-driven hurricane of wind were not enough to defeat them, the sudden stop as they slammed into the unyielding ground did the trick. Subjected to forces they were not designed to withstand, the two ships hit the ground, crunched, bounced, and rolled to a stop, one just east of the Cullasaja Bridge and the other on top of the West Franklin Wal-Mart.

✧   ✧   ✧

Glennis popped her hatch and looked around, shaking her head to clear the ringing. Most of her tracks appeared to be intact, whatever that said about the crews. Anyone who had had a hatch open was probably dead and at least one Abrams looked that way; it had blown out its ammunition relief panel indicating that bad things had happened inside. One of her Bradleys was upside down as well, which probably indicated the crew hadn't made it.

She looked to the east and could just see one facet of one the C-Decs sticking up out of the Cullasaja valley. The facet mounted an anti-ship plasma cannon which was throwing sparks into the air from electrical overload. As she watched the emplacement belched purple fire and blew a thousand feet into the air.

"Fuck this," she muttered. "I want back into intel."

All in all, though, for having been hit by a bit more than the edge of a nuclear blast, they were looking pretty good.

Of course, they didn't have any radios to speak of. And she couldn't have heard one if they did. But all things considered . . .

"So do we drive back and yell at Mitchell?" she asked herself. "Or just stay here?"

She looked around at the devastated landscape and at the crews who were slowly pulling themselves out of their tracks then shook her head. "Stupid question."

"Somebody with a working radio call the SheVa and find out how long until it's up here!" she yelled to the scattered groups of troopers. "We're not going another *inch!*"

She smiled at the scattered cheer and slumped into her seat.

"What a fucking night," she muttered, pulling out a resupply request form. "Let's see, we need about a hundred bodies, a full load of ammunition . . ."

In the end, even with the resupply and the standard rounds and the Reapers and the repeated nuclear blasts, there was nothing O'Neal's battalion could do.

The Posleen, having found a way through the roadblock, had attacked without pause, wave upon wave of the yellow centaurs, climbing over the bodies of their dead to close with the hated suits.

With only 140 troopers left there wasn't enough fire pressure to stop them cold and they came on, meter by meter, against a relentless tide of fire.

"I'm clocking out!" one of the troopers cried as even the seemingly inexhaustible supply of grav-cannon rounds started to run low. "I need resupply!"

The cry went up all down the line as trooper after trooper found his ammo supply running lower and lower, the counters going from the thousands to the hundreds and then zero.

"Breakthrough on the left!" Duncan called, scrambling out of his fighting position and lowering his rifle to fire. The group of centaurs had forced their way through to the remnants of Charlie company and broken the center by the simple expedient of swarming the suits with their boma blades.

The Posleen in the front rank weren't even firing anymore, just hurtling forward, their blades raised. The monomolecular edge could not penetrate the Indowy-forged armor with one strike, but as chop after chop descended on it the armor eventually gave way and the human within was hacked to death.

With the sundering of the line the beleaguered suits seemed to give up hope. Trooper after trooper lifted himself out of his hole, stepping to the rear, those with remaining ammunition firing to try to keep the Posleen at arm's length.

"NO!" O'Neal cried, scrambling out of his own position as the suits in front of him obscured his line of fire. "INTO THEM!" He charged forward through the line of troopers and threw himself on the front rank of centaurs, his own blades out, chopping and whirling in place.

"Captain's down!" a trooper from Charlie called out and was cut off in mid cry.

"Bloody hell, boss!" Stewart cursed, sprinting forward to the side of the commander while laying down blasts from his grav-rifle. "GET BACK!"

"I Am Not Going To Let Them Have This Pass!" O'Neal snarled, chopping sideways. But the tide was irresistible and even he could finally see that. Bravo and Charlie were either falling back or just *gone*. The Posleen had the line and nobody was left to defend it.

The suits still in the line were going yellow then red and dropping off the screen.

"Fall back!" he called, glancing at his readouts. Graphs and charts meant nothing to him now, as indicator after indicator went from green to red. "Fall back on the Reapers!"

Sunday was firing from the hip, flipping out magazines one handed and reloading as each expended mag dropped from his rifle. But nothing seemed to help. The remaining suits were running from the oncoming tide of yellow bodies and no firepower in the world was going to stop them.

"Reapers, prepare for short-ranged volley fire," he called as the Posleen passed the line of holes that had once been filled with ACS troopers. He didn't even bother to try to figure out who was left. It was him and his troopers and that was more or less that.

"Gots to die someplace," he muttered, glad he'd had one last time with Wendy. He flipped another magazine in as Stewart slithered over the side of the hole followed by the major.

"Fall back on the Reapers!" O'Neal called again, flipping around and starting to lay down fire.

"Ammo! I'm out!" One of the Marauder suits scrambled into the supply cache, tearing open boxes, and then cursed. "Reaper ammo!"

"Reapers, open fire!" Tommy called as the front of the Posleen assault came within thirty meters.

The four Reaper suits were each mounted with four flechette cannons, and the hail of metal slivers opened a huge rent in the Posleen mass, even checking it for a moment. But the pressure from the rear pushed the front ranks forward against the tide of fire and the down side to the horrendous amount of fire the cannons could put out was that they ran dry *fast*.

"Clocking!" McEvoy called. "I'm clocking out!"

"Gotcha," the Marauder said, popping open the ammunition container and opening the Reapers' reload bin. "Ammo coming up!" he said, tipping the container up and dumping the contents into the bin.

"*Feed me!*" another Reaper called, laying down a wall of fire to the north.

But as the Reapers went through bin after bin, and the remaining suits, most of them commanders, laid down their fire, the ammunition ran lower and lower and the wall of Posleen closed in on the surrounded hole.

"I'm cold!" McEvoy called, then looked around at the person behind him. "Hi, Major."

"Pick up a rock!" O'Neal snarled as his magazine dropped into the hole.

"Boxes are empty!"

"I'm out!" Sunday called as his last magazine dropped free. He reversed his rifle and swung it into the first Posleen to the hole. The heavy duty stock smashed at the impact, leaving him holding only the iridium barrel. Which he then used to smash the next skull in line.

"Fuck this," O'Neal muttered. "FUCK THIS! I am not going to die in a stinking HOLE!"

"FUCKERS!" Sunday shouted, as the major climbed back out of the hole, slashing and blasting at the centaurs. "Get back here, Major!"

Sunday smashed two more of the centaurs before the first boma blade caught him on the shoulder. He hardly noticed it but then another descended and then another and he could feel himself tiring, trying to slash and crush in all directions, but it was no use, the Reapers were backed up to the rear of the position, trying to beat the Posleen back with their fists and Stewart and McEvoy were down under a tide of bodies and the major was gone and . . .

The sky lit in fire. For just a moment he could see the pupils of the Posleen's yellow eyes tighten down to a pinpoint and the reflection of the Lightbulb of God in their irises. And he hit the ground just in time.

He dug his hands into the ground and focused all his effort onto holding on as, again, the hammerblows descended on his back, lifting him up and slamming him down over and over again. He felt himself lifted up and slammed against the wall of the fighting position and his arm cracked backwards, painfully. He could feel that it was broken, but the suit integrity held. If it hadn't, the fire would have surely killed him. He waited and waited, for a moment, for an eternity, but finally the last echoes of the fire died away and he could look around.

For a time, it seemed like hours, none of his systems could determine anything in his surroundings. But then the sensors slowly came back on-line and he could get some sense of what was around him. Telemetry from suits was coming back first and there wasn't much. A suit here. A suit there.

He looked for the karat that indicated his commander, but it was nowhere to be seen.

Unlike Sunday, Mike had been out of the hole in the Posleen mass when the SheVa antimatter went off and there wasn't much he could do. So for the second time in his life he ended up in the path of a nuclear explosion. This time, at least, he had a moment's warning and instead of trying to grab dirt, which was probably futile, he hopped upward and tucked into a ball wondering where he'd land.

The blast-front picked him up and lofted him south and upward. He felt a brief glance off of something *very* hard; it bruised him despite the undergel and hard-driven inertial compensators. But after that there was, as such, nothing but air.

His sensors were still off-line but he eventually sensed that the blast-front was reducing and he tracked out into what would have been a free-fall position if he was, in fact, free-falling. He got some control over the inertials and used it to stabilize his flight. But since his externals were still reading over a thousand degrees centigrade, getting any coherent data on his location was quite impossible.

Finally the immense power of the nuclear explosion began to dissipate and the return wave came in, catching him and tossing him back, but not as far.

In all he was airborne, or nuke-borne as the case might be, for less than fifteen seconds. It only felt like an eternity. And then he saw open air.

He looked down and broke out in hysterical laughter. He was in a perfect delta track, two thousand feet up and headed down for the ruins of his old high school. Which was swarming with still-live Posleen.

"I always wanted to come back and make a big entrance . . ."

"Sunday."

"*Major?*"

Sunday scanned the map but the icon of the commander was nowhere in sight. Stewart and Duncan were both heavily injured and no other officers were alive. Even with an arm so dislocated and broken the suit could do nothing but numb it he was as good as it got. But he had less than a platoon left so it wasn't a particularly heavy burden of command.

"Yeah. I'm alive. For my sins. I'm heading out of Clayton now. I've contacted the SheVa; it's prepared to deliver on-call fire from now until the local Posleen overrun it or somebody comes to save both our asses. You look like you're clear."

"Yes, sir. No Posleen in view."

"They're reconsolidating by Clayton. I'm calling for fire. But it shouldn't affect your position. Hunker down and hold what you got. You look to be clean for the near future."

"Yes, sir."

"O'Neal, out."

"SheVa Nine?"

"Go, Major."

"One area denial round, UTM North 386187 East 280579."

"Roger. Ah, what's your position, over."

Mike looked down at the ground; he was encased up to his armpits in rock and earth.

"Secure. Please fire the round."

"Shot, over."

"Shot, out."

There was a pause. "Splash over."

"Splash out."

Mike smiled as the nuclear fireball consumed his old stomping grounds.

"I never really liked Clayton anyway."

He waited until the majority of the dust had dissipated then looked around for more targets.

"The problem with nukes is finding a good position to be a spotter," he mused. He dialed up his magnification and shook his head. "SheVa, can you reach UTM North 385846 East 278994. I would swear they're reassembling over by Tiger."

"Ah, negative ACS. Still out of our range. And we're . . . sort of stuck. Again. The crunchies are on the way, though. As soon as they figure out how to get through the radiation they'll be in support."

"555 commander, we can reach that target point. And we'll be there sooner."

The voice was German-accented English and in the background a song was playing, just too faintly for Mike to pick out. As Mike watched a streak of fire like a meteor descended from the heavens and a nuclear fireball, followed by a mushroom cloud, erupted over Tiger.

In the distance he could see beams of light leaping into the sky and more beams, and streaks of fire, coming down. He looked around and the same could be seen in every direction into the distance.

"American Defense Command, hold what you got," another voice entered the net. Presumably all the nets. "This is Vice Admiral Huber, Commander Task Force 77. Heavy fire incoming. Stand by."

In the distance a wave of fire seemed to leap from the ground as fireball after fireball erupted into the sky. It was clear that kinetic energy weapons were taking out every single Posleen ship and settlement for as far as the eye could see. And undoubtedly beyond. Around the whole globe.

Mike looked up and half shook his head as a line of shuttlecraft, seeming half air and half matter, dropped out of the sky. Troopers began spouting from the sides, dropping on pillars of fire then assembling at impossible speed. Their suits, like the ships, seemed only half there, as if one with the land and sky. And on his sensors they didn't appear at all. The air was filled with music and he shook his head and laughed hysterically again as the strains of "Ride of the Valkyries" poured through the air.

He lifted himself out of the ground as a shuttle approached and an armored figure dropped to the orange-tinted ground. He waited until it approached and then saluted the figure with the double star-bursts of a Fleet Strike major general on its shoulders.

"General," Mike said, dropping the salute as it was returned.

"Colonel," the general replied, taking off his helmet. The face was hard, Teutonic and very familiar.

"Oh, shit," Mike said with a half laugh. "God damn, Steuben, it's radioactive as hell out here. Put your damned helmet back on if you would be so good, General, sir."

"'Sorry we took so long, we had a spot of bother on the way,'" the general said, then wrapped the smaller suit in his arms.

EPILOGUE

"Sir, General Steuben's here."

Mike leaned against the rock looking out at the valley that had once been his home. He had seen the refugees and recon troopers extracted from the hole they had been huddling in and then turned his back and left. That hole had been designed for the express purpose of keeping his daughter alive. And when she needed it, she hadn't been there.

"Colonel O'Neal," the general said, touching his arm. "We're about to lift. We're needed in Europe."

"Yes, sir," Mike replied, turning and holding out his hand. "Thank you for your help, sir."

"You had the situation well in hand, as always." The suit turned and looked down across the valley and hills. In every direction there was nothing but an orange nothingness; the very soil had been stripped from the rocks. "I . . . heard about your choice."

"Yes, sir." His voice was cold and distant.

"It was . . . the right choice, Colonel. I . . . don't know that I *could* have made it, but it was the right choice."

"It *would* have been the right choice. But the timing . . . the Posleen couldn't have forced their way through to the Cumberland." Mike stopped. "They couldn't have from the *beginning*. Not with you on the way. You would have arrived before then."

"But to Asheville?" the general asked quietly. "Four million civilians, Colonel. To overrun the SheVa? To wipe out another division of troops? Or two or four or five? And you could *not* know. It was clear that everything that was known to the Earth forces was known to the Posleen. I don't know what they would have done if they had known. Perhaps there was nothing they *could* do. But this one, Tulo'stenaloor, he was too smart. Who knows what he might have done?"

"True," Mike sighed. "But . . . oh, God . . ." He slumped down to the ground and curled into a ball. "My *daughter!*"

The general looked at him for a moment and then sighed. "I think . . . Europe will wait. At least for me."

He reached down and lifted the suit to its feet, taking the colonel by his shoulder and turning him towards the waiting shuttle. "I think, you and I, we will go get very drunk. And cry for the death of a world."

"This is *absolutely* unacceptable!" the Tir shouted then stopped, panting.

I wonder if I could drive him into lintatai? Monsignor O'Reilly thought. *No, no reason to change the plan.*

"How is it unacceptable, my good Tir?" the Jesuit said aloud. "Surely this is a day of rejoicing." In fact, through the doors to the conference room much rejoicing could clearly be heard; O'Reilly thought he was probably the only person in the entire complex who was actually working. On the other hand, while getting the Posleen off their backs was a good thing, to the Bane Sidhe it was just one step in a more complex war.

"Those forces were *not* to leave Irmansul uncovered!" the Tir said, firmly but back in control. "There will be . . . consequences."

"A Fleet issue, I would think," O'Reilly said. "As has been reiterated many times before, the Fleet does not belong to the United States, or even Earth, but to the Federation. Any . . . irregularities in unit dispositions is surely a Federation . . . irregularity." The monsignor smiled thinly then made a complicated hand gesture. "I would consider taking it up with your pet admirals, Tir. The United States government has all it can do to handle the sudden cessation of hostilities."

"So you say," the Tir hissed. "A *Fleet* matter. Obviously the *Fleet* needs to be brought to heel."

O'Reilly smiled darkly and shook his head. These Darhel were *so* easy. What the hell had taken the Bane Sidhe this long to trip them up? "That is, surely, your prerogative, Tir. But for now, there's a victory celebration and I'm missing it."

With that the Jesuit rapped on the table with his knuckles, stood up and went out to find a bottle of Bushmills. Surely the Father Church would permit him one night of celebration.

And tomorrow it would be back to the wars.

Of course, some people hadn't stopped.

Tulo'stenaloor blazed a trail through deep woods, showing his oolt'os how to hack open a path. He didn't know why he bothered; the humans had taken control of the orbitals. Any ship that attempted to lift out was being destroyed. All that he could do was run and hide like an abat. It was humiliating.

He snarled as the oolt'os in the lead stopped, then reached for his rifle. Ahead in a clearing there was a single Indowy standing alone.

"Stop," Tulo'stenaloor said, waving at the oolt'os to lower their weapons. The green ones were never a threat. But what one was doing here, at this time, was an interesting question.

He stepped forward and gestured at the little being, but the Indowy just waved.

"You are Tulo'stenaloor First order Battle Master of the Sten Po'oslena'ar?" the Indowy asked in Posleen.

"I am," Tulo'stenaloor replied, looking around. Suddenly the bushes in every direction spouted armed humans. They did nothing, though, just waited, their weapons bracketing his bodyguards. He waved at the oolt'os to lower their weapons. "Who are you?"

"I am the Indowy Aelool," the little one said with a broad and toothy, and very feral, smile. "And I would like to make you an offer you can't refuse."

"So what do we do now?" Elgars asked the placement officer. The officer was short, overweight, balding and apparently harassed. And clearly in no mood for handling troops that had misplaced their units.

"For right now I'll assign you a BOQ room," the officer said. "And I'll put the two NCOs in the NCO's quarters. Then I'll send a memo up to DA asking them what in the hell to do with you. Until we find out, just stick around the area." He handed each of them a slip of paper and waved at the door.

"This seems . . . I dunno," Elgars said as they walked down the corridor. The Asheville Corps headquarters seemed to have completely lost its head. With the return of the Fleet, half the soldiers expected to be out-processed immediately and all the little routines were gone. Suddenly, no one knew what the future would hold. In a way, it was better facing the Posleen.

"Abrupt," Mosovich said, holding the door open for her in a gesture that was chivalrous rather than rank based. "When you work odd jobs you get used to it. Every now and again you get a heap of thanks; usually you just get ignored. The difficulty of the mission or how well you did it rarely seems to have anything to do with the outcome."

"What now, boss?" Mueller said.

"Well, if the captain can be seen slumming with a couple of enlisted pukes, I suggest we find a bar and get *really* drunk," the sergeant major replied.

"Good idea," Elgars said, looking towards the gates of the compound. "Follow me!"

Mueller chuckled as they headed out, the two males having to work to match her stride. "You seem to be . . . more whole these days."

"I *feel* whole," Elgars replied with a smile. "I haven't had a personality pop up in a few days, everything feels . . . integrated. As if, for the first time since I awoke, I'm *myself*."

"And do you know who you are?" Mosovich asked carefully.

"Yep."

"Who?"

"Anne Elgars," she said in a definite tone. "Just Anne."

"Must come as a surprise in the morning, huh?" Mueller said with a laugh.

Mosovich shook his head and looked at the woman for a moment. Then sighed as if for the death of a friend.

"Yep, time for us to get *stinkin'* drunk, ma'am."

Colonel Garcia got out of the personnel elevator shaking his head like a doctor about to tell the family that little Timmy wasn't going to be coming home.

"There's not much we can do, Colonel," he said to Mitchell, looking around at the group. The whole SheVa crew, plus Kilzer and Major Chan, had gathered to hear the news.

"The engineering area is covered in pebbles," he continued. "It's as hot as I've ever seen. Then there's the battle damage. Given that most of the SheVas are going to be decommissioned, it will probably be left right here. We'll pull the MetalStorms off and anything else that is salvageable, decommission the main gun and then seal it up with a bunch of radiation warnings all over it. This whole area is hot enough it will probably be closed anyway."

Mitchell nodded and sighed, looking around at the devastated landscape.

"I'd hoped for better, but . . ." He looked up at the mountain of metal that had been their home for the last few days and shook his head. "What now?"

"Get some rest?" the repair commander said.

"Will do," Mitchell replied. He looked at Indy and Chan then shrugged. "Ladies, I do believe there is an officers' club in Asheville that is calling our names. Can I buy you ladies a drink? I'm sure we can bum a ride."

"Hey, what about us?" Pruitt asked, gesturing at Reeves. "You're just going to walk off into the sunset with the girls and leave us in the middle of a radioactive wasteland?"

"Pruitt, an officer's first duty is to his men," Mitchell replied solemnly, holding his arms out on either side to the warrant and the major. "You and Reeves have a four-day pass. Report to the 147th G-1 in four days. Don't drink and drive. This completes your pre-pass safety briefing. Have fun." With that he turned around and started walking towards the nearby vehicle park.

"Well, that sucks," Reeves growled. "Where the hell are *we* supposed to go?"

"After them," Pruitt said, spotting Major LeBlanc striding up the hill. "As fast as we can!"

Kilzer spotted her at about the same time and looked around wildly. She was between him and the vehicles, and going back into the SheVa without a rad suit was suicide. But he considered it for just a moment. He suspected he was going to lose his balls anyway, might as well be to some more or less painless radiation damage.

"*Mister* Kilzer," the major said, walking up to him and planting both fists on her hips, "a moment of your time?"

"Yes, ma'am," Paul said.

LeBlanc looked down to where his hands had just naturally fallen to protect his groin.

"I'm not going to kick you in the balls," she said, with a shake of her head. Then when he smiled and moved his hands aside she did exactly that.

"Oh!" she cried, kicking him again as he rolled around on the ground. "I'm *sorry*! My *mistake*! I meant to say 'I *am* going to kick you in the balls!' I don't know how that 'not' got in there! Maybe a side-effect of radiation poisoning?"

"Aaah! I'm sorry! It was a mistake!"

"Yeah, I know you are. Sorry that is." LeBlanc stepped back and shook her head. "Get up, you look like a baby down there whining and clutching your privates in pain."

"Are you going to kick me again?" Kilzer groaned.

"Are you going to be an ignorant asshole again?"

"Oh, shit."

"Get up. I'll let you buy me a drink."

"You're really *not* going to kick me again?" Kilzer said, getting painfully to one knee. "Promise?"

"Not unless you screw up again."

"Damn."

"We have to quit meeting like this," Wendy said softly.

"You've only seen me, what, once before in the body and fender shop?" Tommy said from inside the tank. He was fully submerged in a red solution, but a bubble of air was open around his mouth and nose. He grinned through the nannite solution and pointed to where a darker, more opaque cloud was worrying around his shoulder. "Hey, if only they could increase the size of my cock!"

"You don't need that," Wendy said, looking at the tank and suddenly seeing it as old technology. It was practically magic to most people, able to regrow limbs and heal *almost* any wound short of death. But she had seen *real* magic, for which even death was not an impossible barrier. And she really wondered what in the hell was going to happen when someone figured out what she knew. The world was already a very dangerous place; she didn't need nonrandom enemies.

"I'll be out in a couple of days," Tommy said, when she seemed to have drifted off. "I'll have some leave coming and with the Fleet back, well, I'm not sure what they're going to do in the way of forces. Anyway, I was wondering . . . you wanna get married?"

She looked at her boyfriend and shook her head. "You can't kneel in that condition and it would be hard to hold out the box and then put the ring on my finger. So, under the circumstances, I'll accept the method of proposal!" she said with a broad grin.

"Great!"

"What about Fleet? What are they going to say?"

"Fuck 'em. What are they going to do, send me on a suicide mission?"

"Not anymore, love," Wendy said quietly. "No more."

"Well, I've got to do *something*," Tommy said in a worried tone. "They're talking about cutting back the Fleet and even Fleet Strike. I might be a discharged lieutenant with no training and no future. That wouldn't be fun to be married to!"

"We'll cross that bridge when or if we come to it," Wendy said. "But I'd be just as glad if you weren't working for Fleet, to tell you the truth."

"Well, I've got to do *something*."

"I'm still trying to get straight if you guys are white hats or black hats," Papa O'Neal said, taking a sip of coffee.

The meeting room was apparently *deep* under ground. Now that he had seen what a Himmit ship could do to rock, he was not surprised. What he *had* been surprised by was the briefer.

"The Bane Sidhe would, I think, qualify as white hats," Monsignor O'Reilly said, quietly. "You'll be told some of our history and background. You of course understand the term 'need to know.' You will be told what you need to know. For the rest, well, we're the people who saved you. We have done favors for your son as well. This is in *our* interest, you understand. Michael O'Neal is one of several possible paths to victory over the true enemy in this war. And it is for that that we saved you, in the hope of recruiting you to this great task."

"Uh, huh," Cally said. She had a Coke in her hand but so far she hadn't touched it. "Who is the *real* enemy, then?"

"The Darhel, of course," O'Reilly said. "It is they who waited until the last minute to warn Earth. It is they that, when it was apparent humans were going to be even more inventive than they gave them credit for, slowed production of essential war materials both off-planet and on Earth. They have supplied the Posleen with critical intelligence, without the Posleen's knowledge by the way. On a *personal* note they forced the choice of commanders on Diess that nearly got your father killed, hacked the Tenth Corps data net and did various other things, including sending an assassin after you when you were eight, to make your life less pleasant than it could have been. The only personal loss that is not *directly* attributable to them is the loss of your mother. Random chance does play a role in war. And even there . . . she should have been in command of a cruiser, not stuck with a half-finished, poorly constructed, poorly designed frigate. This, too, could be laid at the door of the Darhel."

"And we can believe as much of that as we like," Papa replied.

"We'll give you some bona fides eventually," O'Reilly said dryly. "I think that after you get to know us the truth will become obvious. And the appearance of Michael O'Neal, Senior, or Cally O'Neal will be cause for some comment. Given that they are presumed most thoroughly dead."

"I doubt that telling them the truth would be a good idea, huh?" Cally said.

"Not particularly. The Terran authorities would take you for nuts and the Darhel would have you silenced in very short order. We have a need for well-trained, highly motivated and self-directing special operations experts. You, Mr. O'Neal, have a long track record of such things and Team Conyers was most impressed on their brief visit."

"I wondered when that was going to come up," O'Neal said, nodding.

"And, with the exception of the experience part, the same goes for Miss O'Neal. If nothing else, the Bane Sidhe have been, from time immemorial, believers that 'blood tells.' And you are of the finest . . . stock imaginable. I cannot imagine you failing to be a *fine* operative, can you?"

"No," Cally said with a grin and a shrug, finally taking a sip of the Coke.

"Both of you have a need, new identities, new lives and . . . trust me, protection in that anonymity. If the Darhel got wind you were alive . . . We have a need, and you are two of the best examples of a round peg in a round hole I have seen in quite some time."

Cally sighed. "What the hell, I'm in. As long as the missions make sense."

"You won't need to worry about missions for a while young lady," the monsignor replied. "You've got quite a bit of schooling, of all sorts, ahead of you."

"School?" Cally asked, aghast. "You're joking, right?"

"No, he's not," Papa O'Neal snapped. "You need to get an education. Even if you're doing this . . . whatever it is, for the long haul, you still need an education."

"School," Cally grumped. "Great. I bet they'll take away all my guns."

"Only to put them in an armory," O'Reilly said with a smile. "As I said, 'of all sorts.' Just . . . try not to kill any of the nuns?"

"Better and betterer. Nuns." But she nodded. "As long as they don't bang my fingers with rulers, I'll let them live."

"Okay, Cally's taken care of," Papa O'Neal said with a frown, staring at the priest. "And I'll come on board too; I'll hunt your Sidhe for you. I'll be the best darn hunter of Sidhe you've got, a fucking Wild Hunt all on my own self." He paused and flexed his jaw as if preparing for a fight. "But I have one condition . . ."

Shari stood in the line of refugees, waiting in another drizzling, cold rain, to get processed into the Knoxville tent city.

Most of the children had already been taken away by social services. After all that sweat and all that suffering and all that fear they had just been . . . whisked away with a disapproving snarl as if it was *her* fault that they had been in the damned Urb or gotten into the middle of a nuclear war. At least they were *alive* unlike . . . God . . . Everyone.

Wendy had gone to the hospital to see her boyfriend, and Mosovich and Mueller had disappeared to wherever it was that troopers go after the fight, leaving her with just Billy and Kelly and Susie. And another tent city. Another batch of frightened, shell-shocked strangers. Another beginning.

She squished forward a few more steps, holding onto Kelly and Susie's hands and keeping one eye on Billy. He seemed . . . better since the whole episode, as if reliving the nightmares had some-how cleansed him instead of making him worse. He probably would do fine. It would have been better if . . .

It would have been better if the Posleen had never come. It would have been better if Fredericksburg had never been destroyed. It would have been better if two million people hadn't died in the Urb or five *billion* scattered across the globe. So thinking that it would have been better if one worn-out old man had not died was just . . .

"Hey, lady, wanna dance?" a voice whispered in her ear.

She spun in place, furious, and let go of Kelly to slap the ignorant, pig-headed bastard across the face but stopped, arrested by his eyes.

"You look like you've seen a ghost," the stranger said, smiling and holding out his hands. He was a little too tall, and far too young and his hair was fiery red and long instead of short, thin-ning and gray. But there was something about the eyes, about the cheekbones . . . Something about the huge wad of chewing tobacco in his cheek.

"Pity," he said, taking her hands and starting to sway. "I'd heard you liked to dance. *'Oh it's a marvelous night for a moon-dance with the stars up above in our eyes . . .'*"

Shari didn't know how she found him through the tears, but she managed to get her arms around him and after that everything was going to be okay. Somehow, beyond hope, beyond reason, it would all be okay.

The End

AUTHOR'S AFTERWORD

David Drake considers explanations of books to be "bad art." Well, I'm going to engage in some bad art as a means of apology.

What you have just finished reading is the ending of another book. I had never intended more than three books in this first portion of the novels that have come to be known as The Legacy of the Aldenata. I believe that a trilogy means *three* books, not four, five or nine. The reason there are four books comes down to the most unpleasant two words in modern America: September 11th.

On the morning of 9/11 I had already completed ninety thousand words on *When the Devil Dances*. And then my brother called me and told me to turn on the television. At that time I was well on schedule for a delivery date of October 1st but from 9/11 to the beginning of October, I failed to complete a single additional word on that novel.

The novel was already scheduled, already announced. My publisher gave me extra time and more time, until it was down to the very wire. We cut some proofreading, it was hastily set and then off to the printer. And, of course, it was truncated. All my fault.

I'll admit that the maximum range of an excuse is zero meters; this is not a request to be excused, I'm just telling you what happened and why. And, like Shari, I will not cry over an incomplete book. Compared to 3,000 dead, thousands out of work and the ongoing war, one book that's not completely up to snuff seems a pretty minor point.

So if you take the two books and put them together, rip out the "and back in the last book" stuff in this one, you have one complete book called *When the Devil Dances*, the originally conceived third book in the trilogy.

Go ahead. Feel free. Rip the back off of *WtDD*, get some scissors and glue . . .

Changing subjects, quickly, people have asked me quite a few questions about this series, and since this "trilogy" is done I thought I'd share a few of the answers in this venue.

The Posleen War was originally conceived sometime in 1985. There was a glimmer of an idea before that but the major pieces, a technologically inept enemy, "friends" that had many levels to them and a major ground war, came to me while I was on guard duty on a mountain in Sinai.

I had been . . . dissatisfied with some of the other novels that had handled alien invasion. Admittedly, if a space-faring species with faster than light travel wants to take Earth they are probably going to succeed. Once a species "owns" the gravity well, there's not much you can do about it.

Ergo, for humanity to survive (and have the book be much more interesting than "and then all the humans died and the evil aliens lived happily ever after") the aliens have to be hamstrung. But, why would aliens with FTL be incapable of using their full potential?

The few novels that had approached this problem I found unsatisfactory. So, to address this, I developed the Posleen. Starting from certain premises I traced the logic back and as I did many things derived *from* the logic rather than forcing the logic. Tom Clancy says that the two parts to a successful novel are "what if" and "what's next"?

What if . . . there was a species that . . . (but that would be telling). And what next?

I originally had intended for them to be able to destroy artillery, for example, but the logic of their origins militated against it. Likewise their enormously resistant physiologies. Yes, any oxygen breather will have trouble with cyanide. But at what concentration? And for what duration? But is it possible to design a species that would be highly resistant to truly weird environmental conditions? Planets where most of the atmosphere is gaseous sulphur, planets with semi-sentient and aggressive biospheres? Take every horror planet ever conceived in science fiction and design a race to survive them, and even *thrive* on them. And, if so, wouldn't they be resistant to any chemical attack?

And so, with some logic in hand and a vague series of images I set out to write a book. It was not intended to be published (indeed, until about three months before I sent *Hymn Before Battle* off to Baen Books I had never considered becoming a published author), but rather it was a book for *me*, something that *I* wanted to read, an alien invasion where the "good guys" (that's us) got to *really* sink their teeth into the bad guys (that's the Posleen). No gray areas, no ambiguity. Victory or death. *Vive le morte!* Once more unto the breach! Take that bunker or die trying!

I mean, if it isn't victory or death, what's the point? (Oh, Art? Excuse me while I laugh. Go read some of the reviews of Dickens.)

At some point in the future there will be stories that expand upon the logic and reveal all the strings behind the curtains. And books in which the focus slides completely off of the Posleen as the enemy and onto newer, more silvery, pastures. And, yes, books that are "grayer."

But, alas, the writing of those books will be some time. I've sort of "burnt out" on the Posleen and I'm going to be writing some other stuff for a few years. I don't think that there will be anything in them that will cause any of my current readers to go astray and I hope that they are more "approachable" to some of the readers who, let us say, don't care for piles of yellow, leaking corpses.

Rest assured, though, Mike O'Neal, Papa and *of course* Cally (as if I was going to kill *her*) will be back. In the meantime just imagine them out there. Mike is retaking planets from the Posleen and Papa and Cally are covering his back. Kickin' ass and not even bothering to take names.

Whether he knows it or not.

Take care and just remember; the good guys *always* win in the end.

John Ringo
Commerce, GA
October 6, 2002

AUTHOR'S ACKNOWLEDGEMENTS

I'd like to thank a bunch of people for help with this book and all the other books.

I'd like to thank Sandra Hearn. Yes, Sandy, I did kill you, finally and permanently. I'd like to thank Doug Miller for giving me hours of good copy. And I'd like to thank Bob Hollingsworth, Tony Trimble and John Mullins for some really great stories. Writing is about taking the world and synthesizing it. Without the input of experience it is very difficult to write well. All of these people have made my life a richer and fuller experience, each in their own inimitable way.

As noted in the dedication, thanks to *all* the Barflies. Baen Publishing maintains a very active webboard community called Baen's Bar. We, and I consider myself a Barfly of long and serious standing, refer to ourselves as the Barflies. (The group is a "buzz" as in "A Buzz of Barflies" and a Buzz of Barflies can be found around almost any collection of good books.)

The Barflies have been out there rooting and pushing for me from my very first book, *A Hymn Before Battle*. I was a Barfly *before* it was accepted for publication and the rest of the gang got out there and promoted it without even being asked. It was like having two thousand sales reps and I'm personally certain that the

Barflies, more than any other single factor, have led to the notable success that I've enjoyed with my books.

I'd like to thank a few of them in particular *and in no particular order, dangit*:

Morgen, for being one of the first friendly faces. Deann, despite DaGiN Ball. Genghis Kratman, newest author Barfly, who's like a brother. Katie/Inga for always being up for a round of groupieness. Wyman for always being out there helping. skippy (sic) for *not* always being around.

I'd like to thank the technical crew, Conrad, Phil, Doug and Ken Burnside for making some vague sense of my technical inanities.

I'd like to thank Russ Isler and Darius Garsys for turning my descriptions into real, breathing, living objects.

Most especially I'd like to thank Joe Buckley and Glennis LeBlanc for being two of the best First Readers in the business and putting up with my various pranks.

Oh, and I'd like to thank Karin my wife for, once again, putting up with me when I was under deadline.

Naturally, I'm going to forget some people, some of whom have made important contributions. To anyone who was left out, I'm sorry I missed you and I'll try to make it up in some other books.

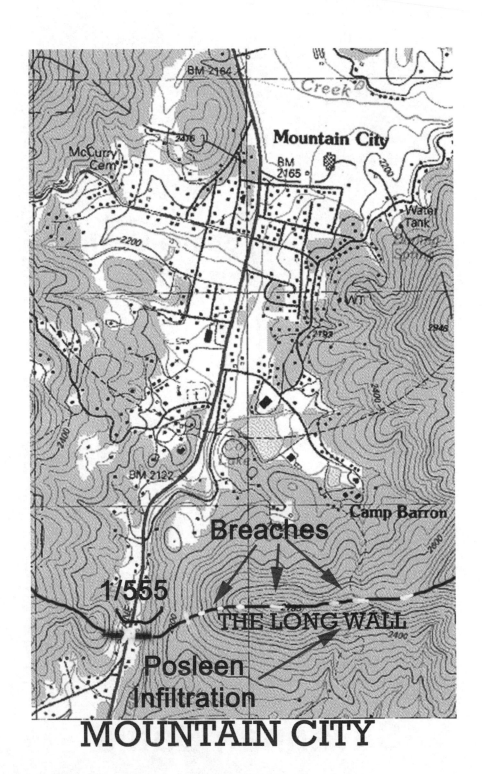

Creek

BM 2164

McCurry
Cem

Mountain City

BM
2165

Water
Tank

WT

BM 2122

Lake

Camp Barron

Breaches

1/555

THE LONG WALL

**Posleen
Infiltration**

MOUNTAIN CITY

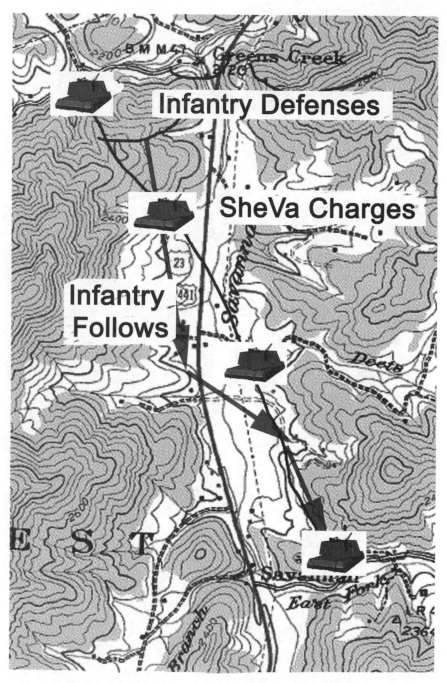

Infantry Defenses

SheVa Charges

Infantry
Follows

Savannah Battle

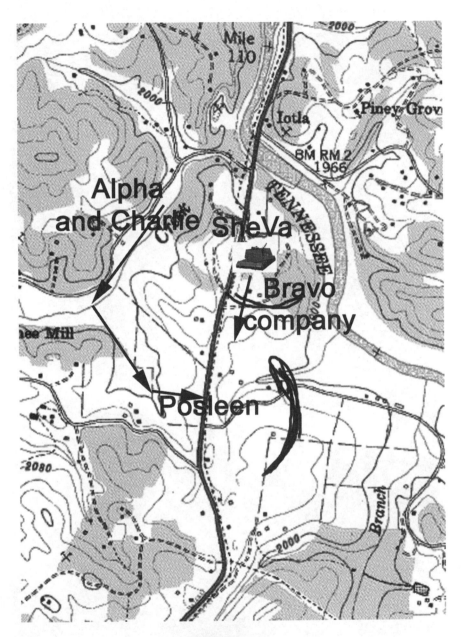

Iotla
Battle

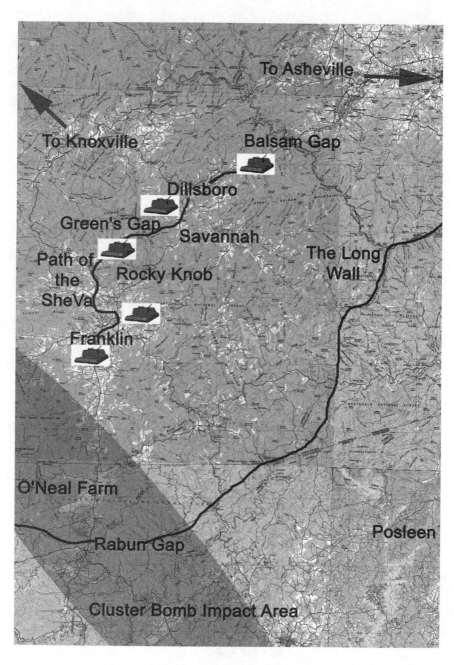

FRANKLIN
AND SURROUNDINGS

SheVa Bun-Bun

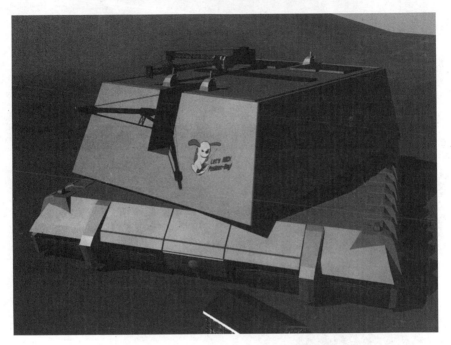

SheVa I specifications:
- Height: 170 ft ground to top of turret
- Treads: four
- Tread height: 27 ft
- Tread width, individual tread: 150 ft
- Weight of individual tread: 37 tons
- Total vehicle width: 385 feet
- Total vehicle length: 468 feet
- Gun Length: 200ft including barrel and breech
- Gun bore: 16"
- Round weight: 16 tons, projectile, cartridge and propellant.
- Cartridge Length: 14.7 ft.
- Cartridge Diameter: 27 inches
- Reactors: 4 Johannes/Cummings pebble-bed uranium/helium
- Drive Motors: 48
- Total Power: 12,000 horsepower
- Unloaded weight: 7,000 tons approximate

Sluggy Freelance

SUNDAY, FEBRUARY 15, 1998
(partial excerpt)

Sluggy Freelance

www.sluggy.com

WEDNESDAY, SEPTEMBER 22, 1999

SLUGGY FREELANCE

www.sluggy.com

THURSDAY, AUGUST 17, 2000

SLUGGY FREELANCE

www.sluggy.com

SLUGGY FREELANCE

IT ONLY TAKES TEN POUNDS OF FORCE TO POP OFF A KNEECAP.

NOT FOR ME. I WENT CHEAP! MY KNEECAPS ARE THE TWIST-OFF KIND! ACTUALLY I HEAR THEY'RE MADE BY THE SAME COMPANIES THAT MAKE THE POP-OFF KIND.

SAME COMPANY, NOT SAME QUALITY. AT LEAST YOU DIDN'T GET TACKY AND GET THAT "KNEE IN A BOX"!

www.sluggy.com

NO FRILLS. I HEAR YOU HAVE TO GET YOUR TENDONS ON THE SIDE WITH THAT.

THE FAMILY PACK COMES WITH **THREE** SIDES, I BELIEVE.

WHAT ARE THE OTHER SIDES?

DON'T REMEMBER THEM ALL. I NORMALLY GET THE TENDONS AND LIGAMENTS.

AND THE THIRD?

CREAM CORN!

WHAT THE HELL ARE YOU GUYS TALKING ABOUT!?!

MONDAY, APRIL 8, 2002

SLUGGY FREELANCE

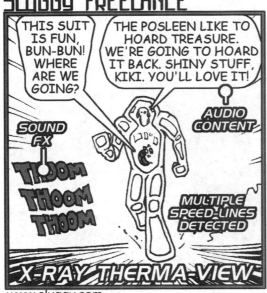

www.sluggy.com

THURSDAY, OCTOBER 19, 2006

SLUGGY FREELANCE

PVT. TORG, YOU HAVE A PLAN TO GET US THROUGH 4 MILES OF POSLEEN ENCAMPMENT UNDETECTED?

www.sluggy.com

ALL IN ALL, MY SHORT-TERM SENSOR JAMMER PLAN *IS* BETTER, TORG.

hmph. SURE, THEY ALWAYS USE **YOUR**, PLANS.